Legacy of the Vermillion Blade

JAY TALLSQUALL

Legacy of the Vermillion Blade by **Jay Tallsquall**

Published by **Bird in the Storm Publishing**

Twitter.com/Tallsquall

Cover By:
Jamie Flack

Developmental Editor:
Donathin Frye

Copy Edited By:
@birdvsplane

Diversity Consultation By:
Maple Intersectionality Consulting

Story Proof-Readers:
@kahruveldesign, CoffeeNick

Free template downloaded from: https://usedtotech.com.
Printed in the United States of America

First Printing Edition, 2022
ISBN 979-8-9869949-1-8

Dedication

Y'all are awesome

Table of Contents

THE CHILD FROM SPRING AND STONE

THE SOUL BETWEEN BLOOD AND STEEL

Author's Note

A fantasy story of love and loss through the lens of Asexuality.

****Content Warning: Mild Gore, Mild Body Horror, Eye Injury****

Map of the Rhymera

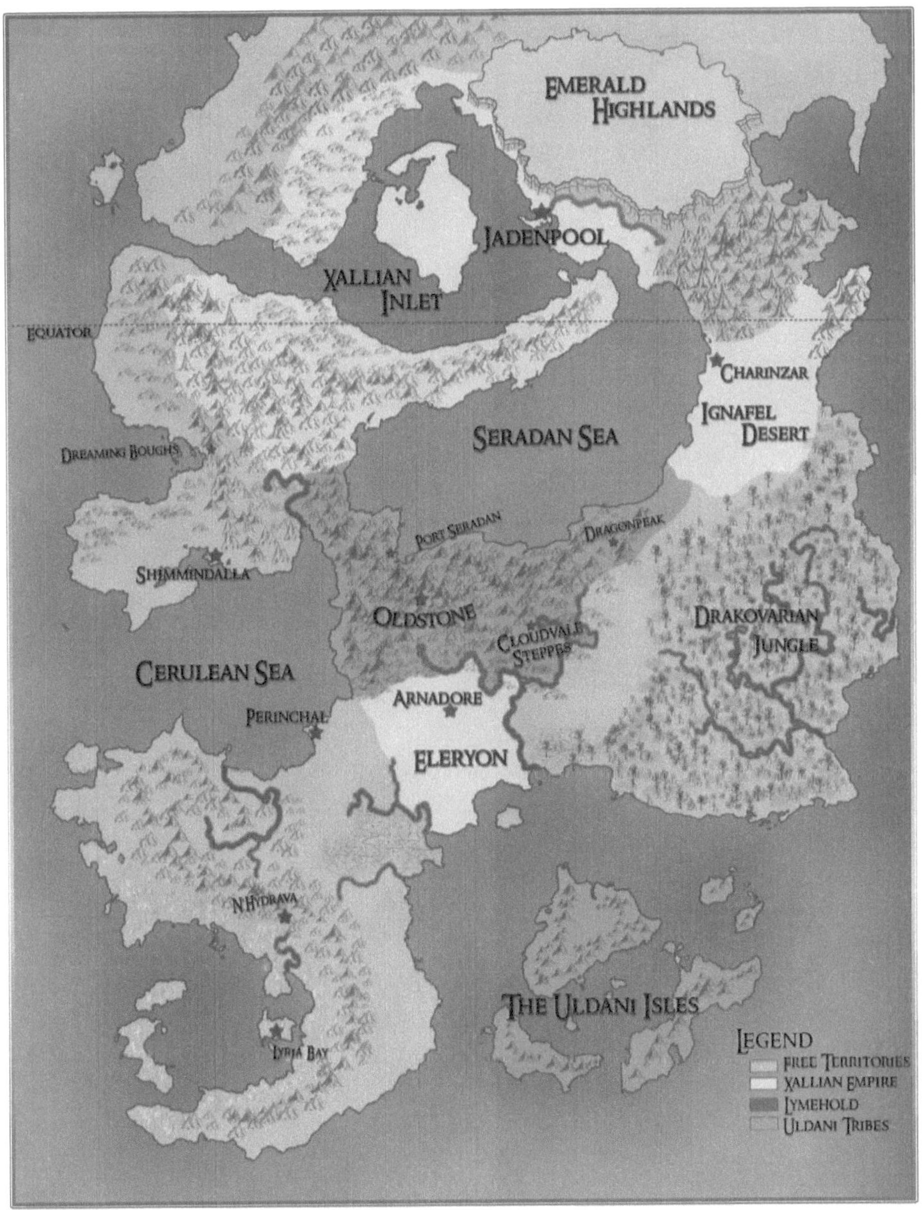

x

PROLOGUE

Year 837 PXF *(Post Xallia Founding) ~ Summer*

Talon Cour-Vermane was born healthy, strong, and wailing like a banshee to Toman and Veronic Cour-Vermane on the hottest day of the Summer. Yet, despite every window being open to catch any errant breeze, none of Talon's wailings were heard outside the walls of the Cour-Vermane estate. For the birth was not occurring in the bedchambers of the manor house; it was occurring within a ritual birthing room hidden deep below.

Only Toman and a single elder midwife, whom Toman would make disappear by nightfall, attended to his betrothed. Talon's squirming form, barely wiped clean, was handed directly from the womb to his father. After inspecting the boy for defects with a severe and judgmental eye, Toman unceremoniously returned him, still wailing to the midwife in exchange for the afterbirth. Striding to the altar, standing prominent in the center of the chamber, Toman placed the blood-filled discarded part of his wife and son into a platinum basin glowing with dark runes and burning with invisible fire. No flare of flame or dramatic effect marked the resealing of the eons-old bargain between the Cour-Vermane family and Darkness for another generation, just an empty and quiet platinum basin - satiated for now.

Silence filled the chamber. Toman's head whipped around at his son's sudden lack of commotion. His eyes narrowed menacingly as, from across the room, he spotted the midwife calming Talon by letting him play with an intricately carved wooden medallion that hung from around her neck.

PART I

The Boy with the Stormcloud Eyes

CHAPTER ONE

Talon's childhood was privileged and mostly carefree. He was chided enough by his elders not to become a brat but was still spoiled unendingly by the staff, especially Ms. Haddington, whom he charmed endlessly with pleading hazel eyes from behind his mop of perfectly unruly hair. Talon spent his days bouncing from playing the part of the perfect student for his tutors to causing mischief around the estate, indoors and out.

As he grew, his daily rounds would take him from his rooms on the 'Sunrise Wing' of the estate down to the main floor, where he would tiptoe past his father's study. Talon was always sure to cause not even a single sound or vibration as he passed the thick, carved doors to ensure he would not disturb his father's maps or the models that covered them.

They. Were Not. Toys.

Even the voice that often spoke in Talon's mind seemed to cower and hide whenever they passed the study, which was good as it tended to constantly suggest that he do things he knew he shouldn't. His arm would still itch when he passed his father's study, a memory of the time he listened to the voice's pleas and barged in through the stately doors. Afterward, he remembered that he had been taken to the surgeon his father employed and who lived on the estate, but curiously Talon remembered little else from that day other than entering the forbidden room.

Once past the study, Talon could freely roam the parlors, library, and receiving rooms on the main floor. If there was indoor fun to be had, he usually found it there. Talon never did any of the really bad things the voice whispered for him to do; most of those scared him and would hurt people. The lesser requests he quite enjoyed, though, stirring anger and frustration between servants and houseworkers, planting discord and causing scenes. Talon liked when their tempers would flare at each other with nowhere to go, biting their tongues for fear that father would hear a raised voice indoors. It was like when he would use one of Mrs. Grawl's sewing needles to pin a moth to the ground and watch the ants come, but with people.

The biggest attraction on the main floor was the dining room; while he was only allowed to join his parents for dinner and sometimes lunch, it was where he could sneak down the servant's stairs to the kitchens. The kitchens always had activity and people coming and going. The gardeners, stablehands, groundskeepers, houndsmen, and especially the cooks always sounded so genuine in their greetings and chats with each other, not like the formalized conversations of the 'upper staff' and his parents. Talon never did bad things to the 'lower staff,' even though the voice sometimes begged him to. Here in the kitchens on the ground floor of the estate, the background noise of the daily running of the household eclipsed the naggings of the voice in his head, and it was one of the few places Talon found he could tell the voice a definitive *no* and not just cajoling it with a *maybe later,* or *we'll do that tomorrow.*

While the estate's half-elf surgeon, Balanon, technically was a part of the upper staff, Talon found him in the kitchens or hallways of the ground floor more often than not. The lower floor of the estate housed Balanon's surgery, as the laborers who worked the grounds more often needed his services than the household staff, and its location also kept any unseemly injury or illness out of the main house. Therefore, Balanon spent most of his day among lower staff instead of with the stuffy maids and butlers above. Talon found the half-elf surgeon fascinating. He had learned from his tutors that although Balanon looked far younger than his parents, the estate's surgeon was actually far older than even his father's father. Balanon was always kind to Talon, and when they would cross paths in the kitchens, he would always listen to and answer whatever question or observation Talon had about nature or elvenkind. So it was not surprising that as Talon outgrew his more childish things, he became obsessed with everything involving the surgery, drawing him like a moth to a flame.

The voice, usually skulkingly quiet when Talon was among the lower staff and exploring the estate grounds, seemed thrilled with this new focus on the surgery. It stoked the innate curiosity in most boys of Talon's young age for the gruesome and gory. Whenever Talon would see a gardener going to the surgery with a leg wrapped in a bloody shirt or a houndsman cradling a hand that had been accidentally bitten while breaking up a ruckus between the hunting dogs, Talon and the voice began to imagine together what circumstance led to the incident and how awful the wound might be.

The voice would even go as far as suggesting to Talon that if a tool were left in an inconvenient place or a poker strayed into the forge at an inopportune time, they might see even *more* people head to the surgery. Talon rejected the voice's plan out of habit, but it did awaken a hint of temptation in him. Its initial outright requests denied, the voice now assured Talon that Balanon always fixed whatever wound or ailment was placed before him. *With Balanon's skill*, it suggested, *it's almost as though these injuries and wounds were merely pretend. Just like other imaginings.* Surely, anything they caused would be just the same? Talon wasn't convinced and wanted to see for himself before deciding on what the voice had suggested, but he couldn't get near the surgery whenever Balanon was treating someone. He once tried to get in under the guise of helping by escorting one of Ms. Haddington's cooks to treatment after they had sliced open their palm, but Balanon shooed him away before he could even get a good look in the door. Talon was supremely frustrated by the chiding of "let the adults take care of this," the surgery door closing in his face. *Perhaps if there were more injured people*, the voice chimed in, *they would need his help*. Talon almost gave into the voice then and there and could feel its glee at his acquiescence, but the smell of Ms. Haddington's ginger cookies baking in the kitchen distracted him and drowned out the voice's influence for a time.

Not two days later, as Talon was sitting at the kitchen's small plain wooden table, effectively ruining his dinner with a snack provided by Ms. Haddington, Balanon approached and sat beside him.

"Your mother has observed your interest in the surgery," he began in his lilting voice. Talon almost choked on his milk. His mother never took any interest in him. Did she know about what he and the voice had been planning? Was he in trouble?

Balanon continued, "She wants you to spend one day a week learning medicine with me."

Talon's heart leaped in his chest, his body quickly following as he jumped from his seat. "Really!?"

"Yes, we begin tomorrow."

The surgery was not at all what Talon had imagined or the voice had claimed it would be. Talon threw up no less than three times before lunch, just from Balanon showing Talon some basics on a preserved pig he had for teaching. However, the most memorable lesson came that afternoon when one of the stablehands was carried in after a plow horse had stomped on his foot.

"Come here for a moment, Talon; this is important," Balanon stated as he waved Talon over to the treatment table where he was preparing his patient. Talon approached and saw the damage the horse had done as they took off the stablehand's shoe. His foot wasn't at all the shape it should have been, and the toes splayed out at odd angles. As Talon got closer, he noted that the stablehand was still biting down with all his might on the leather belt that had been placed between his teeth when he was brought in, but it could not suppress all the cries he made from the pain. The voice jumped front and center in Talon's mind, gleefully observing what was happening, but Talon wasn't sure what to think. This wasn't the fun grossness he was expecting or imagined. This was real.

"Give me your hand, Talon," Balanon said in the gentle manner of physicians everywhere that seemed to elicit instinctive compliance from Talon without thought. Talon, eyes still locked on the stablehand's ashen face and wide eyes, did not hear as Balanon mumbled a few words or see the arcane spark that ignited with them as he placed Talon's hand on the stablehand's wrist.

Talon's physical form was frozen, but his mind, in a dizzying flash of arcane energy, became one with the stablehand. He was on the table seeing his own ruined foot and feeling the excruciating pain. Talon knew the stablehand's fears and suddenly also his name, Gavin. All the uncertainty that filled Gavin was now Talon's to know. Would he ever walk normally again? Would he walk at all? Were they going to cut off his foot?! Everything he saw and felt, physically and mentally, mirrored from Gavin to Talon perfectly. He even saw his own frozen body with his hand on Gavin's wrist, and looking at his own face Talon was sickened by what he saw — the voice had contorted Talon's face into a mask of malevolent joy. Talon realized Gavin saw it too and that the stablehand was both afraid and disgusted by it, adding to his already sizable distress. Talon tried to call out to Gavin, explain that it wasn't truly him with the insidious grin. *It was the voice!* His pleas fell flat, though, and the realization dawned that he could not communicate with his host while in this state.

Balanon left Talon under the spell's influence for the entire procedure required to set and repair the stablehand's foot. While Talon experienced some of the pain-numbing effects of the medicines given to Gavin, he did not share the same mental daze the patient did. Talon was fully aware of every step Balanon did, and Balanon, knowing Gavin was unconscious, but Talon's mind remained awake within him, spoke to Talon as he worked. The surgeon dutifully taught his student the procedure and explained what he was doing, why it was necessary, and the pain it would cause, which Talon still felt even if to a reduced effect.

When the procedure was over, Balanon looked straight at Gavin but directed his words to Talon firmly stating, "You must always consider what pain and distress your actions may cause to others. One day, the roles may be reversed where you are in dire need, and they are the one with the ability to help or harm you."

Balanon released Talon from the spell. He scrambled to his senses, then bolted from the surgery, not wanting to face Gavin, Balanon, or himself.

Talon was furious with the voice, screaming at it in his head. It was the first time he had ever confronted the voice directly. Everything it had told him was wrong. All these things it wanted him to do were not a game. Even if Balanon fixed them, the people they hurt would still have the pain and fear of the event as it happened. That was not something someone could forget.

On top of that, how dare the voice get so much happiness out of that? Talon threw the image of his sinisterly smiling face from the surgery at the place where he felt the voice resided in his mind. The voice which had respectfully cowered at Talon's fury now slyly slunk back into his consciousness, simply pointing out it was his own face smiling that way and no one else's. Talon's fury deflated instantly; he had no counter to that. He and his actions brought him to that moment. Talon did have an answer to it, though. He wouldn't let it happen again.

Talon learned another valuable lesson over the following week: sometimes, you can't undo your previous actions when it comes to people. Try as he might, he found Gavin avoided him like the plague. No matter how kind or considerate or helpful he was, the stablehand wanted no part of it. He felt hurt by the rejection, and the voice tried to twist it into an opportunity for retaliation, but Talon resolutely determined that he wouldn't be listening to the voice for quite some time. Talon continued with his weekly training in the surgery, but now with a whole new perspective untainted by the voice's desire to see and revel in whatever injury may come along, he was there to learn to help people.

Another thing Talon discovered from his continuing time in the surgery was that a cloaked man delivered five healing potions to Balanon every fortnight or so. At first, Talon, who was not overly familiar with magic, just assumed that the potions must not be very effective or were for ailments more than wounds and that Balanon must be using them on the days he was not there. However, the laborers whose injuries Balanon treated still exited the surgery with slings, stitches, or bandages just as they did on the days he worked there. It wasn't until after some subtle inquiries over the course of several months that Talon discovered just how powerful healing magics and potions could be. Still, Balanon never seemed to use them on the staff or laborers. Instead, he always used traditional non-magical medical procedures. So, where were all the healing potions going?

It was quite by accident that Talon discovered his mother was using them, which made no sense to him at all. His mother never did much of anything, to the point where Talon never even thought of her much anymore. There had been a time when he was younger when Talon thought his mother was the most beautiful woman in the world, and all he wanted was to be near her as often as possible. Whenever he would try to get close to her, though, she would ignore him for one of her ever-present books, sternly telling him, "Can't you see I am reading?" Talon quickly learned that there was never a time when she was not reading when it came to him. Sitting as still as a statue in her parlor, silhouetted by the sun coming in through the window in her high-backed chair, she gave not even the slightest hint of emotion or care to Talon. In frustration and rejection, Talon found he stopped caring for her as well.

Talon only discovered his mother's use of the potions because he had lost his favorite pen and, after tearing apart his room to find it, determined it must have ended up in the garbage. Digging about in the rubbish pile behind the estate before it was carted away, he found the empty potion bottle among other refuse from his mother's room. Talon never did figure out why she was using so many of them until much later in life. Young Talon knew his mother was not clumsy; she was, in fact, very graceful, but in the innocence of his youth, he could not comprehend how she would need healing potions so often when the only time she was not alone and in her parlor was when she was with his father.

CHAPTER TWO

Year 851 PXF *~ Early Spring*

Like any privileged adolescent, Talon had the utmost confidence in his 'rule' of the Cour-Vermane estates, staff, and grounds. In the two years since his fight with the voice over the incident in the surgery, he and the voice had come to an accord. The lower staff was off limits. Furthermore, Talon would summarily ignore even minor suggestions by the voice regarding them. In addition, even though his tutoring with Balanon had ended, the surgery and all things medical were forbidden discussion. In exchange, the upper staff was fair game. Talon had enforced an almost two-month silent treatment toward the voice after their fight, but temptation finally got the better of him when the opportunity arose for him to cause some mischief between the upstairs maid and the maids on the main floor of the estate.

He and the voice had a routine with rules they both had to follow and some that, on occasion, could be bent. If any of the upper staff caught on to his manipulations of their lives, or they squawked too loudly, they quickly found they wouldn't be in the employ of House Cour-Vermane for very long. Talon's perceived rule of the estate was uncontested until he was halfway through his fourteenth year. The year when Richen entered his life. The year he understood Love.

Richen was no one of consequence. He was the second son born to a minor metalworking merchant in Arnadore, who then apprenticed him to an artisan blacksmith named Mikal to better learn the properties of metalcraft. Richen accompanied Mikal that day to the Cour-Vermane compound to help with the horses and carry the crates of goods Toman had ordered fabricated. While the Cour-Vermane estate employed a personal blacksmith at the estate, their smith had developed a rot in his joints that had slowly eroded the quality and quantity of his work. A quick inspection of Mikal's goods and an exchange of coins was all it took for the Cour-Vermane's old blacksmith to be sent on his way and Mikal to become the new household smith along with Richen as his apprentice.

Talon heard the news of new 'subjects' in his kingdom that same morning and set it upon himself to make his best impression; that and to make sure they knew who was really in charge (when not following his father's orders, of course). Once the sun burned off the chill near mid-morning, Talon, dressed in his finest hunting wear and feeling that he cut quite an impressive figure, marched all five-foot-one-inch of his almost fourteen-year-old self to the receiving courtyard where the estate's small smithy lay. As he turned the corner, Talon felt he had been struck in the head by a hammer and became paralyzed in his tracks. The whole world turned gray around him, with only a single figure remaining in vivid color.

Standing a good head taller than himself in a sleeveless cloth jerkin and calfskin leather breeches was a boy not much older than himself. Raven-black hair dagger-cut into short thick locks, as was the custom for smiths, shining like polished obsidian in the early morning light. Gray eyes the color of the thunderheads that brought rain and lightning on Summer afternoons. Broad yet delicate features accented by long dark eyelashes and full lips smiling even while doing the menial task at hand. Bare arms and shoulders flexed with the beginnings of the powerful corded muscle that smiths were renowned for, but not yet the bulky swollen mass they would undoubtedly become. Lean and lithe and so full of life stood Richen.

There had never been another person even close to Talon's age on the estate in the entirety of his life, much less a boy. Talon had, of course, seen other children but always from afar and was certainly never permitted to interact with them. Now here was this boy like some character from the historical fictions his tutor made him read. He seemed much closer to being a man than Talon was, even though they were practically the same age. A self-consciousness overcame Talon. He had never felt more silly or more childish or more *like* a child in his privileged life. His clothes suddenly seemed like a jester suit, his body weak and frail, and even his wild, beautiful hair that he was so proud of just seemed like a frivolous ornament. Talon wanted to run and hide before this boy could see him, but it was too late. Richen was already looking up from his task of gathering oak splits to feed the forge. Richen spotted Talon immediately. Talon felt the boy's eyes traveling over him and feared whatever assessments he might have made of him.

"Well, don't just stand there; grab as many splits as you can carry and help me get this forge lit before Mikal gets here." The boy's voice carried a tone of conspiracy and intrigue like this was some forbidden favor and a secret mission he was assigning. Talon's feet moved before his mind could process that he had just been given an order from someone other than his parents. The boy had spoken to *him*. The boy who he now desperately wanted the approval of and to be his friend. The boy he longed to be just like even though he knew nothing about him. This breathtaking boy had said words to him and wanted him to help with this critical task. Talon ran over, grabbed two of the smaller splits of oak (one more than he probably should have carried), and trundled into the smithy behind the raven-haired boy.

"Just put the wood over there with the rest while I get this fire lit." Hearing no verbal response but seeing Talon following directions, Richen continued as he hunched over, looking deep into the firebox under the forge. "I see you know the trick is feeding the fire with the smaller pieces first, so those you brought are perfect."

Talon beamed. He couldn't remember when he felt more satisfaction from a compliment, even though he knew the boy probably recognized Talon had no idea how to light a fire in a hearth, much less a forge.

"Okay, I got the starter kindling going; hand me that split you just brought in... I'm Richen, by the way. And you are?" Richen grabbed the split of oak Talon was offering as he spoke.

There was a long pause as Talon found himself completely lost in the moment of handing the split to Richen, caught in the instant when both their hands were holding the same object. Then, realizing the awkward silence, Talon finally found his voice, "Talon. I'm Talon Cour-Vermane, heir to Toman and Veronic Cour-Vermane." Talon cringed inwardly at his automatic recital of name and title. Before, his title always made him feel bigger, but now in front of Richen, in this smithy, it made him feel small.

"Ya don't say?" Richen said with the most un-shocked tone Talon had ever heard. That, and a long knowing glance at Talon's flamboyant hunting attire sent Talon back into the horror he had felt earlier in the courtyard. Richen's face slid from sly teasing to gentle kindness as he quipped, "Hey, none of that. It's your uniform just like this is mine," standing and motioning to his plain clothes. "And man, I would give anything to be allowed to grow my hair out, and it look like yours... However," he paused for effect, "that sparrow up in the corner is eyeing it as nesting material."

Talon, in a panic, searched for the preying sparrow before the joke finally dawned on him. First Richen, then both boys, erupted in smiles and laughter. Talon's heart nearly leaped from his chest as, all at once, he discovered that a person could feel like they were flying without ever casting a spell or leaving the ground.

The next morning, braving the chill of early Spring not entirely released from Winter's clutches, Talon brought cups of Ms. Haddington's dark spiced tea out to the forge for him and Richen. Steaming earthen mugs in hand with trails of the sweet cream Ms. Haddington dolloped on top dripping down the sides and over his fingers, Talon paused outside the smithy to gather his courage before seeing Richen again.

Talon had convinced himself that he had misread his and Richen's interaction the previous morning, as they had only spent less than half an hour together. After the shared laugh, Talon shadowed Richen around the smithy as he set up the worktables explaining every tool and its function along the way. Unfortunately, Mikal arrived far too soon and was quickly barking kindly orders at Richen, as the new smith of House Cour-Vermane acclimated himself to the attributes and pitfalls of his new space. Talon quickly felt very out of place and in the way, so he left as unobtrusively as possible, once again feeling childish. He couldn't even be sure if Richen saw him go or cared that he left.

The rest of the day, Talon's overactive mind blotted out everything else; certainly, Richen was just being nice to the young lord-inheritor of the estate. He couldn't possibly be Talon's friend. That night, the ever-present voice in Talon's mind took advantage of the quiet in his rooms and the slowing of his thoughts to finally make itself heard. The voice that before had always been an instigator for Talon's actions now took on a different role. The dark voice began whispering in his mind, insidiously explaining in detail Richen's self-interest in befriending him and that there was no possible way he actually enjoyed their time together. In those dark hours of the previous night, the voice was not present as Talon's compatriot but as his saboteur.

Outside the smithy, tea in hand, Talon braced for the inevitable rejection to come; but remaining determined, he silenced the voice, took a deep breath, and stepped through the open threshold of the forge. In his eagerness and sleeplessness, Talon had not registered the earliness of the hour. Dawn was barely lightening the sky, so as he entered the smithy, Talon caught Richen just as he stepped out of the small room where he slept. The apprentice's room was located just behind the flue of the forge and captured some of its warmth as Richen emerged barefoot and shirtless, wearing only the same calfskin pants from the day before. His skin, glistening from the heat of his room, turned quickly to gooseflesh with the chill Talon had let into the smithy. High stepping over to Talon, apparently trying to keep his bare feet from touching the cold cobblestones, Richen wrapped his long-fingered calloused hands around one of the mugs. As he took it from Talon, Richen proclaimed, "You were sent from the gods!" and gulped the steaming tea. "Come!"

Richen over-dramatically pranced back across the smithy, punctuating each step with a clipped exhale as though walking on hot coals, all but diving through the still-open door back into his room. Meanwhile, Talon's mind felt like it was riding an unbroken stampeding stallion. From being mortified at catching Richen just awakening, to stunned at the sight of his naked torso, to melting at his fingertips engulfing his own as he claimed the mug of tea, to terror at being invited into Richen's chambers, his thoughts swirled and bucked in his head. Then, refusing to remain standing stunned in the middle of the smithy, Talon faced the moment, gulped a slug of tea from his mug, and followed Richen.

Richen's room was tiny. There were larger closets in the estate. It housed only a small trunk, a narrow but sturdy bed, and a few hooks on which Richen's tunic and a light jerkin hung. The room was rectangular and not very wide, so with Richen's bed pushed against one wall, there was only a small gap between it and the opposite wall. The trunk took up the rest of the room, leaving only a tiny clearance gap for the door to swing open.

Richen was sitting toward the head of the bed, back leaning against the wall under a small lone window, still shirtless with his feet drawn up onto the bed off the cold floor. He had left a space on the foot of the bed for Talon to join him, and so casual was his demeanor that Talon found himself sitting before his brain could even suggest the propriety of it. He even kicked off his soft leather boots so he could pull his stockinged feet up onto the bed in a similar position as Richen. They sipped their tea in comfortable silence for a few moments before Talon recalled the details of his well-laid plan for the morning. "Oh, I just thought I would come to help light the forge fire again," Talon stated as nonchalantly as he could.

Richen cheerfully replied in a self-satisfied manner, "No need. With my room here in the smithy, I could bank the fire properly before retiring and then feed it midway through the night. So it will be ready for Mikal with only a few pokes and a pump or two on the bellows."

"Oh, uh," Talon floundered, "I guess you don't need help then?" Talon's plan was quickly evaporating. "Um, enjoy the tea." Talon was awkwardly trying to find a place to set his mug so he could free his hands to put his boots back on. Not seeing a home for his mug and not wanting to draw attention to the sparse accommodations in Richen's room, he became increasingly flustered as he tried to escape.

"Oh no, you don't," Richen interjected slyly, folding his crossed legs under him and sitting up straighter. "I need you to tell me all about the rest of the staff and the regular visitors to this estate of yours." The tea mug seemed to settle magically and firmly back into Talon's hands. He'd all but forgotten about Richen's shirtless form being in such close proximity to him as he fell to the subject in which he was an expert: household rumors and secrets. "Well, Tuesday is the day Ms. Haddington..."

Talon had relayed approximately half of what he knew of the staff and all the goings on at the Cour-Vermane estate when, tea long since finished, the boys heard Mikal approaching the smithy. As Mikal preferred to work late into the night instead of early in the morning, several hours had passed, and the sun was well over the horizon. Talon realized he needed to prepare for his morning tutor's arrival, and Richen needed to stoke the forge, so the two parted ways but promised to share morning tea again the following day.

Ms. Haddington, having raised five children of her own, quickly spotted the telltale signs of the budding relationship. The next morning a small satchel of sweet buns sat next to the two mugs of steaming tea. Talon beamed, and Ms. Haddington gave a knowing wink and smiled back, hands deep in a mound of dough she was kneading for pies. Talon and Richen's second morning having tea together went much as the previous. Richen sillily retrieving his tea without a shirt or shoes from the cold main room of the smithy, then the two boys retreating to Richen's small room for Talon to finish relaying all he knew about the estate. It went much the same for the next week. Ms. Haddington providing some new treat along with their tea to break their evening's fast, and the boys recounting the details of each of their days after Talon had exhausted his supply of household secrets. Talon, growing more comfortable with Richen, even began wearing more casual attire to their mornings together; attire his station would never permit him to wear outside his chambers and not even there if expecting company.

Their eighth morning together found Talon, hands around a steaming mug, in a loose-fitting but tailored tunic, scandalously with neither jerkin nor doublet, black doeskin pants, and *unstockinged* feet pulled up onto Richen's bed. In his usual morning shirtless attire and lounging against the wall, Richen looked over to Talon with his stormcloud eyes and asked, "So what are we doing for Hearth's Rest?"

Smiths and cooks across the continent and beyond had the tradition of extinguishing their work fires to take a day of rest every fortnight to honor Caspharian, the Conjoined God of nature and tempest, hearth and forge. What began at hearths and forges in the empire spread from mere laborers up to high-ranking nobles, eventually becoming observed nationally as Hearth's Rest. Relaxation and peace marked the day for even the lowliest servant, as people from all walks of life quickly enshrined the belief that to break Hearth's Rest brought ill fate upon one's house.

As it seemed to be becoming more normal for him than not, Talon found his mind running at a full sprint through all possible outcomes of Richen's simple question. Firstly, Richen had said *we*. Not what *Talon* would be doing, but what *they* would be doing. Was it his intention that they would spend the day together? A whole day and not just a few fleeting hours in the morning? Then came panic about whether Richen would expect Talon to plan a full day of activities for them. After all, Richen was a new resident of the local area around the estates. As hospitality would dictate, it was Talon's duty to show his friend the sights and potentially provide introductions. Did Talon even really know where they could go or what they could do together?

Talon tried to hide the tightness building up in his chest and that his breath was threatening to race away from him. It was Richen's soft, resonant voice that broke his freefall into a panic. "Hey, stay with me here, T," referring to Talon by just that single letter. Richen's bare foot then found Talon's and gently alighted upon it with just enough pressure to remain unintrusive but at the same time feel like a lifeline anchored in the strongest granite. As he always seemed to do, Richen read Talon's thoughts perfectly. "No need to throw a gala banquet. Let's just go and explore these vast tracts of fields and forests I hear your family owns." Richen patiently waited until Talon met and locked onto his reassuring gaze, and when satisfied Talon had indeed calmed, he proclaimed, "We meet at dawn!" but whispered behind his hand like it was a scandal, "You are still in charge of food though, so be sure to talk to Ms. Haddington tonight, or we will have nothing but crumbs." Richen flashed his perfect crooked smile, and with a slight tap of assurance with his foot on the bare skin of Talon's foot, he reclaimed his own and went back to drinking his tea as if nothing had happened.

Filled with excitement, the following day at first light, with travel flasks of spiced tea and a pack filled with Ms. Haddington's best sandwiches and cakes, Talon and Richen stepped out the courtyard gates of the Cour-Vermane estate on their first adventure together. From that moment on, the two boys became nigh inseparable. Lunches together in the courtyard were added to morning tea still spent in Richen's room, at least until the turn of the season drove them outside in search of cool morning air instead of fleeing from it. Morning tea and lunch then expanded into every free moment either could find or steal to spend together. On days he was assigned to read, instead of sitting for direct instruction from his tutors, Talon would relocate to the smithy. Not only did that allow him to be close to Richen, even though Mikal still demanded all of his apprentice's attention, but Talon also found the noise of the blacksmith's hammer and the two smiths' constant banter helped him to concentrate. The voice that had been so prevalent in his life practically disappeared when he was around the forge. Talon found it sublimely comforting to be with or even near Richen, and Richen, inexplicably to Talon's mind, seemed to find delight in his company as well.

The seasons and joys of youth quickly slid by the two boys. Hearth's Rests found them out in the countryside, days that Talon was able found them in the smithy or running errands together into Arnadore for Mikal, and regardless of weather or obligation, every morning without fail, they met over spiced tea.

During their time spent together through the seasons, in their growing mutual comfort with each other, their feet would often find each other's while sitting on Richen's bed, or their hands would find themselves grasped together in an expression of their friendship or solidarity or because it was just lovely to be with each other. Talon loved the feel of Richen's heavy arm draped over his shoulders and his strong hands and forearms next to his own. Similarly, Richen always seemed to find an excuse to let his fingers tarry in his mane of wild hair or wipe Talon's upper lip with his thumb when Ms. Haddington's sweet foam from their tea gathered there. It never seemed to occur to either of them to push their intimacy any further than the simple joy and contentment they had already found with each other.

CHAPTER THREE

Year 853 PXF *~ Early Winter*

Almost three years passed. Both boys grew taller, and Richen notably broader over that time. While Talon's parents did not necessarily approve of the deep friendship between the two boys, as long as it didn't interfere with Talon's studies and courtly duties, they allowed it to continue. On the morning of Richen's eighteenth birthday as ice and the first snows covered the countryside, Talon was where he always was, with Richen in his tiny room behind the forge. Both with a mug of tea clutched in their hands, bare feet pulled up off the cold floor, Talon in a soft tailored tunic and leathers, Richen shirtless and wearing new calfskin breeches. After three years of growth, the two left little space on Richen's small but thankfully sturdy bed as they sat together in conversation. Mikal, now used to having to rouse them out of their morning ritual, looked in from the door unnoticed. Even with their growing size and maturity, he mused that neither of them seemed interested in anything changing between them.

Year 854 PXF *~ Early Summer*

With the Winter holidays behind them and the Spring galas celebrated, the warm breezes of Spring evaporated into the heat of Summer, and Talon's seventeenth birthday approached. With Talon's coming of age in the

Cour-Vermane household the previous year, his and Richen's errands into the nearby city of Arnadore had changed. What used to be Talon accompanying Richen to the trade district to gather Mikal's list of supplies now involved them going separate ways as Lord Cour-Vermane often tasked Talon with visiting the Keep or other noble houses. Due to bureaucracy's slow and grinding wheels, Talon's tasks always took longer than Richen's, so they started meeting up near the end of the day at a local inn by the trade district. That meant Talon usually joined Richen when he was midway through drinks and games of dice with the local butcher's daughter and the weaver's son.

Talon would enter the Sojourn's Rest inn late in the afternoon and see Richen laughing and smiling with the two of them, usually joined by a crowd gathered around and egging them on. The butcher's daughter, Ella, was typically pressed up against one of Richen's arms, and more than once, he spotted Faldan, the weaver's son's arm draped over Richen's broad shoulders. It all was innocent enough. However, there was a camaraderie Richen shared among the laborers that Talon long since realized his name would always exclude him from. When Talon would sit down with Richen and the others, everyone was always kind enough and welcomed him, but Talon couldn't help but feel alone, even surrounded by all these people. Alone except for Richen. A lightning-quick flash from his stormy eyes or a secret smile his way was all it took to banish the clouds over his mood, and he'd jump into games and the fun of the moment with the best of them. Talon was confident in the depth of his bond with Richen, as they both had confessed as much to each other. However, seeing Richen at such ease with others closer to his age and social standing did spark in Talon a fear about the future of his and Richen's relationship.

Talon, of course, knew of sex and heard many a bawdy and lustful tale from the bards in Arnadore over the years, yet none of the stories had resonated with him. While he longed to be physically closer to Richen and felt a need to touch and explore his ever more impressive physique, any sexual aspect of that contact, even as he knew it, was never a part of that vision. Talon's mind testing the waters and even contemplating the fact of Richen having all the male parts he knew he had, squelched any of his other tactile longings toward him. His lack of desire was not due to any shortcoming of Richen's appeal by any account. Richen was already several inches over six feet tall and broadly built, yet still not bulky with a seasoned smith's muscle and strength. Paired with his raven hair and strikingly colored eyes, Richen turned heads wherever he ventured. While they never spoke of such things, and Talon had no evidence of such, he worried Richen might have been lured by either Faldan or Ella to one of the readily available beds at the inn already.

As his birthday approached, the more Talon thought of it, the more the slithering dark voice that had been so long absent from his mind liked to assure him of the truth of Richen's infidelity. Talon would try his best to defend himself against the hissing voice; he was no slouch appearance-wise, after all. While not as tall as Richen and leaner of build, paired with his noble features and famously wild hair, Talon cut quite a picture of virility himself. Partially to his credit, the two of them walking together in certain quarters of Arnadore had all but stopped traffic on occasion. *Certainly, he was as appealing to Richen as Faldan was,* he would throw at the voice, yet it would just sibilantly snicker back at his assertion.

Year 854 PXF ~ Summer

With Midsummer and his birthday fast approaching, Talon, full of insecurity, was determined to face his fears and discover what would lay in store for his relationship with Richen. Accordingly, he planned an overnight hunting expedition into the forests held by the Cour-Vermane estate, close enough for the young men to go alone yet secluded and private enough for "other matters." Sensing his plans, many in the household gave Talon a smile and a wink upon hearing about the trip and his preparations.

23

Only his parents seemed reluctant about the journey, as they were still chuffed from his aloof attitude toward the overly-forward son of a prominent imperial merchant they had tried to pair him with at the planting festival.

The two teens set off on horseback in the morning, riding in a silence unfamiliar to both, often trading fleeting glances at each other and then quickly looking back to the forest or trail ahead. When they arrived at their camping location, a lovely glade near a clear spring deep enough for fishing and bathing, Talon set up camp while Richen tended and watered the horses at the spring. After setting the tent and firepit, Talon went to look for Richen. Horses already tended to, Talon found him sitting pensively on a large flat boulder beside the spring, knees drawn to chest with one arm wrapped around them while the other hand fiddled with pebbles and twigs by his side. Richen looked both strangely vulnerable and strikingly miserable, which was entirely out of character for the person Talon had come to know so well. Talon approached gently, suddenly feeling awkward about this trip, his plans, and just as silly as he had felt the day they first met. Richen, his eyes transmuted into the deepest gray Talon had ever seen, looked at him, not unlike the way he did that morning three years ago, but the words were very different.

"You know I love you, right?" Richen's face was utterly earnest and sincere but also profoundly vulnerable as he asked.

Talon was so shocked he dropped the small loaves he was carrying for them to share. That word had never been used between them in such a direct manner.

Words spilled out of Richen, tumbling over one another, "You do know, Right? I want to be with you night and day. I want to share every part of my life with you. I think you are the most beautiful person I have ever seen, and I want to celebrate and explore every inch of you, but...."

The millisecond pause in Richen's outpouring of emotion stretched into an eternity for Talon. His mind again overanalyzing, turning every fear in his heart to reality; *But I love another, but I only want to be intimate with women, but you are too young, but I am leaving, but...*

Richen finally continued.

"But... I don't like sex. Like, at all. Trust me. It's not you; I swear it's not. Gods, if there were anyone, I know it would be you, Talon." Richen seemed so hurt and ashamed at the confession. "You are every single thing I ever want, mind, spirit, *and* body, but sex is just not something I think I have the instinct for. I know you planned this for your first time, and you have made it so perfect. I don't want to ruin this for you. I even know a trick so that I can perform..."

"Shhhh... Richen. Shush." Talon, crossing to him, placed his finger on Richen's lips, his own words now cascading out in a stream of relief and joy. "Richen, thank the Silver Scribe, I feel much the same way."

Talon gently took both of Richen's hands in his own and waited for Richen to raise his eyes to his as they both knelt on the boulder. "You are everything I have ever dreamed of, but as much as I want to be close to you and touch you and be touched by you, I have no interest in what lies within your under-breaches or having it be within me or mine being within you either."

Silence. Then smiles followed by dawning realization.

Then they let loose a deluge of pent-up laughter as relief overtook them. It was as pure as the laugh they shared that first day, and the two young men now *both* found themselves flying without spells or ever leaving the ground, having somehow found another like themselves within each other.

Talon and Richen spent the rest of the day swimming and laying on the sun-warmed boulder. They talked and questioned and explored each other physically in a beautiful, comfortable way unique to only them, which somehow made it even more intimate because they knew it was indeed totally their own. Finally, they fell asleep that night in each other's arms. Foreheads pressed together after the lightest of goodnight kisses, their lips barely brushing past one another in the gentlest of caresses.

The morning found them in much the same position. Their bare torsos pimpled with gooseflesh skin, and their night breeches hiked up to their calves so their feet could tangle together and caress one another. Fingers still interlaced, they all but opened their eyes as one, looking into the soul of the person they loved most. But, while there was the desire to spend the day reveling in one another, there also was hunting to be done and the journey home.

CHAPTER FOUR

Year 854 PXF ~ Summer

The beast prowled the forest with disdain and nausea as the odors of life filled its nostrils and coated its tongue. Its Master summoned it from the fields of boiling putrescence where it and its kind existed. The Master had bound it with his blood and encased its incorporeal form in bulging flesh and gnashing jaws. The magics of the ritual demanded one task of the beast, which it was impatient to fulfill. Once complete, it would be released, leaving behind the flesh it had been imprisoned in, along with this world of life and hope. The beast lifted its muzzle, choking down another wave of bile as it breathed deeply, and there upon the wind was the scent for which it searched, near the hallowed ground it had avoided but steadily moving away from its protection.

Talon and Richen set out on foot from their camp, backtracking along the game trails which led to the spring. After an hour on the hunt, the two stalked a faint rustling in the underbrush and surprised a prize boar. Talon with crossbow and Richen with his maul dispatched the beast quickly and set about cleaning their kill. Dressed and slung from a sturdy branch, they carried the boar between them and began the trek back to the horses. A disturbing smell hit their nostrils: sulfur, brimstone, and decay. What sprung from the woods Talon could not say - a giant canine form, black as soot with eyes burning like embers. Its jaws locked onto and ripped into Richen's side, shaking his body as if he were no more than a ragdoll.

"NO!" Talon screamed, lunging at the beast with nothing more than the broken piece of the branch they had hung the boar from. He swung wide, missing the beast not because of his lack of prowess but due to the unexpected reaction of the beast to his scream - it cowered like a chided lapdog. The beast guiltily dropped Richen and fled into the forest with its tail tucked. With the clarity of hindsight later in life, Talon would also remember the strangest thing about the beast's hasty retreat; before leaving, it bowed to him.

Richen's grunt of pain brought Talon out of the adrenaline-soaked shock he was in. Talon leaped to Richen's side and examined the wound. While grievous, it did not have the hallmarks of being life-threatening. Talon felt that undoubtedly with one of Balanon's healing potions back at the estate, Richen should have no issue being fine by morning. Talon ripped Richen's shirt off and bound it tightly around his waist to staunch the bleeding. Then placing Richen's arm over his own shoulder to support his weight, the two limped back to the horses. Talon did not even bother to break camp in his haste to get Richen home knowing he could send a servant for their things later.

They were still over an hour away from the estate when Richen swooned and fell from his horse. Talon rushed to his aid, smelling sulfur and brimstone coming from the wound even as he approached, and then saw the angry red color that had stained Richen's skin beyond the makeshift bandage. Talon heaved the delirious Richen onto his horse and mounted up behind him, galloping them both home as fast as the mount could carry them.

By the time they arrived, Richen was burning with a fever hotter than Talon believed any living thing could create. His whole torso was stained an unnatural oxblood red from the wound. Screaming for Balanon, Talon galloped into the courtyard and carried Richen to the surgery - a feat he could never have accomplished at any other time. Unfortunately, even Balanon's most potent potions, which Talon knew could instantly mend bones and cure the most soured wounds, could do nothing but stabilize Richen of the corruption invading his body. Mikal, distraught and wracked with grief at the fate of his apprentice, who he had treated much like a son for over a half-dozen years, hovered at Richen's bedside when allowed. Even so, and not being known as a superstitious man, he still used the commoner's wards against evil before entering and after leaving the surgery to visit. Talon was inconsolable all through the night - unable to even coherently tell the story of what had occurred or how it had happened. Tales of the strange wound spread among the estate staff. However, they miraculously faded with the intervention of Lord and Lady Cour-Vermane to a more reasonable explanation of a direwolf attracted to the smell of the freshly killed boar.

Two days passed with Talon in a haze of exhaustion, grief, and physical pain from the fear of losing Richen. Talon's parents seemed unconcerned with the plight of their son's closest friend and even less so about the strangeness of the corruption Talon and Mikal could see had taken a deep hold within Richen's body. He was only shaken out of his stupor when he saw a stranger stride into the estate's courtyard through the surgery window. An elder Uldani of a high station who greeted Mikal like an old friend.

It was strange to Talon for a human to be so friendly with an Uldani as they were known for their volatile and passionate nature, but the ease with which the Uldani handed over his ornately wrought weapons spoke volumes about their previous business. After a quick detour to drop off the weapons at the smithy, an act that seemed to put much of the estate's staff more at ease, Mikal brought the visitor to the surgery. Notably, neither the Lord nor Lady of the Cour-Vermane estate made an appearance or greeted such a unique visitor. Mikal and the Uldani elder found Talon at Richen's side, forehead on Richen's hand with no more tears to give, left only with the sharp emptiness of grief. He stared blankly, unable to comprehend why Mikal or Balanon, hovering over his medicinal books in the corner, would allow a stranger to trespass in this place.

"This is an old friend, Architavia Therandus, Farseer of the Argutheris. I sent out a message in hopes he could help. He is a champion of Tamul Vigos the Living Breeze, blessed with powerful divine and elemental magics, a holy shaman."

Balanon, who was about to intervene seeing the Uladani enter, bowed ceremonially and recited an elvish greeting upon hearing the introduction.

"Please," was all Talon could say at first. "Please, I can't lose him after we have just truly found each other."

Architavia Therandus' deep voice filled the chamber. A voice that could shake mountains but conveyed a boundless kindness in this moment, "My child, I can make no promises as to what lies ahead, but I give you my word; I will try to bring him back to you."

The Uldani's eyes flashed a bright living green as he examined Richen and his wound. A deep frown darkened his face, belying the fury he could bring to those who stood against him. "Tell me child, everything that happened." Then, looking to Balanon, Therandus continued, "And all measures you have taken."

Under the Uldani's gaze, a deep calm washed over Talon. He recounted every detail of the encounter as though he was reliving it again. He remembered everything clearly except the details of the beast. Try as he might, any element of his memory relating to the beast was shrouded from him. Even prodding from Architavia Therandus seemed to have no effect in pulling back the curtain that had fallen over his recollection of the creature that had attacked.

Upon nodding to Balanon, Architavia Therandus flatly stated to Mikal, "I must take the boy from this place. He cannot heal here."

"Nooooo!" pleaded Talon, "you promised! I can't lose him!"

"Child, this is not a place of healing for what ails him," his eyes making a wary circuit of the space; Architavia Therandus continued, "If anything, it will make him worse."

"I will come with you then," Talon begged.

"Where I travel is no place for you either." There was a finality to Therandus' words as he stood to his full height.

"I won't let you take him!" Talon also stood, facing off to Therandus, mustering every bit of authority he could and felt he had.

"Child, be still!" Architavia Therandus's voice cracked like a whip. "You are part of the problem."

Talon stumbled backward in shock, catching the stool off-center; he fell, tailbone hitting the floor, mouth agape, stunned. It was as though his every fear was being realized. He wasn't worthy of Richen. He never was. The voice slithered into this mind on the attack. "*I told you...*" it hissed and then was gone. Utterly defeated and broken, Talon's mind slipped into an all-encompassing haze. Whether it was for a moment, a minute, or an hour that he remained in the fugue, Talon would never know. All he knew was when he finally awoke from his stupor, Richen and Architavia Therandus were gone.

It was evening before Talon could build the courage to confront Mikal.

"How could you let him take Richen?" Talon wailed, his voice shaking and unhinged.

In a sorrowful whisper, Mikal replied, "This is the way of shamans, son. You saw as well as me that something evil had taken root. He needed a holy place, one of elemental and divine power. If Architavia Therandus had not taken Richen for the help he needed, he surely would have been lost to us or worse." He sighed, "now Richen at least has a chance."

Talon sought answers from his parents, who confronted him with stone-faced indifference. When he demanded answers, all he got was silence. That is when Talon began to train, needing something to fill the void that Richen's absence had left inside him. Knowing nothing better to do, he trained just to become stronger, berating himself for failing Richen out on the hunt and being unable to stop Architavia Therandus from taking him. Through Summer heat and Autumn's chilling rains, Talon trained with the single-minded focus only the young can maintain. Winter came and went, as did the blossoms of Spring.

Year 855 PXF ~ *Summer*

It wasn't until over a year had passed that Talon emerged mentally from his dedication and regimen. It was at the dinner table after finishing the second plate of food he had barely tasted. He stood up as his father excused himself, as was the custom, and Talon realized he was looking him eye to eye with a level gaze, no longer needing to lift his head. An instant of confusion swept over Talon, ridiculously thinking *when had his father shrunk?*

Then, a wave of memory washed over him through the fog of the previous year. Pants being made because his had become too short. New tunics, as the old ones were too tight in the chest and shoulders. Splitting logs and felling trees for the smithy. He had been carrying quarter barrels, then half barrels, and now full barrels across the courtyard again and again. He suddenly felt like his body wasn't his. It was as if he was noticing its new mass and height all at once. What had he become? What had he made himself? Then all those questions and doubts became like a drop of rain compared to the ocean as Richen's face filled his mind. His soul remembered every moment of their years together, and it was crystal clear what the last year was all for - finding Richen.

"Father," interrupting the Lord of House Cour-Vermane's exit, "I require training with weapons." For the first time in his life, it was not a request Talon made of his father but a flat statement of what was to be done. Toman Cour-Vermane bristled for an instant before a slight predatory smile crossed his face.

"I'll arrange it, my son."

CHAPTER FIVE

Year 855 PXF *~ Summer*

Talon's trainer in weapon mastery arrived at the Cour-Vermane estate the following week. A giant of a man even to Talon's new perspective after his year of training and added height. With a glance at Talon, the black armored figure marched into the smithy, setting Mikal to work. He emerged less than an hour later with a flat steel bar as long as Talon was tall with a primitive guard and hilt on one end.

He was a severe man with features that looked like they had been carved of granite and framed by hair the color of brushed steel that hung past his square jaw. He spoke with the authority of one whose words were never questioned and never needed repeating. Throwing the length of steel to Talon, "That is your greatsword. You will treat it like it is the most precious thing you own. You will never be without it, or you shall bear a scar from me to remind you of your folly." He continued directly, "You shall address me as Commander and nothing more. You shall earn another scar if you call me sir or my lord or something equally offensive. Titles such as those are for people who sit on their arses all day in padded chairs."

Talon's training began at that instant. The Commander drew his sword and lunged at Talon more swiftly than a snake's strike. Talon clumsily blocked the attack with his greatsword as he could scarcely lift it into any facsimile of a proper stance when holding it only by the makeshift hilt.

"Again," demanded the Commander.

CHING! Talon retreated, dragging the end of the training sword through the dirt of the courtyard.

"Again!" The Commander was practically chasing Talon now, his long strides carrying him far faster than Talon could scramble away.

CLANG! Talon fell backward, quickly recovered his feet, and grabbed the steel bar just in time.

"AGAIN!" A fury was now entering the Commander's words. Fear and adrenaline coursed through Talon's veins.

CRACK! CHING! CLANG! Over and over, the assault continued.

The Commander was a teacher of little patience and even less tolerance. He demanded nothing short of total obedience and absolute perfection. His attacks were ruthless, and they began drawing blood more times than not. Talon's previous year of self-led training was nothing compared to the grueling first day the Commander put him through. As sunset approached, Talon's whole body was shaking, barely able to stand.

"Good. Tomorrow the real work begins. Here, drink this. It will revive you enough to eat and sleep."

The Commander threw Talon his flask. It contained a watered-down alcoholic liquid with a bitter herbal taste which Talon drank greedily; he then slunk inside, dragging the training sword behind him. Talon ate in the kitchen, being in no state to join his parents in the dining room. Barely able to lift a fork or knife, Talon could only ravenously shovel the food Ms. Haddington and the cooks brought in a stream of plates and bowls directly into his mouth. Sleep came quickly and deeply with only one panicked reawakening when Talon remembered his greatsword, which he promptly recovered from where it was leaning against the dresser and not within arm's reach.

Before sunrise, the Commander in full armor burst into Talon's room, his sword falling to Talon's throat where it stopped, drawing only the slightest trickle of blood. Talon, frozen in fear, found his hand wrapped around the hilt of his training sword, but it had not moved even an inch to block the Commander's blow. "Today, you have died, but your sword is close, so the blame is mine. I shall train you harder." The Commander said before sheathing his sword and turning to leave. "Ten minutes, be in the courtyard. Eat first."

The Commander was true to his word. By midday, Talon's body was shaking, and his muscles were spasming so violently that he fell to the ground with every step the Commander demanded he take.

"If you can't walk, you shall crawl."

CLANG.

"When you can no longer crawl, you shall roll."

CLANG.

"When you can no longer roll, you shall squirm like a worm avoiding the hook."

CLANG.

Each word was punctuated by a fall of the Commander's sword, nearly cleaving off a part of Talon's body. When his frame finally fell limp, unable to respond to any attempt to move, the Commander's voice rang out again.

"And when nothing is left, you shall then be done." The Commander stepped over Talon's body, dropping some hard tack, jerky, and his flask with the restorative elixir on Talon's chest. "We begin again in an hour."

And so the days went—one after another. Talon interacted with no one but the Commander, Balanon, who stitched wounds shut, and Ms. Haddington, who tutted the Commander's grueling training as Talon continued taking his meals in the kitchen. He barely saw his parents; only once did he think he caught a glimpse of his father's silhouette, darkening a window looking down on him from above.

Year 855 PXF ~ *Late Autumn*

It was a month before the training became anything more than a trial of exhaustion and pain. Two before Talon ever blocked a morning ambush by the Commander, to which the Commander dryly stated, "Today you Live. Tomorrow morning I will not be so easy to thwart." Which he was not.

Months after that, as Fall was turning to Winter and Talon was no longer retiring to his room as a zombie from exhaustion, the unthinkable happened when he fell asleep in a chair by the fire. The training greatsword, now covered in nicks and dents, was close at hand as always. Yet sometime in the night, in half slumber, Talon moved to the bed, leaving the sword by the hearth. The morning arrived, along with the Commander's attack. Talon reacted to grab his sword, but his hand landed on thin air, and no block to the ruthless attack came. Instead, the Commander's sword stopped at Talon's throat, drawing blood much as it did the first morning.

"Today, you are Dead, and the blame is yours." The Commander turned, grabbed the training sword from beside the hearth, and walked out without a word.

Not knowing what to do, Talon dressed, ate quickly, and went to the courtyard where they usually trained. A light dusting of snow covered the ground with nary a footprint marking its surface. Talon's breath began to come faster, a tightness gripping his chest. Panic began to enter his mind: had he been deserted once again? Had he ruined his chance to find Richen and bring him home? Talon felt like he was drowning, the courtyard beginning to spin. He could swear he heard a cruel laughing inside his mind but only for a moment.

The attack that hit him was brutal, like being kicked by a warhorse in the chest. Talon hit the hard ground flat on his back, knocking every bit of breath from him. The Commander was then on top of him, knee on his left arm, pinning it down with his full weight, his face filling Talon's vision.

"Today. You. Are. Dead." He clipped each word through clenched teeth. "The dead no longer get the privilege to train. Instead, they have only their scars."

The Commander drew a wicked-looking black serrated dagger from his belt, ripped open Talon's tunic, and cut a deep wound in Talon's chest over his heart. Talon bit back the pain knowing that must be what the Commander expected. Clenched jaw, eyes meeting the Commander's, Talon didn't utter a sound until the Commander poured a white crystalline powder into his gloved hand and pressed it into the freshly opened wound. Until that moment, Talon would have said he knew what physical pain was, but nothing compared to the white-hot fire striking like a thousand bolts of lightning within the wound. The scream that erupted from Talon's throat echoed in the courtyard, broken only by a loud metallic clunk as the Commander dropped a new training sword next to him on the cobblestones. "Tomorrow, we shall see if you live again."

Talon stared at the sky until the chill of the earth in his bones was as painful as the fire burning in the wound on his chest. He considered going to

Balanon but thought better of it. He rolled over and found his feet, his breathing more controlled and the panic from before receding; however, a lilting snicker continued to echo in his head.

"Shut up," Talon said out loud and examined the new 'greatsword' the Commander had left him; his previous flat bar of steel had been augmented and was now a full hands breadth longer, twice as thick as before, and felt double the weight. Without even a sigh, Talon set his jaw and accepted the new reality of the sword.

Before that day, Talon thought he would have given anything for a day of rest from the Commander's training. But instead, after a leisurely breakfast and some time soaking in a much-needed proper bath, he found himself agitated and despondent. Dragging himself from the tepid bath and looking in the mirror, Talon examined the wound in his chest. He found it to be already healing, but as an angry raised red scar compared to the practically invisible razor-thin lines left from the previous cuts that Balanon had stitched shut. The mirror also showed an unkempt *man's* face looking back at him. He had to remind himself that he had indeed celebrated his eighteenth birthday months before and absently wondered about all the courtly duties that used to be a part of his life prior to the Commander's arrival. He also recognized he needed to shave the sparse scruff on his face and neck that was but a sorry excuse for a beard. The thought crossed his mind for a moment to cut his hair. It had become even more wild and tangled and matted, now hanging far past his shoulders. However, the memory of Richen running his fingers through his mane, as Richen had called it, kept that idea from becoming action.

Richen's visage haunted Talon throughout the day, and he realized how it had become almost absent in his life when previously he saw it in his mind near constantly. His name had been a source of constant motivation to Talon, a mantra he recited to persevere through the Commander's relentless training, but now Richen's face, as clear as the morning he awoke by the spring looking into his eyes, seemed to follow Talon's gaze everywhere he looked. Questions flooded his mind. Where was Richen? Did he remember Talon? Did he look as different now as Talon did from the boy who swam in the spring and laid on the boulder by his side? Talon banished the idea of Richen being dead as soon as it formed. He felt in his heart he would know, that his very soul would feel the loss, if Richen had died.

The day passed as Talon bumped around his chambers from distraction to distraction. He acclimated himself to the new training sword, had Balanon give him a shave, brushed and detangled his matted hair, and commissioned the valet to measure him for new dinner cloths, having discovered again that all his jerkins and doublets were hopelessly overtight and his breeches riding up or splitting at the seams.

Dinner with his parents for the first time in five months was predictably bland. His new clothes would not be ready for days, so he had to settle with the old, making him hopelessly uncomfortable and feeling bound and unable to move. The food, of course, was exquisite, but interaction with his parents was relegated to Talon being told of matters of the estate and local politics. His parents did not remark on Talon's presence at dinner, his ill-fitting attire, that he had shaved, or the bar of flat raw steel leaning on the table at his side. The only mention of Talon's activities was Toman's comment, "I see you did not train today. Why is that?"

"I died this morning," Talon replied flatly.

Without missing a beat, his father simply said, "Don't let it happen again."

And that was it. Talon's mother, as always, remained silent and as beautiful as a painting without even a flinch at Talon's statement of dying. Conversation of happenings at the imperial court resumed. Within three-quarters of an hour, his parents excused themselves, leaving Talon alone at the table with a cooling half-shank of lamb.

It was then and there, in clothes that no longer fit, at a ridiculous table of finery he did not recognize, and with a dinged raw steel flat-bar training sword at his side, that Talon realized he was as invisible to his parents as the marks left by the wounds that Balanon had sewn shut. They knew him no more than the stablehands or the gardener, perhaps even less. In contrast, the Commander, as harsh as he was, at least saw Talon and, in his punishments, was reacting to Talon's actions, even if it was his failures or shortcomings.

Before the first ray of sun crested the horizon, the Commander burst into Talon's chambers to find... an empty bed.

CLANG!

The Commander's lightning-fast reactions still stopped Talon's heavy training sword that swung toward his torso from behind. "Ah. Today you live and have learned. Now your education can actually begin."

Relentless. Tactical. Strategic. Precise. Unending. Talon discovered his training truly had just begun. The work of the previous five months was just about brute force; this was about control. Into the Winter, through the Spring, and until the fruits of Summer had come and gone, the Commander refined Talon's skills in the same slow, deliberate process that one tempers and hones a blade. Talon made no effort to interact again with his parents, and his parents were similarly absent from his life.

On a brisk afternoon with the last leaves of Fall crunching underfoot, the Commander, helping Talon up from the ground after a brutal sparring match, held out his other hand and asked Talon for the greatsword that he was still using for training. Taking it, the Commander said, "Tomorrow you rest, and the following day, you begin to learn the ways of the weapon that your destiny demands you wield."

CHAPTER SIX

Year 856 PXF *~ Autumn*

Unlike the previous time the Commander had canceled training, Talon knew precisely what he would do with his gifted day. At first light, with a small pack, he set out on horseback to the spring where he and Richen had spent their last day together. Frost painted the landscape around him in shades of white and gray. The trees that had been lush and verdant in the warmth of Summer were now silent and bare. The solemn scene fit Talon's mood and set the steel in his heart. Through the trees and along the pathways of memory, Talon navigated to the spring.

Leaving the quiet sentinels of the forest behind, he entered the glade where the spring lay. The surrounding holly and juniper, free for the Winter of the shadowing canopy above, burst through the starkness of the landscape with a vibrancy that lifted Talon's heart. He went to the boulder Richen and he had shared and looking into the deep blue heart of the spring, spoke with a strong but wavering voice. "Richen, I am almost ready. I will find you. Somehow, we will still be together again. How could two such as us not be destined to share a life? Even if it takes decades and all we get is to spend one more day together, it will be worth it." Talon fell to his knees, unable to hold back the sob that wracked his chest. The man he had become was indistinguishable in this moment from the boy who kneeled on the boulder, professing his love for Richen and hearing that love returned to him in kind.

A chill breeze ruffled Talon's hair. For an instant, he mistook it for Richen running his fingers through his thick locks. Talon looked up, almost expecting Richen to be there, but alas, it was just a daydream. The breeze turned cold, and Talon watched as it spun a few leaves out across the still water of the spring. As he watched, the leaves became covered in ice, disintegrating into a fall of snow. The flakes fell across the spring's surface, spawning even more ice crystals to form that then spread across the water. The sprays of ice swirled and grew until they covered the spring entirely. Talon knew something beyond natural was happening and barely dared to breathe lest he disturb it. Looking at the now ice-covered spring, he began to discern the features of a face, or perhaps faces, feminine in form yet handsome as well; it wavered and changed as he watched. The eyes then opened and seemed to bore into his own, and an echoing voice spoke in his mind.

> *Talon, son of Toman, your fate is bound to darkness, as your bloodline has been so bound for millennia. While it is true that there is no darkness so deep that the light cannot break it, I am afraid that even the shining beacon of your love will not be enough to free you of the shackles meant to bind you.*

As the chill of those words sunk into Talon's heart, the confirmation of a dread that had lurked in the shadows of his life, a copper-colored flame sparked to life under the ice and the face within it. The reverberating message continued to bore into his mind.

> *Even if you were to become my champion, I still could not fully expel the darkness from your fate. However, I can make it so the darkness within you will never bring harm or pain to your love.*

> *Whether you will be together again or share a life or even another single day is not for me to decide. But, the shattering of the darkness permeating your destiny, even though I cannot sweep all the shards away, can at least give the two of you a chance.*

Talon was overwhelmed not just by the presence of what must surely be a deity but also by the words they spoke: darkness, bloodlines, champions? Yet, what filtered through the churning maelstrom of his thoughts was that this deity could give him and Richen a chance. "What must I do?" barely above a whisper, almost a prayer.

For now, you must disrupt the machinations of a new darkness that will visit itself upon you. This darkness lurks in shadow and creeps in the secret places of the hearts of men. It will neither show itself nor give power to any it suspects that are not of its own kind. Continue your path. The darkness will think it has won, having never lost on its own battlefield before, but when it strikes, I will be your shield that will allow your light to burn all the brighter.

The voice continued.

That will be just the beginning. There will be more for you to endure, perhaps more than I should even ask, but to bind yourself to me is to bind yourself to the seasons and cycles of nature itself. To do so is to surrender yourself to laws far beyond the ken of mortal men.

The ice sheet on the spring shattered, sending shards flying into the air. For a fraction of an instant, Talon came to know the deity to whom he spoke. Haloed in shards of ice, stone, fire, and life was the Conjoined God Caspharian.

Will you be my champion, sworn by this name and all those yet to come?

The force of the question was both a hurricane and the gentle warmth of a shared hearth.

Talon stood, awestruck but with conviction in his voice. "I will be your champion. For Richen, for myself, and against whatever darkness my family has brought to infect this land."

With that, Caspharian was gone as though they had never been there. Talon's knees buckled, and he fell hard onto the boulder, his height and prodigious weight giving it enough impact to slap him back to reality. Had that just occurred? Talon didn't feel any different. What was that about his family's darkness? The more he tried to grasp the deity's words, the more quickly they slipped away, like a dream fading in dawn's light. Looking around himself for any sign of the deity's passing, the only evidence that Talon could find of the miraculous event was a new crack that bisected the boulder he had shared with Richen. There, between the two halves of solid stone, he found a tiny green shoot newly sprouted, poking up through the tight space.

Talon followed a meandering path back to the Cour-Vermane estate. He couldn't have said whether he guided his mount there or if his horse took him to where it knew he needed to be, but Talon arrived at a familiar orchard. Looking out over the orchard from a low rise that marked its northern extent, it wasn't the bare trees of Winter he saw but the colorful bounty of early Autumn from years before.

*3 Years Earlier ~ 852*PXF *~ Early Autumn*

It was the first Hearth's Rest of the season, and Richen and Talon knew their exact destination for the day: Milgran's Orchard. They had visited it in the Spring when the trees were in full bloom and again in Summer to lay in the cool shade beneath the lush foliage of the orchard's boughs. Two days earlier, the boys had been recounting the Hearth's Rest trips of the previous eighteen months of knowing each other, and they had realized a trip to Milgran's had marked the beginning of each season. So, without hesitation, they decided they would keep the tradition and likewise mark this transition to Fall.

As the two crested the rise overlooking the orchard, the heady perfume of the fermenting apples fallen before harvest hit their nostrils. Milgran's Orchard was known for having some of the region's largest and most productive apple trees, and this Autumn was no exception. The trees were laden with fruit, boughs bending under the heavy weight of the bountiful harvest to come. As expected, the farm residents had deserted the orchard for their day of rest; that meant the boys had the sprawling tract of apple trees all to themselves. The two half-ran, half-stumbled, and in Talon's case, half-rolled down the embankment and into the orchard proper. Pulling apples from the branches, they talked of all the upcoming feasts and festivals that came with the harvest season and even a wild scheme to secretly ferment their own cider, which no doubt would be the best to be found far and wide. After a double-dared dip in the already chilly pond near the center of the orchard and far too many apples, Richen and Talon climbed into the largest tree at the center of the orchard. Finding comfortable branches to lounge upon as only youths can, they dreamily dozed through midday and into the early afternoon.

Talon was shaken out of his reverie by Richen's climbing higher into the boughs. "Hey, where are you going?" asked Talon groggily, not quite yet coming to the reasoning that up led nowhere but up.

"I think I have found the perfect apple!" Richen called back down as Talon wondered if Richen had maybe eaten an apple that had already fermented. Richen climbed higher and higher and then out onto a branch that was shockingly small to carry his weight. As he reached up with one hand, stretching out as far as he could, both boys heard the crack of the branch Richen was standing on. It was over in an instant. Richen plummeted down through the tree, hitting limbs as he went. Talon almost laughed at the ridiculous look he somehow saw on Richen's face as he passed by him on the way down. He would have laughed regardless if not for the sickening wet crack he heard as Richen hit the ground and the way Richen's arm bent like it had an extra elbow.

Talon climbed down almost as quickly as Richen had fallen. When he arrived, Richen sat up and looked at his broken arm with glazed eyes like it didn't belong to him. Talon instantly fell into the training he had done with Balanon and spotted Richen was in shock from the fall, the pain yet to sink in. He also knew that it would not last for long. "Richen. Richen! Look at me. Let's get you over here by the tree." Talon instructed far more calmly than he felt as he positioned the still-sitting Richen so he could lean his back against the tree. Richen stared at Talon blankly but followed his instruction.

Talon began to examine the arm, constantly talking to Richen with an even tone of voice, mimicking Balanon's bedside manner as well as he could. "Okay, this might hurt." There was finally a reaction from Richen when he took a sharp intake of breath as Talon probed the break as his mentor had taught him. "Luckily, the break seems clean, and the bone didn't puncture through the skin, so I will just need to set and splint it." Talon recited the course of action more like he was answering a question in the surgery than as any sort of confident confirmation of what he would have to do next. Talon quickly prepared a splint with strips torn off his own shirt and the broken branch that had fallen with Richen. Then, setting the splint aside, he presented a smaller stick up to Richen's eyes - their gray flushed through with bright blue from fear - which had begun to moisten from pain. Richen looked confused until Talon said, "You are going to want to bite down on this," His eyes widened, but he quickly opened his mouth, and Talon placed the stick between his back teeth.

"Here we go, on three. One, two," Talon did not wait for three. With a careful tug and slight twist, he set the bone. Balanon's training had shown him how bone could fit back together like two broken pieces of wood. It seemed to work in Talon's first practical application with a patient that wasn't a preserved pig. Talon splinted the arm and made a makeshift sling from one of the large cloths Ms. Haddington had packed with the lunch they were supposed to have eaten instead of gorging themselves on apples.

"There. We will have Balanon look at you when we get home. We should start heading that way, though; you are going to feel every step as we walk, so we will need to go slow."

Richen looked at Talon with such gratefulness Talon's heart almost fluttered out of his chest. Until this point in the eighteen months they had known each other, it had been Richen always rescuing Talon from his fears, panics, and noble name, but now Talon had done something for Richen when he needed help. For the first time, Talon felt their relationship was one of equals, not Richen always carrying him. He returned Richen's gaze with a smile but watched the gratefulness evaporate into despair. With panic in his voice for the first time, Talon asked, "What is it? Does it hurt? Is there something else?"

Richen, voice full of sorrow, replied. "No. No, it actually hurts very little. It's just that this means I will be leaving."

"What? What are you talking about?" Talon sat back on his heels, not understanding.

"Even if you or the surgeon set it perfectly, this is my right arm. It will take months to be usable again, then months, possibly a year, to regain its strength. We both know Mikal would try to make it work, but he will need a new apprentice, and I refuse to be a burden to him or indebted to your father for healing magics."

"But..." Talon started to interject, but seeing the set in Richen's jaw and the hardness in his eyes, he knew Richen had already braced himself against any argument. Talon would only have one chance to change his mind. "Hear me out. You are right. It is unfair to burden Mikal or indebt yourself to my father, so that is not what we are going to do." Talon smiled cunningly. "You see, because I'm the one who broke my arm."

Talon laid out his plan. First, Richen would need to make it to his room in the smithy with his arm hidden under a cloak with no outward sign of injury. Meanwhile, Talon making a show of his arm being splinted and broken in a sling would head to the surgery to see Balanon as both a distraction and cover for the next part. Once there, Talon would explain the situation to Balanon, and hopefully, Balanon would consent that a healing potion would be the usual treatment for the lord-inheritor of the estate with such an injury. Finally, Talon would walk out of the surgery 'healed' of his broken arm, but with the potion pocketed in his cloak.

Hope returned to Richen's eyes. "But do you think Balanon will go along with it? Wouldn't he tell your father?"

Talon replied as confidently as he could feign, "Don't worry about Balanon. He always spoke of his pledge to fight and dispel pain, physical and mental, and that is what I am asking him to do. We have supplied a perfectly acceptable reason for using a healing potion, so there should be no problem if my father becomes suspicious that one is gone." Continuing, Talon blatantly lied, "And if there is, I do know all about his dalliances with the cleric's wife in Arnadore."

It was the first time he had been anything but honest with Richen. Talon knew that if there were any issue with Balanon, he would bring up the healing potions Balanon was supplying his mother as leverage. He could feel the dark grin of the voice in his mind from both the act of lying to Richen and the anticipation of blackmailing Balanon. He mentally recoiled from the voice's approval and realized Richen was laughing at his proclamation about the cleric's wife. Talon joined in, but his laughter rang nervous and empty. Luckily, Richen quickly stopped from the pain his giggling induced in his broken arm.

Once back at the estate, the plan went off without a hitch. The only tell of something being amiss was Richen's stiff walk to the smithy as every step was agony for him, especially as the splint and sling had been removed to avoid notice. As predicted, Talon's parents made no appearance in the surgery even after word had been rushed to them that Talon had been 'injured.' Balanon, Talon found, had no problem with the plan, so there was no need for blackmail. Though he did not endorse the deception, he seemed to find Talon's problem-solving ability both comprehensive and clever.

After retrieving the potion and nearly running across the courtyard to get to the smithy, Talon found Richen cradling his arm, standing in the center of his room. Trails of fallen tears like they were raindrops from his stormcloud eyes stained Richen's cheeks, and he bit back even more as Talon entered. Whether the tears were from pain, doubt, or worry, seeing Richen this way broke Talon's heart. Without a word, Talon popped open the vial and immediately fed it to Richen. He never even contemplated an awkward attempt at a handoff. His only thought being Richen needed him and that he was in pain. In an unintended pose of complete trust and helplessness, Richen just tilted his head back like a baby bird and drank it down. As is the way with magic and potions, the effect was immediate. Before Talon could even ask if it worked, the strength of both of Richen's arms engulfed him. It was the first time they had hugged, and Talon leaned into the embrace, throwing his arms around Richen as well, now with tears staining his cheeks.

Richen swayed back and forth as he held Talon in his powerful arms and profoundly stated the feelings in his heart. "You have forever changed my life, Talon Cour-Vermane. I knew there was something special in you from the moment we met."

Present Year 856 PXF ~ Autumn

The memory of that embrace brought Talon back to the present. Richen's words that he had uttered three years earlier rang in his ears as if he had just spoken them. "Something special," Richen had said. Talon recognized now that the darkness Caspharian had spoken of was the voice inside his mind. He had always assumed the voice was something from within himself: an inherent ugliness inside him, perhaps even something everyone had to overcome. The deity's words that had slipped away from his recollection before rang in his mind, that he was *bound to darkness* by shackles even a god could not entirely erase. Talon looked inside to where he always felt the voice resided and delved deeper than he had ever dared look before. Guided by the deity's words, what he found was not an entity or an incorporeal voice; he found a black chain fused to his soul that stretched out from him to the horizon somewhere beyond his view. Talon was horrified by the black links that seemed to writhe under his inspection, as though the very act of witnessing them was an offense to their nature. As he searched for how he was bound to such an abhorrent creation, his mind fled from what he discovered. The first link, and presumably all others, was grown from his soul's flesh that blackened into the hard iron links that stretched into the distance.

Talon's psyche slammed back into his body, and he fell from his horse, retching from the revelation. Kneeling on all fours, Talon wiped the bile from his mouth with the back of his hand as he looked out over Milgran's Orchard. He closed his eyes, blocking the sight of the bare tree limbs reaching to the sky like skeletal fingers in the gray Winter light. They reflected the revelation of the dark chain binding him too closely. Taking deep breaths, he concentrated on the memory of Richen's strong arms and warm body pressed against him, their hearts beating almost as one. The deity had said something else that Talon now held tightly onto: "the shining beacon of your love."

Talon arrived back at the courtyard of the estate as twilight darkened the sky. There was still time for him to dress and make an appearance at formal dinner with his parents, but he chose to dine in the kitchen instead. He supped happily with Ms. Haddington conducting the cheerful sounds of the busy kitchen and the endless kindness and servings the other cooks provided, all the while trying to ignore the heavy weight of the chain he now felt binding his soul.

CHAPTER SEVEN

Year 856 PXF ~ *Autumn*

Talon had never felt more naked or exposed as he tried to sleep. Not only was he questioning if his new knowledge of the chain might summon something worse than just the voice he was familiar with, but Talon also had no sword nearby, training or otherwise. He dreaded what that could mean for the morning. He finally settled for sleeping with a long dagger at his side, the one Mikal had gifted him for his sixteenth birthday. Mikal made the blade while Richen was still his apprentice, which Richen undoubtedly knew was intended for Talon. It comforted him to know, in some small way, Richen was with him lying in the darkness. Sleep finally found Talon, a slight smile on his lips and dreams filled with visions of raven-dark hair and stormcloud eyes.

Hours before dawn's first light, Talon lay awake, anticipating what was to come and what he should do. A dagger was no match for the Commander's blade, but he had the element of surprise as the Commander would think him unarmed. Behind the door seemed too expected, and he was too large to hide in the wardrobe anymore. He finally settled on sitting in the chair by the hearth with the dagger hidden to his side. Talon sat and waited. Finally, just after dawn, he heard the Commander's footsteps coming down the hallway. Talon tightened every muscle, ready to spring into action.

KNOCK, KNOCK, KNOCK

The three raps on the door were more unexpected than anything for which Talon could have planned. Then, the Commander's voice through the door, "Courtyard, ten minutes. Eat first." At that point, the Commander could have felled Talon with a feather. Hells, a kitten could have. Confused and not knowing what else to do, Talon got up, grabbed some food, and proceeded to the courtyard.

As he approached, the Commander preempted the questions Talon had etched on his face with a simple fact. "Life and death are in your hands now. 'Safe' is just another word for 'vulnerable.'" He continued, "Now for your weapon. Your height and your strength deserve the weapon of knights and lords." The Commander stepped into the smithy and returned with a polearm over eight feet in length. The top two feet consisted of a broad curved blade shaped like a barbed scimitar, the rest a steel-reinforced ironwood shaft. Talon had seen one of these before: an old imperial glaive of the Shalmecura. The weapon wielded by the knight protectors of Thon'Sangreal.

One scenario he had envisioned as he tried to find sleep the night before was another differently shaped but equally crude flat steel bar as a weapon to train with, but what the Commander tossed him was beautifully wrought, perfectly balanced, and exceptionally deadly. Even with its length and apparent weight, the glaive felt like a feather in Talon's hand. He tried to spin it like he once saw a knight of Thon'Sangreal do when they visited Arnadore. He was even quite proud of himself when he managed a fair approximation of what he thought it should look like. Then, before Talon got too cocky, the Commander put on a display of such dexterity and speed that Talon's jaw almost hit the courtyard's cobblestones. The dizzying theatrics he displayed were not just for flair, as Talon soon discovered when the Commander had the blade stop dead at his throat, giving his whiskers the slightest trim from over ten feet away.

"Now to work."

Once again, the training was wholly different than before. Talon and the Commander rarely crossed blades with their glaives but instead practiced an endless array of forms and stances, maneuvers and blocks. The training in the courtyard looked more like a choreographed dance than battle or dueling. Talon's scoffing at what he assumed would be easy quickly became despair and agony as his muscles began screaming at the effort it took him to match what the Commander made look effortless. Tendons and ligaments long tightened by the bulk of the muscle mass he had added in the previous two years now stretched and strained painfully to even remotely match the Commander's poses. Talon found he needed the Commander's flask of restorative elixir as much, if not more so, than those first training days.

It was three months before Talon had gained enough flexibility and grace to master all the stances the Commander taught him. However, as Talon became more adept at the forms, he found they became a way to calm his mind and gain more control over his new awareness of the dark chain that shackled him. He could not banish it or the voice, but its weight became easier to bear, and the voice became less intrusive. Talon thought his mastery of the stances would allow him to begin sparring with the Commander again, but the Commander then transitioned to instructing him in the art of combinations. String after string of four, then seven, up to sixteen forms and stances one after another without pause or break. The commander drove him through six more months of drilling these combinations and counter combinations before the Commander acquiesced and said Talon was ready. Winter and Spring long since gone, they faced off with glaives held high and shining under the blinding Summer sun.

The Commander began with a slow, wide, main-arm circular attack announcing it by name as he came at Talon. "Arra-fiendal." Talon, surprised by the Commander's declaration, countered quickly.

"Sang'ryteel," the Commander announced again as he slashed back with a twirling off-hand thrust. Talon realized that his previous counter had set up the Commander for this much more advanced attack with few options to repel it. In his resulting mental scramble of identifying his mistake and planning his next move, the Commander's blade struck Talon's shoulder at the armpit. Luckily, the Commander had pulled the force behind the attack, so it did not pierce armor or flesh. Talon knew if it had, his arm would have been disabled, and he'd likely be bleeding out from a sliced artery. The Commander returned to a ready position, patiently waiting for Talon to recognize the lesson.

"Again," was all the Commander needed to say.

Their sparring continued. The Commander announced every move he made as he made them, but as the training progressed, reprimands for repeated mistakes came with a shallow wound. With so many new mistakes to make, Talon made it until near sunset before becoming too bloodied to continue. Unfortunately, the next day was not as productive as Talon repeated many of the mistakes of the day before, and the Commander left him bleeding in the training yard by mid-afternoon. Each day when Talon became too bloodied to continue, the training ended no matter the time or progress that they had made. Finally, after a fortnight of shortened training days due to his own mistakes, Talon felt the challenge of learning it all to be insurmountable. There was too much, and the Commander was too skilled. Talon had tried drilling on his own after Balanon would seal or stitch his wounds shut each day, but it was of no discernable help, and his failures in the training yard continued to mount higher and higher.

The voice that had been sulking since his trip to the spring and effectively silenced by Talon's new mental discipline from earlier in the year gloated incessantly at Talon's frustration with his progress. It relished in pointing out every bloodied and sliced tunic that decorated Talon's rooms and delightedly scoffed as Talon donned his endlessly repaired training leathers each day. The added distraction of the voice throwing suggestions into his already cluttered mind when he was in the ring with the Commander resulted in Talon's skills degrading instead of improving. Furious, having suffered through another week of the Commander leaving him too bloodied to continue before the noon hour, Talon marched into the surgery and grabbed a healing potion without even asking Balanon's leave. Drinking it and throwing the empty vial aside, he stripped off his broken armor and bloody shirt as he strode back into the courtyard, glaive in hand under the scorching midsummer sun. Then, yelling into the sky but directing his words at the voice snickering in his mind, Talon screamed out, "You want to destroy me? Well, come at me!"

He then began his forms, calling out the name of each one as he went. The voice slithered like a serpent through his thoughts, critiquing and questioning each move. It second-guessed and challenged everything Talon did, breaking his confidence and concentration motion by motion. Sweat pouring down his face and into his eyes, Talon became increasingly more frustrated and angrier, and as he did, the courtyard slowly melted away around him, and he found himself on a high rocky plateau under a blood-red sky. Now an incorporeal mist-like serpent, the voice swirled around Talon's blade as he hit each pose. Even though Talon was not actively targeting it, the voice-snake taunted Talon as though he was.

"Enough!" Talon demanded and struck out. In that moment, his mind switched off, leaving his body to channel the months and years of training unburdened by his swirling thoughts. His glaive sought out its target, but that target was not the serpent that taunted him. Instead, it swung out in a sweeping arc for the invisible dark chain bound to his soul. A chain Talon's eyes could not see, but his body knew was there.

CLANG! SZZZZZZNK

Stretching across the tortured landscape, in a clash of steel and a flash of arcane static, the chain binding his soul revealed itself as Talon's blade struck it. Not as the chain he remembered from his vision at the orchard, the single black abomination made of links larger in diameter than his wrist, but an array of smaller branching chains of seemingly endless possibilities. The chains surrounding him covered the plateau in a vast, interconnected, mind-boggling web. Seeing them and their complexity as they stretched out from him in all directions to the horizon, Talon felt the same overwhelming confusion he did when sparring with the Commander, his mind overloaded with input. The chains thrummed with a strange energy and all but called for Talon to examine them more closely. As he did, he saw the links of these chains were somehow forged from all the forms and moves he had learned from the Commander; each individual link a single attack or counter attached to all its permutations.

Talon, surrounded and encircled by the array, chose one of the hundreds that spread outward from him and attacked the first link with the form it represented. As he struck, the link shattered, and around him, the web reconfigured centering on the broken link; some chains fading into a gray mist, others becoming more prominent and glowing with an arcane light. Talon picked one of the glowing chains and, with the prescribed attack, shattered its first link. Again the web morphed, and as Talon looked across the new configuration, he could see where the misty gray chains would lead to weaker attacks; the glowing chains showed a strategy that became stronger and more difficult to thwart. Talon began following one of the luminous strategies in earnest, each link preparing him for the next attack or counter. The path down the chain laid out a strategy, and based on his choices and how well he anticipated his opponent, it could bend the momentum of combat either in his favor or toward defeat. The ends of chains were victory or a setback, some of which were irrecoverable.

As he explored the chains, the array resetting at his will, Talon discovered his mistakes over the previous weeks and months. Delving into the strategies of the chains was like navigating a maze. Before, he had felt trapped between this labyrinth's walls with hundreds of choices and no clear direction. Now he looked down upon the maze, seeing its intricacies clearly, able to plan the clearest path. Talon tested and explored every chain until, against his will, the plateau faded. He tried to hold onto the vision, afraid he would never find it again, but it disappeared, and the courtyard slid into his sight. It was night, and Balanon was holding him up, his tortured body no longer able to support itself. The surgeon poured water on his face as his body shook violently. Talon tried to ask what was happening, but his tongue was thick and his mind cloudy.

"You have been going at it for nine hours without water or rest. You were in a delirium that even magic could not break." Balanon asked with genuine concern in his voice. "You are beyond exhausted; I was worried we would have to have the Commander knock you unconscious if you didn't stop soon. Provided he could get close enough." Talon's eyes could only focus long enough to spot the Commander's scowling outline looming in shadow across the courtyard as consciousness left him. As his mind faded to black, he could not help but recognize that the Commander seemed more disappointed than concerned.

Talon awoke in the surgery the next day. It was approaching lunch if he correctly gauged the light streaming through the windows. To Balanon's protestations, Talon pushed his way out of the surgery and prepared for training with the Commander. Shrugging on his armor, Talon walked out to meet the Commander in their sparring ring. The Commander eyed him with a concern he could not quite decipher as he stepped to meet Talon, who had already assumed the ready position.

"Vari'cah." The instant the Commander announced his attack, the array of chains appeared in Talon's mind, his sight split between them and the courtyard. He could barely process the relief he felt at their return as he moved to counter the swift attack from the Commander. In his mind, the chains on the plateau reconfigured, predicting the Commander's next strike.

"Trel Scykan," the Commander announced his next move, which fell exactly into line with what the chains had foretold, and Talon countered by following the strategy laid out by the chains in his mind. Back and forth they went until the Commander's experience and skill finally defeated Talon, but this time without earning him a wound. Talon was overjoyed with his success, but when he looked at the Commander, he saw only an undecipherable concern along with a hardness and resolve behind the Commander's eyes.

"Again," the Commander demanded flatly, never breaking eye contact with Talon, a deep intensity etched on his face.

"Lin-pal'va." A spinning off-hand feint began the next round.

So it went until the sun began to set; Talon still earned a few wounds but not enough to prevent him from finishing the day. The Commander's attitude did not relent throughout that day or the following week. Talon never spoke of the chains to the Commander, and the camaraderie they had shared before the chains appeared seemed to evaporate as their training became more intense. The Commander became more distant daily, less like the man with whom Talon had enjoyed training and more just a stone golem in a shared sparring ring. It hurt Talon that his success had affected the Commander this way, but the whispered feeling of contempt from the darkness within him colored his perception of it and, in more introspective moments, made him worry about what it could mean.

It took months, even with the Commander still vocally announcing his attacks, but Talon's skill and speed finally progressed to a point where with the chains' insight, he finally bested the Commander. Talon's victories versus the Commander progressed from happening once a week to once a day. When he could finally defeat him regularly under the current training protocol, the Commander changed the process again.

The following day, the Commander flatly stated he would no longer announce his attacks. Talon smugly assumed that the Commander would want Talon to call out his own moves to handicap himself, but instead, the Commander demanded Talon call out the Commander's moves as he made them. Initially, this confounded Talon. Even though he had come to rely on them less each session, the chains seemed to be of little help at all to him now. The Commander beat him soundly again and again. As the morning wore on, the Commander's attacks became increasingly predatory; inflicted wounds were not the surface cuts of earlier months but deep and meant to cause actual harm.

The Commander finally broke the silence he had kept for far longer than when training began that morning. "Get out of your head," he snapped at Talon. "Use your eyes out here. Look at *me*. Listen to what my actions are telling you, not anything else." The Commander's words hit Talon like he had been caught cheating on a test for his tutors. The Commander took advantage of Talon's shock at his words, slamming his shoulder into Talon's chest, putting them face to face. "You have the skills. They are yours. Now trust them." The Commander delivered these words not with the disappointment and stony facade that had marred the last few months but with the camaraderie of the teacher and mentor Talon knew from the time before he discovered the chains. The Commander pushed Talon away and across the ring.

"Again."

Talon took a deep breath and dispelled the chains from his mind. As he did so, an unexpected smug confidence in his imminent failure entered his thoughts from where he knew the voice resided. Talon cleared those thoughts and did as the Commander had said, examining and trusting his senses. The Commander's weight was on his right foot, his glaive angled slightly downward, and his grip forward on the shaft. Only three attacks were probable with that preparation, and the instant the Commander began to move, three became one.

"Sang'thal!" Talon simultaneously announced as the Commander's movements resolved into the attack. Talon's mind forgot to counter after correctly identifying the attack, but his body reflexively not only countered but hemmed in the Commander's next possible moves. Talon felt the Commander's shift in balance through their crossed glaives, which meant only one thing.

"Sang'ryteel," Talon confidently announced and countered.

The smug confidence in Talon's mind began to decay into dismay and disgust as attack after attack, Talon accurately predicted and countered without fail. Finally, the voice itself tried to intrude, but Talon brushed it aside like it was no more than a chill breeze. The Commander did best Talon in the end, but for the first time in months, it was done with an ever so slight curve to his mouth and not a grimace of concern. Through the bright colors of Autumn and the onset of Winter, Talon learned to read and announce the Commander's every action, only relying on the chains occasionally, not as a crutch during sparring but more as a filing system when he reviewed his day alone in his rooms at night. Finally, fifteen months after the first day when Talon caught the glaive tossed to him by the Commander, the tactics of their training changed again, and they sparred in silence as equals.

CHAPTER EIGHT

Year 858 PXF *~ Winter*

The deep chill of Winter still clung to the estate's eaves and icy corners of the courtyard. The Feast of New Dawn's Beginning had come and gone from the Cour-Vermane residence. As tradition firmly dictated, Toman toasted in the dawn of the new year along with his staff. Lifting watered-down cider Toman had dutifully provided, the staff gathered in the courtyard at first light while he, Veronic, and Talon raised their glasses from behind the balustrade atop the main stairs leading to the front doors of the estate. Toman, dressed in heavy fur-lined cloak and festive woolen outer robes, delivered the traditional toast with feigned vigor. Veronic was the picture of vintage New Dawn's Beginning with her attire, cascading curls, and makcup.

Conversely, Talon's attire more closely resembled that of the lower staff, other than being exceptionally tailored and that some of them had actually attempted to look festive. Having taken charge of his wardrobe the year earlier, his dress for the event was functionally formal rather than flamboyant. On Talon's insistence and copious amounts of extra coin, the clothier he retained crafted all of his outfits to his specifications, using only fabrics of plain design with tailoring befitting his size and mass, regardless of current style or trend.

After lifting a glass with his parents, Talon would have preferred to descend into the courtyard to spend the day with Balanon and Mikal, enjoying Ms. Haddington's hearty breakfast fare that she would begin serving from the kitchens soon. There was even a chance the Commander might join them instead of taking his meals alone in his rooms. However, his father's sense of propriety forbade it. After receiving a backhanded compliment on his outfit from Toman, which he did not acknowledge, and a disparaging look from Veronic, Talon followed them inside to the sterile celebration prepared to Toman's exacting specifications by the upper staff for them.

New Dawn's Beginning was the primary holiday observance of the deity known as the Storyteller. One of the very few universally recognized household gods of not just the Xallian Empire but across the world of Valknor, the Storyteller crafted the tales that molded and shaped the present circumstance of people everywhere. Part fate, part destiny, part self-determination, the diminutive deity that traveled the continents was considered a harbinger of great things, good or ill. New Dawn's Beginning was considered the day that the Storyteller turned the page on a new chapter for the world, quill poised above paper to begin writing anew.

After their formal morning meal in the dining room and adjourning to the library for Veronic's recitation of the myth of the Storyteller's appearance at the first Shadowfyre atop Lymehold Peak, Talon was finally able to retire to his rooms. Formalities out of the way, he planned to head to the kitchen in search of more lively company. Just as he finished changing his clothes into something better suited to the downstairs celebration, there was a knock at his door. A member of the upper staff handed Talon an envelope sealed with wax emblazoned with his father's coat of arms. Talon's father had summoned him to his private study. In all his nineteen years, Talon only had the hazy childhood memory of once being in his father's study, but he had never been called to it. Talon considered changing back into his holiday clothes, but as his wardrobe was one of his few acts of open rebellion against his parents, he decided against it. Instead, dressed to his own standard, Talon entered the forbidden study with neither pause nor hesitation and stood before his father's desk, awaiting the cause of the summons.

"I have arranged a duel," his father announced flatly. "It is to be against one of your distant cousins. Do not embarrass me or prove that I have wasted coin on the training I provided you."

Talon bristled at the implication and audacity of his father taking credit for his training, but then he paused. There was something behind his father's words. A cunning and manipulation aimed directly at Talon. At first, he questioned his senses, wondering if he had mistaken the internal antics of the voice as something outside himself, but that was not the case. A predator was in this room stalking prey, thinking itself hidden, waiting to strike. Deceptively, Talon let his original bristling at his father's words remain on his face even though he no longer felt them and, through feigned clenched teeth, replied, "As you say, Father."

"That is all. The duel is three days hence." Talon, taking the dismissal, turned on his heel and left. As he walked back to his chambers and then on to the kitchens, Talon could feel that there was a pressure building, like a boil coming to a head and needing lancing. Talon tried to set it behind himself as he headed down to the celebration below, knowing all he could do was be ready and hope he could meet the challenge.

Year 858 PXF ~ *Winter*

The intervening days passed more quickly than Talon would have liked. Not that he doubted the Commander's training but more Talon knew enough not to overestimate his skills or underestimate his opponent.

The retinue containing his opponent and observers to the duel arrived on the third day just after mid-morning. No fanfare or reception was held at the Cour-Vermane estate, just quiet acknowledgment that their visitors had entered the courtyard. Whatever blood tied these two factions of the Cour-Vermane family together, the animosity they harbored toward each other was no secret. The only exception was a young girl of no more than six years of age who was chided continuously to remain in the visitor's carriage after finding excuse after excuse to leave it. Semi-whispered admonishments of "Cerena!" through clenched teeth and pursed lips were the only noise to break the silent gathering.

Talon entered the courtyard training area to what seemed like a crowd compared to the emptiness of the one-on-one training with the Commander of the last two and a half years. While there were less than half a dozen onlookers, Talon felt the weight of their eyes upon his opponent and himself. His adversary was half a hand shorter than himself and considerably lighter. However, his choice of studded leather armor rather than the chain and breastplate that Talon wore spoke volumes of his speed and agility. Hawklike amber eyes sized up Talon as they estimated strengths and weaknesses, just as Talon's hazel eyes also assessed his opponent. There were no introductions or formalities, just stepping into position and the Commander's voice. "Begin."

His rival made the first attack, glaive whipping out like a lightning bolt. His glaive was shorter than Talon's but still had enough reach for Talon to need to block the strike instead of just dodging. Just as they had countless times before in his bouts with the Commander, the chains of possibility unfurled in Talon's mind, but with this new opponent, the links were blank, just as he intended. Talon retaliated with a wicked spin strike, his opponent having to bend nearly in half in order to avoid it. Strike and counter, maneuver and dodge; the first five minutes brought hardly a blow landed by either combatant. Had Talon been trained by anyone other than the Commander, the untrained eye would have said the two were evenly matched. The experienced eye would even wager that Talon would tire first due to his size and heavier armor, placing their money on his opponent. The only real tell as to how the battle was going was the ever so slight upward tilt to the Commander's lip. He knew exactly what was happening. While the Commander still didn't know about the chains in Talon's mind, he could see Talon's strategy; Talon was learning.

In his mind, Talon was testing and cataloging his opponent's skills on the chains, link by link, junction by junction, discovering the entirety of his opponent's arsenal. Talon forged this knowledge with confidence. When finally satisfied that he knew all he needed, Talon let the chains fade from his mind and began his work. Once he started, Talon's body moved instinctively as though he had faced this opponent a hundred times before. The battle broke quickly and hard—an onslaught of blows without pause or counter. A series so precise and accurate in their intuition, the blade or shaft of Talon's glaive seemed to magically appear in the space his opponent or his opponent's weapon would soon occupy. In less than forty-five seconds, the duel went from looking to be an even draw to Talon's opponent bleeding from a dozen wicked slashes and his glaive laying on the ground ten yards away. With blade to his opponent's throat, Talon snarled, "Yield."

Eyes set, testing Talon's resolve, his rival clenched his jaw and stood silent. Thoroughly finished with the games of his parents, his greater family, and his opponent, Talon leaving his blade to his opponent's throat, broke eye contact. He looked over his shoulder out the courtyard gates and toward the woods where the spring lay beyond them. It was then that he heard his opponent's scoff. Whipping his head around, Talon slammed into his opponent with the ironwood shaft of his glaive, lifting him off his feet and slamming him to the ground. He dropped with his full weight landing his knee on his opponent's upper left arm, hearing both the satisfying pop of the shoulder dislocating and the crack of bone breaking. Then, drawing his dagger, Talon sliced off the chest guard of the leather armor his rival wore, exposing the left portion of his chest above his heart. Taking the blade, he scored a curved line and then another deep into his opponent's flesh, creating a curved 'V' shape like that of a falcon's talon.

Echoed words then came from his throat. "Today, you are Dead. The dead do not have the privilege of yielding. They only have their scars." With but a glance and nod, the Commander threw Talon the pouch of white crystalline powder. Pouring the powder into his hand, Talon then smeared it into the wound.

"YIELD!!!!!" The word was a scream, drawn out and piercing. The young girl, Cerena, covered her ears from the horrible wail, hiding her face in the petticoats of her nurse. Talon stood and strode back to his rooms without even a look to his father or the onlookers. Had Talon spared his father even one slight glance, he would have seen a smile as dark as all the pits of the nine hells contorting his sire's face.

Upon returning to his chamber, Talon bathed and dressed, preparing himself for what was next. It was mid-afternoon when once again a sealed summons came, and Talon proceeded to his father's study. When he entered, he saw that a thin wooden case sat upon his father's desk, long enough to overhang each side by over a foot. The case was ornately carved and made of dark rosewood, unlike any species Talon had ever seen. He could not help but feel the same stalking predator from the previous meeting within the room. His father's well-trained stoic countenance could not hide the calculating malevolence behind his eyes.

Toman began with an even tone and no more emotion than the rehearsed toast he gave for New Dawn's Beginning. "Talon, our family line has awaited this day for many generations. Finally, the day when what should have always been ours by right is returned to us." Toman walked to the case and opened the hinged lid. "The return of the Vermillion Blade of Cour-Vermane."

Toman presented a glaive of extraordinary artistry, the shaft made from the same deep red rosewood as the case. The wood was obviously from an older specimen explicitly cultivated for this usage as the grain was so fine as to be similar to steel Mikal had hardened through folding hundreds of times. The glaive was as fearsome as any Talon had ever seen and seemed to reflect a crimson light that was not present in the study. The blade, consisting of elegant curves intersecting in wicked points and crescent barbs intended to grab and remove weapons and limbs alike, was terrifying and beautiful. It was difficult to perceive the weapon even looking at it directly. The glaive seemed of a bigger scale than the case that contained it. Before Talon could reach out to touch it, Toman interjected.

"To take this weapon is to fulfill a contract. It is not something one returns once claimed. I saw today that you are indeed my son in all aspects; the Cour-Vermane blood flows strongly in your veins. I saw that our ancestral weapon is yours to claim."

With eyes only on the Vermillion Blade, Talon pulled it from the case. Once free of its confines, the glaive revealed its full size. It was over ten feet long, and the terrifying bladed portion was almost as large as a broadsword. The web of chains exploded into his vision around him, resonating in triumph. Talon realized they were not a part of him but of the Vermillion Blade and they had been calling out and assisting him even before he claimed the weapon.

Talon grabbed the glaive's harness from where it lay within the case and slipped it over his head and shoulder as if by instinct. He spun the Vermillion Blade over his shoulder and fitted it on his back. The enchantment on the case seemed to carry to the harness as well. The weapon that had been so imposing in scale in Talon's hand now fit comfortably diagonally across his back, the blade barely a hands width higher than the top of his head.

Offering no thanks, or taking even a moment for recognition from his father, Talon left the confinement of the study to return to his chambers on the floor above. A few minutes after Talon arrived, the case for the Vermillion Blade was delivered to his rooms as he was pacing the floor, lost in thought. A delighted thrill emanated from the place deep inside his mind where the voice resided. The chain, which was usually just a weight on him and one that he had felt he had mastered through his training, hummed with a dull recognition of the Vermillion Blade slung across his back. So disconcerting was that thrum in his soul that Talon did something he had not done for almost two years; he disarmed himself, placing the Vermillion Blade in its case. He left the case and glaive where the servant had put them in the sitting parlor of his rooms and retired to his bedchamber to think. Laying down on the bed, he closed his eyes to summon the calming energy of his forms and stances.

That is when the Vermillion Blade's influence began.

That arrogant prat Rabien never was worthy of such a weapon.

Talon had never heard his opponent's name uttered; he was sure of it, but Rabien was assuredly his name as his own was Talon. The thought that had just passed through his head was his own, but also somehow not. Talon tried to be concerned about it, but the voice assured him it was of no concern at all.

Your mark is the mark of death. It will be feared as you will be.

Talon saw in his mind the curved 'V' he carved and scarred into Rabien's chest and felt *pride*. Pride in knowing this power was *his*. The vision wavered in his mind like a reflection on water; his mark was no longer on

Rabien's chest but on his face. It felt right to be there for all to see - for all to fear. It shifted then from crossing Rabien's eye to gouging it out. Talon imagined pouring the white powder into the empty socket and the screams that would flood forth. On the bed, Talon's now sleeping form smiled at the thought.

Your reputation will grow, and none will stand against you. Your power and might expanding with your stature and strength.

In his mind, Talon saw the Vermillion Blade swing in massive arcs cutting down all who stood in his way. A trail of defeated foes lay behind him as he crossed a vast countryside. As each challenger fell, the Vermillion Blade grew larger, as did Talon. Soon Talon's heroic form was standing head and shoulders above even his most powerful enemies, his glaive defeating whole squads of knights in a single blow. His heroic deeds and stature becoming the stuff of legends and songs. Talon's ego reveled in this newfound vision of strength and power, and even though he found elation in the easy victories, he bristled for a worthy challenge.

While the front of his mind bathed in the majesty of the vision, a tiny whisper, separate from the Vermillion Blade's influence, secretly turned Talon's inner eye backward over what lay behind him. It was not a trail of defeated foes marked and scarred with his 'V' as the Blade directed him to imagine, but one of corpses, viscera, and blood. The defilement he and the Vermillion Blade wrought leached into the fields and forests of the countryside he called home. Wells that once drew clear water now produced only filth and decay with dark figures chanting over their corrupted depths. And above them all, Talon's father, Toman Cour-Vermane, was sitting on a throne made of skulls and gore.

You will free Eleryon from the Empire and then claim the Imperial throne yourself. The blood of the true rulers of this world will rise to their rightful place again with you as their champion.

Talon was now practically a giant within his vision, no longer corporeal but ascended to something glorious and mighty. A vast array of dark chains, identical to the ones he used in battle except for their now massive scale, emanated from him in all directions blanketing the countryside. Huge dark-winged shapes flew over his shoulders, unleashing fire, ash, and poison on the land below. Thousands of banners with his mark emblazoned upon them led his scarred armies beyond count. Leading one of the armies was the one-eyed limping form of Rabien, now his general and attached to his form with one of the massive black chains. At the ends of other chains, far-flung members of the Cour-Vermane bloodline led squads of troops; even Cerena, now grown with wild hair and sharpened teeth, was marching with him. They marched in every direction to flood the cities of Lymehold, Jadenpool, and Lyria Bay; all the continent's capitals and beyond would fall to his might.

As the vision of his armies faded, Talon opened his eyes to the familiar rocky plateau from the day he mastered the chains. Under a blood-red sunless sky, Talon found his normally scaled body wrapped in the web of chains that had once been his allies, but now they bound him and dragged him toward a precipice marking a descent into an endless night. He knew that chasm had already claimed a part of his soul as he finally saw where the original black chain he had first witnessed at Milgran's Orchard led, and the Vermillion Blade was now collecting the balance.

There was no fighting what was pulling him; the chains drawing him closer merged and grew in size as he got closer to the edge. Then, the small whisper that had shown him the truth in the vision intervened again, not as a voice but as a torrent of fire and light. A blinding blaze erupted before Talon flooding the plateau in verdant sunlight, dispelling all but the most robust chains of the web that bound him. As the few remaining chains continued dragging him forward to the edge and the fall into darkness, the heat of that shining sun saved Talon: not by its burning intensity but by invoking his memories.

The heat that washed over Talon was the familiar heat of Mikal's forge. It was the warmth of morning tea in Richen's room behind the flue and the hours upon hours he had spent reading his lessons while Mikal and Richen worked. It was shared jokes, secret ciders, and even uncontrolled coughing as they tried smoking the horsegroom's pipe. Richen and all those he cared about had been missing from every vision the Blade had given him. That omission caused Talon to realize the glaive had no concept of anything outside itself and the dark desires of his family. The warmth of a forge that had somehow become Talon's real home confounded the cursed glaive, for something other than blood relation and self-interest to bind people together was an anathema.

What remained of the Vermillion Blade's web of chains dissolved, leaving just the original dark chain left unshattered. The last chain, locked in place mere moments after his birth, still held tight extending from within him, out over the precipice and deep into the darkness below. However, alone it could not bind his will. Talon was able to turn his back on the plateau, the Darkness, and the Vermillion Blade's promises. He walked away.

Talon awoke with a start and sat up in bed as though his head had been underwater and he had been drowning. He jumped up to check on the Vermillion Blade, but it was still in its case on the table where he had left it. From across the room, the glaive seemed to glower at Talon in anger. From its response, Talon knew the weapon was still bound to him by whatever laws governed it but without the ability to dominate his will. Talon crossed the sitting room to the case and lifted the Vermillion Blade out of its confines, permitting it to grow to its full scale and mass.

"You are defeated. And the defeated have only their scars."

Talon furrowed his brow and willed his mark at the consciousness of the Vermillion Blade. Where blade met shaft, across steel and rosewood, the curved 'V' of Talon's mark grudgingly manifested as though branded there.

CHAPTER NINE

Year 858 PXF ~ *Winter*

Talon was surprised that the first rays of dawn now peeked through his window as he placed the branded Vermillion Blade into its sheath on his back. Ravenously hungry from having missed two of the previous day's meals, Talon dismissed any idea of immediately confronting his father and headed to the kitchens. When he arrived, Ms. Haddington and the cooks were already preparing the day's meals. They greeted Talon with rashers of ham, bowls of hearty porridge, and a full skillet's worth of fried eggs. While there were still many questions for him to answer, there was a clarity to the world that Talon had not felt for many years and his whole demeanor reflected it as he stepped out into the courtyard.

The Commander waited there, blocking Talon's path to the training yard. Dressed in his full combat armor, glaive still undrawn but stance prepared for immediate action, the Commander spoke. "Talon, hold there." It was not a request. Instead, his chiseled expression was deadly serious.

Confused, Talon stopped, then cautiously took a step forward, "Commander, what is this about?" now all but reflexively drawing the Vermillion Blade.

"Hold, Talon. I do not wish to kill you this day." The Commander issued the order as a restrained bark through clenched teeth. Talon now questioned the clarity he had felt just moments prior; he had easily divided his world into friend and foe, but now the Commander acted as an adversary, not an ally. Seeing the same concern in the Commander's gaze that had afflicted it earlier in their training when Talon was relying so heavily on the chains, he realized the Commander was reacting to what had transpired between Talon and the Vermillion Blade. The question was if his aggressive stance was due to him thinking Talon had succumbed to the glaive or if he had subdued it.

Talon proceeded with caution. He took a deep breath, and as the Commander had always advised, he trusted his instincts. Talon refused to believe that a man like the Commander could ever be under his father's thrall, "Commander, it is still me. I defeated the Blade."

Talon took another step forward. Before he could even complete his motion, the Commander's onslaught began. The Commander lunged, holding nothing back from his attack. Talon countered but, having been caught mid-step, had very few options that did not give the Commander the upper hand, which he immediately exploited. Spinning off Talon's blade and around his back, the Commander swung with a lethal attack towards Talon's neck, taking advantage of his blind spot. The only thing that saved Talon's life at that moment was the scale of the Vermillion Blade. Had he been using the glaive that he and the Commander had trained with, Talon would be dead, head severed from his neck. This was not the measured cadence of their training or even the duel with Rabien; the Commander was using a strategy designed to kill or maim his opponent if not blocked immediately and definitively.

Their battle proceeded at a lightning-quick pace, and neither had time to do much more than react to the other. The Commander, having not landed a coup de grâce with his first string of attacks, changed tactics in an attempt to disable Talon. Glaive spinning overhead, he feigned another lethal strike aimed to disembowel its target, and Talon, fearing for his life, fell into the trap with a two-hand chest-level block that fully exposed the back of his right knee. The Commander's mid-swing reversal was perfectly executed, like all he did, and his blade sliced deep into the tendons at the back of Talon's knee. Had Talon not buckled his knee when he did, it would have completely hamstrung him, making his leg useless.

There was no time to speak or explain; Talon knew he must defeat the Commander or die, of that he was sure. In desperation, he summoned the Vermillion Blade's chains. From down on one knee, Talon looked over his shoulder and up at the Commander, his sight now split between reality and the plateau of chains. Talon could see that the Commander recognized what he had done, and he watched any doubt or mercy that the Commander might have for him drain away. A fury ignited in the Commander as he executed his next string of attacks, a spinning flurry of blade and body that seemed to come from all sides simultaneously. The Commander would have slain Talon three times over if it had not been for the chains augmenting his own skills and instincts to block and counter the Commander's assault. Talon knew he could not win this fight, and the pressure from the Vermillion Blade to be allowed to do more felt like it would split his skull. It promised him all the glory and victories from the vision of the night before. It could destroy the Commander for him if Talon would just let it loose.

In the part of his mind that battled upon the plateau among the web of chains, Talon lifted the Vermillion Blade above his head and, with a silent scream, slammed an enormous image of his branded curved 'V' down through the chains, shattering and dispelling them all in a definitive denial of the weapon's corrupted promises. In the real world, with his own eyes and instincts clear of the Vermillion Blade's influence, Talon saw his opening and took it. As he and the Commander spun in opposite directions, both utilizing one of the first combinations that Talon had ever mastered, instead of using the block he had executed hundreds of times before, Talon lifted the Vermillion Blade out of position, exposing his forearms. Lining his arms up with the surgical precision taught to him by Balanon and placing them directly in the path of the Commander's glaive,

Talon let the blade pierce first one forearm and then the other, passing through the flesh and cleanly between the bones. Then, with a twist of his wrists and a grunt from the pain of steel scraping bone, he trapped the blade of the Commander's glaive within his own forearms. Talon yanked his arms in close, pulling him and the Commander shoulder to shoulder and face to face with the Vermillion Blade held horizontally between them at eye level.

"Look!" Talon exclaimed through clenched teeth, nearly shouting but keeping his voice from carrying to the estate's walls, "The weapon bears my mark. My scar. Just as you taught me, it did not take my mind or my will."

The tension in the Commander's muscles and jaw relaxed slightly, but the fury and concern remained only temporarily calmed, not fully extinguished. His glaive, still trapped between the bones of Talon's forearms and forced to remain face to face, blood flowing freely down Talon's arms between them, the Commander growled, "Tell me. All of it."

Talon spat out everything he knew, the chains, the visions, his battle with the Vermillion Blade's will, and how his memory of the forge saved him. Throughout the story, they remained locked together by blood, bone, and blade. And in the telling of it here in the courtyard, looking into the Commander's face and recounting the details of all he had been through, Talon realized everything around him was part of what saved him. The discipline, the integrity, the unending hours and days spent learning and growing, not just as a warrior but as a man. The Commander was not just his trainer but a father that had been absent in his life. As the realization hit Talon, the curved 'V' brand on the Vermillion Blade between them glowed red hot and etched itself deeper into the weapon. He and the Commander could feel the change that came with it as the last bit of will within the weapon became fully bound to Talon and by default his true family.

The Commander stepped back, withdrawing his blade quickly and smoothly from Talon's arms. He removed a small vial from his belt and offered it to Talon, who recognized the healing potion immediately and drank it. "My order sent me to train you to be able to defeat any challenger... and then kill you if you ever claimed the Vermillion Blade."

Talon recoiled as though he had been struck. The Commander continued, "I can see the mark of both gods and demons upon you, Talon. The same as the ones upon dozens of my brothers and many I have slain. Through a deity's grace and the light within you, the Vermillion Blade has not taken you into darkness this day. But have no doubt its evil has not been broken, only bound. Even though you still live while wielding that *thing*," nodding to the Vermillion Blade, "I consider my oath fulfilled: the Blade is defeated, for now. I shall be gone by midday."

Talon was reeling from the Commander's words: that he had been sent to kill him and then the shock that he would soon depart. "What am I supposed to do next? Am I ready to go search for Richen? What about the darkness to which I am still bound? and the..." Talon tested the word, "Demon's mark on my bloodline?"

"You are bound to a god as their chosen or perhaps even their champion, so what your future holds is not for me to say." The Commander turned on his heel and headed to his quarters to prepare for his departure.

True to his word, the Commander rode out the gates of the Cour-Vermane courtyard before the midday meal was served. Talon had so much to say, so much to ask, so much more he needed and wanted from the Commander. But words failed him as he accompanied him along the road, and soon they came to where their paths would part. They paused side by side at the fork in the trail.

"My path is unclear, but what of you?" Talon asked, needing to have some glimpse of what the future may hold for this man who had shaped his life over the last two and a half years.

"I'll return home to my wife, who undoubtedly has missed my sparkling personality." The Commander stated flatly, so devoid of emotion that Talon almost missed the joke. But, before he could comment, the Commander continued, his voice becoming earnest and forthright. "I will also have to let her know that while she bore only two sons, she now has three."

Talon, words bound by more emotion than he could overcome and unable to say all he felt, was finally, with humble gratitude, able to choke out, "Commander, thank you."

The Commander nodded with a grunt of acknowledgment, emotion seeming to catch his words as well. Then, after a pause held out his hand. "Call me Lochlan." Talon took Lochlan's hand with a smile, and for the first time he could recall, the Commander smiled in return.

They then parted ways as each continued on their separate paths, Lochlan to his home and Talon to the spring; Talon could not help but pull up his horse and call out, "Will we meet again, Lochlan?"

In reply, "If destiny sees fit, we shall, but if you have the need before then, send word with your mark to the Lord Protector of Falcon's Spire asking for Commander Lochlan San Barthany Greymonte."

That was the last Talon would see of Lochlan. The world is a vast and unpredictable place; often, the important people in one's life do not always pass your way a second time.

CHAPTER TEN

Year 858 PXF *~ Winter*

Talon arrived at the spring in the early afternoon. Unlike his visit fifteen months earlier, the spring was already frozen over, and drifts of snow piled around the boulder and covered even the hardy holly and juniper plants. The small shoot that had appeared in the crack of the boulder was still alive but remained just a tiny woody sapling of some unknown tree, stunted by its harsh location between the halves of the boulder. Talon sat quietly on the boulder, not knowing what to do to commune with Caspharian.

Perhaps an hour, maybe two, had passed and even Talon's well-trained form was becoming fatigued from sitting on the hard stone for such an extended period. His shoulders ached, his thighs were cramping, and his feet were so long asleep that he wasn't sure they even still existed or would ever feel alive again. But then the clouds parted, and the sun beamed down on Talon's chilled bones bringing with it the same warmth of the forge he remembered from his childhood.

Talon, feeling Caspharian's presence but hearing no voice, posed his questions, "Can you help me find Richen? Where do I start? Do you know where he is?" The requests tumbled out of Talon even though he had meant to ask of his deity only one.

Very rarely are the paths of nature a straight line, and when forced to be, their outcomes are never what was intended. So are the paths in front of you. One is a straight line, forced and rigid, full of hardship and sacrifices, lying partly in shadow. That path bears a single stunted fruit, but it is the fruit you seek. The other is a winding root that grows and changes with the land and the seasons, one that weathers hardship and is strengthened by it. At its end, a flowering tree unshackled from darkness, bursting with blooms and bountiful harvests, and among that harvest, the one you love.

Talon recalled the stories of the gods he read as a child and how often the choices they gave were no choice at all. The memory of his battle with the Vermillion Blade and the knowledge that the last remaining chain of his bloodline still tethered him to darkness remained fresh in Talon's mind. It made his choice clear, "I will follow the path of nature wherever it leads."

Start by guarding this land, away from the influence of the House of Cour-Vermane. You have earned your freedom, now grasp it and see where its winds carry you.

Clouds covered the sun, the warmth retreating along with the presence in Talon's mind. Talon stood up from his place beside the spring and took a long look at the space that had become the center of his spirit. A part of him somehow knew it would be many years before he would return, and that part was not wrong. His ride back to the Cour-Vermane estate, the place he soon would no longer call home, was filled with planning about how best to leave it.

It took the better part of a fortnight for Talon to sort the belongings he wished to take with him and arrange a flat of rooms in Arnadore. The Cour-Vermane name opened many doors in the city, and his coin and credit were readily accepted. With everything in order, Talon first went to Mikal to tell him about his departure.

"I am leaving. I now understand the words of your Uldani friend when he took Richen. This house is not a place of healing for those in need of the

Light. I am leaving so I can find him again. I do not know how long it will take, but I will spend my life searching. Your presence here has helped me more than you know." Talon placed one hand on Mikal's shoulder and the other on the hilt of the dagger Mikal had gifted him. "I will carry this with me always."

Mikal, never a man of many words, said only, "I will always be here for you, my boy, even if it is just here," Mikal laid his calloused hand over Talon's heart. Then, he turned back to the forge and his work. Talon respected Mikal's desire to be alone with his emotions and quietly left.

Talon's next stop was to Balanon to thank him for all he had done, from the lessons he taught to the healing potion for Richen to the seemingly hundreds of stitches and bandages he had given throughout Talon's training with Lochlan. The half-elf looking completely unchanged from even Talon's earliest memories, smiled at him with a far too knowing look in his fey-touched eyes. "We shall meet again, Talon Cour-Vermane, if not in this life then in your next."

Lastly, of the people who truly mattered to Talon, was Ms. Haddington. Before he could speak, she shoved a pack filled to the brim with all his favorites into his arms. "You tell Lolly I will have her apron if I see you all scrawny in a couple of months." Talon wondered how Ms. Haddington knew who Lolly was, then realized that, of course, she would have checked up on the proprietor and cook of the inn where he had rented rooms.

Talon reached down and embraced the tiny plump woman in his massive arms, finally ending up on his knees in front of her as the moment's emotion overwhelmed him. Still hugging her as he knelt before her, he wept with his head on her shoulder. This tiny mountain of a woman had raised him and nurtured him through all the joys and pains he had endured. She was the bedrock upon which he had built his life and himself. The crushing immensity of her no longer being a part of his everyday life struck him like a landslide. Her comforting words filled the space between them as she stroked his always wild hair that cascaded over his shoulders. "Oh, Talon, it won't be the same here without you, but you will always be the same in my heart as I hope I will be in yours." Cradling his face in her loving hands. "Now finish up with that," wiping his tears, "you still have your father to deal with, I suspect."

Talon stood up and was transported from being the twelve-year-old mischievous and lonely little boy who still couldn't reach Ms. Haddington's stash of ginger biscuits above the stove to the towering man who had conquered the Vermillion Blade. He squared his shoulders and took a deep breath, steeling himself for what was to come, looking every inch like a warrior heading into battle. However, he still grabbed a ginger biscuit before he left the kitchen, receiving a swat one last time from Ms. Haddington's cooking towel as he did.

With neither invitation nor summons, Talon, Vermillion Blade slung across his back, opened the door to his father's private study and walked in. An unthinkable act a mere two weeks ago was now done without hesitation. Without looking up from his ledger, his father spoke, "You were not summoned."

Talon calmly stated, "I am leaving. I will be joining Duke Issul's guard at the Keep."

Toman replied boredly, "You will do no such thing. It is beneath a Cour-Vermane to serve thusly."

"It is already done."

For once, a slight pause from his father. "Then undo it." An edge now in Toman's voice.

"I will be gone by nightfall."

"I forbid it!" Toman stood hands on desktop, eyes flashing with malice and invoking words he expected to have power. "As keeper of this bloodline and master of House Cour-Vermane, you shall not leave."

Talon felt an ephemeral pull on that remaining chain that tied him to darkness and realized who had shackled him so. In his bottomless malevolence, his father must have bound his blood to the family's demons and expected the Vermillion Blade to seal his control over Talon. Toman had intended for Talon to become a weapon he could wield. But now, without the Vermillion Blade's reinforcement of that original chain, Toman held no power over his son.

Taking on the formality that his tutors had drilled into him as a child, Talon spoke, "You cannot forbid me of anything, father. I shall do this, and you will not dishonor my name in my so doing with your forked tongue." The words struck Toman like a slap across his face, but Talon also saw something else: a flash of fear in his father's eyes. Talon realized the Vermillion Blade held influence over *all* Cour-Vermane blood, and its power now pulled on Toman, trying to bend him to Talon's command. Neither man bowed to the force of the other's will, even with the magics that assisted each of them, but both acknowledged their uneasy stalemate.

Toman first broke the silence and his gaze by sitting back down at his desk. "Do present and carry yourself as befits your name if you insist on pursuing this work you have chosen. Your mother will expect you for Last Friend's Remembrance."

The dismissal was absolute. Talon took it as such and left Toman Cour-Vermane's private study and the Cour-Vermane estate with no intent to ever return.

PART II
The Man of Simple Passions

CHAPTER ELEVEN

Year 871 PXF ~ Autumn

The rooms of Talon Cour-Vermane were much as she expected them: well-appointed in a minimalist vein suited more for function than style or decoration but still with enough elegance and pomp to be deemed appropriate to one of his name and station. The flat of four rooms took up the back corner on the third floor of the Sojourn's Rest inn, arranged in an 'L' shape with the bedchamber on the short leg and the other three social rooms making up the longer one. Before entering through the window she had pried open, the darkly clad figure made an intricate set of delicate forms with her fingers, sparking a vivid purple arcane flash in her pupils. Within the rooms, multiple items and sigils ignited with their magical potential in her augmented sight. There was power to the wards and enchantments, but nothing someone of her skill and training couldn't handle and easily cover up after completing her task.

While darkness was always an ally, she hadn't needed to rely on it. It was the Night of the Drowned Moon; the autumnal celebration dedicated to the Undrowned Mistress, the goddess of mystery, exploration, and the foolhardy. Elsewhere in the empire (especially near the Seradan Sea), the festival had a more nautical flare, as foolhardy exploration was the bread and butter of most sailors. Here in Arnadore, it had a darker feel tied to the fogs that flooded the lowlands this time of year. The festival called upon the Undrowned Mistress' domain over mystery, intrigue, and unexpected demise. It was still early evening, and contrary to the deity's aspect, there was no mystery surrounding the rowdy crowd of revelers flooding the streets throughout the city, especially here in the trade district of Elery Square and the surrounding Trellis Market. Citizens had donned costumes, both arcane and mundane, and the amount of benign magic the festival attendants were casting would cover any real spells she might need to utilize. Climbing to Talon's suite from the alley had been a breeze, and entering uninvited into the rooms before her was just as simple.

The intruder knew she needn't worry about bumping into the room's inhabitant as the lauded travels of Talon Cour-Vermane were well known and documented. Currently, he was hundreds of leagues away chasing a watery devil beast that was harrying the town of Perinchal over on the coast. Still, she didn't tarry, as one never knew when someone might get a hankering for their home and teleport in unexpectedly. Her objective wasn't to steal anything, as it often was when breaking into people's abodes. Her goal was far more esoteric. She was here because she needed to get a feel for the man who was to be her adversary, and over the years she had found the best way to do so was to invade her quarry's most private places. The places they felt safe, where they could let their guard down and, most importantly, be confident they were alone.

She quickly found what she was looking for: something personal yet not so loved that it would be routinely examined or handled. She crossed to a small curio mounted to the wall that displayed a handful of badges and medals that must have been from Talon's first assignment to the guard at Arnadore Keep. Like most, she knew of the lord-inheritor of House Cour-Vermane's meteoric rise through the guard's ranks in his younger days. While these early accolades would be too sentimental to discard, they would not hold the emotional value of ones earned in later life. The curio was also in a perfect position, located in the corner of the 'L' shape of his rooms, to let her view everything that occurred within.

The spell she cast was one of her most prized creations, effectively undetectable by magical means because its power lay not in enchantment but in the single component it required. Selecting a dark bronze medallion not much larger than a gold coin, she laid it carefully on the top of a nearby bureau. She then withdrew a long hollow needle from her cloak and inserted it directly into her eye until it pierced the delicate veins at the back of her eyeball. Leaning over the medallion, needle extending out of her eye, she patiently waited until a single drop of her retina blood splashed onto the bronze medal. As the blood sank into the cracks and crevices of the medallion, she extracted the needle and cast minor healing incantation on her eye, careful not to completely heal the full extent of the damage as it was part of the spell's requirement. Her crimson blood was easily visible on the medallion as she replaced it into the curio, but it would practically disappear by morning as it darkened.

Work complete, she did not leave by the window she entered through. First listening at the entrance to ensure there was no activity beyond it, she confidently stepped out the door of Talon's room into the inn's upper hallway. Then, with a flick of her wrist, her black leathers and dirks sheathed at her ankles were concealed by the rotting petticoats of a macabre costume befitting the Night of the Drowned Moon. With another quick motion, she released her hair from its binds, letting it cascade freely down her back as she descended to the main room of the Sojourn's Rest. After finding a chair at a small table nestled near the stairs and waving off any overzealous revelers seeking to woo her, she ordered a mead from a strapping young tavern lad.

Before leaving, she wanted to be sure her efforts weren't for naught, and it would take a moment for her to silently invoke the ritual to activate the spell connecting her to her eye's blood in the room above. Concentration had never been an issue for her, and anyone watching would think her just another festival goer swaying to the music of the bards playing on stage. The very astute might catch a bit of eyeshine in her left eye like that of a predator caught in the light when prowling the darkness, but on a night like tonight, most would likely think it just a bit of glamor. As expected, the spell worked perfectly, her patron's arcane gifts allowing her full view of Talon's rooms and even the ability to maneuver her point of surveillance around them to some extent. Her mead arrived just as she severed the connection to the spell, and she almost got up to leave until the bards onstage announced the title of their last song before their break: *Ballad of the Crimson Falcon.*

She was familiar with the song as bards all across the Xallian Empire sang their own or other's compositions chronicling the exploits of Talon Cour-Vermane. However, she had no interest in the performance itself; her goal was to hear the conversation after the song. In his home inn, people would potentially know him more personally or even from before his time in the Arnadore guard, which could give some valuable insight. The song ended to a round of applause, and, as expected, before the bards even fully left the stage, talk began amongst the tavern guests.

"Is he really that big?" she heard from an overloud reveler in smeared skeletal face paint two tables over.

"He's a big lad for sure, always has been, but taller than a dire bear is probably a bit of a stretch," a more sober voice answered over his shoulder one table away.

"Strong though," another wearing a skinned boar's head as a hood chimed in, "and that glaive of his is a wicked thing. I served on the Crimson Sentinels with him, and a swing of that blade could probably cut a dire bear in half." A cacophony of agreements and disbelief muddied her ability to hear for a moment until another voice cut through the din.

"Whatever did happen to Councilwoman Darlis? Is she still locked up after Cour-Vermane caught her with a hand in the treasury?" a woman wearing a rotted noose around her neck asked from across the room.

"Nah, her family finally bribed her way out at least three years ago. I hear she looked a wreck after almost a decade in the dungeon though, lost all her teeth!" A shout of "serves her right!" was met with raised flagons and goblets.

"Where's he now, then?" slurred the drunkard with the smeared skeleton makeup.

"I heard Duke Issul has let him take a break from all that envoy-ing he has been doing acting as his personal messenger pigeon. He has assembled a new group under the banner of Falcon's Grasp and headed to the coast to kill another one of those devils he chases," the man wearing the boar's skin replied. Nods and grunts of agreement filled the room. "Gonna make it an even dozen sent back to the Nine Hells by my count if he gets this one." Lifted glasses filled the air again.

A well-dressed laborer in an immaculately woven silver tunic asked the room with little hope, "Speaking of devils roaming about, did he ever find Mikal's boy?" Mutters of "nah" and "shame" and "he still pays well for any word, though," and other condolences quieted the room for a moment.

A large busted woman, deep in her cups, wearing hardly more than scraps of bandages as a costume, leaped to her chair. Finding it the most opportune time to make a spectacle, she announced, "I bedded him once!" while shaking her prodigious bosom.

A bard breaking every string on their lute mid-song would have brought a lesser reaction. The main room of the tavern went silent. The woman's friend, face hidden, tried to drag her down off the chair while at the same time trying to hide herself under the table.

"What? Talon not like the ladies? Well, he liked me, I tell ya!" she reiterated, doubling down.

The sober man who had answered the drunkard in the skeletal face paint earlier stood up and in the stern voice all fathers seem to be able to channel, "Sir Cour-Vermane, and you will address him as Sir, does not 'bed' anyone. Of all half-truths and tall tales told of him, that one thing remains fact." The thief in the corner was surprised to hear the number of "here heres," "got that right," and "good on him, I says," from the locals to rebuff this now obvious visitor to Arnadore. She wondered if Talon had any idea of the amount of validation and support he had among his neighbors.

As the stern gentleman sat back down and the busty woman was dragged out of the Sojourn's Rest by her friend, a reveler who hadn't spoken before playfully added, "Now to the reason he never beds, that is still up for debate!"

The smear-faced skeleton jibed, "All that noble blood gave him all the stature but none of the size," extending his pinky and shaking it about, receiving some nods and general laughter.

"I would say the opposite!" chimed in the soldier in the boar's head hat, "I've seen him in the baths, and I wouldn't head to his bedchambers without at least TWO healing potions!" which was met with uproarious laughter.

The thief had gotten the insight she needed; sliding a gold coin into the rear pocket of the young tavern lad who had served her, she exited the Sojourn's Rest and blended into the celebration of the Drowned Moon.

$$\backsim\!\!\infty$$

CHAPTER TWELVE

Talon sat alone in his flat of rooms at the Sojourn's Rest. Night was finally pulling its cloak across a day that Talon wished had already ended. Most people found their birthdays a time for celebration or at least nostalgic, sentimental reflection. For Talon, those things had faded from his birthdays long ago. Even as darkness fell across Arnadore, the heat of mid-Summer still permeated every nook of the city, and Talon's rooms were no exception. His impressive form was not built to shed heat effectively, and certainly not when the air was as warm as his skin. His damp tunic clung heavily to his shoulders, and rivulets of sweat traced their way down his back as he sat on the large bed in his room, feet firmly planted on the floor. His head rested in his calloused hands, his hair creating a curtain behind which he could hide from the world and what he could only label as his failures.

He turned thirty-five this eve. A new year of his life toasted in with ale and a table full of his favorite dishes from the Sojourn's Rest kitchens served up by Lolly Kelderman. Lolly, as always, was a wellspring of kindness and good cheer, carrying nearly thrice the amount of joy that should fit in her tiny halfling frame. He graciously put on a show of happiness and thanks to all involved and invited. Talon brightly asked for second helpings from Lolly's seemingly bottomless serving dishes at the meal, even though the familiar foods held a bitter aftertaste for him. The guilt of Ms. Haddington having gone to her final rest two years earlier while he had been away on an envoy mission for the Duke still gnawed at him. After far too many slaps on the back and "old mans," Talon made his escape upstairs, though not before spotting Faldan and Ella across the main room of the inn. Now married with a half dozen children (one practically an adult already), their happy family all lifted a hand or mug in acknowledgment of his celebration. Talon claimed they couldn't see the effect their friendly gesture had on his face due to the dagger he felt plunge into his chest from it. As Talon turned and continued up the stairs, his mind dwelled on how his jealousy of Ella and Faldan initially spawned the idea of his hunting trip with Richen. Added to everything else of the evening, it sent Talon into the downward spiral in which he now found himself.

Back in his room sitting on the bed, Talon desperately needed to take his shirt off to relieve his body of some of the heat oppressing it, but he found he couldn't. Every thought of making an attempt roused the ghost of Richen sitting shirtless on that tiny bed in his room behind the forge. Talon found his feet were likewise nailed to the floor no matter how much he knew stretching out might help cool him. As he stared down through the spread fingers supporting his head and at the feet that had carried him thousands of leagues in his search for Richen, it was incomprehensible that he now couldn't move them even a few inches to put them up on the bed. Talon's mind retreated from the fear that if they found their way there, he would crave and perhaps even feel the comforting caress of Richen's foot against his own and, like a drowning man who can't breathe yet still craves air, Talon wasn't sure he could survive it. So Talon sat in a soaking wet tunic, thick mane of hair lank and damp hiding his face, feet firmly locked to the floor, frozen in the misery visited upon him by the echoes of his past.

Though Talon's body was frozen, the slithering voice in his mind, still with him after all these years, loved to take these opportunities to strike. Eighteen years had passed since the Farseer had taken Richen, almost fifteen since Talon had gained the skills to begin his search for him, and what did he have to show for his efforts? Currently, it was an inability even to put himself to bed. Talon knew the voice was a part of the last remaining dark chain still attached to his soul, but that knowledge wasn't helpful at times like these. Why couldn't Talon be normal like everyone else? Over the years of interacting with and observing the patrons of the main tavern room of the Sojourn's Rest, Talon had seen rebounds from crumbled relationships happen in less than an hour. The voice guided Talon's musings to the fact that, for many, sex did seem to be the magical peacemaker. For reconciliations or broken hearts, the panacea for all ailments of the human heart seemed to return to that one single act. On many an occasion, when caught in public or private gatherings deep in his dark thoughts, someone would believe they were the one who could provide that universal cure for him if just given a chance, that they would fix Talon of what ailed him.

He did try once. As that thought entered his mind while his body remained frozen on the bed in his rooms, Talon felt a ghostly arm wrap around his broad shoulders. He leaned into the phantom embrace and was transported back in time to a warm starry night years earlier on the shores of the Seradan Sea.

8 Years Earlier ~ 864 PXF *~ Late Spring*

Talon was following a lead he had picked up in Jadenpool while escorting Duke Issul to the Exposition of Arcane Wonders there. The Exposition was a marvel of the age, with magics and artifice the likes of which Talon had never seen. Mages from as far away as Bal'Ethera and Qual'Vareen exhibited sorcerous feats of incredible beauty and breathtaking power. Bards from the competing musical schools of Highmount and Falwynari took not only to the main stages for compositions of dazzling complexity but also to the corners of almost every thoroughfare for more simple tunes, filling the atmosphere of the Exposition with a constant ebb and flow of music. The Duke seemed to enjoy the wonders on display but was acutely aware of their power and troubled by them. Due to this, he cut his trip to Jadenpool short, leaving the city and the Exposition unexpectedly, long before his scheduled departure, after attending a private meeting with the Emperor that left him in a sour disposition.

While strange, the Duke's early departure was a boon to Talon. He had never been to Jadenpool, and with the number of visitors the Exposition drew, he had uncovered many rumors and tales regarding fiendish incursions and Uldani shamans in the surrounding regions of the Empire. The most promising one centered around reports of an Ignitherris, a demon made of sand and fire, nesting near the port of Charinzar in the far eastern reaches of the Empire. Begging leave of Duke Issul with the promise of even more renown for his small southern duchy, Talon, with the blessing of his liege, remained behind while Duke Issul returned to Arnadore with the rest of the guard. Spending far too much coin, Talon enlisted the help of a down-on-his-luck mage and teleported to the far reaches of the Xallian Empire, where the Seradan Sea met the Ignafel Desert and the city that lay between, Charinzar.

While now inhabited mainly by human citizens of the Empire, the city was indisputably not of their construction or design. Scholars who spent lifetimes studying its architecture would argue endlessly about its elven influences, dwarven motifs, or, most controversially, even pre-dragonborn draconian elements. Most locals, though, attributed their city's construction to the enigmatic people of Qual'Vareen, who came from across the vast eastern sea. There was no direct evidence of the connection, mainly due to Qual'Vareen's harsh one-way immigration laws and policy of seclusion from the societies on the western continents, but locals would speak of the familiarity tourists from Qual'Vareen would have with Charinzar and the frequency of their visits.

The architecture of Charinzar was alien to every other city in the 'known world,' though that moniker seemed to be getting more extensive and increasingly diverse with each passing year. Nevertheless, Talon had never seen anything like the port city nestled between sea and desert. Impossibly thin towers soared into the sky, connected by bridges that defied gravity. Every structure looked like it was created out of tinted sand and stained glass spun and woven by some giant hand making castles on the beach. The city's lack of symmetry, recognizable forms, or cohesive color palette added to its haunting beauty. As the sun moved overhead, the interplay of shadow and light through the woven buildings and shifting colors changed the city's aesthetic hour by hour. It was in this dream-like cityscape that Talon encountered Rahmed.

Talon had been less than subtle in surveying the city, both in trying to make sense of its layout and keeping his ear out for rumors of the Ignitherris. He also had kept his eyes open for anyone he could hire as a guide or convince to join him on his search for the fiend. That was when he found Rahmed, or more accurately, Rahmed found him.

Rahmed intercepted Talon while he ate an intricately spiced local dish under the stretched fabric awnings of an outdoor marketplace. Talon spotted him when he approached, as Rahmed was hard to miss. Against the backdrop of the flowing structures of the desert city, Rahmed was a striking figure in his well-used brass armor and flowing white robes; his attire offsetting his smooth dark skin, the color of shipwright's teak, and shining eyes of polished sandalwood.

"I hear you are looking for the demon of the dunes and possibly a guide? I am Rahmed, and you need to look no further." Rahmed, uninvited, confidently sat down at Talon's table across from him and helped himself to a piece of the soft flatbread off the corner of his plate. Talon, who would have usually been put off or possibly offended by such forward behavior, couldn't help but be intrigued and captivated by this stranger's demeanor and the bright smile he flashed while chewing a bite of the pilfered flatbread.

"Perhaps," Talon replied coyly. Though, if honest with himself, he had already made up his mind.

"It is settled then," replied Rahmed reading Talon's intent. "Of course, if you need a more physical demonstration of my talents, that can be provided," Rahmed added luridly and seductively. Talon must have inadvertently projected his weariness and fatigue of such advances as the swarthy stranger immediately corrected his trajectory. "Or we can talk about the business at hand and the skills I can provide."

Boundaries set, and Talon still needing a guide and partner, the two discussed a strategy for tracking the Ignitherris. They spent the rest of the afternoon and well into the evening at that same table, Rahmed guiding them through a veritable mosaic of food and drink as they traversed easy conversation and details of the coming journey. Their tête-à-tête finally turned to Talon's real reason for being in Charinzar and his search for Richen. Over the previous seven years of his search, Talon had discovered he needed to approach the subject warily. The topic of Uldani and shamanistic traditions could tread on many people's prejudices, religious beliefs, and imperial biases. So, without too many details but in an attempt not to sound overly vague, Talon inquired of Rahmed if he had heard of anyone using elemental magics in the area.

"Yes, yes I have," Rahmed's voice dropped to a conspiratorial whisper. "A fierce warrior of the sands wielding both sword and the elements with unmatched aptitude and prowess." Then adding, "Quite handsome, I hear as well."

"It's you, isn't it?" Talon asked. Try as he might, he couldn't hold back the smile his charismatic companion inspired in him, and Rahmed gave him a sly wink as confirmation. Talon did not inquire any further about shamans or Uldani. Even if this was a dead end for finding Architavia Therandus, there still was a fiend that needed to be sent back to the Nine

Hells, and one never knew what clues it might have in its hoard or what secrets could be coaxed out of it.

With Rahmed's help, Talon spent the next few days securing supplies for their trek into the desert. Rahmed seemed to know everyone whose shop they visited, and Talon accepted that even if it was some elaborate con to bring business to his friends, they were getting good equipment at not ridiculous prices. It did ease his fears that it seemed truly *everyone* knew Rahmed, not just the vendors they bought from or taverns they visited. From folks living on the streets to nobles passing by in their palanquins, all seemed to lift a hand in greeting or shout out a hail of friendship to Rahmed. The swarthy desert warrior's easy manner was infectious and lifted spirits wherever they went. Finally, well-provisioned and sure of their course, the two headed out into the Ignafel Desert. Not only to search for the Ignitherris, but Talon still hoped for any crumb of information that might help him locate the Farseer or Richen.

Traversing deserts, involving moving primarily at night and finding or creating shelter during the day, makes for lonely travel without a good companion. Luckily for Talon, Rahmed turned out to be one of the best. Witty but not overbearing, serious when the situation called for it but still a showman when circumstances allowed, Rahmed made the nights of travel over the dunes seem less arduous and kept their days of rest hiding from the sweltering heat more bearable. Over the long weeks of travel, they learned much from each other and of each other's lives. However, Talon held his tongue when it came to Richen, keeping his stories to ones of his life in the Duke's guard or times before Richen arrived at the estate.

Time and distance become a strange viscous liquid in the desert, sometimes moving as slow as glass and others with the speed of oncoming lava. Talon grew accustomed to and welcoming of Rahmed's affectionate nature, and Rahmed, with astute insight, never pressed beyond quick moments of friendly contact and platonic camaraderie. It took months, but the duo finally caught up with the Ignitherris in one of its multiple lairs throughout the region. Between Talon's prowess with the Vermillion Blade and Rahmed's skill with his dual scimitars and totemic magic, they finally defeated the demon after an extended battle. Talon attempted to extract some knowledge from it before it dissipated back down to the lower planes, but to no avail. The hoard turned out to be nothing more than stolen treasures and trinkets from desert caravans it had ambushed. He left looting the hoard to Rahmed as he dejectedly turned and left the cave, hopes dashed that this might finally be the lead he needed to find Richen.

After the battle they waged during the daylight hours in the depths of the lair, the two traveled under the blazing sun a short but safe distance away from the Ignitherris' corrupted den and made camp. Rahmed must have picked up on Talon's weary and wounded spirit after the battle, and he suggested they stay for the day and camp for the night as well instead of moving on. As they sheltered from the afternoon heat, Talon could not initially place why he felt so emotional and distraught over the day's outcome until he realized the date. It was nearly ten years to the day from his hunting trip with Richen at the spring. The realization crushed him like a boulder from the sky. How had a decade passed? Yes, there were other distractions in his life with his responsibilities for the Duke, but how had his search dragged on so long, and why couldn't he seem to either make progress or finally let it go? Talon sank into the darkness of his mind until Rahmed spoke.

A quiet "What troubles you, friend?" from Rahmed as he handed Talon some cool conjured water was all it took for Talon to unburden himself. He told his companion about his lengthy search and the details of his old relationship with Richen. Rahmed was the perfect listener as he recounted the lengthy tale, never intruding on the story but asking clarifying questions, not only to help him understand but also to assist Talon in organizing his thoughts. Twilight was fading into night when Talon finally was out of words and had reached the part of his tale where Rahmed entered it.

Rahmed, after a long silence, took a deep swig of his water and began to speak. "In my culture, where we are not so obsessed with marriage and bloodlines and heirs, relationships such as yours are not uncommon. We consider them as blessed as any other and as interchangeable." He continued, "How one feels and reacts towards one person is not always how they will react toward another." Rahmed paused as though remembering some past pain. "Every connection between two people is unique, and while a lost love can never be duplicated, it does not mean a new relationship can't be just as powerful."

Talon heard and felt the honesty of the words but still instinctively braced himself for what might come next; in his experience, people expressing such openness and candor did so with an expectation of physical response and an inevitable seduction. However, none came. Rahmed left the tent and wandered away from the camp into the night. Talon wondered if this was a part of a ploy as well, to have him follow and things to continue from there, but he did not have the energy for games this night. If there were hells to pay in the morning, so be it.

Talon was surprised and relieved that he and Rahmed's camaraderie and regular jovial interactions remained unchanged in the following days. As they traveled under the night sky on their return to Charinzar, Talon thought more deeply on Rahmed's words and their possibilities. At the end of the first week of travel, over their morning meal before camping for the day, he took a deep breath to gather courage equal to what he often needed to face the greatest of foes, "Rahmed, may I ask for your help?"

"Of course, my friend." There was no hint of subterfuge or the smug success of a predator after a long hunt, just a genuine desire to help.

"I need to find out if I can be with someone other than Richen," Talon confessed painfully. "I can offer no promise of a present or future together or that this will get any further than the intimacy of this conversation, but it has been a decade. While I am willing to search decades more, I am ashamed to admit, I am so tired of being lonely."

"My dear Talon," Rahmed paused, voice filled with empathy, "may I begin by just holding you?" Rahmed's voice was a balm as Talon silently nodded. Rahmed went to his side, gently wrapped his arms around the larger man, and slowly rocked him as Talon crumpled into his embrace.

As their journey back to civilization continued, Talon opened himself to Rahmed's affections, and with the progression of their romance and physicality came an excitement and intoxicating exhilaration for Talon. Richen and he had only had a single day and night to explore their sensual relationship, where he and Rahmed, while at a much slower, tentative pace, explored theirs for nearly three weeks. Rahmed, in many ways, was objectively more aesthetically beautiful than Richen; much of that was from a masculine maturity and confidence, but also his physical form was as near perfection as one could imagine.

Over their weeks together, Talon tested and crossed many of the self-imposed boundaries he had placed upon himself out of fear of them leading to an inevitable and immediate press for sex from a partner. With consent from his patient and willing confidant, he finally allowed himself a tactile exploration of Rahmed's body. He experienced it the way a sculptor appreciates a masterpiece; every nuance and line examined and admired. Talon did not anticipate the pleasure his ministrations would give Rahmed, and a creeping disappointment and recognition began to enter his mind as he did not experience the same. When they were two days out from Charinzar, early in their night's travel, Rahmed led them to a high outcropping of sandstone where the city's lights and sea beyond were visible. Rahmed looked to Talon with a not-so-innocent raised eyebrow, and Talon returned it with a nod of feigned confidence.

The night was full of stars, and a crescent moon rose over the Seradan Sea. Even though the newness and thrill of his explorations with Rahmed were wearing off, Talon promised himself he would not back away from this final step. He needed to know, and Rahmed, somehow, by the blessings and light of the Silver Scribe, was willing to help him find out. Under the moonlight, they kissed passionately; at least, Talon hoped that was what Rahmed was feeling. They then disrobed and lay down on the rugs and blankets from their packs. Talon began to let his fingers dance across Rahmed's body. As always, he was physical perfection; beneath the moonlight, Talon found every inch of him profoundly and breathtakingly beautiful. But even as Rahmed's body began to react to his touch and the caresses were returned, Talon's own body refused to respond to him and could not ignite any desire or connection to Rahmed in his mind.

Feeling Talon's disinterest and rising distress, Rahmed offered to help Talon however he could. Talon tried with every part of his being to get to a place where they could continue but finally had to say no. Talon sat up and pulled away, his mind now filled with shame, guilt, and the projection of all he was and wasn't and couldn't seem to be. Rahmed, gods bless him, sat up with him and gently wrapped the blankets around them as they looked out to the sea and the rising moon. Rahmed held Talon and gently rocked him as years of frustration and pain, loneliness and loss poured out of him as stifled choked wails into the night sky.

That had been eight years ago, and there had been no one since.

Present Year 872 PXF *~ Summer*

The moon over Arnadore was high in the sky when Talon found he could move again, demons content in the amount of turmoil they had collected from him. Talon stood and peeled off the soaked tunic, which fell to the ground with a wet slap; breeches soon followed. Wrapping a light robe around himself, Talon padded down to the private kitchen reserved for the rooms under a long-term contract. From the well spout, he pulled a tankard of water conjured from the deep cisterns under Arnadore and was drinking deeply when a knock came on the kitchen door that led to the connecting alley. It was a messenger from the Duke. The sealed letter he carried summoned Talon to Arnadore Keep at first light. Talon paid the messenger handsomely for the late-night delivery and was happy Lolly hadn't been awakened to receive the message for him. Then, knowing he should get at least some rest before whatever lay ahead with the morn, Talon returned to his rooms. He donned a light pair of sleeping britches and, clearing his mind, lifted his feet off the floor and stretched out on the bed. Talon wished he didn't see Richen's raven-dark hair and stormy eyes as he exhaustedly drifted off to sleep, but he did, accompanied by the maudlin memory of the aroma of Ms. Haddington's spiced tea.

CHAPTER THIRTEEN

Year 872 PXF *~ Summer*

 As is the case with all urgent news coming in the dark of night, the message was not a happy one. The captain of the Duke's personal regimen, a woman with whom Talon had served, and a newer addition to the guard that Talon did not know had succumbed to a virulent disease and had died in the night. The Duke, without leave or pause, promoted Talon from his position as the Duke's Envoy to Knight Captain on the spot and had pre-selected a replacement for the other guard that only awaited Talon's approval. Having no real choice in the matter, Talon accepted the position, took the oath always to protect and obey the Duke's commands, and then asked for the candidate to be brought in.

The new guard was a young Uldani, shockingly so. While full grown and most likely the same age in years as Talon, the long-lived Uldani rarely let one so young outside their territories. His young age, while not as apparent physically, was more than conveyed by the effort he needed to exert to maintain control over the sometimes-volatile impulses and passions that were a hallmark of his people.

The Uldani had once been elves. For time immemorial, the elves glacially moved through their lives as other inhabitants of the material world bloomed and faded like the seasons. While the majority of elven people were content with their peaceful and measured existence, a faction amongst them was not. The Uldani realized to live on such a scale, seemingly in defiance of all but the geologic cycles of nature, was to live apart from life itself. They cast off their ties to the eternal groves and valleys of the elves, instead binding themselves to the elemental forces of nature and embracing the shamanistic traditions of the other races.

The Uldani found that by so doing, their blood began to quicken. Their emotions didn't just bloom; they flourished, and as they fed their newfound passions, embracing the rush and vitality they brought, the fires of their lives burned ever hotter and brighter. No matter the emotion, be it rage, love, kindness, spite, or any other, it was to be savored and embraced, fueled to the height of its potential.

To live as such was not without cost; to live so brightly, even for a species as inherently magical as elves, was to live briefly. The Uldani, in a trade they would happily repeat, began living only half as long as their elven brethren. What was at first only cultural, over the eons, became biological as the elves and Uldani diverged even further. For the Uldani, the porcelain delicacy of the elven countenance and physique evolved into a more rough-hewn and rugged visage and appearance. With their fey ancestry, elemental ties, shamanistic ways, and lives still four times the length of humans, the Uldani were a stunningly handsome albeit volatile people often misunderstood. While sometimes admired, the Empire's inhabitants more often disparaged them and their culture.

The candidate before Talon appeared to be in his late teenage years if one measured on a human scale. Talon knew while he could be younger than himself, due to his heritage, he just as easily could be older. He had dark brown curls close-cropped on the sides, but they were allowed to bunch into a mound on the top of his scalp and over his prominent brow and deep-set eyes. A lantern jaw and defined cheekbones framed a well-proportioned nose and thin tight lips. The young Uldani guard kept having to adjust the stare he had leveled at Talon from across the room as he approached. First, raising his eyes and then his chin as well, having misread the taller human's scale and height when he entered the large chamber. As he approached, Talon could read in the young Uldani guard's eyes and posture both defiance and ambition, emotions tempered with a hopeful need for purpose and direction. Talon saw a glimpse of himself in this Uldani, both as a child looking up to Richen and as a young man looking to Lochlan.

"What's your name?" Talon asked.

"Osman. I have not earned any other," the young guard replied.

Immediately setting roles, Talon responded, "You will call me Captain and nothing more. Not sir or my lord." With a pause and a glance to the Duke on his throne, Talon reconsidered using Lochlan's words, "those are titles I do not wear."

Talon led Osman out to the central yard of the Keep. With the Vermillion Blade sheathed, he drew only his long dagger gifted to him by Mikal. "Show me your skills." Osman drew his longsword and proceeded to engage Talon. The Uldani swordsman was a capable enough fighter but no match for Talon, even while wielding only a dagger. Talon corrected him without humiliation, but it became evident that Osman did not have the speed to rely on his longsword alone.

"Tomorrow, we begin your training to wield two weapons at once... Unless you prefer a shield?" Talon watched the emotion rise in Osman's eyes at the suggestion of a shield. The goading remark allowed him to get a sense of Osman's self-control, a potential concern. "Have the armory find you something suitable for your off-hand. Be here at dawn. Eat first."

Talon surprised himself with how quickly he fell into the role of "Captain" and realized Lochlan must have done the same as "Commander." While Talon felt he was not being as brutal and relentless as Lochlan, that could not be surmised by the look on Osman's face by midday, much less by how he barely drug himself to the barracks that night. Talon considered ambushing Osman the following morning the way Lochlan had ambushed him at dawn in his bed, but Osman was not a child handling his first weapon as Talon had been, so he decided against it.

Within a few months, Osman's daily training had changed from Talon driving him through a drudging grind of exhaustion and the frustrations of learning to dual wield to an exuberant sporting match between two combatants quickly becoming equals. The young Uldani warrior throttled his volatile personality into a mix of razorlike focus and unbridled ferocity that could change instantly and without warning. Even Talon wielding the Vermillion Blade and with his years of experience could find himself quickly on the defensive as Osman's tactics changed moment to moment mid-fight.

Year 872 PXF ~ Autumn

As Autumn's last leaves fell, Talon recognized that Osman had made few connections or friends within Arnadore, his Uldani heritage labeling him an "outsider" and "embarrassing unpredictable" to the often milquetoast sensibilities of the local human nobles and peasants alike. Talon, likewise having spent far too many nights with only Lolly as company, approached Osman as he was sheathing his swords after an especially challenging round of sparring.

"Captain, may I help you?" Osman inquired tentatively, his breath fogging the crisp air of the autumn evening.

"Call me Talon," he answered with an outstretched hand. "Lolly at the Sojourn's Rest is making an old favorite of mine for dinner. Why don't you join us."

Osman looked a little shocked and increasingly reluctant until something clicked, and then, overcoming his hesitation, he grasped Talon's hand enthusiastically. "That sounds amazing! I have been living off alley stew, and let me assure you, it is as awful as it sounds!"

Talon suddenly concerned, "Have you not been receiving your wages?"

"Oh, I have plenty of coin," Osman confessed, "or enough, at least," and then, with unabashed candor, "It is just many establishments won't accept it from me, and I got tired of being turned away or served with a concerned wariness."

Now it was time for Talon's temper to flare, "Are you telling me that a member of the Duke's personal regiment has been denied service within the walls of Arnadore? I will personally-"

Osman interrupted him with words wiser than his young face should possess, "It is a common misconception, but the Uldan people also embrace peacefulness and calm as much as rage and passion. Acceptance will come." He added with a mischievous grin more in line with his boyish looks, "And if not, the bastards will be long dead before the first gray hair marks my brow." Then, with a flourish, Osman dramatically pulled a single silver strand of hair from Talon's scalp to drive home the point and defuse his still-growing temper.

It was the first time a deep and pure belly laugh had escaped Talon's lips in years. The laughter was infectious, and soon the two of them were howling like jackals not only at the original joke but also at the absurdity of neither of them seemingly being able to stop laughing. Finally, breathless with arms clutching cramped sides and wiping away tears from their eyes, small guffaws threatening to start the whole spectacle all over again, the two headed out of the Arnadore Keep and to the Sojourn's Rest.

The evening had begun raucously at the Keep and only became more boisterous as the night went on. Dinner was ravenously consumed and vocally lauded, with first Osman and then Talon standing on their chairs proclaiming to the blushing then exuberant Lolly of the uncontested "deliciosity" of the meal. The evening moved from the inn's private kitchen and dining area to the main public room and tavern. Feeling more intoxicated from the unbridled chaos of Osman's personality than ale or spirits, Talon allowed Osman to drag him onto the stage to join the bards performing there. The two of them elicited roars of laughter as Osman played the fool to Talon's well-known stoic reputation. It was well after two in the morning before the whirlwind that was Osman quieted, landing them at a table with half a dozen empty and half-drunk tankards of ale.

Talon had a more than general knowledge of Uldani culture and territories through his childhood tutors and his search for Richen. Most notably, their custom of having to earn their surname. Once earned, it was of their choosing and not necessarily related to a family connection. It was one of the main things that had hindered his search for the Farseer. As they wound down at the table, feet up on chairs opposite them, Talon almost asked Osman if he knew of Architavia Therandus, but the night had been such a welcome respite from all the weight Talon had burdened himself with for nearly two decades; he instead remained quiet and gave himself permission to just be happy for a moment.

After that, Talon and Osman became fast friends, often taking meals together at midday and in the evenings. Around Arnadore, the two became well-known for their antics and high spirits. Establishments that had once shunned Osman now begged the two to visit not only for their own copious consumption but also for the crowds that followed them and stayed deep into the night. There were even taverns that attempted to hire them to make appearances. While flattering, that kind of commitment was not in Osman's nature, and Talon found it to be an inappropriate proposition for the Knight Captain of the guard. Instead, on Hearth's Rest, the two would put on elaborate displays of acrobatics and fighting skills, the likes of which many in the region had never seen. Their duels would begin in front of the orphanage in the silliest way imaginable and then range throughout Elery Square and the Trellis Market. Over rooftops, through the fountains, across wagons, and into taverns, exiting with a featured ale in hand and lauding endorsements of the establishment. For hours they would delight the gathered crowds and especially made sure to include the children of Arnadore in their schemes. The spectacle was the talk of the town for days, and as each Hearth's Rest approached, it seemed like all discussions centered around what the two could possibly do to top their previous outing.

On the cold midwinter eve of Richen's birthday, Talon's life slowed enough for him to reflect on his growing relationship with Osman. The bond between Osman and him was not unlike the depth of his bond with Richen but entirely different in its emotion. From the first moments, Richen had been his love, infatuation, and, eventually, his soul mate. On the other hand, Osman was his best friend, a comrade in arms of times both serious and silly, and like a brother he never had. If asked, Talon would unhesitantly say he loved Osman, but he was not *in* love with Osman. As Talon's mind became more settled and assured in his feelings and the slithering voice could find no purchase even on this night when it was usually its most vocal, Talon blew out a single candle and wished Richen, wherever he was, a happy birthday.

Through the rest of Winter, the Knight Captain and young Uldani guard quickly became the most sought-after guests at all of the season's festival gatherings within the city and the surrounding estates. Finally, as the weather turned more temperate, just after the first Hearth's Rest of Spring, an engraved and wax-sealed letter Talon had been dreading might arrive finally did: an invitation to the Festival of Blossoms Gala at the Cour-Vermane estate.

CHAPTER FOURTEEN

Year 873PXF ~ Early Spring

Talon had to admit the manipulation was masterfully done. The invitation was from his mother with no indication of his father's hand. She had even used the ancient Vermane family crest in the sealing wax to indicate it was from the Lady of the house and separate from his father. While not directly stated in any way, the invitation gave every indication his mother sent it in defiance of his father and as some form of rebellion against his iron control of the estate. The Festival of Blossoms Gala was, of course, the perfect choice, just as was every aspect of this outreach from his family after fifteen years. The gala was large enough that Talon and his parents could keep direct interaction to a minimum but intimate enough that Talon's presence both as the Cour-Vermane heir and the 'must-have' guest of the upper echelon of Arnadore society would be well and duly noted by all. And the final masterwork stroke, the gala, as always, was a masquerade.

Talon was absolutely not going to attend. It was a decided issue in his mind. He was not about to again fall into his family's web of deceit and control. He was about to throw the invitation into the hearth when Osman burst through the door to Lolly's kitchen so violently that he almost knocked it off the hinges.

"We're going to a Masquerade!" he proclaimed at a volume that if it had been a battle cry, would have been more subtle.

All Talon could do was sigh under his breath, "Masterfully done, mother. Masterfully done."

Unsurprisingly, Osman had never been to a gala, much less a masquerade. Talon, of course, had attended the gala as the lord-inheritor of the estate during his youth. However, later when training with Lochlan, he had always managed to excuse his absence by claiming some injury, feigned or actual. Even though the gala was weeks away, Talon knew they hadn't much time. If invitations were already in people's hands, the tailors and the mask makers especially, would receive commissions this very morning if they didn't already have them from the nobility who had planned ahead.

Talon knew, as all good warriors do, that when the odds were against him, when he was on unfamiliar battlefields, the best tactic was simply to cheat. He grabbed the first courier he could lay a hand on, bellowing as only he could to get one's attention. A young girl appeared at Lolly's kitchen door lightning fast, beating many of the other couriers who weren't as quick on their feet. Looking her in the eye, he pressed a gold piece into her hand, nearly ten times the usual fee, assuring her that it was hers to keep and another as well if she beat all other couriers to her destination. He then handed her a small pouch of three dozen more gold coins for her to deliver to the old clothier he used at the estate, along with a summons for him and all his supplies to come to Talon's rooms at the Sojourn's Rest. Then, to even further bend the rules in his favor, he sealed the parchment with his Knight Captain's signet, marking it as an official summons.

The clothier's carriage arrived mid-morning laden with bolts of fabrics, stacks of leather, and two assistants in tow. Talon had prepared a small fitting space for the clothier in his rooms, along with securing and outfitting an adjacent room as a workspace. Taking a note from his mother's playbook, Talon intended not to allow the clothier to leave the premises until the work was complete. He knew full well that as soon as the clothier returned to his shop, another noble would flood his pockets with gold to displace their outfits from the front of the line.

Osman was effervescent with excitement, his spirits more full of bubbles and froth than a keg of ale that had rolled down three flights of stairs. Talon had never seen this side of his friend's personality. Osman didn't just embrace the giddy joy of this new experience; he fed his childlike wonder of each moment to absolute bursting. The air of Talon's rooms became positively electric with the charged possibility of each new bolt of fabric and skin of leather the clothier and his assistants brought over the threshold.

When everything was finally in place to begin, Talon, with a sigh and a bored voice hiding the playful malice behind it, said, "Well, I guess I should go first." Talon's words hit Osman with more impact than the full-force shoulder checks he had thrown at him in training. He abjectly deflated to the point Talon worried there might be tears. "Osman, get over here. Of course, you're going first."

Osman's rebound was like a firework exploding on a midsummer eve. He practically launched from his chair to stand on the small dais the clothier had set up in the middle of Talon's rooms. There was a long pause as Osman realized and then sheepishly asked, "What am I supposed to do?"

The clothier and his assistants, who had likewise been infected with Osman's exuberance, with a sparkle in their eyes, replied, "Tell us anything and everything you want this outfit to be, and we will make it happen."

"Anything?" Osman confirmed. "Everything?!" making sure he had heard right.

The clothier looked over his shoulder to Talon to confirm he was aware of the costs. Talon nodded in the affirmative.

"Anything within the realms of the mundane, arcane, or divine." the clothier stated matter-of-factly, adding a spark of arcane energy between his fingers with a flourish.

The Festival of Blossoms traditionally had been an occasion to celebrate the coming of Spring, fertility, and blessings for a good harvest. Falling on Hearth's Rest meant the whole of the populace could participate in the picnics and parades and the prominent wearing of their favorite flowers and blossoms on their clothing and oversized hats. However, through the years, the homespun festival became more and more gentrified by the nobility to its current form in which one had to have powerful connections, social status, and, most importantly, vast amounts of money to participate fully. Noble houses would predate upon one another to win who had the most extravagant, best attended, most talked about party of the season.

If for no other reason than the nobility's blood-thirsty attitude towards the whole blossom social season, Toman Cour-Vermane would have had nothing to do with it. However, after one ill-aimed jab at the House Cour-Vermane thirty years ago, Toman set loose Veronic on assuring no other house would ever dare to challenge his house again for hosting the pinnacle event of Blossom Festival. Thus the Cour-Vermane Blossom Gala was born. While mostly invisible for the rest of the year, Veronic became the tectonic force behind shaping the Gala and all things Blossom Festival in Arnadore. Her ruthless hospitality and vicious pleasantries eviscerated all who crossed her during the planning season for the Gala. Where social manipulation did not fulfill her needs, money was applied liberally, and if still unsatisfied, she would leverage the full political weight of House Cour-Vermane against the offender. Treaties between empires had been scuttled over an embassy daring to plan an event opposite the Gala. Veronic not only didn't take prisoners when it came to the Gala, but she would also hang her rivals' metaphysical social corpses on her tea parlor wall as trophies.

After rigorously enforcing a 'flowers only' theme at the Gala for a decade, even Veronic recognized its limitations. Hence, she expanded the theme to the more accommodating one of 'nature and the seasons,' which allowed the Gala to truly flourish, becoming grander and grander each year. Talon was sure this year would be no exception, so when Osman could not decide between an outfit representing Summer or Fall, Talon, as offhandedly as he could muster, suggested, "Why not both?"

Naively, he had not expected Osman's spark of inspiration and exclamation of, "Or all four!" And so was born the outfit that would affect the wardrobe at the Gala for the next decade.

The creation of Osman's outfit took the better part of two weeks, involving the recruitment of tailors, embroiderers, leatherworkers, and even enchanters and artificers teleported in from Bal'Ethera. Platinum coins spilled from Talon's accounts like a waterfall, but to be caught up in the purity of Osman's unbridled joy of its creation was worth every copper twice over. Moreover, Talon never had a younger sibling to spoil and witness having new and exciting experiences for the first time. With it happening now, this late in life, Talon seeing Osman's thrill at every step of the process opened the overflowing and pent-up floodgates on a need he didn't even know he had.

Talon's outfit, by contrast, took a little over a day to complete. What he commissioned was not without sentimentality, though. It consisted of a dark slate-gray jerkin over a contrasting granite-gray doublet and rich forest green leathers, all to evoke the boulder by the spring where he and

Richen spent their last day together. He matched it with a fitted leather mask ornamented with the bright green leaves of an apple tree in Spring and a single apple blossom above his left brow.

The day of the Gala arrived. With all accounts paid, Osman's swords and Vermillion Blade polished (as the guests would no doubt expect for them to have one of their outrageous duels) and outfits donned, Talon and Osman mounted and headed to the place Talon once called home and where he had vowed never to return.

*Year 873*PXF *~ Spring*

Osman was determined to gallop to the Cour-Vermane estate at full speed, but Talon convinced him the later he arrived, as long as it wasn't too late, the more people would see his entrance. He relented but was practically bouncing in the saddle by the time they were in sight of the gates to the estate in which Talon had grown up. Even at their impressive scale, the gates seemed small to Talon. In fact, the whole estate seemed smaller than Talon remembered. Not that he had grown physically any larger since leaving, but his world perspective now encompassed continents instead of just a few leagues of estate-held lands. Even the vast influence of his father's political ties was insignificant in relation to the larger world. Luckily, there was a short queue of carriages and horses delivering guests to the Gala, which gave Talon a moment to collect himself and gave Osman time to prepare.

Talon gave all due credit to Osman. He did have a sense for the dramatic, and the embracing of his emotions allowed him to heighten this moment, *his moment,* to one of sublime radiance not only for himself but for all those around him. The two of them dismounted and entered the courtyard gates. All eyes instantly went to Talon. His presence after such a long absence, paired with his size, elegant but subdued clothes, brute physical presence contrasting the feminine delicacy of the mask he wore, and ornate thick Uldani braiding that flowed through his hair cascading down over his broad shoulders, stopped all conversation. No one gave a second thought to the Uldani beside him in his plain black walnut-colored doublet, leggings, and matching eye mask - until the first stitches of green silk embroidery appeared at the shoulders like the first shoots of Spring appearing on a fallow field. The patterns being made by the looping strands of light green shimmering thread spread and grew, becoming verdant green vines as they scintillated over the fabric that now looked more like rich topsoil than the flat brown of its first impression.

As if on cue, the golden light of twilight illuminated the courtyard spotlighting Osman like the lead actor on a stage. More and more guests began to note what was unfolding across Osman's clothing. The green embroidery began sprouting tiny leaves, some integrated with the fabric while others at the neck and cuff became three-dimensional accents. The vines lifted off the material at the shoulders, curling and weaving themselves into cap-pauldrons made of Uldani knotting. Similarly, his mask had sprouted into a woven structure of organic complex knotting and tiny leaves to match the rest.

Every eye was now on Osman. There was a pause, and just as people were about to turn away, the vines began to bloom. First, with tiny white jasmine flowers filling the evening air with their fragrance, the jasmine grew into gardenias whose color then deepened as they changed to roses. Flower after flower bloomed and faded, the changing of the blooms washing across Osman in waves like Summer breezes bending long grass in a field. With each successive varietal, a longer and longer cape with an ethereal echo of each bloom grew from the pauldrons on his shoulders and flowed down his back. Finally, the waves of Summer flowers began to slow as lavender, the hallmark of Summer's end in the region, replaced all the blooms across Osman's outfit. Then, as if blown by an invisible breeze, the cape of ethereal flowers detached from Osman's pauldrons, rose into the air, and burst apart, the flowers scattering into a flurry of ghostly petals that swirled over the heads and then showered down upon nearby guests in the courtyard.

By the time they looked back to Osman, the vines of the pauldrons were transforming into small silver-barked branches to create a mantle that sprouted into a canopy of perfectly formed maple leaves. His mask also transformed to match the change in his clothes, the body now looking like it was crafted from birch bark with maple leaves spreading out as accents over his left brow. Across his torso, the vines coalesced in a motif of forest trees leading to Osman's shoulders, their now shedding branches lending their leaves and color to the mantle. There, leaves turning from green to gold to scarlet cascaded from the canopy at his shoulders, falling back toward the ground and creating an autumnal carpet around his feet.

To Talon's consternation, to end the presentation of Autumn, Osman insisted on bringing some fun to what, at this point, had been a potentially overwhelming display. In each hand, one by one, a veritable cornucopia of the products of the local harvest began to appear. Overflowing with aplomb and charm, Osman, with lewd expression or raised eyebrow, then handed a piece of local produce to a surprised party guest, often with an uproarious result. When Osman made his way back toward Talon with a mischievous grin, all the while setting up the crowd for something outrageous, Talon instead turned the tables on him and promptly pulled an apple out of his pocket and, with a wink and smile, took a bite, leaving Osman holding an over-large pumpkin and nowhere to put it. The guests lost all decorum as Osman pawned the pumpkin onto a startled stablehand who had just entered the gates, unaware of anything that had transpired.

Talon dared a glance at his mother, wondering what hells he and Osman might have to pay for this incursion into the usual stately mood of her Gala, but he found her looking back at him with a genuine smile on her face. A smile with a tenderness toward him he had never seen before. The emotion was fleeting as her customary stately rigor reasserted itself overtaking her expression. Talon and his mother then turned their attention back to Osman as Winter was yet to come.

The last scarlet leaf fell off Osman as frost began to form and spread across his mantle and mask, at first from the tips of the branches and then extending to the cuffs and neckline of his doublet. His outfit's rich brown base fabric changed to a deep glacial blue. The silver barked branches at Osman's shoulders dissolved into a flurry of snowflakes that dusted his dark brown curls, whose tips at their touch became frosted snowy white. His mask color changed from white birch to the hue of the blue spruce trees that grew in the mountains to the north. The leaves changing from maple to holly, complete with their red berries. The tail of his jerkin lengthened from being cropped at the waist to extending to his knees with an elegant drift-like split bisecting it. As the frost spread across Osman, it stitched into the fabric ornately embroidered ice-crystal beading, accenting every edge and seam in the impossible knotted patterns of the Uldani shamanistic tradition. The deep blue base fabric, still visible beneath the fantastical beadwork, highlighted every nuance of the design. Osman's outfit finally came to rest, leaving its wearer looking every inch the epitome of an eldritch prince of frost and ice.

Osman spread his arms wide as though to hug the world, took a final turn, and eyes to the twilight heavens let out the most joyously pure laugh many in the gathering had ever heard in their pretentious and privileged lives. Talon, emotion caught in his throat seeing his best friend, his little brother, have such an experience, simply began to clap the way he used to clap for Ms. Haddington's pies emerging from the oven when he was a child. The rest of the party did the same. Osman's purity of spirit washed away many of the prejudices against the Uldani people that night. To live with passion is not just to live with turmoil and embarrassing unpredictability; it is also to live with unabashed joy for life's experiences and feed the moments you have with your whole soul.

CHAPTER FIFTEEN

Everyone wanted to meet Osman. The crush of people complimenting him, asking about his outfit, and even a few wishing to learn more about the Uldani knots and their cultural meaning stretched on for almost half an hour. Osman's outfit continued to change from season to season but now at a far slower pace and without the fruits and vegetables appearing in his hands. Throughout the night, as each season emerged, another person would approach to comment on details they had missed before. Talon happily faded into the background, having less than a handful of people approach him. Being this inconspicuous even in his former home, he took the opportunity to slip into the lower levels of the estate and head to Mikal's room. Walking down the narrow hallway past Ms. Haddington's kitchen and to Mikal's chamber was like stepping back into his childhood. By the time he reached the door, he wasn't the towering Knight Captain of Arnadore but a shaking teenage boy terrified of what fate might await behind the blacksmith's door.

Talon was in a panic. Mikal had found their plan. Did he break their secret code and know everything? Ms. Haddington had told him over lunch that as soon as he finished eating, Mikal wanted Talon to come to see him in his rooms. The stern and, even worse, disappointed look that she gave Talon spoke volumes about the nature of what was to come. As he walked down the long narrow hallway on the lower level of the estate, a fresh panic entered his mind. Had Mikal told his father?

Talon timidly knocked on Mikal's door.

"Come in, Talon." Mikal did not come to the door himself, instead leaving Talon to work up the courage to turn the handle and enter on his own. As he took a deep breath and swung the door open, he saw Richen sitting on a chair next to Mikal's desk, pale as a sheet and his back straight as an arrow. There wasn't just worry in his eyes; there was fear.

"Close the door," Mikal stated calmly. Once done, he held up exactly what Talon had expected: the note. "Would you care to explain this?"

Talon's tongue suddenly seemed three times too large in his throat. His mouth opened and then closed, but nothing came out.

In the absence of Talon's voice, Mikal continued, "I can plainly see it is your writing and his," head motioning to Richen. "I thought better of you spreading such scandalous filth about good people. Do you even understand the consequences if your father found out about this? He is a man of far more severe justice than me, and it would very well be within his rights to ask for Richen to be expelled as my apprentice for being a part of such slander."

Talon saw Richen look to the ceiling and bite his lip to hold back the emotion welling up. The thought of losing Richen set loose his own tongue.

"But it's not slander," Talon blurted out. "It's just a story to hide our secret code." Mikal looked confused and a bit taken aback, leadingly asking for Talon to continue.

Talon tumbled over his words, hoping the faster he could get the truth out, the more chance there would be to save Richen. "We were planning to go back to Milgran's Orchard to pick apples to make fermented cider, and we didn't want to get caught, so we wanted to code our message, but it was too obvious, so we came up with that." Talon finally took a breath and pointed to the note while internally cursing the tittering giggle emanating from the slithering voice in his head that had suggested the plan.

Mikal just stated, "Show me."

Talon explained how the coded message was just a simple word swap, but to distract people from noticing he and the voice had created a scandalous tale about the upstairs maid and the gardener to hide their real message. The account spilled out of Talon's mouth like a rushing stream until he finally concluded, "... and we knew no one would really believe it for real because the gardener is the most pious man in town and Betsy loves her wife more than anyone, but it would keep them from looking for our message."

Mikal sighed deeply. "So you were worried about people finding out about you two making some hard cider and didn't even consider what this story could do?"

Talon nodded, and Richen chimed in, "That is why we made it so ridiculous. With half a thought, people would realize it couldn't happen and throw the whole thing away as rubbish."

"Boys, listen to me." Mikal now positioned them both in front of him, looking them in the eyes. "You have to learn, most people don't spare any thought, much less half a thought, when it comes to scandal. Worse, they will believe a lie about a good man or woman long before accepting the truth about a wicked one." He continued lovingly but strictly, "You must never spread lies like this again. I truly could have done nothing to keep

Richen here had this gone any further than me." The boys began to smile, but Mikal interrupted, "And you will both clean every tool in the smithy as well as sweep the flue and rotate the woodpile." Groans from the boys at their punishment were interrupted by Mikal slapping them hard on their outside shoulders, so their other ones knocked together. "Now get. And save me some of your cider. You can use the old quarter keg in the smithy store room."

Present Year 873 PXF *~ Spring*

"Hello?"

A voice answered from beyond the door, pulling Talon back to the present. He turned the knob and entered the chamber he had not been inside for two decades. The room was much the same as he remembered. As Talon's focus shifted to the man hunched over the desk doing ledgers, his first thought was, "Who is this old man, and where is Mikal?" It wasn't until the figure at the desk turned to him that Talon recognized it was indeed the blacksmith he had known so well. There was no hiding that the years had begun to take their toll. Mikal was only fifteen or so years older than Talon, but smithing is a hard life.

His body still held all the power it once had, built more akin to a hundred-year-old oak than a human, but his face did not have the vitality it once held. Wrinkles and sagging skin come with the territory, but the melancholy in his eyes caught Talon off-guard. Mikal always had a spark of purpose and determination in him, lighting the darkest times. Even after Richen was taken, he was a solid force of determination that Talon leaned upon when training with Lochlan. Often late in the day, when Lochlan had pushed Talon further than he felt he could go, and the Commander still demanded even more, Talon would look to the smithy door and find that Mikal would be standing there. Always watching and silently caring,

Mikal, with just a nod and a flex of one of his mighty arms, would renew Talon's determination to keep fighting and stay on course for his goal.

"Talon?" Mikal questioned, squinting over a small pair of half spectacles, seeming to doubt his own eyes. "Is that you, my boy?" Talon had forgotten he was still wearing his mask, and probably that for the first time since knowing Mikal, his hair was styled and not its usual free-flowing mess. "But who else could it be filling my doorway thusly?" Mikal added with a smile. "Ah Talon," now standing up and crossing to him, then placing his right hand on Talon's chest near his heart, continuing with a bit of wistfulness, "It has been an age, hasn't it?"

Talon felt Mikal was no longer referring to just the passing of time. Mikal examined one of the thick Uldani braids, running his hand down it. "This is new. Something has changed in you, my boy, for the better, perhaps even?" In answer, Talon embraced Mikal in a giant bear hug, first creating shock in the shorter man experiencing a hitherto unknown act of physical affection from Talon. But then Mikal leaned deeply into it, returning the embrace and letting all the pent-up sadness and loneliness flow out of him. The two men, who each had the power to crush ale kegs in their arms with a similar act, held on to each other powerfully and tenderly, letting their contact say all the words that needed to pass between them.

When they finally let go, Talon began, "I haven't given up on Richen, but I have met someone..." Talon told Mikal all about Osman, up to the moment that had just occurred in the courtyard.

Mikal, immediately understanding, interjected before Talon could explain, "I always said you would be a wonderful big brother, and now you are one." Talon realized that perhaps the ways of his Uldani brother were rubbing off on him as he felt his eyes well with moisture under the mask and his throat close a bit. Mikal, perfectly reading the moment, knew it was time to change the subject. "I think your father is up to something. I am crafting far more weapons and light armor pieces than are normal for our exports to the northern duchies and Lymehold for trade." A seriousness overtook his tone, "and he is not putting them on the shipping caravans headed north. He is sending them south in local wagons. I have not found evidence of something amiss, but it is strange."

Talon thought a moment. "Perhaps we should begin a correspondence, casual conversation, but if you have something to report," Talon looked around the room, lost in memory again, "use Richen's and my old code." Mikal chuckled unexpectedly, being transported back to the same memory.

"That will do nicely." Then, slapping his hips as though looking for his missing set of etching tools, Mikal added, "And you should get back to the Gala before your parents miss you or your absence intrudes on Osman's experience.

With smiles and slaps on each other's shoulders, Talon left Mikal and returned to the Gala.

CHAPTER SIXTEEN

Returning into the courtyard, Talon, surprisingly, could not immediately find Osman. There was a brief moment of panic where Talon thought something might have happened, but his fears were allayed when he spotted him off at the edge of the party near the grounds where he and Lochlan used to spar. He was not alone. Standing with him was a lean woman of almost his same height wearing a slender midnight blue gown covered with the sparkling stars of the night sky above. Her mask was of the same starry motif but also adorned with a large moon lotus over her right brow. With Osman's outfit currently displaying Winter, the two made a striking pair. Spotting Talon approaching, Osman waved him over. "Talon, I would like to present to you Cerena…" Osman stumbled in his introduction and looked at the young lady at a loss, "I am so sorry, I don't believe I know your last name."

With a familiar predatory smile that Talon immediately placed, she rescued her floundering Uldani companion, "That's alright, dear, he already knows."

Talon stepped in, as a part of him was his mother's son after all. "Osman, may I present to you Cerena Cour-Vermane."

Osman began to choke even though he was neither drinking nor eating. "Your sis-"

Talon interrupted, "Cousin." Shooting a sidewise glance at Cerena, "Definitely, cousin." Talon now fully engaged in social fencing with Cerena. "So, tell me, how is dear cousin Rabien?" Adding "her brother" to keep Osman caught up with the relationships.

"Oh, here somewhere. Probably skulking about in shadows or smithies. I'm surprised you didn't bump into him," Cerena purred. Then added, voice dripping venom, "Aren't those your normal haunts?"

Osman had spent enough time dueling Talon on the training field to know the steel he saw in Talon's eyes and set of his jaw meant he was about to deliver a devastating string of attacks that would end whoever was on the receiving end, so he jumped in to defuse the moment, stepping between them. "Cerena," he paused, looking to each of them, then cleared his throat and continued. "Cerena was just telling me she is staying at the estate until late Summer." Then, closing his eyes and cringing slightly, he continued, his voice sliding up in timbre, "I invited her to join us sometime in Arnadore for an evening of frivolity."

Cerena chimed in maliciously, "Yes, Osman here said to join you *whenever* I wanted." Then, putting her hand on Talon's chest and patting it lightly, "That I was *always* welcome."

Talon refused to rise to the bait, "But of course, dear cousin! I can even send a carriage to pick you up."

"I would hate to trouble you, cousin. I can ride in myself. Osman here tells me you like to be spontaneous with your plans, so I'm sure it will be no problem if I appear at your door unannounced."

All but shattering his teeth, knowing he could now have no knowledge or control over her comings and goings, Talon grumbled back through a clenched jaw, "That would be fine."

"Good. It's settled then. See you around, cousin." And with that, Cerena sauntered off back into the throng of the Gala, her cascading hair swinging back and forth as she walked.

Talon turned to Osman, ready to unload a tirade of epitaphs regarding his cousin, but held his tongue, immediately spotting the problem.

Osman was smitten.

The social aspects of the rest of the Gala were uneventful relative to all that had already occurred: hands shaken, glasses lifted, small pleasantries exchanged. The only other event of note was when Talon did finally spot Rabien well in his cups, eying the Vermillion Blade covetously from across the Gala's dance floor. Talon was concerned there might be a scene for a moment, but before he could plan accordingly, he caught out of the corner of his eye a nod from his father to some of his 'invited associates.' Rabien was then briskly and discreetly assisted to the guest house on the far side of the grounds without incident.

As the Gala stretched into the evening and began losing some of its momentum, Osman and Talon initiated their duel, not only to goose the crowd but also as their exit strategy. As all great duels do, it began at the bar, Talon muscling Osman out of getting a drink with his greater size and mass. Then, with a shrill, "Excuse me, Sir!" Osman confronted Talon. "I demand satisfaction for this besmirching of my honor!" Talon shrugged and turned away unbothered. "Well, I never!" Osman continued, and as his outfit was currently showcasing Fall, he mock-drew a zucchini from his scabbard and thwacked Talon across the shoulders with it.

Talon, bewildered, turned to Osman and, with a far more haughty voice than Talon ever used, retorted, "Have you just struck me with a zucchini, my good man?"

Indignantly Osman replied, "And what if I did?"

"Well," Talon, now drawing the Vermillion Blade in a single slow motion, revealing its full horrifying scale, "I would have to retaliate." The crowd gasped as the terrifying edge of the Vermillion Blade swung down on the unarmed Osman holding only a lone zucchini for defense. Lightning fast, Osman dove between Talon's legs hitting him right in the codpiece with the oversized squash, pausing just a beat for the joke to sink in, then rolled to his feet with both swords in hand, and the duel was on.

As had come to be expected, the duel was an exposition of unparalleled athleticism, acrobatic skill, and deadly blademanship, and Talon took great pleasure in making his father's house his and Osman's playground for their battle. From the outside bar, Talon let Osman press his attack, pushing the heir of House Cour-Vermane up the main entry stairs to the very threshold of the estate. There Talon posed gallantly for the party guests making a 'heroic last stand for the aristocracy' defending his ancestral home from the raging Uldani invader, and promptly got full chest-kicked through the front doors by Osman.

In the creation of his outfit, Osman had not forgotten the duel. Now as he and Talon fought, a seemingly unending bag of tricks poured forth from it. Combined with Osman's acrobatic skill, Talon's athleticism, and the multi-tiered atrium of the entry foyer, the duel became more akin to stories of theatrical productions from the forests of the Fey. Gala guests crowded the main floor as their contest took to the air above them, leaping from railings, banisters, and chandeliers against an ever-changing backdrop of flowering Spring vines, cascading Autumn leaves, and gusting flurries of snow and ice.

Perhaps too caught up in the moment, Osman's exuberance, or the memories of his childhood, Talon glanced around, trying to lay eyes on Toman. Talon had lived long enough under his father's roof to know Toman was livid, but not the tiniest spark of that rage marred his smiling face as he was trapped by circumstance, knowing that any show of disapproval in front of his guests would mark him a 'poor sport' and 'curmudgeonly host.' Talon made sure his father saw his gaze and intent, and with a smile worthy of a Cour-Vermane, he leaped from a third-floor banister down to the grand staircase leading from the foyer to the upper floors.

Talon allowed himself to be driven up the stairs by Osman's furious onslaught of icy attacks bolstered by an illusionary blizzard conjured from his outfit. Talon swung the Vermillion Blade in wide arcs with far more flourish than necessary, always careful to displace not even a speck of dust from the estate's art or his mother's precious décor. Osman, followed by the Gala's guests, pushed up the grand staircase and around the upper walkway, forcing Talon ever backward, who begrudgingly gave up ground to Osman's two lightning-quick blades and threatening rose vines covered in thorns. Then Talon arrived precisely where he wanted to be, the large landing overlooking the foyer with his back pressed against the carved wooden doors of his father's private study. Toman caught Talon's eye, giving him a smug smirk of confident victory; the heir of House Cour-Vermane then did something he would have sworn he would never do in a million years - he gave his father a sly wink. With a loud arcane knock and the sound of shattering magical seals, the doors to Toman's study flung inward, now open to the party.

As though they had rehearsed it, Osman, looking through the doors, spotted the colossal desk and floor-to-ceiling window behind it and, in an acrobatic maneuver that startled even Talon and drew gasps from the party guests, used the Vermillion Blade as an anchor to vault across the study and land squarely in the middle of Toman's desk. Again, Talon spun around to face his Uldani foe but instead got slapped in the face by a huge, brilliantly colored sycamore leaf, this time not an illusion but conjured into reality by Osman's autumnal cloak. A whirlwind of vibrant leaves filled the entire study and blew out the open doors toward the guests. Talon heard "oohs" and "ahs" and wonderment from the party goers behind him as leaves blew past him, and he couldn't help but smile as he examined the sycamore leaf that had hit him in the face. There on its burnt orange and scarlet surface in gold leafing was the Cour-Vermane crest imposed on a beautifully rendered magnolia blossom, the well-known favorite of his mother. Duel still unfinished and without a finale, Talon braved the storm of leaves, noting how the squall had thrown his father's maps of the duchy, labeled with its pre-imperial name of Eleryon, and his dozens of regimens of neatly arranged models into disarray. Seeing the sheer number of maps and models raised a feeling of dread in Talon's throat, but he didn't have time to explore the emotion as it was dispelled by the satisfaction of the study also filling with what would become one of the most desired party gifts of the season and the braver guests inching around the duel to claim one.

"You, sir, shall no longer defile this fine home! Out I say!" Talon, sheathing the Vermillion Blade, broke into a dead sprint at Osman standing on the desk whose arms were held wide like a conductor leading an orchestra. Then, lowering his shoulder and wrapping his arms around Osman's waist, Talon slammed into him with enough force to carry them both crashing through the giant window. But, at the last possible instant before they collided with the segmented glass wall, Talon cast his last bit of shamanistic magic, a gift he had learned from Rahmed. In a flash of arcane fire and desert sand, they disappeared from the office and, for showmanship, reappeared just outside the window to plummet to the courtyard below.

In their moment of freefall, Talon quickly checked Osman and asked, "You good?"

His joyful smile spoke for itself, but Osman answered with a nod as he pushed out of Talon's grasp and began to flip mid-air, "Better than good!"

There was a scream of alarm as one of the few guests that had not followed the duel inside saw Talon and Osman falling from the second floor amidst a maelstrom of colorful sparkling autumn leaves. Talon kicked off the outside of the estate and muscled his way to the ground catching one of the high arbors of the courtyard wall. Conversely, Osman seemed to spin and dance through the air as he fell, using every surface on the way as though he was as little affected by gravity as the leaves tumbling through the sky around him, finally ending up on the opposite courtyard wall from Talon. The two stalked each other slowly toward the main gate to allow the guests to make their way back outside and hopefully give them time to disturb Toman's study even more in a rush to grab their party favors.

Osman, as the heel of the duel, proclaimed, "I am defeated and bid you adieu, my worthy opponent." The guests cheered until Osman added, "And with so many noble personages here, perhaps there are easier homes to defile than this," to which the guests played along with mock gasps and ladies swooning.

Osman leaped off the wall into the night, to which Talon then assured the crowd, "Fear not, the Knight Captain of Arnadore shall protect your homes and your honor!" purposely not using his title as the Cour-Vermane heir and pursued the villain into the darkness.

As they galloped away, Talon and Osman could hear the cheers and din of the crowd and then a final gasp as Osman played his last trick. A magical missile shot into the sky and then exploded into a burst of arcane writing with a message from him to the partygoers:

"Goodnight, Dear Friends! Be Well, Be Happy, and Be Kind."

Had they looked back, they might have spotted a lean feminine form tracking their exit from the now-lit window of Toman's study, tapping a finger thoughtfully on the wine glass in her hand.

CHAPTER SEVENTEEN

Year 873 PXF ~ Spring

The two arrived back at Talon's rooms in the Sojourn's Rest just after one o'clock. Osman had been retelling every moment of the evening on the ride as Talon just rode in silence, smiling and utterly content. Talon started stripping off his mask and formal clothes the moment he entered the door of his rooms after climbing wearily up the inn's three flights of stairs, while Osman plopped into a chair still fully dressed. His outfit had returned to its basic pre-gala form, but he was making no move to take it off even though he had dressed here and his street clothes from earlier in the day were on a nearby hook available to change back into before heading home.

"Are you just going to wear that forever now?" Talon asked jokingly. "It's not exactly dress code for the Keep. Not to mention, you smell."

"I. Do. Not!" Osman retorted, acting far more offended than he was. Then sniffing his armpit, "Oh gods, I do! Why didn't you tell me?"

"It is just from the duel. You were fine beforehand." He added slyly, "Smelling like a bed of roses, in fact." Talon threw the unlaced sleeve of his doublet directly into Osman's face with devastating accuracy, the armpit landing directly under his nose.

"Ugh! You smell worse than a horse's ass."

"That is why I am headed down to the baths," Talon replied smugly.

"Wait, there are baths here?!" Osman queried excitedly, jumping up and beginning to undress.

"Where have you been bathing, Osman?" Talon asked. "Osman?"

Osman, who had stripped out of his outfit in record time, headed out the door stark naked, only reaching back in and grabbing one of Talon's dressing robes off the hook behind the door as an afterthought. "Downstairs, you say? On the main level, or is there a basement I don't know about?" Osman called over his shoulder, Talon's borrowed robe dragging the ground and sleeves almost wholly obscuring his hands.

"Just. Wait... Oh, I am... Just..." Talon couldn't get a word out as he was now struggling to get out of his remaining garments and track where Osman was going by looking out the open doorway. Finally, free and stripped down to his breeches, Talon grabbed a robe and pursued Osman before he ended up in the main room of the tavern wearing only a robe or even less.

Talon caught Osman just in time and guided him to a private stone staircase behind the towering hearth's chimney that led to the cellar and the baths. Three large pools were located in the stone chamber styled after the baths of Bal'Ethera. One was heated to near scalding, another of moderate temperature, and the last one chilled; magical runes keeping the temperatures set and the water clear and pure. Osman immediately dropped his robe and sank into the warmest tub with a contented "*Ahhhhhhh.*"

"No, really, Osman, where have you been bathing?" Talon asked again as he finished disrobing and sank into the hottest tub as well.

"You really don't want to know," Osman stated flatly.

"Are you still having troubles with people, even now, after all we have done for businesses here in Elery Square? Not just as patrons but as the Duke's guard as well?" Talon was puzzled and frustrated by even the thought of it.

"Turns out, while people are happy to take your coin and lift a glass with an Uldani, they draw the line at sharing bathwater with one." He threw a small splash at Talon. Then Osman paused, still gazing at Talon, face becoming both serious and tentative at the same time. "I have been away from my lands for a long time, and you are the first to treat me as an equal, even more so. Before you, even things as simple as bathing and eating had become exercises in loneliness and exclusion. Of course, I tried to relish it, as is the way of my people, but there is only so much you can learn from isolation and only so much of it anyone can bear." In an almost ceremonial voice thick with emotion, he said, "Thank you, Krolh'dran, for accepting me."

Talon kept his face open, awaiting the full meaning of what was being said. He understood just from the tone of the word that he did not recognize that something profoundly personal with deep cultural significance was being bestowed upon him.

"It means soul brother." Osman explained further. "In the Uldan culture, we choose our family. It is as core to who we are as our chosen name. A Krolh'dran is a mentor, a guide, a protector, but above all, he is the brother you look up to. The one you lean upon in times both fair and foul."

Talon couldn't keep the smile off his face. "Just tonight, a dear friend, as I told him about you, said that it seemed like I had found the little brother I always needed in my life, and I wholly agreed."

They couldn't help but give each other a quick embrace even though both were naked as the day they were born and neck-deep in a steaming tub.

They parted and sat back on the ledge of the pool. Osman broke the silence, "What a night!"

"Quite." Talon, however, was more interested in the conversation they had begun earlier. "Why don't you take the room we secured from Lolly for the clothier's use and move in here?"

"Oh, I could never afford it," Osman replied

"I assure you that you can. I do know your salary after all." Talon was again bewildered. "Are you aware of how much you make compared to most in this town?"

"Well, I am aware of how much I am paying for the tiny room I have now, and it eats up almost all my salary as it is," Osman said dejectedly.

"You are joking. *Please* tell me you are joking." Talon questioned playfully, then his voice dropped to a deadly serious tone. "You're not joking, are you?"

Osman just stared at him.

"Alright. It is settled. You are staying here tonight." Then, adding through clenched teeth, "We will be visiting your current landlord tomorrow."

Osman's whole body seemed to relax, and as Talon watched, it was almost as if a piece of Osman's life that had not quite fit fell into its proper place. As was always the case with Osman, his emotional state washed over Talon, releasing the tension that had built up in his shoulders over the discussion regarding Osman's soon-to-be former landlord.

His voice now deeply relaxed, Talon requested, "Little brother, they truly are absolutely stunning, but could you please get all these knots out of my hair."

"Come here, Krolh'dran" Osman turned Talon's shoulders so his back was facing him and began to untie the intricate ceremonial braids.

As they sat in the steaming bath, Osman's fingers running through Talon's hair undoing the knotting he had so meticulously put in earlier in the day, Talon fleetingly recognized that this whole scenario would be completely different if it were Richen here in the tub with him. With Osman, it was different, just two brothers unwinding and relaxing after a spectacular evening being the glitter of the gala at the social event of the season.

CHAPTER EIGHTEEN

Year 873 PXF *~ Spring*

Once they made it back upstairs, Osman immediately set to making the room they had secured for the clothier his own. It was just one door down from Talon's rooms, and while not as large as Talon's suite of rooms, Osman claimed it to be palatial. At first light, Talon, with Osman in tow, paid a visit to his current landlord. The tiny room Osman had rented was located over a dilapidated brothel and was even smaller than Richen's room in the smithy. After much badgering along the way to where he had been staying, Osman finally told Talon how much he was paying, nearly triple what his new room at the Sojourn's Rest would cost.

After Talon had 'a conversation' with the landlord, a truly despicable man who spat his disdain for the Uldani people with every look and gesture, not only was Osman's dodgy five-year lease broken; the landlord returned a generous refund to him. Later that day, Talon penned a letter to his mother, thanking her for the beautiful Gala, and asked if she might turn her gaze on the establishment that had so wronged Osman. Talon had no doubt and even internally winced at what the outcome of her attentions would be.

Lolly was thrilled to have Osman as a resident. Not only for his unending lauding of her meals, always praising every morsel of each dish for the masterpiece of flavor that it was, but also for the cheer and levity he brought to each morning, which Lolly would vocally admit was not her favorite time of day. Three days later, sitting over plates of hearty morning hash and cups of coffee, Osman finally asked, "So what can you tell me about Cerena?"

Before Talon could answer, Lolly chimed in as she was heaping another serving of hash onto Osman's plate, "Oh now, who's this Cerena? Has someone caught your eye, Osman?" Seeing the deep red blush flood Osman's face, she bantered on, "Well, now that answers that. Look at you! You are as red as a tomato ready for sauce!"

Talon sedately answered as Osman could not seem to find his tongue, "Cerena is my cousin. She and Osman met at the Gala."

Seeing Osman's further distress, Lolly decided to turn up the heat. "A noble woman! Good for you, lad!" She elbowed Osman with her plump arm and continued, "She'll make a fine bride. Check her hips first though, to see how she will do with birthing heirs."

Talon spat his coffee out before it came out of his nose. She gave the two a wink, "Gotta be able to take what you dish out, boys!" and headed back to the stove, chuckling to herself over the two men still squirming at the table.

Once he regained his composure and wiped up the sprayed coffee with his napkin, Talon admitted he didn't know much. Just his relation to her and the details of his duel with Rabien. Osman sighed at this a bit despondently, "Do you think she will actually join us one evening here in town?"

Talon, with a hint of foreboding, "I have absolutely no doubt that she will."

It was less than a week later when Talon's premonition came true. Just as Talon opened the door of his rooms for him and Osman to step out after a grueling day at the Keep, there was Cerena.

With a sigh, Talon greeted her, "Cerena."

Equally aloof was her reply, "Cousin."

Osman ducked under Talon's arm, "Cerena! I am so..." pushing the unmovable mass of Talon out of the way and not succeeding, instead leaning halfway on him and the doorjamb. "So..." Osman now awkwardly tried to look dashing, "Glad to see you. We both are, in fact."

"Osman, dear!" giving him a faux kiss on the cheek and pushing her way into Talon's rooms, "I took you up on your offer and am here to see all the fun there is to have in Arnadore. It's such a quaint and charming city." Her tone left no question that she thought the city was neither quaint nor charming. Talon felt a tinge of unease at the familiarity and comfort Cerena seemed to have with being in his rooms. Before he could comment, Osman, not allowing the two cousins to begin sniping at each other, grabbed Cerena by the wrist and dragged her out the door and to the stairs, regaling her with all they would see and do.

Whether by Osman's infectious presence or by design, after an hour or so, Cerena did seem to begin having fun. Her initial attitude of just haughtily playing along with the city's provincial customs melted into an actual good time. By the night's end, even Cerena and Talon were somehow getting along, albeit both were deeply inebriated.

As the evening wound down back in the main room of the Sojourn's Rest, Cerena conspiratorially shared with Talon, "You know he absolutely *loathes* you."

Talon jokingly, but also truly curious, questioned, "Which one?"

"Rabien, of course." With only a slight slur to her late-night words, she continued, "He scowls at that scar in the mirror for hours. He went to every cleric in Jadenpool to try and heal it, and when they had no success, he petitioned the archmages of Bal'Ethera. Nada, nothing, no one could budge it." Her words just plowed forward with the story, "Ya know he tried to cover it with a tattoo but had to have it magically removed because it looked so terrible." Her voice now getting a bit louder, "He even cut it out once." swigging some ale for emphasis, "Still grew back."

Talon had no idea the scar had such power, his hand absently drifting to his own chest where his scar was.

Cerena added as final punctuation, "Nine hells level, *loathes you.*"

Osman, who always seemed able to go from deeply intoxicated to sober in a blink of an eye, took charge. "Okay, let's get you a carriage to get you back to the estate." Helping Cerena up from the table, he continued, "We'll have them stable your horse here, and you can send a groomsman for her tomorrow." Then, as Cerena protested, "She'll be fine. Yes, I will make sure she has extra oats... and an apple in the morning," confirming he would follow everything Cerena was demanding as he escorted her out of the inn.

A few moments later, Osman returned to the table, looking every inch as sober as a judge. Talon was baffled at his condition as he knew Osman, at half his weight, had drunk at least twice as much. "How?"

"Did you not know, Krolh'dran? Uldani are unaffected by alcohol."

Talon's mouth opened and closed several times like a fish caught on shore. "All this time...?" he asked, realization setting in, "Bastard."

"Come on, big brother, I can't carry your huge ass up the stairs if you pass out," Osman warned as he helped the larger man up from the table.

Talon felt a rush of alcohol hit his head as he stood up, swayed, and defensively retorted, "I'll have you know my ass is quite the talk of Arnadore. Have you not noticed when I am in uniform?"

"Yes, yes, Krolh'dran, your ass is lovely. Now up the stairs. That's it, one step at a time..."

CHAPTER NINETEEN

Year 873 PXF ~ *Late Spring*

The next Hearth's Rest was just under a week away. As usual, Talon and Osman were ready for it. While this duel was not as magical as their one at the Gala, it was still a spectacle and, as always, started and ended at the Arnadore orphanage as they truly performed it for them. The only surprise this time was that after almost three hours of dueling, stunts, and acts of whimsy all through the Trellis Market, as the course was on its return approach to the orphanage, there was Cerena. Osman, intent on including her, even if just for a moment, pulled the fight towards where she sat at a garden table of the most upscale tea parlor of Elery Square, dressed to the nines in skirts, bodice, and corset, sipping a cup of afternoon tea.

With superb accuracy, Osman allowed himself to be disarmed of one of his swords, sending it flying into the air. The sword arced high into the sky on a perfect trajectory to embed itself vertically into the lovely display of tea cakes on Cerena's table. It landed right on target with a twang into the table's wood and perfectly skewered a lovely cake in the process. Cerena dutifully played the noble lady, shocked by such a startling event, as Osman began a string of handsprings to retrieve his sword. However, before reaching his destination, Cerena ripped off her skirts, revealing a tight-fitting pair of black leathers, claimed Osman's sword for herself, and drew a long dirk from her ankle. Both Osman and Talon drew up short, for once, without a quick-witted response.

"Ah, ah, ah, boys. No one defiles my cakes!" Cerena announced with aplomb and proceeded to duel the two of them at once. The children from the orphanage, who had already gathered to see the return of Osman and Talon, cheered with delight at this new development. Neither Osman nor Talon held back nearly as much as they anticipated they would need to against Cerena's attack. She displayed both skill and improvisation levels that avowed extensive weapons training. After a prolonged finale in front of the orphanage involving Osman and Talon battling more as a four-armed demon than two separate men, the duel ended in a three-way stalemate as children and adults alike cheered at the performance. Talon, at first a bit miffed at Cerena's intrusion, couldn't stay that way for long when he witnessed what he knew was a genuine show of emotion from his cousin. It happened after the duel had completed when a young girl from the orphanage handed Cerena a meticulously crafted and colored paper rose and asked, "How do I become just like you when I grow up?"

Talon suspected much of Cerena's interaction with them since the beginning had been part of a ploy, even her tipsy moment at the end of the night earlier in the week, but this moment with the little girl seemed an honest one. Perhaps her ties to the Cour-Vermane heritage could be broken just as his were with a bit of guidance.

Year 873 PXF ~ *Summer*

After the duel, Cerena began appearing at the Sojourn's Rest more and more often, and over the next two months, the duo of Talon and Osman slowly grew into a trio. Cerena opened up to Talon, becoming more relaxed and enjoyable company, and while she and Talon would never be the best of friends, they developed a playful yet cutting repartee and appreciation of each other.

On the other hand, Osman and her relationship escalated quickly. Soon it was not the door to Talon's rooms she arrived at but Osman's. The first night Osman and Cerena went out without him was actually a welcome one for Talon. Since the Fall, he had let many of his duties at the Keep slide as he focused on regaining some semblance of a social life by spending time with Osman. With the bit of respite and quiet his offices at the Keep provided, it began to enter Talon's consciousness that the much-needed distraction Osman brought to his life also had deafened him to any whispers of new fiendish intrusions into the realm or information regarding Richen. As he began to ponder that, his curiosity piqued at how something so important was so easily set aside; he was distracted by yet another urgent and overdue requisition request. Yet, strangely, Talon's mind somehow couldn't seem to find its way back to his concern.

As weeks passed, Osman and Cerena spent more nights out in Arnadore without him. While Talon sorely needed the recent focus on his position as Knight Captain, he had to admit, there was a bit of a sting when, as Spring turned to Summer, the trio's nights he could attend began getting canceled so that Osman could visit Cerena at the estate by himself.

As the heat of Summer progressed, so did the heat between Osman and Cerena; if the noises Talon heard emanating from Osman's room early in the morning and late at night were any indication. While Talon saw Osman outside of work less and less, he focused on how lax he had allowed his skills and the skills and conditioning of the other guards in the Duke's personal regiment to become. By Talon's own rules, "training for one meant training for all," which therefore included Osman as well and meant the extra time at the Keep became time away from Cerena.

In the last month before Cerena's departure, Osman confronted Talon. "You're keeping us apart on purpose, aren't you?"

"What?" Talon, only partially hearing Osman, asked as he perused an official scroll while standing behind his study's desk.

"All this extra training, keeping me here late into the evening half exhausted. It's because you don't want Cerena and I spending time together." Osman grabbed the top of the scroll. "At least look at me, Krohl'dran."

At the use of the ceremonial title, Talon gave Osman all his attention. "Truly, I could care less about you and Cerena. Have you looked at the others? Yes, you might be half exhausted, but they are half dead. Less than a year ago, you could have done the training, run to the estate on foot, and still performed for Cerena in bed." As soon as he said it, Talon sorely wished he hadn't.

"And there it is." Osman spat back ruefully, "I don't give two wet farts what you are into or not into, but don't hold it against me that I want to bed the woman I love." Then, Uldani emotions flaring, Osman stormed out of Talon's study.

That next month Talon hardly saw Osman outside training and rounds at the Keep. He even took to staying at the estate instead of his room at the Sojourn's Rest. The next Hearth's Rest came and went with Talon left waiting outside the orphanage for Osman and Cerena to show up. Neither made an appearance. To avoid disappointing the children, Talon dueled with them in the streets and alleys of the Trellis Market instead.

Finally, the morning of Cerena's departure arrived and went with no sign of Osman returning to the inn. Talon was left unsure if he would actually see his little brother ever again until later that evening when Talon heard the door to Osman's room open and shut. Knowing what that must mean, he walked down the hall and, after a soft rap, said through the closed door, "I am here. Whenever you are ready or need me." There was no response.

Long after moonset, in the darkest hours of the night, Talon heard a light tap on his door. Upon opening it, Osman just fell into his arms, sobbing uncontrollably. "She wouldn't stay and even forbade me from following her," was all he could choke out.

Talon held him tightly, knowing the pain of abandonment. Then, fully supporting his weight with his prodigious arms wrapped around him whispered, "There is no pain worse than heartbreak, little brother. Not on earth nor in the heavens."

CHAPTER TWENTY

Year 873 PXF *~ Late Summer*

Living in proximity to a heartbroken Uldani was to suffer through it to some degree yourself. It was not that Osman was invasive with his feelings; it was more that seeing a person of such vibrant personality as Osman so subdued and gray set a pall on everything around him where they had always brought light before. Osman threw himself into training for distraction from the pain he was feeling, and Talon had to be equally as dedicated to keep up with the intense focus Osman was putting into it. The other four guards of the Duke's regiment seemed to find themselves similarly driven, the entire squad not just excelling in their skills but far exceeding their previous level. Duke Issul lurked like a vulture over their training grounds with sunken eyes, not only taking note but seeming to be intent on their progress with an ever more watchful intensity.

Before Summer's end, the Duke bid Talon to expand his focus to all guards in the Keep and the city's Arnadore Watch. To fulfill such a monumental request, Talon made Osman his second-in-command to lead the training of the Watch. By happenstance, becoming peers and wrestling with similar issues with their subordinates but not being so fully entangled in each other's lives did much to bring the two back closer together. Over time their relationship healed as time heals all things, and while the bonds of brotherhood had not been broken, they had undoubtedly been strained.

Talon suspected it was not just from the words that had passed solely between the two of them.

20 Years Earlier ~ 853 PXF *~ Late Autumn*

It had been three days since Talon dared approach the smithy. After their lecture and punishment from Mikal over the coded letter, everything had seemed fine between Richen and him; they had even snuck back to Milgran's Orchard on the next Hearth's Rest with the quarter barrel from the smithy storage shed and filled it with late-season apples for their cider. He and Richen had laughed and joked their way back to the estate; both had even gotten sour stomachs from all the apples they ate along the way. But then, a few days later, everything changed.

Talon had come down to the smithy after a particularly long and tedious lesson from his tutors to wait for Richen. Mikal had sent him on some of his regular errands to Arnadore but, due to his studies, Talon had been unable to join him. Talon was surprised that as the afternoon faded and the gloaming of twilight approached, there was still no sign of Richen. It was unlike him to return so late; even when they were together and lost track of time, they always made it back to the estate before darkness fell, if only barely. Finally, an hour after sunset, wobbling in the saddle and with only the barest hint of color left in the sky, Richen passed through the gate of the Cour-Vermane estate. Talon jumped off the crates in front of the smithy and ran to Richen, thinking he might be injured, but the stench of hard alcohol and smoke immediately let him know what was wrong with him. Talon began to laugh and help Richen off his horse, but as soon as Richen was on his feet, he shoved Talon back, knocking him to the ground. "Get *away* from *me!*" he slurred.

Talon, hurt and confused, responded from the ground, "Richen, what is it? What's wrong?"

Richen, swaying over Talon, spat back, "You are just a rich kid slumming with the staff of his 'oh so noble' parents." He continued his diatribe, "I have almost lost my livelihood because of you twice!" Richen held up two fingers. "You know, they talk about you, right? They say something evil lurks within you. That bad things happen around you." Richen paused, turning his head away, seeming suddenly more clear of thought. "You think I haven't seen it? The way your eyes unfocus and then propose one of your pranks or some hurtful idea comes flowing out of your mouth." He now barely whispered, almost like he was repeating something he had heard, "Regular folks like me can't afford the trouble you bring with you, so just stay away."

Richen, swaying side to side, walked to the smithy leaving Talon sitting in the dust of the courtyard. Talon was too shocked to cry; he couldn't because everything Richen had said was true, except for the part about him 'slumming with the staff.' But the rest, the evil within him, the bad things he had caused to happen, and the ones that seemed to follow him without his help, they were true. His anger now rising, Talon stood up and marched up the front steps of the estate, not even taking his usual path through the kitchens. His fury increased with every step. Through the front door and across the threshold, he crossed the foyer atrium continuing up the stairs past his father's study, not even bothering to lighten his steps as he climbed the last flight of stairs to his room.

He closed the door with controlled precision, belying his internal rage, and screamed into his mind, "*YOU!*" throwing his fury at the voice. It emerged with a snickering laugh. Talon pictured the voice as a piece of black parchment and then ripped it in half, fueling the vision with his anger. The voice's giggle choked to a halt. "We are done. It's over as of right now." The voice scoffed at his assertion. Talon took the two halves of ripped parchment in his mind and ripped them into quarters. "I will not be doing ANYTHING you say ever again. Do you hear?" A weaker snort of derision came from the voice. Talon tore the quarters into eighths; the voice screeched in pain. "You. Do not. Control. ME." In his mind, he ripped the parchment again and again into smaller and smaller pieces. Until he felt the voice bow in acquiescence, leaving its scraps tattered and quivering on the floor of his mind.

Back in the courtyard three days later, Talon was lurking near the outside wall of the surgery as far as one could be from the smithy and still be inside the outer walls of the estate. He hadn't dared come with tea these last three mornings as it implied an invitation and seemed too invasive for an apology and to say what he needed to say. He and Richen hadn't even made eye contact over the previous days, and it was the longest that they had been without each other's company in over two years. Richen finally emerged from the smithy to get more wood for the forge, and Talon crossed the ocean of the courtyard to intercept him.

Richen turned as he approached, looking for a way to escape the encounter, but Talon got there before he could retreat. "I'm sorry. You were right." Richen's face soured at that, but Talon continued, "Not about the slumming with the help part, but everything else. Something bad is inside me. I can't explain it, but it is real, and you should run far, far away from me." Talon's voice became more measured, "It talks to me, Richen. I don't have to listen to it, and I can silence it, sometimes even for months, but when it does speak, sometimes I can't tell if the ideas it has are good or bad."

Talon took a breath, Richen's face now curious and concerned. Talon continued his confession. "It used to be easy to tell whether what it suggested was good or bad when I was younger, but now it is trickier with its ideas. More sly with its manipulations. So yes, I should get far away from you and stay away. But, before I go, I want you to know you were the best and most honest thing that has ever happened to me. When I am around you, how you make me feel, I know I am *seen;* not just as I am now but as the person I long to be." Talon lowered his eyes and walked away.

Richen's voice floated over Talon's shoulder after he had turned to leave, "Is it gone now?"

Talon turned back to Richen, tears welling in his eyes but not falling. "No," he choked out.

"Will it ever be?" Richen asked, staring into Talon's eyes.

"I don't know," Talon replied, lowering his face to look at the ground, not wanting to meet Richen's gaze.

"Is it here now?" Talon could hear Richen walk toward him as he asked.

"No," he sniffed back unfallen tears, "I ripped it up a few days ago."

"You what?" Ricken asked bewildered

"I ripped it up and threw the pieces into the far corners of my head." Talon looked up at Richen, who was now right in front of him. He let his gaze fall to Richen's stormcloud eyes, drinking them in, knowing this could perhaps be the last time he saw them up close.

"Look, I don't understand what you are talking about, with something in your head speaking to you and ripping it up, but you are right, I do see you. You light up my world when you are near. I don't care what other people see or say about you or me. I am the one who should be apologizing to you for how I acted the other night. I don't know why I listened." Richen looked away abashed. "Something happened, and I was embarrassed and angry and ashamed, so their words got under my skin, and I decided to blame everyone but myself, and you were the easiest target." Tears were welling in Richen's eyes now. "Please forgive me."

Talon snorted and let out his held breath simultaneously, causing him to choke. Taking Richen's hands in his, Talon asked earnestly, "Richen, of course, but are you sure you want this?"

Richen, squeezing Talon's hands, replied, "Just promise me no more trouble, and if your voice tells you to do something, just ask me first and let me know where the idea came from so we can figure it out together." Talon smiled and nodded, unable to create words. Richen then added, "Oh, and also promise me you will start bringing tea again; mornings in the smithy are as cold as Icefel this time of year."

Present Year 873 PXF ~ Fall

Fall came early that year, and Winter threatened to arrive ahead of schedule as well. Osman had returned to more like his usual self with only an occasional sigh or pause at the places he and Cerena visited during the Spring and Summer. Then, just as Lolly began to tire of putting harvest spices in every dish and beverage and instead adding it to just half of them, the first letter arrived. It was from Cerena addressed to Osman, and it took every bit of Talon's will not to throw it in the fire before Osman could see it. However, knowing that no good could come from him even casting his shadow on anything concerning Osman and Cerena, he just sat at Lolly's table and pretended that he didn't see it.

There was a tiny spark in Talon that hoped that Osman would do the very thing his own first instincts told him to do, but alas, that was not the case. Osman almost floated around the room as he read Cerena's letter, and thus the season of pining began. Talon and Lolly couldn't decide what was worse, Heartbroken Osman or Pining Osman, so after a month of Pining Osman, Talon went to the Keep to cash in some favors.

That night at dinner, between Osman's sighs as he re-read the two-week-old most recent letter from Cerena at the dinner table, Talon cleared his throat and then, needing to rap his knuckles on the table to get the love-sick Uldani's attention, spoke. "Osman, I have gone to some great lengths to do it, but I have secured your use of the Duke's teleportation circle." At the word 'teleportation,' Osman almost leapt out of his chair. Talon continued, "Slow down, that only takes care of one way. I have also gotten you this." Talon produced a granite stone the size of a goose egg with a rune on it. "This is a returning stone, keyed to this hearth. It takes a fortnight to recharge, but that will get you two monthly trips to see Cerena."

Osman now did, in fact, leap over the table to hug Talon so firmly around the neck that it almost choked him, and was not at all bothered that his legs were currently splayed across his own and Talon's dinner.

"You are not to miss any of your duties at the Keep or in training the Watch, or the Duke has said he will replace you himself, and I have asked the transit mage to check the return stone is charged before you leave, so no games."

"Of course!" Osman ran out of the kitchen to presumably contact Cerena but then poked his head back in, "Thank you, Krolh'dran." It was the first time Osman had addressed Talon as such since the Summer, and while it didn't seem to have the same weight behind it that it had on other occasions, it was nice to hear.

Year 873 PXF ~ Early Winter

The Winter of that year was harsh, and some said the worst in a century. Snows buried Eleryon deeper than any in Talon's memory, yet by order of the Duke, it was not to curtail the rigorous training schedule for the Duke's forces within the Keep and surrounding city. Through freezing rain and drifting snow, Talon and Osman pushed the city's forces, never having the opportunity to lighten the intensity as Duke Issul's watchful eye was ever present lurking over them from the balconies of his rooms.

After the first fortnight, Talon and Osman were going to confront the Duke to ask for his reasoning behind this new obsession, but before they could act, the Duke doubled the pay of all guards and issued an edict to the taverns of Arnadore that he would pay for them to provide free rations to all guards in his service on training days. Suddenly being a guard became the most sought-after position in the city, and guards requested the extra training days instead of greeting them with moans and grunts of disapproval.

Talon had to admit that what would have been a slim season of tightening belts for almost all businesses in Arnadore now became a boon for the city. And neither Osman nor Talon could deny the Duke's forces had never been in better shape. Before this new focus on training, they had all but become a farce that nobles and commoners alike snickered about behind their hands, but now there was a level of pride and respect among the guard that lifted the morale of the whole city. Braggarts among the guard boldly stated the Arnadore Watch was even a match for the Emperor's elite Jadenarme forces, and Talon could not for certain say they were wrong.

Osman was still able to spend time with Cerena, but they were quicker jaunts than the extended visits earlier in the Fall. Talon never asked any details about Osman's time with Cerena, as things between him and Osman were practically back to normal with their relationship. The only thing Talon couldn't help but notice was that while he assumed Cerena was at her family's home in Jadenpool, the clothes and other things Osman arrived and departed with, including parchment-wrapped bundles of clothes from the clothier they had used for the Gala, spoke of a climate more like their own than that of the temperate capital by the sea.

Just before Last Friend's Remembrance, a friendly half-elf named Castian appeared at Lolly's. With the harsh weather across the countryside and the boom of prosperity within the city, they ended up spending the remainder of the season at the Sojourn's Rest. Talon and Osman surmised that Castian must spend all their day in Lolly's kitchen, as every time the two left for or returned from their duties with the guard, they could be found sitting, feet up, at the kitchen table. Castian was somewhat guarded about the details of their past but was good company and shared many stories of their adventures and the foes they had vanquished. The conversation could not help but turn to the unprecedented level of activity within the city with such a harsh Winter raging over the rest of the region. Talon could offer no explanation other than the Duke's own; it was to help bring prosperity and security to the city in preparation for the Emperor's visit in early Spring. Castian countered with a statement that stuck with Talon. "In my experience, nobility doesn't give out their treasury freely. They are *always* buying something."

While not uncommon in the Winter months, Talon began to notice an unprecedented level of traffic through the Duke's teleportation gate. Casual inquiries informed him that most of the travel was between nearby cities within and outside the Xallian Empire, many of which were the same cities he had hand-delivered the Duke's overtures to while he was Envoy. Talon had always been a bit perplexed by the Duke's insistence that he be the one to deliver such letters while outfitted in the Duchy's formal regalia, which was loosely based on the historic regalia of the region when it was known as Eleryon. Of course, he complied, and as always, he carried the Vermillion Blade with him. At the time, he often mused if he was as much the message as the scrolls he carried. Talon wondered if there was a connection or if it was just a coincidence, but keeping up with Duke Issul's and his guard's requests for extra training did not allow him to investigate further.

Year 874 PXF *~ Early Spring*

The harshness of deep Winter finally broke, and while Arnadore had remained active through the season, the areas across the rest of Eleryon were just beginning to thaw. Correspondence that had been blocked from traveling now flooded into Talon's study at the Keep and soon overflowed into his rooms at the Sojourn's Rest as well. Envelopes and scrolls quickly piled in stacks upon nearly every surface. Multiple letters from Mikal, which up through the Fall had remained light and casual with no coded messages, were left unread along with dozens of others that had arrived in the deluge.

Spring was just around the corner when a courier hand-delivered a message to Talon. It was from Mikal, relaying he was leaving the employ of Talon's father. Knowing a courier-delivered letter was unlikely to be intercepted, it talked openly of Toman becoming more secretive and people coming and going from the estate at all hours of the day and night. He referenced his letters that Talon had left unread from over the Winter that he had coded with messages regarding Toman redoubling the demand for weapons and armor to be made. He was now even more concerned about the armaments as he had no idea where they had ended up, but all were headed south. Mikal closed with his plans to travel for a short time but then would be securing a smithy in Arnadore. He requested they meet in two weeks' time to discuss things in person. With the Duke's sudden interest in the guard's training, the travel through the teleportation gate, and his father's activities, Talon also grew concerned but couldn't fit all the pieces together into a defensible theory.

It seemed to be a time for messages as a small skin, tied in Uldani fashion, arrived for Osman two days later, something that Talon could not recall ever having happened before. Osman excitedly opened his message at Lolly's table after supper that night. Unfortunately, his excited expression immediately dropped.

"My father is dead," he said flatly. Lolly gasped and Talon began to offer condolences, Osman continued, "No, it is fine. He was ill, and I hardly knew him as he continued to travel, even with the wound that caused his illness. If I saw him once a year as a child, that was a lot. When I did see him, his wound was such that it drove him to silence lest the pain of it cause his emotions to storm into a rage."

"Was he wounded in battle?" Talon asked.

"Of a sort. He had the wound for as long as I can remember, but my father called it a 'wound of the soul' when he could speak of it. I do not know how he came to earn it."

"All those who carry their scars deserve remembering," Talon pronounced loudly. "Let us lift a glass to your father's name."

Even Lolly lifted a small glass of cooking sherry. Osman raised his glass as well. "To my father, Architavia Therandus."

Talon's cup hit the table, dropped from his grasp. "Who?"

"Architavia Therandus"

"Architavia Therandus the Farseer is your *father*?" Talon asked again.

"Yes."

"I have been looking for your father for over two decades, and his son has been here with me for over a year!" Talon bellowed. Grabbing Osman by the front of his armor and pulling him across the table, he yelled at the Uldani, "Have you known of Richen all this time!? A man possibly when you knew him? A human with raven hair and stormcloud eyes! Tell me!" Talon was manic in his questioning.

Osman broke Talon's grasp, shouting, "No! Get off me!" His heightened state caused his emotions to begin to swirl into a storm.

Talon could see the signs but kept pressing. "You must know! You call me your brother, and you kept this from me! Your father took him! He promised he would heal him of the corruption rooted in him so we could be together. Yet, with all the times I talked of Richen, you sat there silent!"

Talon tried to grab Osman again, but as he lunged forward, the table still between them, the emotional tempest took Osman, and he threw an elbow directly into Talon's nose, eliciting a sickeningly wet crunch.

"I don't know anything about your damned Richen other than you brood over him like an old mare put out to pasture." Blood rained on Lolly's table and the remnants of dinner. Then, with a tenuous hold on the emotions consuming him, Osman sprinted from the kitchen, out into the alley, and fled into the night, but not before adding, "And you never once asked me of my family or my damned father!"

As Talon stood fuming and looking out the door into the night, the slithering voice in his head, seemingly absent for so long, made itself heard again, filling his mind with a smug gleeful snicker of schemes fulfilled.

CHAPTER TWENTY-ONE

Year 874 PXF *~ Spring*

It had been years since Talon had been in a fugue the likes of which he found himself trapped. The world drifted by him like shadows in the fog. He went through the motions of life, but none of it touched him. He continued training the guard, attending briefings, eating, and sleeping, but all were just shadows occurring in the background as his mind raced with the thoughts that plagued him.

He felt betrayed. By Osman, by Caspharian, and primarily by himself and the damned chain his father had shackled him with. The previous years on 'the winding natural path' now felt wasted when the direct path to the person he sought had been sitting across the table from him for eighteen months, living under the same roof and calling him brother! How could he not have known, heard, or felt by divine guidance that a doorway to Richen was so close? Why had he allowed himself to put down the burden of his search and be so protective of the distraction that Osman offered to never even ask about Architavia Therandus? And how could Osman not have been moved to say something? Surely Talon had mentioned it was an Uldani shaman that had taken Richen? Surely he had, *hadn't he*? Now the only person who could give him answers about Richen was dead, his corpse presumably half a continent away.

The fugue continued, nothing registering in Talon's troubled mind. Reports from the southern border, the impending Imperial visit, locals creating militias reflecting the training of his guards and the Arnadore Watch, the cleric setting his nose, unspoken apologies never exchanged with Osman, the old flags of Eleryon flying over the city, Lolly asking if he wanted seconds. Yet, along with the daily noise, something else itched in the back of Talon's mind. He should be paying attention to something he had seen. Something that was in plain sight and was connected to the doubts that plagued him, but whatever it was kept slipping through his fingers. He attempted to probe his mind for the voice and demand answers, but wherever it had hidden itself, Talon could not find it.

Three days? A week? A fortnight? Talon could not have told a soul even with a dagger to his throat. He finally woke up as he stood in the pre-dawn darkness of early morning along with his guards in the Duke's council chamber. "What was that?" Talon asked.

Unaccustomed to repeating himself, the Duke tersely and waspishly answered, "You are to take Lieutenant Fredric's militia via the teleportation circle and attack the Imperial forces raiding our southern villages."

"I am to attack the Imperial army?" Talon repeated, sublimely confused.

"Yes," replied the Duke, now growing angry.

Talon blinked twice, running the command through his mind that was just emerging from the fog that had shrouded it, making sure he heard correctly. Suddenly, a flash of understanding washed over him. Seasons worth of weapons his father had ordered Mikal to make headed south, people coming and going from the Cour-Vermane estate at all hours. The training of the guard and his envoy missions across the countryside. The use of the ceremonial uniforms and the Eleryon flags flying over Arnadore.

His father was starting a war to secede from the Empire and had been instigating it for years. The Imperial army would never attack from the south; there was nothing to gain, but the south of Eleryon was secluded enough that planning a false flag attack by the Empire would inflame the provincial residents of the Duchy. When the Emperor eventually did send troops to settle the unrest and keep the peace, what was a false invasion would become a real one; there would be no stopping the violence once it started.

Talon glanced to his side and registered what Lieutenant Fredric's bannerman was holding: a red standard with a curved 'V' shaped like a falcon's talon emblazoned on it. Talon was thrown into his vision from his contest of wills with the Vermillion Blade years before - him leading armies carrying the same banner and leaving a trail of bodies in his wake. Through Duke Issul and even without the Vermillion Blade's control, his father was still planning to wield him as a weapon. It would be Talon under the banner carrying his mark attacking the Empire! What had been itching in the back of Talon's mind rushed to the surface: the brand he had willed onto the Vermillion Blade was gone, along with the control it represented.

"No!" Talon exclaimed, both to the realization about the Vermillion Blade and the Duke's order.

Before he could get another word out, the Duke launched into a fury, "You defy me and deny your oath?"

oathbreaker

Talon retorted, his voice booming in the council chamber, "This is treason, and treason under false pretenses at that." He turned to his guards, but their gaze would not meet his own. "Osman, do not do this. It is sedition." Finally, Osman met his gaze and took a step toward Talon, looking for guidance. "It is all my father's doing, a plot." Talon's eyes widened in fear. "Osman, is Cerena involved? Are *you* involved? What have you done?" He thought now of Osman's trips and the garb and parchment-wrapped clothes – could they have been imperial uniforms?

"Will you abandon your oath and your liege so easily?" the Duke spat out at Osman, stepping on the tail of Talon's words. "I should have expected as much from an Uldani." The Duke's comment, combined with Talon's accusation, landed true. Osman, with a set jaw and eyes of stone for the man he once called Krolh'dran, stepped back to join the other guards, turning his eyes away from Talon and staring silently forward.

"Talon Cour-Vermane, you have broken your oath to your liege and your house. I..." The Duke continued, but Talon heard none of it. Instead, another voice now filled his head, the voice of the Vermillion Blade.

Oathbreaker.

In his mind, Talon felt the remaining black chain connecting him to the darkness grow taught and tighten around his heart. Overlaid with the council chamber, he saw the iron web of the Vermillion Blade's magic joining the chain, pulling him toward the dark precipice. An overwhelming urge to draw his cursed weapon began to overcome him, and all it wanted was to cut down everyone in this room, painting the walls with blood. Most disturbingly, the glaive showed him Osman's head on the end of its blade mounted there like it was on a pike. Desperate to reject the vision, Talon gathered every ounce of will he had, not to fight the Vermillion Blade as before but to turn and flee, putting as much distance between him and Osman as possible.

He turned and ran from the room, hearing the Duke's voice command, "Stop the Oathbreaker, stop the traitor to Eleryon."

Half-blinded by the vision and the pull of the Vermillion Blade, Talon didn't even look back as he used the small amount of magic he had to slam and seal the council chamber doors with a binding of desert glass. If they heard the Duke, the startled guards in the outer halls must have thought that their Knight Captain was chasing some invisible enemy as they stepped out of his way when he careened past them. The Vermillion Blade filled his head with its desire to be drawn and lay waste to every living thing they passed. Talon struggled to keep his hands away from the cursed weapon with each new guard or servant he passed. Finally, arriving at the stairs, he dove down them, doubling back at their base to reach the service door that exited the Keep's outer yard just behind them. And then Osman was there blocking his path.

Osman landed, swords drawn in front of him, having leaped from the second floor through the stairwell. "Stop, Talon. You don't know what is going on. You've been distracted and unwilling to see." He confronted Talon with a harsh but pleading voice, "I can show you. She can show you."

Talon wanted to scream and as his anger rose, so did the urgent need to draw the Vermillion Blade. "Osman, you don't know my family. You don't know who we really are—even me. You can't fathom the darkness my blood holds and the absolute *evil* that resides in my father." Talon spit his words through clenched teeth, the whites showing around his crazed and vision-clouded eyes as he stalked forward closer toward Osman, fingers flexing in their desire to hold his cursed glaive. "You saw what Cerena wanted you to see, what she needed you to see." Talon nodded his head along with his following words to get the affirmation he needed, "Everything was justice and righteousness as she had you train those soldiers over the Winter down south. You perfectly fell into my father's plan and web of deceit as she drove a wedge between us."

Osman's face was wracked with conflict as he tried to reject Talon's words, but some part of him couldn't completely discount them. It was all Talon and his blade needed, just a moment of hesitation. In all his training and duels, Osman had never had an opponent go for the kill on the first strike and therefore was utterly unprepared for Talon's attack.

Talon's blade sank deep precisely where his training with Balanon guided it, through the ribs and deep into the lung, deflating it and hitting a grouping of nerves to induce excruciating pain. Talon thanked whatever gods were assisting him as he had somehow been able to draw Mikal's dagger instead of the Vermillion Blade. Osman crumpled in his arms, Talon leaving the dagger in place as it would keep him alive, and the way it bit into his ribs, no 'helpful' guard could easily remove it, allowing Osman to bleed out.

As Talon lowered Osman's head gently to the floor, his wide eyes panicked, looking up into Talon's. Talon had so much he wished to say, how he hoped Osman would see the truth and understand one day, but all he choked out was, "You will not die this day, but it will leave a scar." As Osman tried to grab his arm, Talon rose to leave, gently adding, "You will always be my little brother."

Talon then stood quickly, knowing he had tarried too long.

Oathbreaker.

The word echoed in his mind. Talon ran out the small door behind the stair and made his way to the stables. The Vermillion Blade overcame his emotions that had suppressed its will and demanded it be drawn and wielded, its web of chains now engulfing Talon, his sight shimmering between reality and the rocky plateau. Jumping onto his mount, he galloped out of the Keep heading in the only direction he knew to go. Unfortunately, the news of his actions seemed to travel even faster than his horse, as before reaching the outskirts of Arnadore, Talon met shouts of "coward," "traitor," and "Oathbreaker," along with residents throwing spoiled food at him in equal measure.

Oathbreaker.

The Vermillion Blade's voice rang again in his head. The urge to have it in his hands was now impossible to deny. He drove his mount even harder. Across fields and recklessly into the forest, he flew until, without warning, the Vermillion Blade was in his hand, Talon having drawn it without a thought. With one swift motion and a massive downward strike, he cut the legs of his mount out from under it, sending them both crashing into the ground. The horse screamed in pain and terror, but Talon could no longer hear it.

Oathbreaker. Eternal Walker. Thrall to the House of Heart's Vermin

The vision was familiar but changed. Talon strode the land wielding the Vermillion Blade as he had before striking down his foes. However, in this version, Talon was now an undead skeletal monstrosity. He would take a piece of flesh from each body he cut down and stuff it into his decaying form, adding it to his own. Every limb and organ added to his mass and writhing size. The figure now standing head and shoulders above his adversaries was not the heroic version of Talon the Vermillion Blade presented before but a horror of screaming undead faces and rotting limbs. Every footfall of Talon's vile form corrupted the land he trod upon. To Talon, trapped in despair, the images lasted for years, decades, and centuries; the pain of his own screams in the real world finally pulled him out of it.

Talon, still alive and human, covered in his mount's blood, was running through the forest as he awoke out of the vision; his hands, welded to the shaft of the Vermillion Blade, burned within arcane black flames. The skin and flesh on his hands blistered and melted, falling away, exposing seared muscle and charred bone. His legs somehow had kept him on track for the spring while his mind was absent. The spring was the only place Talon hoped there might be help or, in light of this new vision, rest for his corpse so that it could not rise to become the horror he had witnessed. Finally, as the spring came into view, the Vermillion Blade tried to wrest his mind away from him again. He sprinted forward with all his might and will. Legs churning without ever slowing, Talon leaped off the familiar boulder, his and Richen's boulder, and dove deep into the waters, not knowing if he would ever breathe of the air again.

Hands extinguished in the coolness of the spring surrounding him, Talon dove deeper and deeper, kicking with all his might, the cursed glaive held before him, still welded to his hands. As he descended, eyes wide open, he searched for the bottom and a rock or outcropping to wedge himself and the weapon underneath, trapping them both here, hopefully for eternity. Upon the shaft of the glaive, an inscription appeared before Talon's eyes in fiery runes:

To break oath is to be doomed even beyond death to walk this land as a blight upon it.

The curse now seen and believing his fate sealed, Talon closed his eyes and accepted his doom, praying that whatever divine force the spring might have would keep him from rising again after death.

He did not see the grain of the Vermillion Blade's rosewood shaft twist and contort under the hand of Caspharian, to whom all of nature bowed. The Conjoined God's divine touch, unable to erase the words, reformed the runes into a new inscription before their cursed magic left the shaft of the Vermillion Blade and sunk deep into the flesh and bones of his ruined hands.

CHAPTER TWENTY-TWO

Year 874 PXF *~ Spring*

Talon awoke face down on the familiar boulder beside the spring, clothes damp but not soaking as they would be if he had just emerged from the water. His eyes opened upon a tiny version of a full-grown tree: the sapling he had seen sprout so many years ago. The weak Spring sun did little to warm his bones but managed to do even less to warm the cold void in his spirit. Consciousness also brought an aching, itching burn to his hands which he had to steel himself to look at. Horribly scarred, covered with just the thinnest layer of skin and mottled tissue, his hands barely seemed like they were his. He flexed his fingers to see if they would move at all and while weak and stiff, they shakingly obeyed his basic commands. Talon could only hope that he could ever use them in battle again. The Vermillion Blade was nowhere to be seen.

Talon sat up and looked to the sky, the spring, and the verdant forest around him and said only, "Thank you."

Talon Cour-Vermane is dead, and a new man must now walk his paths and wear his scars.

The conjoined aspects of Caspharian spoke with a finality that brokered no discussion. While using similar words to Lochlan, the deity's pronouncement was far more profound. The implications of which Talon did not still fully understand.

The last chain binding you to darkness is gone, and the cursed blade has no hold over you, but not without cost and consequence.

He looked inward to where the black chain that shackled him to the darkness had always been and recognized its absence. It was odd for it to be missing. *Does one mourn when a part of themselves since birth is shorn away, even if it is a hated part?* The void in his spirit he felt upon awakening was not just for what had occurred at the Keep but also for his freedom from the chain. He scrambled to the water's edge and gazed at his reflection in the spring, looking for something profound, a physical manifestation of the change he felt and knew was real, but Talon's same face looked back. Peering into Talon's eyes, captured on the surface of the spring, he knew that his old name was no longer his, that it did not fit who he was now, and that the chains of his history no longer bound him.

Caspharian's voice continued.

You are without a noble name or house and wear the form and face of a known oathbreaker, traitor, and proclaimed coward. I can hide you from magics that may try to find you, but your physical presence, you must conceal on your own if you are to survive.

But I will not send my champion weaponless into this world. Draw forth the tree from the boulder you and Richen discovered your love upon.

Not fully understanding, he wrapped his hand around the tiny tree trunk that perfectly fit his damaged hand. He pulled gently upon the small plant and then more forcefully, biting back the agony it caused in his ruined appendage. It came free and revealed a sickle, blade grafted onto the roots and trunk of the tiny tree. As he held it, he felt his senses awaken to every living thing around him, feeling them and seeing through them as if they were an extension of himself. Hanging from a loop of vine entangled with the sickle was a seed much like an acorn. He placed the pendant around his neck and could feel its magic cloak conceal him.

Your place on the Moril'tha, the great world tree, is yours to decide. Whether that is to be bark or thorn, root or leaf remains to be seen. My gifts that you have already received, both boon and bane, are all I can offer you.

However, another, as ancient as I, has hidden what was your true birthright in your path. It lies in the place Talon knew as home.

The man who once was Talon knew he had saved only himself. His own chains to Darkness were shattered, but others still existed or had been newly forged by his father's designs. And while the Vermillion Blade was nowhere near, he somehow knew it had escaped from Caspharian's spring and still moved through the world.

In answer to himself as much to the deity, he stood at the edge of the spring, shoulders straight, sickle in hand. "I shall be a thorn, as it both protects the tree and injures its foes." He rolled the word around in his mind, before declaring, "My name is Thorn."

Thorn could not tell if Caspharian was satisfied with his choice, but for once, perhaps the first time in his life, he did not care about any other's opinions or expectations of him, even a god's. Thorn stood in confident solitude on the boulder that had driven so much of his previous life, Talon's life, but now it was Thorn's choice if it would guide it any longer.

PART III

The Child from Spring and Stone

The dark, hunched figure shambled slowly across the landscape. Road debris and moss matted and clung to the once well-maintained skins they wore; their journey had taken them far from home. They plucked a bit of lichen off their cloak and pushed it into their awaiting mouth with two wrinkled, swollen fingers. Their lips puckered and nose scrunched at the taste; the gray-green lichen was a biter supplement to keep them moving but not suitable for much else. Their journey continued. If one were to cross the path they walked in the coming days and were observant, one might wonder at the sparse trail of ghost-white snowdrops flowering in a meandering line following the sun from East to West.

They had been drawn onto their journey by the whispers that had called them. The voice had summoned them to bear witness to a birth just as many of their kin had been called before them. A mundane request for one who had ushered so many into the world from their mother's wombs, but this call was from someone not to be denied. It was not unexpected for the journey to be of such magnitude, for what was distance and time to the one who had called? The figure was, however, mildly surprised by their path leading them into the wilderness and away from nearby settlements, but they had delivered a child under worse circumstances; perhaps a hovel lay ahead or a hag's shack? What they did not expect to find at their destination was a man.

The man was lying on a boulder by a spring, soaking wet, looking as if he had just crawled or been flung out of the water. As the figure watched, cloaked in magic and wards, wondering at their purpose here, the water in the spring began to turn blood red, and the surface started to bulge unnaturally, like a woman who had held a pregnancy too long. Whatever was trying to escape this spring's womb bucked and kicked from deep within it mercilessly. For over an hour, the labor of the birth continued. Then, with the same horrifying rip that no person in a birthing room ever wants to hear, the Vermillion Blade escaped in a geyser of blood and water.

Once above the surface, the weapon vanished in a flash of arcane crimson light. The observer, bewildered at what they had seen, brought the carved medallion around their neck to their lips in reverence as they turned to leave, their task complete, but then the man on the boulder began to stir, and the watcher realized they were here to witness the birth of twins.

CHAPTER TWENTY-THREE

Year 874 PXF *~ Summer*

The events of the revolt and secession orchestrated by House Cour-Vermane swept across Eleryon like a brush fire in late Summer. It began with the militias attacking the 'imperial forces' invading the South. These soldiers, the Emperor's interrogators would later discover, were sellswords outfitted in uniforms and trained in the style and tactics of the Imperial Jade Guard. When word reached the Emperor of general unrest in Southern Eleryon, occurring only hours before his visit to Arnadore, he doubled the forces in his retinue that would be arriving with him via teleportation circle. On orders from Duke Issul, the Arnadore Keep guard sprung a well-planned ambush on the Emperor and his Jadenarme as they emerged from their magical transit, and the Arnadore Watch did prove to be their equals as the braggarts had claimed over the Winter - until the magic users arrived. The fiery arcane explosions ripping through the Keep and word of squads of Imperial troops arriving in large numbers in the heart of Arnadore set off a panic among the citizens. The tide of the ambush turned quickly at the teleportation circle, so in response, many of the city's citizens took up arms alongside the Duke's now highly-trained and prepared Arnadore Watch in defense of their home. With the support of the Jadenarme's war mages to protect the Emperor, the massacre that inevitably occurred at the Keep enraged tempers across Eleryon.

With the teleportation circle secured, the Jade Guard flowed into Arnadore unopposed, fulfilling the fears of an Imperial invasion that House Cour-Vermane had been stoking for years. The outcome was assured, but the process of the Jadenarme and Jade Guard securing Arnadore as they fought skirmishes street to street took a heavy toll on the city. The Eleryon rebellion did have some victories, but without the Vermillion Blade and a champion to wield it, their fate was ultimately sealed. Outside Arnadore, rolling waves of uprisings attempted to retake the capital but finally began to subside when Duke Issul was publicly captured and arrested for treason and taken to Jadenpool for trial. Minor revolts popped up here and there, but with the militias decimated, the Emperor's Jade Guard peacekeepers quelled them quickly. Finally, the Emperor, having no ambitions in Eleryon of any sort, ordered his forces to return to Jadenpool, destroying the teleportation circle behind them.

All who remained in Eleryon were left in shocked disarray as the Jade Guard withdrew; most citizens had no idea what had even occurred other than the destruction of the city and countryside around them. The Emperor sent his ambassadors and agents to try and inform the populace of the truth as facts were discovered during Duke Issul's trial, but the distrust, confusion, and lack of any leader in the region made their efforts fruitless. Eleryon, once the bountiful cornucopia of the empire, in a little over a month had been decimated. The loss of life and property, field and orchard, made the Xallian Empire's southern Duchy of little worth to the empire, which had more pressing concerns looming than the rebuilding of one distant province. While Eleryon did still remain part of Xallia, it was largely abandoned and left to regain enough stability and governance on its own to return to the Emperor's graces.

As tempers calmed and passions quieted, Thorn, under cover of darkness and draped in a heavy cloak with his face hidden under a dark hood, snuck back into Arnadore and headed for the Sojourn's Rest. Thorn was heartbroken walking through the city he had so often visited while growing up and called home as Talon for seventeen years. The battles that raged in Arnadore had left building after building in ruins; in some places, the fighting had so completely destroyed whole blocks with their fire and magic that Thorn could scarcely find the path the streets once took through them. As he approached Elery Square, Thorn worried for his friends and feared for their fate, especially that of Lolly, Mikal, and the rest of the regulars at the Sojourn's Rest. Thorn braced himself, expecting the worst as he turned the corner to approach his old home, but it stood intact. The Sojourn's Rest was not without scars, scorch marks darkened the roof and walls, and several windows were boarded over, most notably the ones to his old flat of rooms. Nevertheless, Thorn stealthily made his way around the back of the inn to the alley that serviced the kitchens and, face hidden from any stray light source, tapped quietly on the door.

Lolly tentatively answered the soft rapping on her door. Recognizing the scale of the figure and with confirmation by his face turning into the light spilling out the door, she rushed Thorn in and turned off the lantern leaving only the flicker of the low burning hearth to light the kitchen. She offered Thorn food and tea as always and filled him in on the news he hadn't learned already. The Emperor's inquisitors, after lengthy questioning, revealed Toman Cour-Vermane's hand in the plot, but he found leniency with the court by turning evidence over that implicated the Duke and showed himself as an unwitting pawn. Regardless, the Emperor threatened House Cour-Vermane with being stripped of all land and fortune, but Toman's cooperation stayed the sentence for one generation if they could prove their loyalty and dedication to the Empire. For all anyone knew, Toman was still in Jadenpool, having been ordered to witness Duke Issul's execution as a warning to him and his family. At the mention of the execution, Lolly looked at Thorn with haunted eyes.

"All of the Duke's personal guards were taken with him to Jadenpool. The last news we heard is that they were to be executed alongside him." Her voice caught in her throat, "Osman was among them."

The news hit Thorn like a blow; he was grateful for confirmation his dagger had not killed Osman but dismayed about his sentence. He had hoped that somehow after their altercation and his escape, Osman would have come to his senses. However, if Osman was as entangled in Toman's plot as deeply as he feared, the Emperor would have his justice. Thorn choked down the emotion in his throat, feeling another tie to his old life sever from him. He asked thickly, "Is there news of Mikal?" Lolly had not heard of any, but laborers that drank in the inn's tavern whispered that a blacksmith had a part in tying Toman to the Duke's treachery and was currently in hiding.

With at least that bit of relief, Thorn asked Lolly if she possibly had something for him, hoping that surely the place Thorn had lived for nearly twenty years would be the home Caspharian had referred to, but Lolly could think of nothing. Stutteringly, she confessed and profusely apologized that she could not stop rioters from raiding his rooms and taking all his belongings to burn in the streets. Thorn assured her it didn't matter as those were no longer really his. He didn't elaborate any further about his new identity but instead took his leave, not wanting to place Lolly in any further danger and feeling the need to escape the news he had been given about Osman. Perplexed by Caspharian's message, Thorn knew he had to go to the only other place he might call home and headed to the Cour-Vermane estate.

CHAPTER TWENTY-FOUR

Year 874 PXF *~ Summer*

From afar, the Cour-Vermane estate looked deserted but for a single light shining in Veronic's parlor on the third floor overlooking the courtyard. The estate and surrounding buildings seemed no worse for wear, having predictably escaped the damage its lord inflicted on the region. Thorn checked his surroundings for any unseen threat. Then, cloaked in darkness and armed with his intimate knowledge of the estate, he crept across the still-manicured gardens and over the high wall of the courtyard. Thorn landed in a crouch, hidden by the deep shadows of the training yard where Talon and Lochlan used to spar, and skulked toward the main house where his childhood rooms were. Thorn was halfway across the open expanse when a glint of light from the smithy caught his eye, and at that moment, he knew where Caspharian had referred to as his home. His silent form changed direction and padded its way into the deserted space, carefully closing the wide door behind him. Looking around the cold and empty smithy, he couldn't help but absorb some of its chill into his spirit. The stark contrast between its current state to the sanctuary it once was to him years before was profound and heartbreaking.

Shaking away encroaching memories, he found he was staring at the forge, and he could not recall a time in his memory when it sat as cold and lifeless as it did now. Trusting the deity had not led him astray, Thorn searched every nook and cranny of the space but could not find much of anything left behind by Mikal or anyone else. Despondent and with a fugue threatening to overtake him, the man that was once Talon sat alone in the darkness. His mind wheeled as it would in his younger days, projecting what the remainder of his life might be. Here he was, starting over with nothing, burdened with the face and form of the years he had lived, but everything else he built now crumbled and gone. Nearing forty years old, with the search for the love he lost, molding twenty of them. Was the search for Richen even something he, as Thorn, should pick up? Or should it die along with Talon Cour-Vermane back in the spring? The audacity of even considering continuing the folly that had shaped over half of Talon's life almost made him laugh. This was his escape. Thorn could walk away from Richen just like he was about to walk away from Eleryon and everything else that had been Talon. As the conversation with himself about his two selves continued, he had to tamp down a creeping sense of hysteria that threatened to bubble up inside of him. Thorn felt that letting it loose might overwhelm him and break his mind.

Across from Thorn, the smithy door slowly crept open on its hinges, moved by some errant breeze he neither felt nor heard. It revealed the crumbling woodpile outside like a curtain drawn to reveal a stage. By some delirium or ghostly haunting, as clearly as if it was happening at that moment, he watched the first day he met Richen replay in the courtyard, but now from his current vantage point inside the smithy.

There young Talon was in his flamboyant hunting attire, frozen by the sight of the mysterious, beautiful boy at the woodpile. Gods, how small and lonely he looked. And there was Richen, looking all elbows and knees compared to what he would soon become in just a few years. Thorn remembered just how desperate he was for someone to want him—even though young Talon would never admit it, his ego still wrapped up in the idea of being his father's son. Then he watched it happen, the moment Talon's life changed. Richen looking up and asking for Talon's help to carry splits of wood. From this vantage point, Thorn saw the gulp young

Talon made and the slight shaking of his hands. Richen turned and walked into the smithy just as he had in the memory, but now he was walking straight toward Thorn. Even at this young age, Richen was just as beautiful as Thorn remembered him, but now he could see what young Talon never did. Richen whispering to himself, "Please let him want to be my friend, please let him want to be my friend." There was no way Talon could know what Thorn was now seeing, but in his heart, he knew it was the truth of that moment so many years ago; Richen had needed Talon as much as he needed Richen. Thorn stepped out of the way of the two memory ghosts as they began to light the fire and play out the rest of what had occurred, and as Richen looked deep into the firebox, Thorn realized the one place in the smithy he hadn't looked for the gift a god had left for him.

The apparitions of Richen and young Talon dissolved as Thorn dropped to his knees and looked into the cold firebox under the forge; far in the back corner, there looked like what was just another mound of coal and ash, but for the slight metallic glint it gave off. Grabbing a long poker Thorn was able to hook it and drag it forward to where he could reach it. Whatever Thorn had found had not been disturbed for a very long time as parts of it were wholly covered in molten slag and sand turned to raw, blackened glass. Thorn broke apart the brittle detritus that encased the object, and as he did, he found that it unfolded like fabric. Turning it and spreading it across his soot-covered hands, he discovered it was a chainmail shirt made of the finest links Thorn had ever seen.

At first, Thorn thought it must be made of dwarven lymdian due to its light weight and ability to survive in the burning heat of the deep forge fires for gods only knew how long, but it was far too dark and did not carry the bright sheen of the prized gleaming metal of the dwarves. As he examined it, the shirt, which was sized more for someone of Osman's height and lighter build, seemed to conjure additional links and chains until it soon was of a size to fit his far larger frame. Tears in his eyes, Thorn could not help but reflect on the memory of his little brother and his outfit at the Gala, which had been held here on these grounds a little over a year before. Thorn whispered under his breath, "Enchanted, of course," and held the chain mail close to his chest. Gods, how could a year change the lives of so many so completely?

Knowing this was what he came for, Thorn, caught in the emotion of remembering Osman and the satisfaction of the discovery, tucked the mail shirt under his cloak. He was fully prepared to walk back into the courtyard, closing the door on another pain-filled chapter from the life of the man he had been before. But that was not to be. Instead, the willowy form of Veronic Cour-Vermane, carrying a shrouded lantern in one hand and one of her ever-present books in the other, stepped into the smithy.

CHAPTER TWENTY-FIVE

"This is, of course, where you would come," Veronic intoned as her eyes scanned around the room. She wore a heavy, dark green dressing gown with embroidered orchids at the lapels, something she usually would never be caught outside her chambers wearing, much less outside the house. She slid the small tome she carried into one of the outside pockets so she could pass her less than perfectly manicured hand over one of the smithy's worktables. Thorn at first thought the expression she wore was of rueful disdain but then realized it was one of envy and wistful disappointment. She continued, eyes finally meeting her son's. "This and dear Ms. Haddington's kitchen was always your true home, not the sterile halls and rooms of the upper floors that your father and I inhabited." There was a bite to her words, but the warmth returned as she added, "Here was the home you deserved."

"Talon," Veronic paused, looking deep into the eyes of the man before her and then seeing a truth behind them. "That's not who you are anymore, is it?" She sighed, "Of course not. How could you be? You no longer have the Vermillion Blade, yet you are alive, and even after all you had already lost, your father has taken even more." Veronic closed her eyes, seemingly searching for a place she had long ago walled off from everyone, including herself, "That is where we are alike, you and I."

She walked around Thorn, past the forge, and to the narrow door beside the flue that led to the tiny room beyond it. While still tightly controlled, Veronic spoke with a passion Thorn had never heard from her before. "He took you from me the moment you left my body and made sure I could never take you back." Veronic's hand went absently to her cheek, remembering past offenses she had endured. "But by the gods, I tried to find the people who could provide you what I was incapable of giving myself." Then, laying her hand on Richen's door, she added, "But even that, he found a way to steal from you."

"Mother, what are you saying?" Thorn asked with the horrifying unspoken question shaking in his voice.

"Toman has many skills," Veronic crossed back to her son and took Thorn's ruined and scarred hands in her own, examining the damage, "and as you already know, they are tied to the darkest forces of this world." Veronic could not meet her son's eyes. "I wish I could have been capable of being more to you, my son, but sometimes the only act of love one can manage is to step aside so others may do what they cannot."

Thorn was torn between striking Veronic and embracing her but finally only said, "You will not see me again."

"I know," Veronic confirmed, "but that does not mean you are without family completely. I might not have been able to do anything about your father's schemes, but that does not mean he has taken all of those you love from you." She paused. "Osman is alive. He was in the infirmary recovering from a grievous wound at the time of the battle of Arnadore Keep and never actually took up arms against the Empire. At first, that fact did not matter to the Emperor, as he wanted to make an example of all those closest to Duke Issul. Fortunately, something must have jogged his memory of the last conflict between the Uldani and the Empire, and so as not to give offense to the Uldani Isles, he instead commuted Osman's sentence to twenty years of exile."

194

Veronic then turned and left the smithy, retrieving the book from her dressing gown pocket as she left. A book Thorn now recognized and knew quite well from his youth: *200 Years of Blood: A History of the Xallian-Uldani War.*

Veronic drifted out into the night like a leaf on an autumn breeze. Thorn, who had been so ready to throw away all that was Talon's life and start anew, was now not so resolute in that course of action. His body feeling as unsteady as his mind, he sat down on the edge of the forge and opened himself to the memories and ghosts that haunted this space. Half a dozen fleeting images of young Talon and Richen materialized around him, reenacting snippets of memories of their time together. As one would fade, another would appear. There wasn't a square inch of this place that their presence had not touched. They really had been inseparable, and young Talon was so happy; no, *he* was so happy. Thorn's eyes became trapped looking at the door to Richen's room and Veronic's hand resting there. Had Toman sent the creature to attack them that day? Was it all part of his plan for Talon to become his weapon, to become this?

Thorn looked down at the body he had inherited from Talon. Its strength, its mass, and its size. The years of training and fighting and honing his skills. With disgusting clarity, the image of the undead horror the Vermillion Blade showed him of what Talon would become filled Thorn's mind; it taking pieces of the dead to bolster its strength and size, and now all Thorn could imagine was Toman feeding Talon pieces of Richen to create the weapon he became. Thorn retched at the truth of it. All the fiendish incursions over the years keeping Talon's skills sharp and developing his ability to lead others - *was Toman's hand in that as well?*

Thorn wanted to reject the thought of it, but as the pieces came together in his mind, it made far too clear a picture for his father's hand not to have been behind it all. Thorn was ready to storm into the estate and demand more answers from Veronic but knew in his heart getting more than she had already offered was unlikely without extreme methods, and he was not going to become shaped by his father in that way as well. It was then the last ghost appeared in the smithy—Richen, just as Thorn remembered him from the morning of their hunting trip.

"Mikal, I don't want to lose him." Richen's voice was shaky, but hearing it again sent a shiver down Thorn's spine.

"Richen, my boy, what the two of you have," Mikal's disembodied voice paused while gathering his thoughts, "it is like nothing I have ever seen. It is what you hear about only in the great tales and songs of bards. So, whatever happens today, just be honest with yourself and each other, and let love do the rest."

"But what if he wants something I can't give? What if he doesn't find me..." Mikal interrupted Richen's worried words, "Richen, love always finds a path between two such as you. Always."

The memory of Richen looked right into Thorn's eyes. And repeated Mikal's words with a reassured voice, "Always."

The ghosts around Thorn dissolved, and he was once again alone in the smithy but no longer a man with nothing. Yes, Talon Cour-Vermane was dead, but Thorn now understood that building a new life did not mean you couldn't bring the best parts of who you were to create the foundations of who you would become.

As the ghosts around Thorn dissolved, a sleeping form a world away whispered into the night,

"Always."

Thorn spent several more months living in the forest surrounding Arnadore; he even claimed that he was waiting and hoping for things to die down in the region so he could do something more to help. Of course, he knew not what that might be, but if he told himself that helping was the reason and not that he was waiting to confront the Lord of House Cour-Vermane, it made him feel better as he watched another day turn to night with him still in the borders of Eleryon. Unfortunately, what information did reach him even as he skulked around the forests and orchards was not welcome news. By design or ill fate, Talon Cour-Vermane and not his father had become synonymous with all things that ailed Arnadore and the surrounding region. Whether from his actions of breaking oath and fleeing the Keep, Toman's schemes being attributed to the only Cour-Vermane they knew, or his not wielding the legendary Vermillion Blade and leading the Arnadore Watch against the invading Jade Guard, all that had befallen Eleryon was the fault of Talon Cour-Vermane.

No matter the care he took, eyes would often linger too long upon him even from afar. After one too many close calls, Thorn, with eyes closed and breath held tightly in his chest, had taken the sickle to his hair to at least remove one of Talon's distinctive features, and the only one he had any control over. But even now, with his wild hair haphazardly cut nearly to the roots, his face and form were far too infamous, and Thorn knew it was beyond reckless even to consider facing his father. All he had was Caspharian's sickle and the armor from the forge that he wore under his plain roughspun tunic, and they would be no match for whatever guards or mob might rush to the aid of his father. Still, a deep need for further closure kept him from moving on and away from Arnadore, so Thorn waited. Finally, his third month in the forest reached its midpoint, and the first chills of Autumn reminded him he would need to find shelter before Winter; Thorn had a visitor.

Whistling brightly as though they had no care in the world, Castian Varo, the half-elf who wintered the Sojourn's Rest, strolled into his camp. Thorn had hidden deep within the brush upon hearing someone's approach but was still close enough to keep eyes on his ramshackle refuge. Castian looked straight at him without a search and said, "A package was delivered for you at Lolly's." Thorn stood up, knowing there was no sense pretending he was hidden from Castian's keen eyes. "She also mentioned you are not you any longer. So who are you now?"

Thorn followed Cas' dizzying logic and introduced himself. "Thorn. You can call me Thorn."

"Well, Thorn, for a man the size of a small mountain and a face as easy to spot as a newly painted tavern sign, you have done a humanly adequate job of making yourself scarce. Anyway, here's your box." Castian expertly threw a rectangular package from out of the pack over their shoulder at Thorn.

Thorn caught the small, well-made plain wooden box that Cas tossed to him. Opening it, he recognized what it was and what it meant. Within the box was the ball-peen smithing hammer that Richen had made to win his apprenticeship. Mikal had used it nearly every day and kept it in his belt at all times. It could only mean one thing for it to come to Thorn: Mikal had died. Emotion filled Thorn's heart, but strangely it was not as crushing a blow as he expected it to be. Just like he learned regarding Richen, Mikal would always be a part of this new person he was creating and becoming. Mikal might have taken his journey with the Last Friend, but he would also be forever with Thorn as a foundation of who he was. Perhaps this was the closure Thorn needed, not the confrontation with the lord of his old house he desired.

Cas broke the silence of Thorn's introspection. "You'll be needing something more than hedges and trees for shelter come Winter. You should head up to Lymehold. Old King Stoneanvil owes me a favor and does not care about the winds of the Empire's political seasons. He will put you up for the Winter, maybe longer if you make yourself useful. Find a deep enough place in the mines, and the human world need not see you ever again."

Cas continued, "Welp, I need to be getting home for the Winter myself, and it's a long walk. See you around, kid." Castian stood, picked up the tune they were whistling at precisely the same note they left off on, and strolled out of Thorn's life for nearly a decade.

CHAPTER TWENTY-SIX

Thorn had not truly been out on the road since before his thirty-fifth birthday when the Duke had promoted him to Knight Captain, and he couldn't help but be invigorated by having a destination beyond the horizon and a journey before him. Of course, he had to stay well off the main roads and paths through Eleryon, and luckily that spared Thorn from witnessing most of the destruction the rebellion had visited upon the region. Still, the magically withered fields and orchards spoke of the burned-out farmhouses and barns that lay over almost every rise in the distance. Thorn vowed to return and somehow help bring the land back to what it once was, but how long into the future he might have to wait, he did not know.

Eventually, the ground began to rise beneath his feet, and the lowlands of Eleryon started to turn into the foothills of the Lymehold Range, the ancestral homeland of the dwarves. Thorn began to trust using the roads as he got further away from his old life and deeper into the evergreen woodlands that spread out hundreds of leagues from the towering limestone cliffs and peaks of the dwarven capital. Even in his past life as the Duke's envoy, Thorn had never visited Lymehold as the King of the Dwarves dealt mainly with the Emperor himself via their treaty of accommodation. The histories he studied as a child marked Lymehold as the oldest settlement on the continent and perhaps the world, the latter unquestioningly being what the dwarves believed. The city beneath the white peaks was immeasurably vast, and cartographers more accurately described it as four cities, with Oldstone being the central hub of the sprawling metropolis. If Thorn were to plead for sanctuary as Castian had advised, he would need to go there as that is where he would find King Stoneanvil.

As Thorn traveled higher into the mountains, the seasons seemed to transition league by league. Where it had been early Fall in the lowlands, the chill of Winter was ever present when he arrived at the dwarven capital. The etchings Thorn had seen in his mother's books were but a dim reflection of the immensity and grandeur of the gates of Lymehold that stood before him. Recessed into a three-hundred-foot white cliff face and towering a hundred and fifty feet high themselves, the massive arched gates stood open in all their vaulted majesty. Divided and sub-divided into thousands of carved motifs and buttresses, the craftsmanship and detail were all but incomprehensible to the human mind. Still marveling at their grandeur as he walked toward them, Thorn, who had been rehearsing a way to gain entry to the city, was without even a question allowed to pass unhindered by the two dozen ceremonially armed dwarven guards at the entrance. Thorn did not precisely know what to expect of Lymehold or Oldstone in particular, but Sunhall Cavern was absolutely not it.

Dwarven settlements and stories had always conjured dark and claustrophobic spaces for Thorn. However, even accounting for this being their capital and on a larger scale, it still did not prepare him for the bright and airy magnificence of Sunhall. Utterly massive in size, far larger than Arnadore's Keep, Elery Square, and the whole of the trade district combined, the cavern walls and architecture blended natural rock formations and carved stone structural aesthetics into an otherworldly and breathtaking tapestry. Thorn, having entered near the midlevel of the cavern, was awestruck as he realized the cityscape within Sunhall soared at least a dozen levels from its dizzying heights to its floor below. Still, without question, the most striking feature was the overwhelming presence of natural sunlight. Sunlight that was not magically conjured but ingeniously redirected from the outside and focused through quartz stalactites and vertical columns of smooth flowing crystal-clear water that passed from the uppermost levels down to the river winding through the floor of Sunhall far below.

If being a human of his size among a population consisting primarily of dwarves didn't set him apart enough, his provincial gawking and standing stunned in the middle of the thoroughfare certainly would have. However, after being jostled at least a half-dozen times, Thorn finally came to his senses when a young ginger-haired dwarf wearing an official-looking uniform and well-polished spectacles asked, "Can I help you find something? A tavern or inn? I can recommend several that can accommodate humans of your stature."

"Oh, um, no... sorry." Thorn had to jog his own memory as to his purpose, so distracting were his surroundings until he finally could conjure out of his windpipe, "Right. Yes. I need to see King Stoneanvil."

The young dwarf eyed him suspiciously as they stroked their thrice-braided beard. "What business do you have with the King?"

"I was sent by Castian Varo. He said the King may be able to help me." Not knowing the nature of the favor or how Cas might have earned it, Thorn felt discretion was the best way forward until candor was needed.

The young dwarf knowingly nodded at the mention of the name. "Castian Varo, huh? Yes, I do believe the King will want to meet you." Thorn wasn't sure what he might have stumbled into, but with his current lack of provisions and Winter looming, he had few remaining options.

The young dwarf introduced themself as Darvis and a member of the Oldstone Historical Society and Visitor Welcoming Guild. "You would be amazed at the number of visitors we get to Oldstone; even among residents of greater Lymehold, nearly half have never made the journey," Darvis offered affably. "Not many humans, though. I guess the Emperor likes his magical forms of diplomacy rather than visiting face-to-face," Darvis added the last bit distastefully but recovered quickly by adding, "Don't get me wrong, I love a magical doodad as much as any dwarf, but over the centuries, we learned that some things just need the personal touch."

Darvis led Thorn higher and higher in the cavern, explaining how many of the original first homes of the dwarves were long gone, now replaced by ornate guildhalls, embassies, and residences of honored citizens. On these higher levels, Thorn even crossed paths with several dragonborn who stuck out equally as well as he did among the dwarves, some being even taller and broader than himself. Following Thorn's gaze, Darvis did not hesitate to recount how the dwarves and dragonborn's histories intertwined not only with each other but with Lymehold itself. They finally stopped in front of an unimposing open arch that, compared to the rest of the architecture Thorn had passed, was quite plain. Only two well-equipped guards stood to either side of the opening who did not intercede as Darvis gestured for Thorn to enter.

"This is where I take my leave. Good luck." Darvis was gone before Thorn could even thank them, disappearing into the bustle of the thoroughfare.

Thorn stepped through the arch into a dimly lit space, his eyes struggling to adjust after being in the bright sunlight outside. A long straight hallway led deep into the rock, well carved and adequate for his height but just barely. Finally, after a hundred feet or so, he came to an open chamber not much larger than the main tavern room at the Sojourn's Rest. A well-provisioned table laden with food and drink filled the center of the space in front of a small dais atop which sat a carved stone throne.

A well-groomed older dwarf with salt and pepper hair and a single braided beard that hung long enough to be tucked through his belt leaned on the table facing Thorn. Upon his brow sat a simple but finely crafted circlet of lymdian. He held a frothing tankard in his hand, and with a grizzled voice, he asked while gesturing with his mug, "So what has Castian sent to me this time?"

In the dim light, Thorn quickly spotted a magical effect flash into existence, illuminating the King's eyes as he examined Thorn. Stoneanvil's left eyebrow slowly raised as his eyes roamed over his visitor's form. "Well, what you wear speaks far more loudly than any words you might say, so what is it you want? Speak plainly, as I have no interest in fencing with your niceties."

"Shelter. Sanctuary if it comes to that, but I think most believe me dead, so I anticipate no one to come looking for me." Thorn's words startled even himself; it was the first time he had vocalized how alone in the world he now was. In Talon's days with the Crimson Sentinels and Falcon's Grasp, no matter the risk, there was a shared pledge; someone would always come, even if only for your corpse. Knowing no friend or ally cared to know the fate of Talon Cour-Vermane felt like a hole had been bored in Thorn's stomach. Thorn wrenched his mind away from the thought in time to catch the King's words.

"You may Winter in Oldstone, but I ask you not to travel to the outer cities of Lymehold. There are still empty quarters in the Pillars from the departure of the dragonborn to found Shimmindalla. Darvis will show you to one." Thorn was startled to find Darvis standing by his side as the King continued, "Once Spring arrives, if you wish to remain, you will need to find a way to earn your place here, but until then, consider yourself my guest. What shall we call you?"

"Thorn is my name," After a pause, he added in the manner of the Uldani, "I have not earned any other."

King Stoneanvil gave a knowing nod of approval and of dismissal. Darvis escorted Thorn out of the chamber, but after he left, the King's voice echoed down the entry hallway, "And when you see him tell Castian Varo we are even!"

Darvis led Thorn down from the upper echelons of Sunhall Cavern past the grand entry hall towards the lower levels. The winding path of ramps, stairways, and natural stone arch bridges over the river below took the better part of an hour. At first, Thorn attempted to act unaffected by the wonders of the cavern around him, but he couldn't stop thinking about how he wished Osman could see it all.

He then realized that Osman had always been Talon's excuse: an excuse to show emotion, embrace joy, and be happy. Thorn decided he would not live this new life relying on outside justifications to live fully and as he wanted, and while not as exuberant as his Uldani little brother, Thorn gave himself permission to experience the wonder of Sunhall. He would later insist over mugs of ale that the length of his first trip down to the River Rock district was not due to his stopping in slack-jawed amazement and wide-armed proclamations of the vistas and artistry of the architectural composition the dwarves had created but the wink and wry smile he shot to those around him, assured them that it was.

To keep Thorn moving, Darvis tried to distract him with some facts and details about where he was guiding him. "Below us is the Silvervein River, and built along the banks is the River Rock district. That is where you can come for meals and drink. While there are other options, if you have no coin, you can always partake of the King's Fare, which every brewery and food hall carries a version of on their menu." Darvis looked longingly at the dwarves who were already gathering for a midday meal and ale out on the sprawling patios and decks of River Rock. "But," he continued mournfully, "that's not where we're headed. We need to go upriver to the Pillars."

Leaving River Rock behind them and following the wide boulevard that paralleled the Silvervein, Darvis led Thorn to a massive crack in the outer wall of Sunhall Cavern. Nearly fifty feet wide at its base, the vertical crevasse extended in a jagged triangle roughly half the height of the cavern. The Silvervein poured out through its center in a cascade of white water while the boulevard they were on narrowed to a winding ramp that climbed into the darkness beyond.

At the top of the ramp, the narrow passage, relative to the caverns' size, emerged into another enormous space filled with columns of stone reminiscent of a dense ancient forest. While not as tall as Sunhall, between the lower light level and the pillars of limestone, Thorn's eyes could not discern where the furthest extent of this cavern lay. There was no sunlight in this cavern, but a soft blue-green rippling phosphorescence emanated from the Silvervein river, which had widened into branching and meandering streams and ponds throughout the cavern. As Thorn and Darvis moved further into the space, it was apparent that the Pillars must be where most of Oldstone, and perhaps even greater Lymehold, conducted their commerce. Every pillar housed multiple storefronts and vending stands. Looking upward, Thorn saw that these establishments extended up to the tops of the columns, and as his eyes adjusted to the rippling light, he spotted bridges and walkways suspended between the pillars high above.

Thorn garnered a few second glances from vendors and customers alike, but Darvis' presence seemed to quell any badgering or undue curiosity. Thorn did not spot any other humans among the throng of people in the Pillars, but many different species of humanoids were represented, and their presence seemed accepted and welcomed here.

The deeper they traveled into the Pillars, the more Thorn began to notice a deep roaring sound in the distance coming from the direction they were traveling. Darvis chimed in without Thorn having to ask. "That's the Mist Market. Don't worry, that's not where your abode is. It's way too moist." Darvis didn't elaborate, and Thorn didn't have time to query further as Darvis began leading them up a set of stone stairs that curved around the outside of one of the limestone pillars. After no more than a quarter turn around the column, the two came to an open landing with a door leading into the stone face. "Here we are. A quite large ruby dragonborn lived here before heading out to Shimmindalla, so you should find everything to your scale if not a little oversized."

Thorn was skeptical about the latter statement as it had been decades since he didn't feel overly large and cramped in most indoor spaces, but he was quickly proven wrong. The abode consisted of three rooms and a privy, and while the scale didn't look visually off, Thorn discovered the difference almost immediately as he moved around the space. In the kitchen, not only were countertops and chairs at a more comfortable height for Thorn's size than he was used to, but they also seemed to be just a tad too high in some cases, giving him a strange sense of dissonance between his self-perception and the scale of things around him. As he explored his new accommodations, he was surprised to find a large balcony that opened off the central great room and stretched around to the main bedroom giving an expansive view of the main flow of the Silvervein. A small study with a desk and bookshelves completed the apartment's rooms.

Interestingly, most of the larger furnishings in the rooms were carved directly out of the pillar's stone. Only a few high stools and a matching table in the kitchen were made of wood. Darvis chimed in again, "There should be a delivery coming with bedding and some essentials to stock the kitchen as a welcome from King Stoneanvil. You'll want to find your bearings sooner rather than later, though, as you will need to adjust to life here in Oldstone for the Winter without the King stepping in all the time.

I can usually be found in Sunhall if you need additional assistance." And like an errant breeze, Darvis was gone leaving Thorn alone in his new living quarters.

Thorn hopped up to sit on one of the high wooden stools in the kitchen, an action he had become unfamiliar with over the years with more human-scale furnishings. The silence in the apartment was both comforting and oppressive. The single small lantern in the great room did little to light the space, and the Silvervein River's mesmerizing light flowing in from off the balcony seemed to dissolve away the walls of the rooms. Thorn allowed his mind to fall into the rippling light and reflect back over the day. He had assumed he would find some anonymity in the dwarven halls of Lymehold, a place to hide in dark, cramped mines and scrape out an existence. A part of him felt he deserved some form of penance or hardship to shape the man-who-was-to-be Thorn, but that certainly was not what his first day presented him. Sunhall's bright thoroughfares, boisterous meal halls, and endless dwarven wonders didn't leave much opportunity for a lone human to skulk around, certainly not one of his scale. Yet, strangely, standing out so much lent him its own kind of invisibility. He was another passing oddity in a place full of wonders, activities, and destinations for tens of thousands of people; it felt like his incongruency in their lives didn't even register with most citizens of Oldstone.

There was a strange freedom that came with that revelation. Thorn was not only unbound from Talon Cour-Vermane in this place but also unencumbered by his learned and self-enforced tenets of Arnadore and human society. It had felt so good to be like his Uldani little brother and embrace the experience of exploring Sunhall. Of course, in the past, Talon had sometimes leaned into Osman's exuberance in their times together, but always as an observer or tag along to them, not the instigator of the experience. His inhibitions had always chained him to Talon's role as Knight Captain or even just the "big stoic serious one" of their duo. As unintuitive as it might seem, his being ridiculously larger, at nearly twice as tall as almost every citizen, gave him more license to physically convey his emotions as he pleased. There was no way for him to *not* be an outsider and different from everyone around him. Blending in was and would never be an option for Thorn. The dwarves he had observed on his trek through Sunhall had personalities far more expansive than their size, and he was free to be a personification of that on an even grander scale. Here in this city, he was unknown—an unwritten story in the lives of these dwarves, or more likely a minor footnote considering their long lifespans.

Thorn felt liberated by that idea as he sat in his kitchen, finding comfort in the new and varied branching options it gave to his new existence. With a sigh, he smiled and relaxed into the feeling of dissolving into the hypnotic rippling of the light on his walls. Thorn's mind moved in its dreamlike state back to his meeting with the King. Some form of magical sight had certainly informed Stoneanvil's decision, *but what exactly did he see?* Thorn assumed his sickle would carry some mark of the Conjoined God of nature, but what enchantment lay on the mail shirt he wore under his roughspun tunic and threadbare cloak? He had no idea of what it might have shown the King.

As the rest of the conversation played out in his head, Thorn came to his own statement that no one would be looking for him and the emptiness it left in his gut. His mind had danced around the thoughts behind that emptiness, avoiding them at every turn where they appeared. Finally, long overdue, it was time for him to face the question that haunted him; what would Thorn do about Richen?

The question left hanging in his mind seemed to bring the world to a stop around him. Now asked, Thorn had to face it and the ramifications of it. It was one thing for Thorn to adopt Osman's zest for life and experiences; it was quite another for a thirty-seven-year-old man to shape his life around a love he lost over two decades earlier when he now had a perfect opportunity and reason to leave that burden behind.

Perhaps the answer was for Thorn not to erase his love for Richen and its loss but to carry it, much like his scar from Lochlan. An indelible mark inherited from the late Talon Cour-Vermane, but not something to continue to pursue. Thorn chewed on that idea and tried to swallow it but couldn't seem to choke it down and accept that as a course forward. The feeling from Thorn's own words, "no one is looking for me," kept that easier path, the wiser path, the sensible path blocked to him. Thorn hated the emptiness those words left in him and could not bear to think of Richen feeling them now. Thorn knew that it was likely Richen had felt the impact of those words for the last two decades when day after day no one ever came, but just as he knew Richen was still alive, Thorn hoped Richen too knew Talon had been looking for him.

And now Thorn would continue looking as well.

CHAPTER TWENTY-SEVEN

Thorn was broken out of his thoughts by a knock at the door. As promised, a group of rowdy dwarves herded by a demanding dwarven matron whose demeanor shifted from honey-sweet toward Thorn to thunderclap fury toward 'her boys' delivered bedding, blankets, and 'stylish accents' along with provisions to his new abode.

Once satisfied with her work, the matron demanded of Thorn, "Get down here, boy, and show some deference to your elders," indicating for him to bring his face closer to hers. "Now, not too much drinking or carousing and keep your nose clean of the funny business that this city has far too much an abundance of. If you need coin, you come to see old Margren," introducing herself with a wink. "I could find good use for someone your stature." She gave a pat and then a harder but not painful strike to Thorn's cheek, emphasizing it with a finger pointed at his nose. "And stay out of the dice parlors, or you'll end up indentured to the Icebeards and working the Frostforge Depths."

Margren took her leave, leaving Thorn stunned but free to putter around the apartment and his new additional furnishings. He was thankful for the bedding as he wasn't sure how he would have slept on the stone bed otherwise. He was happily surprised that after Margren's ministrations, the bed was one of the more comfortable he had laid on. Thorn decided to take up Darvis on their advice and get his bearings within Oldstone as nothing else remained to occupy him within his rooms.

As Thorn left his apartment, the Pillars was teeming and bustling with the constant activity of the city's commerce. As he explored the district, he saw everything from small everyday transactions between residents and grocers to negotiations of mineral and jewel shipments at the brokerage cafes along the Silvervein's winding course. Later, as his stomach began to inform him that dinnertime was approaching, Thorn headed downstream back into Sunhall and the meal halls of River Rock. As he emerged from the Pillars back into the towering vaults of Sunhall, Thorn was once again reminded by sunset's ruddy glow washing the limestone walls that the light here was not a conjuration. Thorn approached River Rock with some trepidation, not knowing the custom to receive the King's Fare that Darvis had described as he was down to his last coppers. Thorn chose the first of the meal halls that he came upon as it was on the fringe of River Rock and did not seem as crowded and loud as those further ahead. The Lamb's Shank was a tidy and well-kept establishment with a large outdoor seating area laid out in front of its open windows. As he entered the meal hall, Thorn was deeply contemplating the efficiency of windows needing no glass when buildings were inside a cavern and so was, therefore, surprised by his encountering a dragonborn behind the low counter separating the small 'indoor' common area of the Lamb's Shank from the large kitchen.

The dragonborn was of a mottled green and black coloration with a long serpentine neck that placed their head above even Thorn's. While Thorn had seen dragonborn in his previous life as Duke Issul's envoy, it was mainly from afar and never one-on-one. With a quick assessment of Thorn's ragged clothing and still road-worn appearance, the dragonborn offered, "One King's Fare, I'm thinking?" The dragonborn's accent was thick but intelligible.

"I would appreciate it," Thorn replied, "But I don't know the custom here yet and would hate to short you of the coin."

"That's not the way it works here. No matter how many I serve, I get paid for a certain number of K.F.s, so it won't be any scales off my back." The dragonborn added, "By the looks of you, you are in sore need of some sustenance."

"Thank you, friend. I am Thorn." He extended his hand in greeting.

The dragonborn reached across the counter, grasping Thorn's hand. "I am Malkidan. Not many humans in Oldstone; most stay to the south in the Cloudvale Steppes, but you are welcome here, especially if you enjoy dragonborn cuisine. I'll hold off on the hottest of the spices for you this first time."

Thorn graciously took the meal Malkidan offered him, a hearty stew in an orange-yellow sauce that, if the dragonborn had spoken truly, just the smell told Thorn to be grateful for him holding back on the spices. Exiting, Thorn found a table outside that was unobtrusively placed against the outer wall of the Lamb's Shank. He had selected one of the few seating arrangements scaled for species other than dwarves, which served the dual purpose of comfort and begging off any companions as he felt self-conscious, having been reminded of his appearance.

The stew was delicious, but Thorn thanked the gods more than once for the tankards of stout dwarven ale that Malkidan kept bringing to his table. While supping, Thorn let his mind switch gears from the loftier existential thinking of earlier in the day to the more everyday matters: finding the baths, earning some coin, and getting some new clothes for his time here. All that would need to wait for tomorrow, though, because for the first time since fleeing Arnadore Keep and ridding himself of the Vermillion Blade, Thorn had the closest thing to a place he could call a home.

Within a few days of his arrival, he had settled into a routine. He was quite surprised by the dwarven versions of baths; with the abundance of falling water both in the Pillars and Sunhall, baths consisted of standing beneath a rushing torrent of water instead of submerging in a pool. Depending on the coin you wanted to spend and the luxury you desired, you could have the cascading water heated, smoothed, converted to tiny raindrops, or even jets of pressurized steam, though the steam option was mainly for dragonborn due to the scalding heat. Overall, Thorn found visiting the cascades, as the baths were called, more refreshing than traditional bathing, but once in a while still missed his long soaks in the heated pool beneath the Sojourn's Rest.

True to her word Margren found Thorn work enough to keep him busy and provide him enough coin for two new sets of clothes and other niceties. Thorn continued to visit the Lamb's Shank and even tried some of Malkidan's other dishes, but most often came back to the ever-spicier King's Fare, insisting he be allowed to pay for it when he was able. Thorn also began dining at the large common tables more centrally located outside the Lamb's Shank. They were a bit undersized for him, but they offered some company, and he found he was a welcome guest with several of the groups of dwarves that came for dragonborn cuisine once or twice a week.

Year 874 PXF ~ *Early Winter*

The arrival of Winter, even in all its harshness this high in the mountains, did little to impact the lives of Oldstone's citizens. The only real noticeable change was the ever-reducing hours of daylight in Sunhall and the occasional dwarf arriving at River Rock just in from the outdoors with ice still in their beard. Cold months are much the same anywhere regardless of the actual climate one has to experience, a time for hearty soups, dark ales, and tales told by hearth fire. As the nights grew longer and the moonlight seemingly brighter in Sunhall, more and more of the citizenry of Oldstone filled River Rock each night. Every square inch of the boulevards and patios on the banks of the Silvervein River sprouted braziers, seating areas, and tables for friends to gather together and share a story. The Lamb's Shank was no exception, and as a regular patron, Thorn somehow found himself nightly having a seat saved for him among the central tables on the patio. Thorn, being a newcomer to Oldstone and not being of dwarvenkind, was harried for tales of himself or the human lowlands. He spent weeks insisting he had no stories to tell, and if he had no escape from a particularly insistent group of tablemates, he shared only the news of the unrest that had occurred in Eleryon.

However, Thorn was fascinated to hear the tales of the dwarves. Their cultural stories and histories were far richer than what his tutors had taught, and they came alive when heard as told by the dwarves instead of being read in a history book or recited by rote. The dwarves' connections to this world, the primordial dragons, and the dragonborn were all mere footnotes in human histories of the world of Valknor, if included at all. Hearing them here in Oldstone, where that history actually happened, and being able to, within a few steps, lay hands on the places referenced in tales that were tens of thousands of years old gave Thorn a whole new perspective of the world. He discovered, for being so short-lived, that humans certainly had a way of twisting history to make it seem that it revolved around themselves and no one else.

Mid-winter was quickly approaching, which meant Richen's birthday was nearing as well, and while he had celebrated it every year, this would be the first time as Thorn. As he sat in the kitchen with a sweet muffin that was a standard of dwarven fare, it was strange to think that two years earlier, he had been sitting in the Sojourn's Rest contemplating his relationship with Osman. Now he had lost Osman as surely as he had lost Richen. The two loves of his life, while very different, were absent from his own existence.

What lay ahead for Thorn was a mystery, but those two foundations of Richen and Osman would guide his path wherever it may lead. Ironically, perhaps this Winter also marked Thorn's birth; while he may have been spat out of the spring and into this world months ago, it wasn't until recently that Thorn had actually begun to come alive as his own person. When he blew out the candle on the muffin, Thorn knew what must come next, and it was the season to do it properly.

Every culture views death in its own way, but on the continent of Rhymera, whether dreaded or welcomed, most people regarded the God of Death as the 'last friend' they would ever know. As such, people treated Death with deference to the many customs of hospitality that governed their cultures, even if done so ruefully. Those different customs created a tapestry of traditions that blended into the universal observance of Last Friend's Remembrance on the shortest day and longest night of each year. For the dwarves of Oldstone, it was the one time of the year the dwarves shrouded the multitude of apparatus and inventions which brought outside light into Sunhall Cavern, plunging it into darkness. No brazier, candle, or lantern was lit; instead, each resident carried a spherical vial of the luminescent water of the Silvervein River with them through the darkness. They gathered on every level of Sunhall and, in groups small and large, told the stories of those they lost to the Last Friend through the years.

On this Last Friend's Remembrance, Thorn, a globe of Silvervein water in hand that he collected from the tributary just outside his home, walked solemnly downriver out of the Pillars and into Sunhall. He found a seat waiting for him at the tables outside the Lamb's Shank, where Malkidan, Margren, and some other regulars he ate with were already seated, having somehow anticipated the coming moment; the time had come for him to lay Talon Cour-Vermane truly to rest.

"I am not here to tell the story of a hero, though there was a time some thought of him as such. Or the story of a traitor and oathbreaker as he came to be known as well. Just the story of a man I knew and who is now gone."

Thorn's voice faltered, not from loss, as many who were listening assumed, but from fear that speaking of Talon might conjure his return. At that moment, he finally realized he wanted to live as Thorn and never again as the person he had been. The self-assurance of his own right to live as himself and not an echo of Talon gave Thorn the confidence to continue.

He began by telling stories of the Crimson Sentinels and Falcon's Grasp, not as adventures he lived but as though they were stories of another person, recognizing now they indeed were. He left out details that only Talon would know, including all of the inner struggles with the Vermillion Blade but included everything a third-party observer would have seen or experienced. His stories of Talon were cheered and lauded in their times of triumph and met with shock and dismay as they approached their conclusion. Each tale was absorbed and respected by those around the table as they continued to spill out of Thorn through the night, and when dawn broke, and light returned to Sunhall, marking the end of the Night of Last Remembrance, mugs were raised to a life well lived, sending the fallen hero, or perhaps villain, Talon Cour-Vermane to peaceful rest.

CHAPTER TWENTY-EIGHT

Year 875 PXF ~ *Winter*

Thorn's stories reached one individual in particular. A young pewter dragonborn of just over two centuries named Nazge Berylston. Thorn had crossed paths with Nazge on a few occasions at the Lamb's Shank, but after Last Friends Remembrance, Nazge seemed by happenstance to be everywhere Thorn went. Whether in the Pillars or Sunhall or even the silent sanctuary of the Cavern of Echoes, Nazge was always close by. Knowing that his face and form were still easily tied to his past identity, and with the timing being so soon after his stories of Talon, Thorn decided to confront Nazge. Thorn had learned early in Talon's life, one should never underestimate the reach and resources of Toman Cour-Vermane.

Over his scant few months in Oldstone, Thorn had taken the time to investigate the Mist Market that Darvis had mentioned the first day. It didn't take much intuition or experience to recognize the district as a den of illicit activities. Located adjacent to the cacophony of the Silvervein River's plunge from hundreds of feet above into the Pillars' cavern, the constant roar made the Mist Market a perfect place for shadier individuals to conduct discrete negotiations without fear of eavesdroppers. In addition, since continuous rain from the falls bathed the district, as a courtesy, the Mist Market supplied all visitors with waterproof full-length hooded cloaks and ingenious portable awnings on sticks to keep their personal clothing dry. So not only could people be unheard in the Mist

Market, but they could also be unseen for all intents and purposes with the anonymity the cloaks and awnings provided. As with all such districts, the Mist Market needed to be home to legitimate businesses so that not all visitors would be automatically considered suspicious. Accordingly, the district was home to many fine purveyors of exotic wares, importers of rare and hard-to-get items, and Oldstone's most upscale gambling establishments and private drinking clubs.

One early evening, Thorn, with Nazge not so subtly tailing him - he was a pewter dragonborn in a city of dwarves, to be fair - lured Nazge deep into the pouring rain of the Mist Market. With little effort, Thorn, shrouded in a dragonborn-sized mistcloak, confounded Nazge in the narrow alleys and shopfronts. He then easily ambushed the dragonborn, slamming him against a wall under a downspout and yanking back his mistcloak's hood so the water would pour down his face. Finally, placing his sickle to Nazge's throat while still pinning him to the wall, Thorn snarled, "What do you want from me? Why do you haunt me like my shadow?"

"Peace, friend. Peace! I am an enchanter and artificer; my only interest is in the sickle you wield." his eyes darted down to the blade at his throat. He added, sputtering through the water pouring down his face, attempting to calm Thorn and reading his concern, "Dragonborn live many lives over their time walking this world; we think nothing of laying one to rest and picking up another." He narrowed his eyes. "What might seem strange or suspicious to those with such a brief time before meeting the Last Friend is but the change of the seasons to those descended from dragons."

Thorn pulled the metallic dragonborn out of the water flowing from the downspout. "What of my sickle?"

"May I?" Nazge requested to hold the sickle.

"How about with eyes first, and then we will see about hands," Thorn replied.

"As you wish. I suspect you know this, but the blade was not wrought by any craftsperson; it is god-touched. And while it looks like metal and," he pointed to his throat where the sickle remained, "certainly cuts like metal, I doubt that it is." Nazge continued, "It is not just the grip that is alive… you do know the grip is alive, right? The blade is as well, and in case you weren't aware, both are in need of some water and sunlight." He added with a draconian smile and overly familiar tone, "Perhaps we can get your weapon some sustenance and then some of that ale and bread you purchased this morn for ourselves?"

For some reason, the strange dragonborn put Thorn at ease. Whether it was his faltering reptilian smile or the black crest that furled and unfurled with his emotional state, he could not say, but he took his sickle from Nazge's neck. Then nonchalantly, acting like it was some regular practice, Thorn held the sickle under the downspout of water, having been chided for not caring for his unique weapon properly. However, Thorn was fooling no one. Nazge watched with a side-eye glance, and Thorn meeting his gaze, knew he had been caught. Both chuckled at the absurdity of the picture they must make. Then Thorn, with a smile, placed a hand on Nazge's shoulder and led them back out of the Mist Market to his nearby residence.

Thorn offered Nazge a towel upon their arrival to his abode to apologize for placing him under the downspout back at the market, but Nazge hardly needed it. His pewter scales had repelled most of the flow, letting whatever remained to fall away by the time they arrived. Once to his apartment, Thorn tapped the small keg of stout he had picked up that morning, laid out a few loaves of dark bread with sweet butter, and set them up at the tall wooden table nestled between the kitchen, great room, and balcony overlooking the Silvervein. Thorn took the time to examine Nazge's unique coloration as they settled in. While Thorn had still not met many dragonborn, he had yet to see one with scales like Nazge's. They had a brushed metal look instead of the bright mirror-like polish of all the others he had seen.

Nazge noticed his scrutiny and chimed in, "I have a unique heritage, bit of a mutt really. I have a great-grandmother on my mother's side who was carnelian gem-born, and my father was chrome-scaled. While not as flashy as some, I quite like it. You wouldn't believe how much time scale polishing takes."

Thorn couldn't help but smile, knowing firsthand how much time it had taken to maintain Talon's hair when he bothered. He absently reached for the missing mane of locks he had in his previous life finding only the short chopped remains from his decision when living in the woods of Eleryon.

Nazge's scales weren't the only thing that made him unique, he was taller and leaner in build than most dragonborn Thorn had seen of his size, and unlike Malkidan, his short wide neck almost blended into his broad bony shoulders. Nazge held himself with a bit of a slouch, but Thorn could empathize as when one interacted with folks of half your height most of the day, it was hard not to become permanently hunched in your stance.

Thorn found Nazge to be an excellent conversationalist who had knowledge of a vast array of topics and asked intelligent questions on the subjects Thorn was versed in and could easily discuss. The night slipped away, and both soon found themselves yawning and yearning for rest. As Thorn escorted Nazge to the door, he inquired, "Nazge, you obviously were able to discern much about my sickle, but can you tell me anything of my armor?"

Nazge replied, "First, only my fathers and mother call me Nazge. Call me Naz. Second, for the chainmail, not without the equipment in my lab. I didn't want to pry or impose by asking, but what you have there is not of this world."

"What?" Thorn asked, overwhelmed by the statement.

"It's not dangerous from what I can glean; in fact, it vouches for your character. You see, no one of evil intent could possess it, or so it seems. But with items such as it, crafted in places far from our own world, concepts such as good and evil might not even exist." A yawn interrupted Naz's thought, "I could talk another four hours on this, but instead, why not come by my workshop when you get a chance, and we can see what it's all about?"

Catching Naz's yawn and echoing it himself, Thorn said, "Sounds good, I have a job with Margren which has me tied up for the next few days, but I'll come by soon after. Where can I find it?"

"Inventors Grotto, most anyone can point the way. It's downstream from River Rock, two levels up." Naz recited as he headed down the stairs. "See you then!" Thorn's first job with Margren led to another and then another; it was almost a fortnight before Thorn spotting Naz at the Lamb's Shank, approached him, apologizing profusely, and promised to come by the following day.

Inventors Grotto, while still a part of Sunhall, was recessed back from the main thoroughfares and, unlike the rest of the cavern, was only three levels high, being tucked under an overhang of the main structures of Sunhall and hidden behind consecutive curtains of waterfalls. Hearing some of the alarming noises echoing in the grotto, Thorn correctly assumed the waterfalls were part of a system to protect the populace of Sunhall and perhaps even all of Oldstone from whatever activities and experiments were conducted here. With just a few inquiries, Thorn was pointed to Naz's workshop on the middle level of the Grotto in what seemed to be a prime location near what appeared to be a large semi-mechanical semi-arcane teleportation arch.

Like many of the workshops in the area, Naz's shop had an open front most barns would be envious of. Beyond the wide entrance was an open workspace large enough to fit three wagons side by side, and to one side of that, there were two smaller, fully enclosed rooms with a true rarity in Oldstone, glass windows looking out onto the workshop floor.

At first, Thorn could not find Naz and wondered if he had accidentally wandered into the wrong workshop, but then from behind what looked like a pile of brass plates and scrapped gears popped up Naz's familiar black head-crest and frills, followed by his wide draconian eyes. It struck Thorn that even how different humans looked from dragonborn, he could immediately register the excitement and kind welcome Naz had in his expression that Thorn had come to visit him in his workshop. So much so that he wondered if Naz had been equally disappointed when Thorn hadn't arrived when promised.

"Greetings, friend Thorn!" Naz exclaimed, standing up to his full height as he rubbed some type of grease or other arcane fluid off his hands onto his trousers. As Naz walked toward him, hand extended, Thorn watched as the stains that he had just smeared on the fabric of his pants disappeared as well as any remaining smudges on the tiny metallic scales of his hands. Naz shook Thorn's hand and pulled him in for a quick embrace keeping their hands still clasped between them. At first, he tensed up but then was glad for the casual, easy contact with someone, something he hadn't had since Osman's heartbreak over Cerena's leaving two Summers before.

"Don't mind the mess. I always have half a dozen projects going at once, and even on the ones that look finished, there is always more to do." Naz guided Thorn around another contraption with multiple mirrors and lenses, "careful of that one; it is one of the Sunhall raycatchers; they sometimes have a mind of their own." Naz then led the way to one of the doors to the smaller rooms with the glass-paned windows. Ushering Thorn inside, he closed the door behind them, an action that made Thorn's ears pop.

"Not to worry, just a precaution when delving into the secrets of unknown magics," Naz said nonchalantly. "I assume you have the armor shirt, so we can take a look at it?" Thorn handed the shirt over; it had been very strange for him not to don any type of armor that morning, as he had practically lived in armor for most of his adult life, but he also didn't want to have to undress here at Naz's shop.

Seeing Thorn's trepidation, Naz offered, "Oh, you don't have to worry about it getting damaged. It is far more likely that it will damage my equipment or shop or the whole district for that matter, with whatever it is that is making it tick." Naz added, deadly serious, "No, really."

Naz took the chainmail shirt and gently placed it on a round platen that he slid under a multi-armed crystal jointed apparatus that looked much like an inverted spider. He then began casting a series of sigils and runes with intricate hand motions and guttural words in a language Thorn did not comprehend. Springing to life, a shining sphere made of light and sparking arcana surrounded the spider-like apparatus holding the armor shirt.

Naz began to recite what he learned from the casting as he identified the armor's secrets. "Well, not unexpectedly, its power is divine in origin... and the metal is not any found on this world, at least that the dwarves know of, so highly unlikely it exists here on Valknor. It has the telltale signs of arcane translocation, which I have seen before with items coming from the Lyrian Gulf..." As Nazge spoke, he manipulated the arcane sphere around the apparatus, focusing it more acutely on the armor. "My question is: is it telling me the truth?"

Naz's concentration furrowed his brow, and the dark frill across his scalp began to fold back from the strain as he now seemed to be fighting the sphere of arcane energy. The armor lit up with silver light as a shrill noise suddenly built in the room around them. Nazge was so deep in concentration he either couldn't see or was blind to the glow around the chainmail shirt coalescing into an ethereal barbed dart. As the sound of the ritual crescendoed, Thorn dove forward, knocking Naz away from the machine. The spell broke just as the divine bolt Thorn had seen forming shot out of the armor to where Naz's head had been, ripping through the machine along its path.

Nazge and Thorn fell to the floor in the corner of the room, both looking wild-eyed up at the not-insubstantial glowing molten hole in the wall of the small lab above their heads. "Perhaps I cut that a little too close," Naz blithely commented as he pushed his taloned finger through a hole in his head-crest, "but it was enlightening. The armor is a relic of the Silver Scribe, not the deity as we know her, but a different aspect of her as she exists on another world." Nazge stroked the elongated obsidian-like scales on his chin. "Our Lady of the Scrolls is most known for her domain of knowledge and medicine; this other aspect's purview seems more akin to secrets and maintaining the vaults that lock away the things that mortals should never know." Naz added a bit nervously, "And I trod right upon that sacred space."

"Uh, do we need to be worried... or running right now?" Thorn asked a bit lightheartedly but also ready to spring out the door.

"No need. We would already be dead if it wanted us to be," Naz said flatly. "The other thing I confirmed is that this other aspect of the Silver Scribe does align themself with the forces of good, in fact, zealously so. Here, take a look."

Nazge got up and lent Thorn a hand as he rose to his feet as well. The dragonborn tossed some of the broken arms of his machine out of the way and retrieved the now benign-looking armor from the platen it occupied within the array. Spreading the shirt out on the workbench, Thorn noticed it was now closer to the smaller size it had been when he found it under the forge and, with its longer drape, would probably fit Nazge.

Naz went to a cabinet, retrieved a deeply runed lead box, and placed it next to the mail shirt. Grabbing a pair of tongs, he opened the small chest, revealing half a dozen dark coins. "These are from the Nine Hells, utterly evil in every possible way." Pulling out a coin with the tongs, he then dropped it onto the chainmail, or more correctly, tried to. "Ok, wow." Naz exclaimed as the coin completely disintegrated into a fine mist before ever touching the links of the armor. "I was thinking at best the coin would glow like in a furnace, perhaps melt a little... hum, interesting." Naz began to reach into the chest for another coin, but Thorn grabbed his hand.

"Perhaps we shouldn't play games with the relic of a divine entity we don't fully understand, and that could evaporate us as easily as that coin, yeah?" Thorn commented pointedly.

"You make a good point," Nazge conceded, "but now we do know neither one of us is evil, apparently. So where did you say you got this again?"

"I didn't," Thorn replied with a firm finality to that line of questioning in his tone.

"Ah, got it." Changing subjects, Naz asked, placing a hand on Thorn's shoulder, "So do you want a job? The work is good, and I will give you a percentage of commissions you assist on plus a weekly rate. It is better than hauling furniture and harvesting cave lichen, I would suspect."

"Regular work would be a boon, but I have just the barest amount of magical skill, and it is shamanistic in nature," Thorn confessed.

"That's the point! You can be my apprentice. I'll teach you!" Naz replied with his fanged draconic grin.

Thorn almost said no, but why not? He had been a leader and trainer for decades; why not learn something new and be the student once again? "When do I start?" Thorn asked.

"Right now. Grab this, and I will show you where the to-be-repaired pile is." Naz indicated the broken spider-like machine. Nazge led Talon out of the small lab and into the main workspace. At the far side of the large room, he pointed to a wall of shelves containing at least three dozen machines and constructs in various states of disrepair. "As I said, I need the help."

CHAPTER TWENTY-NINE

Year 875 PXF *~ Spring*

Winter dragged on as it will in the mountains, well past when Spring would have unfurled in the lowlands of Eleryon. Even so, Thorn found having a routine immensely satisfying. Every morning having somewhere to be and a schedule to follow finally gave him something to which he could moor this new life. Also, having a co-worker and mentor relying on him and expecting him each day broke Thorn out of his swirling introspection, and he began to think of more than just his own needs.

Thorn proved to be 'not terrible' at the arcane. He would never reach anything like Nazge's skill, but between the little bits he had learned from Rahmed, and what Naz was teaching him, he at least felt helpful. He learned to shape metal and even manipulate the size of components so they were easier to work on. A steady stream of conversation filled Naz's lab as they worked, ranging from the mundane to the magical and, eventually, the personal. Thorn could not help but be reminded of the easy and constant conversation that filled the smithy between Mikal and Richen. It made him smile to think that he now had that kind of relationship with Naz.

Eventually, as Winter in the mountains turned to Spring, even though to Thorn it should be approaching Summer, he realized it was time to tell Nazge all the details of his two lives, past and present. Not only because he longed to have a confidant in this new life but also to learn more of the Vermillion Blade, and Naz knew more of enchanted armaments than anyone he had met. One evening at his apartment, he told Naz everything over a mini-keg of stout and dark loaves of bread with creamed mushroom cheese. Naz took it all in but, other than his support and empathy, had nothing immediate to offer regarding the Vermillion Blade. His draconic features wore a strange inquisitive look but, for whatever reason, he held his tongue instead of speaking.

Year 875 PXF ~ Early Summer

As the months wore on, Thorn began to feel restless under the mountains of Lymehold. A trek to the main gates of Oldstone became a daily ritual to see if the snow here in the high peaks had finally melted and the passes through the mountains cleared for unencumbered travel. He anxiously felt as though Summer must surely already be half over, the calendar telling him it was well after planting season in the lowlands of Eleryon. Feeling more sure of his identity and himself as a person, Thorn resolved to tell Nazge he was going to leave Oldstone and return to the lowlands. To what end, he wasn't sure, but something was drawing him back toward the region of his birth, and he felt he needed to follow it. Thorn picked the day after Hearth's Rest to break the news to Nazge, but when he approached his mentor, Naz jumped into conversation first.

"May I be intrusive for a moment or two?" Naz asked almost coyly. "I have been thinking on your tale of your past life, and something I have noticed."

Never knowing Nazge to be shy about most any subject, Thorn was intrigued but also concerned. "Yes, I suppose."

"Your hands are healing." He paused for emphasis. "You told me those burns came from the fires of a powerful cursed weapon, the Vermillion Blade, correct?" As Thorn nodded, Nazge continued looking deep into

Thorn's eyes with probing concern. "Cursed wounds like that don't heal. It just doesn't happen. Ever. Not in my experience or study. Not without the help of magics or miracles more powerful than I know and I would wager more powerful than most in the city know." He continued, "Even the divine energy of your sickle and chainmail combined would not have the power to manifest such a feat passively."

Thorn looked down at his hands. He had realized they were more functional than when he lived in the forest and indeed even more so now than when he first arrived in Oldstone, but he hadn't registered the scar tissue had been slowly receding until this moment. His fingertips were now almost devoid of any evidence of their horrific burns. Nazge, seemingly embarrassed at asking the question, inquired, "May I read you? Take a deep look at whatever energies are manifesting in you?"

Over the last half-year, Thorn had hoped and felt that supernatural and magical forces were no longer shackled to him personally. The mention of 'manifesting energies' inside him made him want to run and flee from even the question of it. However, fear trapped Thorn in place. The familiar feeling of panic overwhelmed him. His breath came too quickly, his chest tightened, and his sight was forced into narrow, claustrophobic tunnels in front of him. From the moment he was thrown from Caspharian's spring, Thorn had felt the influence of the Vermillion Blade but could not track its presence. But what else could it be that still had a physical hold on him? Was the Blade or perhaps Toman still trying to transform him into a weapon for their purpose?

Thorn saw that Nazge could see his distress but also that the dragonborn did not know how to help him as the panic kept rising and started to choke off his air.

"Thorn, may I use magic to calm you? I don't know how else to help." Naz asked, beginning to panic himself. Thorn couldn't speak and, hanging on the edge of consciousness, could only give a weak nod of consent.

Thorn felt the wave of calming energy flow over him, his breath easing and sight returning to normal. He knew it was an arcane suppression of his panic but was thankful for it nonetheless. Clearer of mind, Thorn was able to contemplate the question Naz had asked. If he could face the answers it might give. He still almost said no. However, the secrets of his bloodline had cursed his previous life, and he wasn't ready to risk another to its influence, so he relented to the request.

Nazge brought Thorn into the lab opposite the one where they analyzed his armor; a series of complex runes and sigils formed concentric circles on the floor and walls, covering almost every surface. Nazge placed two plain wooden chairs facing each other in the center of the arcane etchings motioning for Thorn to sit in the one further from the door. He then exited and returned with two palm-sized intricately etched crystals, placing one in each of Thorn's hands. An irrational panic began to rise again. Even though he saw the other chair in front of him, he feared he would have to go through whatever was about to happen alone.

"Don't worry, I'll be with you the whole time," Naz assured him as he sat in the opposite chair. He then took Thorn's hands and began to mutter a long incantation bolstered by the runes and crystals. Even Thorn's limited training told him this ritual was far beyond the spells Naz had used to read the armor in the other lab. Around Thorn, the runes on the walls and floor began to glow and rotate in their circular paths, and a brilliant white light began to shine from between his and Nazge's fingers.

When Nazge looked up, his eyes shined like pools of liquid mercury with glowing runes spinning within them as he peered into Thorn's gaze. Thorn could see the twitching of Nazge's scales and the rapid rotation of his mirror-like eyes as he read whatever was etched onto his soul. Finally, Naz shuddered, then gently withdrew his hands from Thorn's, taking the crystals with them as the sheen on his eyes faded. Setting the crystals aside, Nazge then took Thorn's right hand in one of his and placed his other hand over it, and in a tone Thorn knew from Balanon's training long ago,

Nazge delivered the news. "You are still cursed." The words fell on Thorn like a sledge, but the worst wasn't over. Nazge continued, "It's like nothing I have ever seen. Ancient and degraded, but somehow twisted and remade. It writhes like an eel caught in a net, not wanting to be discovered but longing to be seen. The curse is alive."

Nazge's words mortified Thorn as the idea of a living curse twisting inside him settled in. Nazge continued somberly, answering Thorn's unspoken question. "I do not know what it is doing to you or what it has done already. I dare not break it or probe further, as it has found a tenuous balance within you. All I can tell you is that it is neither good nor evil in nature, but at the same time, it is also both." Nazge squeezed his friend's hand comfortingly. "As I said, balance."

How Thorn got back to his apartment in the Pillars, he did not know. Naz must have guided him there and brought him to his bedroom. Thorn sat on the edge of his bed, his shoes somehow off, and a soft tunic had replaced his work jerkin and chainmail shirt. He saw and heard Naz as he stood at the bedroom door. He said sternly, "I *will* check on you tomorrow. I'll bring fresh sourdough and creamed mushroom cheese for breakfast by the time Sunhall begins to wake."

Thorn sat on his perfectly normal bed that he had freshly made that morning, surrounded by the rippling light of the Silvervein that always filled his apartment, yet he felt like he was plummeting in a freefall. His stomach was in his throat, and the world was sliding past him in a dizzying blur. His morning had started with plans to travel back to the lowlands and a notion of even checking in on Arnadore, but now that all had evaporated.

Cursed. *Still? Again?* Thorn couldn't even keep track. Was he becoming that horror from the Vermillion Blade's vision or some other foul nightmare of its creation? Thorn looked at his now unscarred fingertips, and while they seemed a blessing, he couldn't be sure of anything anymore.

Would he forever be a danger to all those he knew or would ever know? Thorn looked at the chainmail shirt and thought of the coin he had seen it destroy. Ripping off the tunic Naz had put him in, he donned the armor and let it lay against his bare skin. In that moment, Thorn couldn't have said if he was looking for assurance of the good within himself or the release that was demonstrated on the coin. Standing in his bedroom whole and unburnt by the armor, Thorn sighed. *What should I do?*

Dark thoughts whirled around in his mind, but the one that stuck with him was Castian's words from the previous Autumn: "Find a deep enough place in the mines, and the human world need not see you ever again." Thorn considered packing and heading to the Frostforge Depths on his own or purposefully losing at the dice halls in the Mist Market so the Frostbeards would indenture him, but he knew Nazge would find him or pay his debts to have him released. Not to mention to cross the Frostbeard clan was its own form of curse. So, still wearing the armor, he sat back down on his bed and waited for Nazge's arrival the following day.

Thorn had eventually laid down, curling into as near a fetal position as a man of his size could form. He had already been awake for hours when he heard Naz come in and start puttering around in the kitchen. As Thorn lay in his bed, the oversized dragonborn furniture his eyes fell upon seemed much larger than they really were, and he felt so much smaller. Talon had years of life before facing the trials of the Vermillion Blade and his bloodline, but Thorn felt like little more than a child. How could Thorn survive this? Would he have to fade away to allow Talon to return to solve the problems that now burdened Thorn? If that happened, could Thorn, as he was now, ever return?

With a sigh filled with the exhaustion of his thoughts, Thorn reluctantly sat up and forced himself out of bed. Stepping into the great room, he saw Naz had tidied up and set out the food he had promised, luring Thorn to the table. They sat mostly in silence, Nazge being a quiet comforting presence instead of trying to fill the space with one-sided conversation. As he packed up to leave, he promised, "I'll be by tonight with stout and the King's Fare from the Lamb's Shank." Thorn almost asked Naz to stay but then realized he was going into the workshop and couldn't add the guilt of keeping Nazge from his job to everything else, including that there was no way Thorn could join him.

So it went for nearly a week, Naz stopping by twice a day with sustenance and company as Thorn's mind processed his fate. Then, finally, the depression broke with the arrival of a branch of high-mountain apple blossoms carried in by Nazge one morning as he brought breakfast. The smell filled Thorn's small residence and transported him to the Autumn long ago, lounging in the limbs of Milgran's Orchard with Richen; a twenty-two-year-old memory from a person who no longer existed. That an aging yet somehow new person such as Thorn could still be moved by such was both ridiculous and silly, but sometimes that is what hope takes: the impossible folly of faith.

After eating, when Naz usually tidied up before heading out, Thorn got off his stool at the high table in the kitchen and said, "Let me grab some clean clothes. I need to stop by the cascades, but I will meet you at the shops."

With a relieved smile he could not hide, Naz replied as offhandedly as he could, "I could use a steam myself. Mind if I join you?" Then, without any undue fuss or concern for perceived fragility, Naz and Thorn fell back into their routine. The only change was Thorn's voracious focus on learning about the enchantment of objects and armaments.

CHAPTER THIRTY

Nazge was an excellent teacher and Thorn a gifted student, but the ways of enchanting are arduous and time-consuming. Over the following five years, Thorn had advanced from being merely an assistant in Nazge's work to having laid enchantments of his own as a final test to graduate from apprentice to a journeyman. When Naz had asked what Thorn wanted to enchant as his test, Thorn knew it must be the ball-peen hammer that Richen had made for his apprenticeship trial that he now carried as Mikal had before him. So Thorn had laid upon the hammer spells befitting its function, a way to heat metal without the need of a forge and a force magnifier to give its light weight the same striking impact of a larger sledgehammer when required.

Nazge presented the hammer to the guild council for assessment, and when their certification came, Naz declared a celebration was in order. Thorn invited Naz over to his apartments, which over the intervening half-decade had become more personalized to the style and taste of a cosmopolitan artificer living in Oldstone than the refugee from the lowlands who first had moved in. Thorn had on occasion considered returning to Eleryon, but the fear of the curse residing within him escaping and whatever its ultimate effects might be, held him close to the resources and protections Oldstone and Naz could offer.

As it was close to midsummer Thorn added to the celebration of his journeyman status an acknowledgment of the end of his forty-second year of being alive. However, he placed only five candles on the cake in recognition of Thorn's life, not the cumulated time of this life and the previous one. Over the candlelight, Naz stared a bit too long into Thorn's face, and Thorn gave him an acknowledging nod in return, knowing the question he must be about to ask.

Thorn had begun to notice it a few months after Naz had discovered the curse. At first, it was just little things, like that as his hair was growing back out, the strands of gray that had been apparent since he had first become Knight Captain were no longer there. Then, six months after that, by the time his hands had healed to the knuckles, Thorn, in a spate of contemplation while staring into the mirror, noticed the crow's feet around his eyes seemed less prominent. He had deluded himself that perhaps it was due to the diffuse light in Oldstone instead of living under the unfiltered bright sun. Eighteen months after that, as he stood shirtless in front of the mirror, the weight and muscle mass he had lost was undeniable. Thorn had not become soft; his physique still conveyed strength, but not in the overwhelming way Talon's had. He attributed that to his focus on his apprenticeship and his more leisurely lifestyle under the mountains with no daily training. With some satisfaction, Thorn realized one of the things that would make him undeniably Talon back in human lands was fading. But now, five years on, looking over the birthday cake at Naz, he could not deny what was occurring.

Thorn answered the unasked question in Naz's eyes, "I know. This is not the face of a human five years older than the day we met. I will assure you it is my face, though, or I should say, his. This is how Talon looked when he was first assigned as envoy for Duke Issul. His form was much bulkier, carrying nearly thirty more pounds of muscle, but this was indeed his face as I remember it."

Nazge sighed with concern, "I couldn't be sure. To my eyes, humans seem to decay as quickly as Summer fruit left forgotten in a cupboard, but I didn't think my eyes were deceiving me so badly as not to recognize the lack of change in my closest friend."

As Thorn blew out the five flickering candles, an uneasy silence followed as they both knew the root of what was happening and where it might lead.

The truth now spoken about the curse affecting him more than just by healing his hands, Thorn began training again. At first, he started with just Caspharian's sickle but having trained and battled for so many years with a glaive, he quickly realized, like Osman, he would need an offhand weapon. Having nothing else readily available, Thorn began using the ball-peen hammer he had enchanted as a training stand-in for whatever weapon he decided to replace it with later. He knew he could not hide in Oldstone or even all of Lymehold forever; he would eventually have to face his demons again.

Year 880 PXF *~ Autumn*

The snows of coming Winter had already begun to fall outside the gates of Oldstone when three young dwarves, all with glacial-blue hair and beards, dumped the large ice-covered contraption on the doorstep of Naz's workshop.

"Where's the dragonborn?" the shortest of the motley group demanded. "Drovan said there would be a dragonborn here," he added aggressively.

Thorn replied, "Nazge is delivering some raycatchers to the upper ingresses; I am his partner. How can I help?" Thorn had almost said apprentice but caught himself, remembering his new rank and was sorely glad he did so with this crew, who were obviously from the Frostbeard clan.

"Tell the lizard the boss wants this fixed." The short Frostbeard kicked the machine as he spoke and then stalked away. Thorn bristled at the slur they had thrown but knew better than to stir up trouble for himself and Naz by drawing the ire of the notorious mining clan. Thorn dragged the icicle and frost-covered machine into the workshop. He sliced his hand on the sharp crystals in the process, and the melting behemoth left a trail of snowmelt across the floor for him to mop up. Thorn wrapped his hand to keep from tracking blood around but knew by morning the cut would be hardly more than a memory due to the mysterious workings of the curse churning within him.

Nazge returned a few hours later, right before closing time, and, seeing the twisted machine dripping water all over the floor as the ice melted, let out a disgusted grunt. "Ugh, Drovan's kin drop that off?" He walked to one of the smaller worktables where Thorn was cleaning and re-etching runes into a large heating plate for a tavern's stove.

"Yeah, while you were out. Not a very friendly bunch. I assume it is a rotary miner from down in the Frostforge Depths, but hard to tell with the damage and ice." Thorn replied over his shoulder, eyes and concentration still on his work. He added, "Be a couple of days before it fully thaws, I suspect. I placed some totems I learned from my time in the desert around it that draw moisture to help with the mess."

"We'll take a look at it after Hearth's Rest then." Nazge affirmed and asked, "You have any plans?"

Thorn spun around on his stool, having come to a stopping point for the day. Standing up he replied, "I was hoping you had something we could do. Maybe hit Cascadia and the canals of the Cloudvale Steppes?" Thorn suggested.

"Now that could be fun. You know they celebrate the Night of the Drowned Moon for a whole fortnight there, and they observe Hearth's

Rest as a time of opening your hearth to others and hospitality, so…" Naz's frills widened and flexed in anticipation of home-cooked cuisine on the canals of Cascadia. Grabbing his belongings to head out he added, "I'll book the transit gate, so we don't have to use the public teleportation circle, and I've got a couple of returning stones charged, I think? Oh, and we will need masks. It is all about masks in Cascadia for Drowned Moon."

Smiling ear to ear, Thorn said, "I'll take care of masks; I know a thing or two about costumes."

As they left Naz's shop, neither one could see the melting ice slowly, drop by drop, depositing Thorn's blood on the machine's metal. After the first drop, the thawing metal seemed to hungrily await more and greedily absorbed each subsequent drop into its framework.

Naz and Thorn entered the workshop the morning after Hearth's Rest, laughing and reliving tales from their Drowned Moon jaunt to Lymehold's Cloudvale Steppes region and its lively central city of Cascadia. Singing along at tables over hand-crafted ales bled into remembrances of tasting samples of residents' culinary delights served from outdoor kitchens attached to their homes. Side by side, nudging each other with their shoulders at particularly embarrassing or outlandish memories, they were all smiles until the looming hulk of the Frostbeard mining apparatus reminded them of the task ahead.

The machine was a monstrosity of intermeshing mining gears and augers meant to break through the magically frozen stone of the Frostforge Depths. The mining head sat upon four spider-like legs with serrated tips to pierce and hold tightly within the icy ground of the Frostbeard's mines far below. The arachnid feel of the contraption was completed by the dual-purpose counterweight and ore bin that hung off the back like some bloated abdomen. Even from across the room, the two artificers could tell the augers and gears were racked and off their axes, while the damage to the legs appeared to be more from blunt force, most likely from being kicked and beaten with mining tools by its owners after it failed.

With a simultaneous sigh echoing Naz's, Thorn offered, "I'll dispel the power out of its runes and get the casing off while you make the coffee. Double strong, double hot," Thorn called to the retreating form of Nazge. The pewter dragonborn lifted his arm in acknowledgment, his frills still drooping to one side in his pre-coffee morning state. Thorn set to work on the rotary driller by first dispelling all the magic from the sigils that powered it. Overall, it was a mess. The anti-corrosion runes had long ago been damaged or had worn off, so all the fasteners between the outer shell plates were fused in place with rust. When rust wasn't the problem, the beating it had been given by the Frostbeards when it failed proved to be. The precision plates which had been aligned when new were now twisted and warped, no longer unlocking from each other as intended. As often as not, Thorn was forced to damage them even more to give himself and Nazge access to work on the axles of the mining head.

Nazge returned with the coffee, which he had spiked in the dragonborn style with Bronzepyre root. Handing Thorn a mug of the near-boiling dark liquid with a coppery sheen floating on the surface, he noted, "Always the same. Not a frill of maintenance, and they wonder why it broke." Naz walked around to the front of the machine, squatting down to get a better look at just how bad the augers were off-angle.

As Thorn finally wrested the last panel off the drill head, exposing the last axles and back side of the gears, he could immediately see the problem: a black rock a bit larger than his fist had jammed itself between the gears bending their axles. He started to reach in to retrieve it, but as he did so, a memory from Talon's life screamed in alarm. It wasn't a stone but a petrified obsidian heart: a demon heart. Before Thorn could even make a sound, the right front leg lifted off the ground.

Skthunk!

With the sickening wetness of a knife plunging into a ripe melon, the machine's razor-sharp serrated leg thrust through Nazge's thigh, emerging out the other side and sinking into the polished rock floor of the workshop. Nazge tried to scramble away from the machine as it came alive, tendrils of demonic essence now flowing out of its every joint, but the machine's leg pinned him to the ground through his own. The automaton then lurched sideways. It slammed into Thorn, throwing him off his feet and causing him to skid across the smooth floor. Thorn watched in horror as the rotary driller stood up on its three remaining legs lifting Naz into the air with the fourth and drawing him close to the now wildly spinning augers and gears.

Nazge thrashed like a fish on a hook, but the durability of his own scales and the barbed serrations of the machine's leg held him trapped. Seeing Naz held aloft by the demonic being inhabiting the mining rig, Thorn was momentarily frozen by the similarities to how Richen looked when the hellhound shook him in its jaws decades earlier. Talon's voice screamed in his head, breaking him out of his paralysis. *Not again!* Thorn dove forward, thanking the gods again for Lochlan instilling in him the need always to have his weapon at hand and sliced through the already damaged spider-like leg of the machine at its joint. Naz and the portion of the machine's leg still embedded in his own fell to the ground with a clang.

"Pull it through the other way, like you do with an arrow!" Thorn shouted at Naz as he drew the demon driller's focus.

"What?!" Staring in shock at his skewered leg, Nazge panickedly yelled back, "I've never been shot with an arrow! I've never even been in a fight!"

The possessed rotary drill lunged toward Thorn on its three legs, hitting him with one of its augers which ripped through his jerkin. His chain shirt stopped the pointed edge, but Thorn saw the automaton seem to wince backward as it made contact with the divine armor's links. Naz, either not having the stomach to pull the bladed leg through his own or thinking he had a better plan, began to cast a spell.

"Naz! No!" Thorn cried, recognizing what Nazge was casting, and from his experience as Talon knew of demons' unique abilities regarding magic. It was too late. Naz reached out and touched the back leg of the machine, and as the arcane energy flowed into it, Thorn readied himself for the opportunity he knew was about to come. They were going to need a new plan.

The silvery arcane energy of Naz's casting flowed over the arachnid-like form of the possessed rotary driller and became corrupted by its fiendish power. The spell meant to reduce its size to a more manageable scale began to enlarge it instead. Thorn seized the moment as the automaton grew larger to dive under its legs, grab Nazge, and drag him into one of the windowed labs sealed with wards slamming the door behind them.

"I- I- I- I, I was trying to help." Naz stuttered, trying to explain.

"It's okay. It's okay. You didn't know. Demons like that one warp magic to their benefit," Thorn tried to explain while at the same time calming his mentor. He reached into one of the cabinets and pulled out a healing potion that Naz kept on hand for emergencies.

"Get ready to drink this once I pull that out." Thorn handed the potion to Naz and grabbed the machine's serrated leg. "On three. One-" Thorn didn't even wait until two to yank the leg the rest of the way through his friend's thigh. The dragonborn hissed in pain and then downed the potion, which, while not healing the wound fully, got it into much better shape than it had been in. "Okay, we need a plan."

A loud crash came from the now huge drilling machine as it tore apart the workshop making its way toward the lab Thorn and Naz were sheltering in. Its new size confounded it momentarily, but that wouldn't last for long. Thorn began to remove his jerkin. "I know the spellbook, but any chance you've got a trick to make a divine chainmail be affected by a spell?"

"What? No. That is crazy and impossible," Naz scoffed as he pursed his scaly dragonborn lips. "You know better than that," He chided, always the teacher.

"Well, then we have to get really crazy. I need you to make me bigger." Seeing Naz shaking his head and about to say all the reasons why that was an even worse idea, Thorn pressed on. "The shirt will size itself to whoever it is bound to, and we need it big enough to throw over that thing." He motioned through the window with his head to the possessed machine, now slamming its full weight into the door protecting them. "I know the risks. You told me all the horror stories of people trying to change the scale of living things. But if the curse could heal my hands, it can certainly heal the damage from a simple spell – eventually at least, and there is one potion left just in case. I just have to time things to throw the shirt before the spell incapacitates me so it can destroy the demon like it did the evil coin."

Naz was about to object when through the window, they saw the demon-possessed driller turn away from them, hearing the noises outside the workshop coming from Inventors Grotto. It turned and started to walk toward the opening leading to the causeway. "This is crazy. You could die." Naz stated matter-of-factly.

"If we don't stop that thing right now and all the artificers start throwing magic at it, *lots* of people *will* die." Thorn didn't hesitate any longer. Now with bare torso and chainmail shirt in hand, he stepped out of the lab. He looked over his shoulder at his best friend and mentor, "Hit me, Naz! Do it! Have that potion ready in case I pass out." Thorn braced himself as he looked Naz in the eyes. "I trust you, *brother.*"

Naz looked to the machine headed toward the door and then to Thorn with his analytical arcane eyes comparing the scale of the two. "I'm sorry, it is going to take a double cast. Brace yourself." Both of Naz's hands pressed into Thorn's back, and magical energy flowed into him.

"ARGH!" Thorn tried to hold back the cry of pain as the world began to shrink around him. He felt the bones in his legs begin to crack under the strain of his increasing weight, and the world started to go fuzzy as his eyes' focal length started to warp. Knowing he only had fractions of a moment before the spell fully resolved and his body's new size would tear itself apart, he threw the chainmail shirt like a fishing net. As he continued to grow, his connection to the armor kept its expansion a mirror to his own increasing scale.

The spell's effects proceeded on their merciless course. Thorn's tendons ruptured and tore off their bones, having exceeded nature's intent for their maximum size. His muscles burst, their volume increasing far more than their organic structure's ability to contain the expanding fibers. Thorn's now massive form crumpled to the ground. Thorn felt his heart begin to falter in its labor to pump blood through his still-expanding form. As his head hit the stone floor of the workshop, his eyes could barely make out the massive shape of his shining armor as it draped over the demon-possessed mining machine. The armor-turned-net disintegrated the demon-inhabited construct in a bright golden flash of divine power. The pain that had wracked Thorn's body had turned to numbness as his nervous system became overloaded with the agony of his body's scale destroying itself. The last thing Thorn saw before passing out as he lay on his side on the workshop floor was Nazge coming into focus as he ran toward him, barely taller than his shoulders were wide at his gigantic size. Then there was nothing but darkness.

CHAPTER THIRTY-ONE

Thorn woke up in his bed back at his apartment to the smell of simmering dragonborn spices wafting to him from the kitchen. His body ached, but he could at least feel all of it, and it seemed whole from what he could tell. As he started to stir and sit up in bed, Naz came through the open door of his bedroom.

"Take it slow. It has been a couple of days," Naz informed Thorn. "I have been feeding you potions, but the curse has done the majority of the work. It has been remarkable to witness." He continued, "With the stigma around what we did and the damage it causes so recognizable, I dared not call a cleric once I saw you were stable."

Thorn, still sitting on the edge of the bed, began checking the functionality of each limb and joint as he reassured Naz, "You did the right thing. The spell and the curse's influence would have been undeniable, either in the moment or as I healed in ways beyond anything but extraordinary magics." Other than some range of movement issues, his upper limbs seemed to be doing alright. However, upon standing, he realized his knees were not functioning fully, and his balance was entirely off-kilter. Naz rushed over to help him, putting Thorn's arm over his shoulders. Then, in a half-limp, half-stagger, they moved to the kitchen, where Naz helped Thorn into one of the higher bar chairs and helped him prop up his legs to support them.

"My research says you will have to rehabilitate your walking. Unfortunately, your legs got the worst of it. They looked like they had been crushed under a landslide." Naz paused, head lowered and nictitating membranes closed over his eyes in shame, "Thorn, I am so sorry." Genuinely dismayed, he added, "You trusted me, and my spell ripped you apart."

"Naz, there is no one in this life I trust more, and I knew exactly what the spell would do and in whose hands I was placing my survival." Thorn looked into Naz's draconic eyes. "I called you brother, and I meant it. You are the first piece of family I—" Thorn patted his hand on his heart twice, "*this* me, Thorn, has." Emotion caught in his throat as he said the words aloud.

"Brother." Nazge seemed to taste the word. "Dragonborn have clutch siblings, which is more a statement of generation than emotional connection." Naz tried the title again, "Brother. I think it would be nice to have a brother." Naz's frills stood proud, reflecting his happiness and satisfaction. He continued, "So *brother*, I am wondering, would it be too much to ask you to teach me to defend myself? I can't help thinking had I known what to do in the fight, all of this could have been avoided."

"Well, I'll need to be able to walk first, but yes, I would be more than happy to," Thorn glanced at the stove and the large pot simmering there, "but can we eat whatever that is you are cooking in the meantime?"

Naz smiled. "I'll break out the lichen milk. You're going to need it."

Thorn was back on his feet and stable enough to navigate around Oldstone independently less than a week later, although at a measured pace. By the next Hearth's Rest, he began the process of training Naz in the art of combat. Naz wasn't exaggerating that he had never been in a fight, so the correct weapon choice for him became vital. After trying multiple options with comical and sometimes disastrous results, Nazge, in a stroke of inspiration, suggested creating a whip from one of the telekinetic ropes they used in the shop. After some modifications to the length and enchantments on one of the lengths of magical twine, Naz crafted a sixteen-foot whip that responded not only to his physical manipulation but also to his mental commands.

Training Naz proved the perfect thing for Thorn as well. He quickly discovered he had lost much of his flexibility and coordination as an aftereffect of the enlargement spell, and as such, it paced his and Naz's exercises to a level where they were on equal footing. Thorn immensely enjoyed training as equals instead of the unbending rigor and demanding style of Lochlan that Talon had experienced and used to train Osman. They were brothers walking the same path together, side-by-side, instead of an expert pushing and driving the beginner.

Year 881 PXF *~ Early Summer*

While Blossom Festival occurred in Spring in the lowlands, Thorn and Naz had taken to celebrating it in early Summer here in the Lymehold peaks when the high-mountain apple trees came into bloom. They sat in one of the dwarven wild meadows deep in a protected valley where the trees flourished independently without the tending required in the lowland orchards. Opening their Blossom Feast basket, Naz let out a groan. "Seriously, brother? Lamb's Shank King's Fare again?"

With a playful punch to Naz's now meatier shoulder from nearly a year of training, Thorn shot back, "Hey, not my fault. You were the one who lost at training last night, and 'the dead don't get to pick Hearth's Rest provisions,'" Thorn stated playfully with a wicked grin from ear to ear.

Naz laughed and added, "I think you are the only person who eats this. You know there are much better dragonborn meal halls and cuisine than Malkidan's King's Fare, right?"

"Oh, I know, but sometimes you just want comfort food. No matter how it tastes, it is the memory you crave," Thorn mused.

"But you crave this three to four times a week!" Naz lamented.

"I guess you shouldn't lose so much in training," Thorn said lightheartedly. Naz opened his jaws, pretending like he was going to breathe lightning at Thorn, who immediately surrendered, "Whoa, whoa, whoa... that's cheating. We've talked about this."

The taller dragonborn took the opportunity presented by the distraction of using his lightning breath to grab Thorn's head and give him a noogie through his human brother's wild locks of hair. He rolled his eyes and suffered the humiliation. Thorn reminded himself how much he regretted teaching the dragonborn about noogies by doing the same to Naz and his frills, only to find out just how much his scales were like a cheese grater on his knuckles. Ever since it had become Naz's most often form of physical affection, and if he admitted it, the silly brotherly hazing always gave him a smile.

In actuality, Naz had become quite adept in his training and, with Thorn drawing upon his past life's knowledge, had created a unique fighting style with his whip. The enchanted whip could not only be used traditionally, but with its magical properties and Naz's concentration, it could also double over on itself and become as rigid as a quarterstaff for close-quarters fighting. Thorn could honestly say he had never encountered something quite as versatile. Paired with the dragonborn's lightning breath and leaping ability, Nazge won as often as not in their sparring, leaving Thorn the 'dead' brother left to Nazge's dining whims for the night.

In addition to their training, they had also begun a new project. Naz, able to find inspiration anywhere, had contemplated how the demon had co-opted the rotary mining construct as its body. It had been able to manipulate it as though it were its own flesh, even though all the runes and sigils etching every surface had been nullified. He pondered if he could create an internal rune and enchantment-based core that articulated clockwork joints and actuators without the need for the hundreds upon hundreds of laborious surface etchings they now utilized for the same.

It was an undertaking unlike any Naz had ever tried. Due to the precision and arcane balance needed to create a stable core of such impermeable powerful runes, he enlisted Thorn to help. Much like their training had been a partnership, this new feat of artifice was as well. Naz had two centuries of experience, but this was new territory, so experiments were collaborations in design, execution, and safety.

The two alternated their evenings between training and magic. Each shared their own expertise and learned from the other's, growing their skills together as a team, pushing each other to new places they could not have reached alone. It forged a bond unlike any Thorn had experienced in his previous life as Talon. While Osman had been a little brother and Talon his Krolh'dran, Naz was his equal. Each could be the guide and mentor, as well as the one needing guidance and teaching. There was a balance between them as strong and profound as the balance of nature itself.

Sitting in the verdant valley surrounded by blooming trees and wildflowers, Thorn couldn't help but reminisce about the lowlands and Richen. The acute reality of the curse was always with him and what it likely meant for the duration of and how he could live the rest of his life. If he had any intention of finding Richen, he would need to start contemplating that path, as it now seemed to have an endpoint regardless of the outcome. However, the deity who had saved him and made him their champion had promised that a route existed to a tree bursting with blooms and a bountiful harvest that included Richen, so he kept faith that it was true.

But, for now, he had his pewter-scaled brother, spicy dragonborn stew, and dark dwarven stout in a meadow full of Springtime's hope and beauty.

Year 882 PXF *~ Early Winter*

Living with people as timeless as dwarves and dragonborn, seasons become like weeks and years, no more than months. A year and a half slipped away as Thorn and Naz trained, invented, and deepened their bond of brotherhood both in the workshop and on their transit portal trips across the length and breadth of Lymehold. Thorn had adopted the hammer he enchanted as his permanent offhand weapon for sentimental and practical reasons, and Naz's core, while not yet functional, was still holding the promise that it was a viable idea.

They didn't speak about the curse that continued to churn inside Thorn and wherever its insidious course might lead. They were acutely aware of drawing too much more attention as word of what had occurred with the possessed mining construct had leaked out. The two were spending far more time and energy tamping down either rumors of Naz using forbidden spells or that something strange was happening to Thorn than either of them liked.

The feast of Last Friend's Remembrance was approaching again, and precisely a fortnight before was a day that not only Thorn celebrated but Talon had celebrated before him: Richen's birthday. Richen would be turning forty-seven this year. A lifetime had practically passed them by, and while Thorn had long ago lost hope of a life together, he still held hope for that single day he had requested of Caspharian decades before.

Thorn should have been long in bed. He had wished Richen a happy birthday hours ago and blown out a single candle on the small honey muffin he had purchased for the occasion. But try as he might, he could not find rest. Instead, Thorn's reflection in the small mirror above the washbasin kept haunting him, catching his eye every time he passed it. As he made the sixth or seventh lap around his rooms, from balcony to great room to kitchen to bedroom, he faced the reality that the mirror was a problem. Well, not actually the mirror, Thorn mused, the face in it.

The visage reflected there was not that of a human who had lived over forty-five years; it now looked like thirty was still years away. The changes in Thorn were beyond explaining away as a glamor or aesthetic charm to the citizens of Oldstone, especially with the closer scrutiny after the enlargement spell and miraculous recovery. The number of clerics, magic users, and those who used glamors was too numerous for rumors not to grow, and where rumors sprouted, there were always ears to hear them and darken them with fear and superstition. Even the casual friends he had known for eight years at the Lamb's Shank no longer held a seat for him when he would venture there alone, and the anonymity he had enjoyed as just 'being human' was gone. Instead, he was now branded with the whispered label of 'cursed.'

Thorn suspected this would be his last Winter in the dwarven city he had called his home for nearly a decade. Thorn added ruefully that the blessing, or the curse of it, was that the face in the mirror he could honestly say was no longer Talon's face at the same equivalent age. Thorn wanted to believe the difference he saw in his visage was the lack of the strain of Talon's training with Lochlan and the bulk of Talon's body. However, a part of him was beginning to believe the horrific revelation he had had at the smithy: that his father and the black chains that bound Talon had exerted some unknown influence over his strength and size. Thorn could find traces of Talon, peering into the mirror while manipulating his face with his fingers, but the young man that looked back at him was now distinctly Thorn. One might think of them as cousins or, with what should be the age difference, uncle and nephew, but not the same person. The only thing that remained identical was his fully regrown mane of unruly hair and the scar Lochlan had placed upon his chest.

At the first sign of Spring, before the tensions regarding Thorn could rise like sap in the maple trees, Nazge appeared at his door with an old friend. Looking the same as always was Castian, sly smile on their lips and two pairs of snowshoes in hand. Throwing a set to Thorn, he stated, "The passes are mostly open..." He looked to Thorn for the first time, adding, "... old man. So get packed, and we will be on our way tomorrow."

Nazge tried to explain in stuttering, tumbling words that he had planned to gently talk Thorn into the idea of heading out of the city and how much he wished he could stay, between every phrase shooting daggers with his eyes at Cas. Thorn just smiled, "This is exactly as it should be and I might add well timed." Thorn presented his leg and showed a small gap that had formed at the back of his shoe and that he had to hike up his pants about half an inch. Nazge and he shared a silent glance, both knowing the pants and shoes had fit him perfectly at the end of the previous Summer.

Once Nazge overcame his horror at Castian's lack of tact, he began processing this new development. He stated urgently, "I think you must somehow find the Vermillion Blade. It is the only clue we have to the origin of the curse and how it is," Naz paused, searching for the correct least damning words, "diminishing your age." Crossing to Thorn, he added with pain clouding his eyes, knowing what he might be signing up for, "If you can't find the Blade or a cure, come back here before it is too late. I will care for you until the end if necessary." Naz pressed a returning stone into his hand. "This will get you home, brother, when the time comes that you need me." With a tight grip on Naz's shoulder, showing his deep gratitude for the offer, both hoping it would never be needed, they left Thorn's apartment and headed for the River Rock district.

The trio ignored the stares of other patrons and celebrated their last night at the Lamb's Shank with tankards of stout, Kings' Fare stew spiced to blazing heat, and sourdough liberally spread with creamed mushroom cheese. Malkidan came to their table, which had formed a halo of empty space around it, and silently deposited an enchanted sealed crockpot for travel simply labeled, 'King's Fare – may the gods walk your journey with you.'

As they dined, Thorn looked around him, the conversation and companionship of his friends fading into the background. The towering majesty of Sunhall cavern soared above him, still bustling with the activity of tens of thousands of souls. On his first night, he mused in his apartments that he would not even be a footnote in the lives of the citizens here, and with a maudlin sigh, it sank in just how true that was. But, he reconciled with himself, isn't that the way most anywhere? In any form it may take, only love makes you real in someone else's story.

The following day Thorn took his leave of Oldstone by way of Sunhall. Thorn only looked back once, which was more than Talon ever did when he left the Cour-Vermane estate. It had been a good childhood for Thorn here under the mountain, blessed with friends, a brother, and the roots of a new life.

PART IV

The Soul between Blood and Steel

CHAPTER THIRTY-TWO

Year 883 PXF ~ Early Spring

Castian led Thorn out of the deep drifting snow of late Winter in the high mountains and into the fragrant Springtime breezes of the human lowlands at the southern reaches of the Empire. Castian left Thorn to his own travels once they had descended out of the mountains and into the foothills, himself heading on a course toward Perinchal on the coast of the Cerulean Sea.

As Thorn followed the roads into the lowlands and Eleryon proper, he was shocked to find much of the devastation from the rebellion remained even though a decade had passed. Farmsteads that had been still smoldering when he left remained abandoned, now just crumbling derelicts surrounded by fallow fields. Even the road he walked was in disrepair, and broken-down wagons rotted where they had run afoul like carcasses of long-dead animals. Mile after mile, Thorn found more of the same, and while he felt the urgency to begin his search for the Vermillion Blade, he also couldn't help but wonder what had happened to leave the countryside of Eleryon so desolate and unrestored. With no small amount of trepidation, Thorn redirected his path to Arnadore to try and find some answers.

When Thorn saw Arnadore and its remains after the rebellion, there was a certainty in his heart that the place he called home would rebuild and, free of the yoke of corruption and intrigue, would flourish. But, arriving at the gates of the once welcoming and vibrant town, Thorn was dismayed to find that dream had been a false one; whatever wealth and leadership that could have led Arnadore's reconstruction had instead forsaken it. In the districts whose buildings the battles had decimated, the rubble and ruin had barely been cleared, and instead of new homes and businesses, shanties and makeshift hovels had sprung up. Any buildings that had remained standing had now fallen into squalor and decay: windows broken, doors off hinges, and the evidence of looting apparent everywhere. The few sallow faces he did see peering from shadows and through protected cracks and hiding holes were filled with desperation and fear. Poverty, hunger, and disease were everywhere, and the Spring thaw filled the air with the miasma of the people and creatures that had not survived the Winter.

Thorn choked back tears as on his way to check the Keep, sun waning overhead, he came to Elery Square and the Trellis Market, both now unrecognizable. However, the most devastating blow came when he saw that the Sojourn's Rest was now only a burnt-out husk, even Lolly's stove reduced to rust and slag. The flood of Talon's memories of his life inside those walls and under that roof crashed into Thorn. For a brief moment, the Sojourn's Rest stood once again, a homespun jewel on the corner of Elery Square, and then dissolved away like the last trail of smoke from a blown-out candle.

Thorn explored the ruins for some clue or hint of what had happened. Lost in the cracked memories of the debris, suddenly curiosity struck him, and he made his way to the hearth where the path of the stone stairs that led to the baths would be. Due to their construction, the stairs were still somewhat concealed as they had never connected to the inn's main floor and looked like just more of the inn's collapsed oversized hearth. After two failed searches, he finally found a path through the massive hearth's semi-intact rubble to where the stairs began their descent. At the bottom, he was surprised to see a newly installed, heavily bolted, reinforced door. As he approached, a small eye window glowing with arcane protective energy slid open, and two roughly almond-shaped eyes looked out at Thorn.

"Are you hurt? Is someone injured or sick?" a voice asked.

Thorn replied, shocked to his core, "Balanon? Is that you?"

"I am known by that name," the voice from behind the door responded tentatively. "Do I know you?"

"You used to, from a time when I was someone else." Thorn pulled down the collar of his shirt and the chainmail beneath, revealing the unmistakable scar Lochlan had placed there.

The eyes looked at the scar, then traveled over Thorn's face, finally widening with recognition, "Gods! How can it be? I thought you dead." Along with Balanon's voice, Thorn heard the sounds of arcane muttering and the displacement of large bolts sliding back. "Come in quickly."

The door swung open, and Thorn stepped inside. The physical room housing Sojourn's Rest's baths was much the same, but now it had been converted into a surgery for Balanon to practice medicine. The mid-temperature pool had been drained, and its basin now housed multiple examination tables and cabinets of healing supplies. The hot pool still steamed with its crystal-clear water, but Balanon had sectioned off a portion where the water now boiled, its roiling surface revealing the shine of his tools and linens soaking in the cleansing heat. The chilled pool now had dozens of pipes dipping into it like oversized straws that bent and curved their way out of the chamber through either walls or ceiling.

Balanon's visage was as timeless as ever, looking to be not much older than Thorn appeared. However, his complexion had lost its ruddy glow of vitality and had dulled to an ashen gray. The surgeon had taken to shaving his head, his scalp showing a week or more's worth of stubble, and his clothes, which had always been so exacting in their upkeep, were disheveled and damaged. Looking them over, Thorn could spot how Balanon, at some point in the past, had kept up with their repair by hand with his meticulous stitching, but more recent damage was left without care.

Thorn did not hesitate and grabbed the half-elf surgeon - his friend, his first mentor - in a full-throated embrace. A suppressed shudder of emotion wracked Thorn's body as he held his friend and mourned the state of Arnadore. Balanon let Thorn grieve for a few moments, then pulled away and looked up into the face of the new man before him.

Thorn began with an introduction, "I am Thorn now. Talon Cour-Vermane died the day of the revolt."

Balanon nodded in acknowledgment, testing the name out. "Thorn. It is a good name," he continued, "I am ready to hear whatever you are willing to share of the rest."

Thorn told his mentor everything. He ended his tale with, "But most of this was not something I was immediately aware of; it has been slowly unfolding over the last decade." He spread his arms and turned around. "The curse seems all-encompassing in its course, not just the wounds the Vermillion Blade gave but even the vast amounts of damage caused by an enlargement spell cast on living flesh. The only one remaining is this," pointing to his chest, "from his crystal powder."

Balanon took in all the information like any good practitioner of medicine would, but even he seemed overwhelmed, especially by the information regarding the healed damage from Naz's spell. As though he could soothe his mind with a touch, he pulled his fingers across his eyelids and pinched his nose when Thorn completed his dissertation of all that had occurred. "It is fascinating, and in my years, I have not heard of the like. However, my profession is to care for the common ailments of regular people, not the curses of weapons and heroes." After that disclaimer, Balanon switched to a more technical assessment. "I do agree with your observations, though. You look to be a human of twenty-five years, no more than twenty-seven." Then, grabbing a light and lens from his desk, Balanon approached and, after getting a nod of consent, shined the light and looked through the lens into Thorn's eye. "You say you have recently lost some height? And, of course, your mass is far less than that of Talon when I saw him last at the estate or even from afar as the Duke's envoy or Knight Captain. It is interesting, though, that your face is not a clone of Talon's at this same age, and the difference is more than can be explained by a change in weight and lifestyle."

"I can't explain my face other than it feels like it is mine. This is Thorn's face, not Talon's. The height is just recently, within the last three months. The rest, with your confirmation on age, seems to me that for the years I should have aged forward, I have aged almost twice that backward." As Thorn finally said it out loud, Balanon, at first, just said an offhanded "ah," and then the implications hit him as well. He pulled away and gazed at Thorn.

"And there it is, yes?" Thorn asked rhetorically. "A forty-five-year-old human in this day and age should be able to count on another thirty years of life, fifty if he is lucky, and with magic, perhaps even eighty years." He continued with the calmness of one who has resigned themselves to their demise, "In less than a decade, I could be barely a teenager. Five years more, and I will need someone to act as my parent. Beyond that..."

Balanon cut Thorn off. "We don't know that yet. And just because the artificers and enchanters of Oldstone didn't have answers doesn't mean they don't exist."

"Perhaps," Thorn stated flatly. Then, changing the subject, he asked, "What has happened to Arnadore? To Eleryon? Why has nothing been rebuilt?"

"That is a long story with many versions and finger-pointing at who is to blame. I will make us some tea." Balanon, in deference to their previous subject, patted Thorn on the shoulder with a look that conveyed the empathy of someone who had spent a lifetime learning to help and knew there was nothing they could do.

Balanon relayed to Thorn the story of the years after the rebellion. When the fighting stopped and the shock of Eleryon's failed secession wore off, the noble houses of Arnadore began to position themselves as the rightful heir to the Duchy. Receiving utter silence from the Emperor, they began to seize power and gather influence where they could. Not unexpectedly, it wasn't long before the houses' ambitions began to grind against one another, and bloody feuds erupted over Eleryon's scarce and decimated resources. In the first five years after the rebellion, sabotage, assassinations, and policies of salting the earth in retaliation for losses led to the fall of the nobles and even further destruction of the countryside.

Even House Cour-Vermane did not emerge from that period unscathed. Trying to appease the Emperor and claim the Duchy, the house split, expunging Toman's side of the family. The house was retitled House Vermane after Veronic made an advantageous remarriage to a wealthy but titleless shipping merchant in Jadenpool. There were brief rumors that Toman attempted to legitimize 'House Cour,' but it gained no traction and dissolved.

After the fall of Arnadore's nobles, the farmers and laborers tried to organize a guild-based government. It began well, but the need for funds to rebuild far outstripped the taxation that could be levied without animosity. So, to remedy their tax burden, the last pockets of concentrated wealth aimed packs of roaming mercenaries at those who would 'steal their profits and give them away,' eventually tearing the guild council apart. And that left Eleryon where it is today, broken and sucked dry of hope or promise for a better future.

Balanon concluded, "There are a few pockets out in the countryside where the seeds of renewal are sprouting, but they are always in jeopardy of being trodden underfoot by those who would take and destroy rather than try to rebuild." Thorn couldn't help but shake his head in disbelief but reluctant acceptance. Balanon continued, "As for me, I do my part for those who still cling to life here in Arnadore. I can keep up with injuries, but the disease is another matter." He motioned to the chilled pool with the piping. "Clean water is the best I can offer as restoratives are beyond my power with so much life leeched out of the region."

Having recounted the history, Balanon seemed to recall something. "Thorn, perhaps there is someone who might help you. There was a hermit, or some even say a hag, that made their home near the spring you spoke of. Some went to them as much as they came to me for medical attention in the early days after the rebellion. Those who visited called them the Watcher of the Waters as they would sit at the spring and watch it for hours without end." Then, becoming aware of the hour, Balanon added, "But you must stay here for the night. No one should be caught in the city without shelter after dark."

The two retired, and while he felt secure within Balanon's sanctuary, alarming sounds from above still filtered down to the underground baths. Thorn sprung awake at some early hour before dawn to a loud arcane jolt and retreating whimpering after being dimly aware of some loud growls and a claw scratching at the sturdy door that Balanon had installed. Just after dawn, Balanon awakened Thorn and supplied him with some of his scarce provisions for his trek to the spring, reminding him to either be back at his door before sundown or to camp well outside the city so as not to attract the beasts who scavenged the ruins for carrion by night.

Instead of heading through the city to exit through the eastern gate adjacent to the Keep, Thorn left via the southern gate closest to the remains of Elery Square, wary of the creatures he had heard through the night. While he was confident in his skills, he was not foolish enough to falsely believe that a skilled warrior couldn't get overrun by a pack of starving beasts. As Thorn circled to the east to head for the spring, many of the homes and small businesses outside the perimeter of Arnadore he had once known had disappeared or were in ruins. The missing landmarks confounded his sense of direction from time to time, but like the day he fled with the Vermillion Blade, his legs seemed to know the way back to the spring.

Thorn found the spring and surrounding glade to be remarkably much the same, not just from the last time he was here a decade ago but even from that magical first visit with Richen. As he approached, he could almost imagine two young boys lying on the boulder, exploring their connection and falling into a love that, at least for one of them, would last a lifetime. After the despair and destruction that marred the rest of his homecoming, the untouched spring seemed almost surreal, like it somehow existed in a place outside space and time.

They were so still, and their clothing so covered in detritus, moss, and lichen that Thorn would not have spotted them had he not been so familiar with the spring and its surrounding features. His mind first registered the Watcher of the Waters as a large rock that had somehow appeared at the water's edge on the opposite side of the spring from the boulder until he spotted the eyes peering out from under matted gray-green hair focused solely on him.

"Good morn to you. I come as a friend. Are you the Watcher of the Waters?" Thorn raised a hand in greeting, holding his other hand out to his side without a weapon to show his peaceful intent. When he received no response, he took a different tact, believing that no one of ill will could invade this place. "I am from this spring, born by it. I carry Caspharian's blade." As Thorn unsheathed the sickle and raised it, blade down and clearly showing the small tree that was the hilt, the reaction was immediate. The hunched figure stood up and began to glide across the water's surface toward him.

CHAPTER THIRTY-THREE

Year 883 PXF *~ Early Spring*

The hunched figure drew closer, leaving only the smallest of rippling footprints behind them as they approached, padding easily across the water's surface. Thorn was unnerved as the Watcher approached, their form seeming to ripple and shift as much as their reflection in the waters of the spring. The wrinkled face that was nearly indiscernible from gnarled bark across the stream resolved itself far more than could be accounted for by the relatively short distance they traveled to reach Thorn. So too, their clothing shifted from looking like little more than a moss-covered rock to robes, smock, and tunic. By the time they reached Thorn, an elder androgynous figure stood before him. Their face, while heavily wrinkled, was almost beautifully so. Time had not marred it with its burdens but instead imbued it with its unending stories and experience. They had lank hair as wild as Thorn's own that hung to their elbows, and many seasons had filled it with its fair share of leaves, twigs, and dried blossoms. A cloak not very different from the forest's carpet draped over the Watcher's hunched back that, if straightened, would mark them as human in height, but in their current bent state, they came only to Thorn's mid-chest.

Pointing a curved finger and looking up into Thorn's face, the gnarled voice of the Watcher spoke prophetically, "I was witness to your birth and the choosing of your name. But that is not all I witnessed. I also saw your twin's birth that day."

Thorn would have fallen had his and Richen's boulder not caught him. "I have a brother?!" Thorn questioned, awestruck as he leaned against the boulder for the support to stand.

"Oh, this was not a twin of flesh and bone. It was a twin of blade and blood and steel, but a twin nonetheless." Thorn felt the blood drain from his face as any fear he had about the Vermillion Blade paled in comparison to this revelation. He wanted nothing more than for the Watcher to stop speaking, to be silent, and never utter another sound, but they continued. "At least when I saw it born, it had neither flesh nor bone, but that may no longer be true. One such as it will always find a host, even while a part of it remains forever bound within you." The last was said with the finality of the grave, the Watcher's voice seeming to reverberate menacingly even in this open place.

"Forever bound..." Thorn echoed back the Watcher's words. "I don't understand. The Vermillion Blade's curse is making me younger, does it somehow..." The Watcher interrupted before Thorn's thoughts and words could spin up like a child's top.

"Hush, child. No one expects you or I to know the whims of the gods, but we can learn to read their footprints, especially when they make sure we are present to witness them."

The Watcher motioned over the spring's waters with a staff that seemed to materialize in their hand. Words began to appear on the rocks at the water's edge, sometimes even seeming to etch themselves into the water's surface. The letters were written in a shimmering script the color of the sunset, their forms archaic but legible.

To break oath is to be even beyond death. To walk this land as doom to
the blight upon it.

The Watcher gazed at Talon as recognition and confusion came to him simultaneously. "But that's not the curse I saw written on the Vermillion Blade as I dove into the spring. It said, 'To break oath is to be doomed even beyond death to walk this land as a blight upon it.'"

"Perhaps, but *this*," the Watcher motioned with the staff again, "is the echo of what was imbued in you at your birth, most likely by Caspharian's will." The Watcher continued now as though teaching a lesson. "In my experience, Gods cannot or will not unmake another's creation, but they often meddle and twist the intent of their brethren, especially when it comes to those they have chosen for a larger purpose."

Moving to lean on the boulder next to Thorn, they expanded, "Which leads us to you. Most people wrongly believe their walk with the Last Friend comes at the very end, in the last breaths of their life. But, in truth, it begins much earlier. Once one is no longer growing to adulthood is truly when their walk with Death begins. For you, *"to be even beyond death"* is to never have begun your walk with the Last Friend, and that, my child, is where this curse is taking you." The Watcher peered at Thorn with their bottomless eyes to see if there was understanding.

"So... But..." Thorn had so many questions, but the Watcher chimed in.

"There are no definites in divine mysteries such as these. The mark of two warring divine possibilities, the curse and Caspharian's binding, shine from you like the sun for those that can see, and I have nothing more I can add regarding the details of that dichotomy." The Watcher paused. "However, I believe my summoning here to witness your birth was to tip the board in Caspharian's favor."

The Watcher of the Waters moved from where they were leaning on the boulder next to Thorn and began walking around the spring, motioning for Thorn to follow. They continued speaking as they walked. "Your twin, the cursed blade, has a portion of its power tied up within you, captured by Caspharian's will, but as Caspharian's champion, you have some sway over its direction. Is the visage you now wear the same as it was in your life before, or is it a new face reflective of your new identity?"

Thorn subconsciously brought his hand to his face as he followed the hunched figure, "It is not the same, and it does feel true to who I am now, but I can't say this is what I willed it to be or necessarily what I would have chosen had I known."

The Watcher chuckled over their shoulder at Thorn. "That is because your form did not conjure itself from some errant wish or fantasy; it is a mosaic of the pieces of your life that are *True* and *Real*. It is the person you have chosen to be and that you are still sculpting, now made into flesh by the Conjoined God's will, as tenuous as it might be through the web of the divine powers trapped within you."

A shadow seemed to pass over the sun, and the light around the spring plunged into that of nighttime instead of midday. The Watcher whipped around faster than their age should have allowed. "But, just as you are influencing the curse, your twin can do so as well. It is the Blade's power, after all. If it has indeed found a new master, not only will it search you out to reclaim the part of itself trapped within you, but the strength of its curse will also increase. It may yet undo what you have created as this new person within the protective halls of the dwarves." The Watcher motioned with their bony hand from Thorn's head to feet at the last statement.

"If it is searching for me and could begin changing me, how do I find it first and destroy it?" Thorn asked overconfidently. "I am sick and tired of people and things and gods having control over my life. If it means I die in the process, so be it. What sense is there in living if my life is not mine to live?"

The shadow passed, and daylight returned to the glade and spring. The Watcher continued their circumnavigation of the spring, tutting Thorn through their teeth. Their prophecy resumed, "The deity you serve's power stems from forge and hearth, field and forest, but look around this land; corruption has diminished Caspharian's presence, a decay of which your twin is only a piece. To face the Vermillion Blade on such hostile ground so devoid of the Conjoined God's grace would be folly, yet meet it here you must."

"So I am doomed. Fine. Point the way," Thorn said snidely, turning back along the path the Watcher had led him on around the spring.

Thorn could hear the Watcher stop and turn behind him but refused to look back, keeping his eyes ahead. Their strained voice called after him, "But will you doom all others as well?"

As though created out of fog and mist, the shape of Balanon appeared. Thorn, refusing to allow the Watcher to manipulate him, waved his arm through the illusion and kept walking. Next was Nazge's form standing in his path. The Watcher's voice, now seemingly in his head, whispered, "Do you think corruption such as this knows borders or kingdoms?" The Watcher's speaking in his head was far too reminiscent of the voice from Talon's life and hardened Thorn's will. He did not even bother to wave Naz's form out of the way but plunged through it head-first. Thorn's steps faltered as Osman now appeared before him. He was older, looking to be almost the same age as Thorn appeared now. He was stalking something with Talon's dagger, the one he had stabbed him with at their last meeting. There was a wary readiness in his eyes, belying an underlying concern and fear.

"Stop your tricks! Are you watcher or witch? You speak in riddles and impossibilities without answers or direction. If you are to help me, then speak plainly." Thorn reluctantly brushed the misty shape of Osman away with the back of his hand.

In answer, the Watcher's voice rippled across the water of the spring, "I, like you, am the product of who I serve, the Conjoined God; sometimes of one mind, sometimes opposed. Yet, bound as one. Friends, rivals, siblings, lovers... the only sin is to pull them asunder."

As Thorn returned to the other side of the spring, the last of the Watcher's illusions was there to haunt him. Sitting on the boulder, one arm wrapped around drawn-up knees, the other to the side, drawing shapes with their fingers, was a man's hazy outline. Thorn took a sharp intake of breath at its appearance. This was not the memory from three decades ago. The shape was larger than the teenager he had been, and while the details were vague, as the head looked up, Thorn would know the eyes anywhere, the eyes of storm clouds before the rain.

"Richen!" Thorn ran to the boulder, unable to stop himself, but the image of Richen dissolved as though dissipated upon an errant breeze before he arrived. "*TELL ME!*" Thorn cried out in anguish, collapsing to his knees in the gravel beside the boulder, "Tell me what to do!" He looked back to where he had left the Watcher, but there was only a large moss-covered rock where they had been. Faintly, rustling through the trees above him, he heard their voice, "Begin healing the land. The Blade will find you."

CHAPTER THIRTY-FOUR

Year 883 PXF *~ Early Spring*

Thorn rolled from his knees and sat on the ground leaning his back against the boulder. He didn't know where the tears on his cheeks had come from. It was more like he was leaking than sobbing or wailing from the shock of seeing the image of Richen. His eyes were clear, and his breath wasn't wracked as he had always experienced crying before, but tears continued to fall nonetheless. Was the image he saw how Richen looked now? Or some other time in all the years that had passed? He tried to piece together details he thought he might have seen. *Was that the image of a forty-eight-year-old man?* There was nothing for his memory to grasp though other than the eyes, his beautiful stormcloud eyes still clear and full of reflected dreams.

Thorn stood up, not bothering to wipe the trails of moisture off his face. Looking at the sky, he knew he had to get moving to make it back to Balanon's sanctuary below the Sojourn's Rest before sunset. But, before leaving, he dipped the blade of his sickle in the spring to give it the sustenance it required, and as he did, there on the tiny branches of the tree, he saw a miniature bloom. Barely larger than a grain of sand but unmistakable in its shape and color, it was the first bloom Thorn had ever seen on the living weapon he carried. He gave the sickle a little smirk, and instead of sheathing it, he hooked the blade under his armpit, positioning the little tree to ride on his shoulder to get some sun. At first, Thorn had to concentrate on keeping the sickle in position, but the longer he walked, it seemed to anchor itself in place and rode steadily on its new perch.

Thorn arrived back at Elery Square just as the sun was setting. As he traversed the open square, he could feel eyes upon him, but unlike yesterday it was not the eyes of the curious. Instead, this was the gaze of a predator. The hairs on Thorn's neck stood up, and his senses opened to the world around him. Thorn hadn't felt the magic of the sickle to this extent since the day he pulled it from the boulder. The sickle seemed to plug his nerves into every living thing around him in the split second before the attack came. It was as though his body were connected to a vast network of roots and branches that radiated outward around him, covering every surface and feeling even the slightest movements in the air and earth. Thorn grabbed the tree-like hilt of the sickle, unhooking the curved blade from under his arm. He wasn't sure exactly when or if he closed his eyes, but Thorn no longer needed them. The filaments of his and the sickle's life force radiating around him gave all the information he needed about what was stalking him.

It was hungry, but not only in the natural sense, maliciously so. Its need came not just from an empty belly but from an instinct poisoned by corruption. As a hunter, it was exceptional, approaching its unwary fleshy prey from downwind, six legs slinking in the lengthening shadows without so much of a whisper of a sound. Even its heartbeat was slow and steady, with no rush of adrenaline causing blood to pound in its ears. Thorn should have been dead, killed instantly by the jaws clamping around his neck from behind, the long canines puncturing the arteries there as they found purchase. The leap was the perfection of tens of thousands of years of nature refining its apex predator and the corruption molding its form into a perfect killer; nevertheless, it did not find its target. Instead, in a motion one would think belonged to a tree limb springing back from an unexpected gust of wind, Thorn spun around with the sickle while simultaneously bending his body backward, and as the shadowy feline form passed over him, the living edge of the sickle passed cleanly through the beast's neck, severing it from its body.

Thorn followed through with the momentum of his evasion and returned to a standing position as his senses retreated back into his body, no longer reaching outward and encompassing all around him. Before him lay the corpse of the beast that had stalked him. It would have been a beautiful creature if not for the sores biting into its skin and the webwork of abnormal veins burrowing through its fur and feeding vestigial tentacles emerging from its back.

The flesh at the site of the decapitation drew Thorn's eyes. At first, he thought he was witnessing some kind of foul magic as glowing blue-phosphorescent fungus and lichen grew in the wound before his eyes, accomplishing in seconds what should take weeks or months. But then he saw their true purpose. They were drawing the poison and corruption from the corpse, filtering and processing it. As a result, the sickly gray flesh of the beast returned to the more natural color of game freshly killed, and the vile tentacles withered away. Thorn looked to the sickle for answers but found none other than the single bloom, glowing in the approaching twilight among its canopy of branches that acted as a pommel stone for the weapon. Hooking the sickle back under his arm, Thorn, intrigued and curious about the process happening within the corpse, wrapped it in his cloak and brought it with him to Balanon's sanctuary.

Placing the corpse on an examination table, Thorn assisted as Balanon worked to confirm Thorn's theory. There was a strange déjà vu as the two worked side by side, Thorn immediately falling into the training Balanon had given Talon. By every analysis, including a blessed lens to detect any disease, poison, or corruption, the lichen and glowing mushrooms that had spread across the body had cleansed the creature's flesh. Balanon even caught the decontamination process in action at the feline's haunches furthest away from the decapitation wound.

As they worked over the corpse, Thorn told the surgeon of his encounter at the spring and the new information he had gleaned. In light of what they witnessed with the corpse, healing the land might not be as impossible a task as Thorn had imagined.

Thorn assisted as they carefully harvested the lichen and mushroom samples for Balanon to try and cultivate. The surgeon explained how he hoped he could create a way to use them to help fight the disease outbreaks in the city. However, Balanon, ever the realist, stated flatly, "One creature rid of corruption and some helpful plants are not the cleansing of the whole of Eleryon." Then he asked, "And if the Vermillion Blade is only a part of the source, where to then?"

Thorn just looked at him and replied, "I have one cleansed creature more than I had hours ago, and the faith that nature wants to be healed if we can give it a helping hand." He glanced at the small tree on his shoulder. Thorn took a moment to think, then continued, "But you are right. The answer is not to go on an extermination spree here in the city. Not yet, at least. I'll need to start somewhere else, somewhere secluded, and I know just the spot."

The following day, Thorn headed out, breath clouding in the predawn chill of early Spring. Along with all his belongings, he took some medical supplies and a hefty share of salted meat from his kill the night prior. He arrived at his destination in the early afternoon and looked down from the bluff he had perched upon so many times a lifetime ago. Before him stood the diminished but by no means devastated acres of Milgran's Orchard.

Thorn surveyed the orchard with relief. There was still time to prepare the trees for their first growth. It was also evident that someone had cared for the trees over the last decade, but most likely, too few people trying to care for too many trees. Thorn suspected who was responsible for keeping the orchard from dying but could tell within a few seasons it would still not be enough. Thorn descended from the bluff into the orchard as Talon had done so many times before, walking among the trees and assessing their condition. Slowly he made his way through the orchard toward the farmhouse and workshed barn ahead.

He noted the ground would need to be cleared around the trees before Spring truly arrived, and far too many trees had sappers growing from their root bases near the trunk along with unproductive vertical branches higher up in their crowns that had to be pruned before first budding. Walking the trees with a critical eye reinforced the daunting task ahead, but nothing worth doing should be easy. Thorn finally came to the center of the orchard and the largest tree at Milgran's, where Richen had broken his arm. The tree was far from prime condition but had weathered the neglect better than many others around it. Thorn laid his hand on its trunk and greeted the tree like an old friend, assuring it that he was here to help. He scanned the branches looking for some sign from Caspharian that he had made the right choice to begin his task here, but no blossom magically bloomed or apple miraculously appeared. Sometimes all you had in life was blind faith; that it's not always about making the best choice, just making a choice and doing the most good you could with what you had.

Ahead of him, the roof of the large combined workshed barn that had housed field equipment, sorting tables, and crating bins, along with bunks and rooms for workers during harvest, had caved in. The walls seemed intact, but the sliding double doors facing the main house were off their rails. Compared to the many buildings Thorn had seen when traveling across Eleryon from Lymehold, the Milgran farmhouse looked in remarkably good shape. Besides some porch railings that needed replacing, missing shingles from the roof, and one boarded-over window on the second floor, it looked habitable. Heeding Balanon's stories of bandits and ne'er-do-wells that plagued the countryside, Thorn approached the house carefully, arms raised as he called out, "Hail in the farmhouse; I am here in good faith."

BOOM

The sound echoed across the open space between the house and Thorn as the bark of the apple tree next to him burst apart as though a thousand pebbles hit it. A puff of white smoke revealed where the thunderous sound had originated from. Thorn would have assumed magic if not for his time with Naz in Oldstone. Whoever was in the house was wielding a blunderbuss. Thorn smiled as his suspicions were confirmed. He had met the woman behind the gun decades before when she was just a girl.

30 Years Earlier ~ 854 PXF *~ Spring*

The stone hit Talon square in the left cheek of his buttocks and stung like hell. He had been strolling hand in hand with Richen through the Trellis Market on the first warm afternoon of Spring, the day before the Blossom Festival on the coming Hearth's Rest. His mother's gala had been a few nights before, and regardless of Talon's pleading, he was not allowed to bring Richen as his date. Instead, he had to play host to the son of some shipping merchant from Jadenpool. But that was all behind them. Tonight was theirs, and tomorrow they would celebrate with a picnic on the Square. Like most strolling the market this night, they were browsing for things to fill their Blossom Basket, not that they needed anything as Ms. Haddington would have their basket packed to the brim with all their favorites, but it gave them an excuse to walk together holding hands in the golden light of a Springtime evening. As they walked, Richen took no end of pleasure rubbing in how he had spent the evening of the gala in the kitchens gorging on all the hors d'oeuvres that had returned on only half-empty serving dishes while Talon had been stuck in a receiving line and trapped in the company of 'Marco,' who he pantomimed by mocking his roaming hands pinching Talon.

The attack on Talon's bum had occurred as he and Richen had walked past the trellis occupied this evening by Milgran's Orchard. They both spun around to see a girl's face, a bit younger than themselves, tongue stuck out of her mouth, dart behind a stack of crates, and make a break for a nearby alley. Richen and Talon exchanged looks, almost letting the affront lie without reprisal, but they were both still young enough that they could be baited into a good chase. They tore off after the girl, skidding around the crates under the trellis and sprinting for the nearby alley. Charging into the shade of the alley, they had only gone a few yards when both slammed to a stop at the girl's voice behind them. "I know who you are, thiefs."

Talon's eyes went wide as Richen glared at him before they turned around. After their fight over the Winter, Richen had laid down the law; Talon had no more chances. If this was more trouble, Talon knew he would lose Richen forever. Talon faced the girl nervously, saying barely above a hissed whisper, "I don't know what you think you know, but we haven't stolen anything."

"I know you stole a barrel's worth of apples last Fall from our orchard. I saw you do it," the girl said matter-of-factly.

Talon's breath began to come faster as dread filled his belly. Richen, knowing his part in this particular bit of trouble and in less of a panic than Talon at the given moment, began the obvious negotiation that had started the moment the girl had pegged Talon with the rock, "What do you want? You obviously want something, or you would've pointed us out to your parents back under the trellises. So what is it?"

"I happen to find myself needing a bit of help." She didn't look into Richen's eyes, suddenly looking almost embarrassed.

"What kind of help?" Richen countered. "We aren't doing anything illegal, or that will cause us more trouble,"

The girl suddenly got defensive, "I'm no thief. I just need some extra hands tomorrow to finish my... chores."

Richen didn't let the pause before the 'chores' go by without comment. "Oh, I know all about 'chores.'" Richen made air quotes around the word, "You got punished and didn't do the work. Whatcha do?"

"I sure as heck didn't steal a barrel full of apples!" She shot back, her voice rising. Talon, in a panic, started shushing her and found his voice, "What're the chores you need done?"

"Well, it's gonna take all of us because I will have to teach you two, but we gotta clean up some trees before first bud," she admitted.

"So we help trim a couple of trees, and you don't rat us out ever?" Richen asked leadingly, "How many trees?

"*Well...*" the girl got bashful again.

"How many?" both boys asked in unison.

"Two dozen." She whispered.

"TWO DOZEN!" Richen and Talon nearly shouted. All three dove behind some empty barrels in the alley when several heads turned their way from out in the Trellis Market, reacting to the noise.

Richen sizzled off a rebuff in a strained whisper, "What could you have possibly done to get such a punishment to complete in one day?" The girl scrunched up her face. "Wait a second, how long have you had to do this?"

"*Well...*" the girl rubbed her elbow, not wanting to answer.

"How long or no deal," Talon took the reins as Richen was seething.

The girl finally confessed, "A week."

"And how many did you get done?" Talon asked coaxingly

"Four." The girl started tumbling words out, "You see, it was twenty-eight trees because that is how the rows are divided, and I had a plan to get them all done with plenty of time, but I got distracted."

Richen, who was always better at math than Talon, chimed in with the numbers, "So you were supposed to get four trees done a day for seven days, and you only got four trees done total over the week!? What the heck have you been doing all this time?"

"Oh, practicing!" the girl said quite proudly, producing out of her pocket a miniature dwarven slinger.

Talon exclaimed, "Hey! Is that what you hit me with? It hurt, you know!"

"*Shhhhhhh*," both the girl and Richen hissed at the same time.

"Okay, here is the deal," Richen sounded like he was Mikal bargaining for supplies. "You are in a heap of trouble with the amount of work you have to do, and if we are going to knock out a week's worth of work in one day, not only on Hearth's Rest but Blossom Festival, that is worth way more than making up for one barrel of apples from last season." Hearing no objection as of yet, Richen continued, "So if we do this, we get a barrel full of apples *each* next season without sneaking around or stealing. Straightforward labor barter." Richen finished with a finality that brokered no argument, saying, "That's the deal. Take it or leave it."

The girl, whom Talon finally looked at as more than just an extortion artist, was probably no more than thirteen. She gnawed on a braided pigtail, eyes darting back and forth, torn between her current predicament and whatever she would have to do when harvest came to meet her end of the bargain. "Deal," she finally said. "I'm Gwendolyn Milgran," and spit on her hand in the most binding of youth contracts before extending it. "You can call me Gwen."

"Richen," he stated, spitting on his hand and extending it.

"Talon," he followed suit before awkwardly spitting on his hand and extending it.

The girl looked at Talon questioningly. "Talon? Talon Cour-Vermane? Why the heck are you stealing apples? You're rich."

Talon wanted to crawl under a rock. He at least was thankful the voice was still in hiding after their altercation last Winter. Withering under both Gwen and Richen's stare, Talon did manage to change the subject, "So how did you get in trouble?"

"I shot someone with my slinger," Gwen replied proudly.

The day went surprisingly well. Talon sent word to the estate that he and Richen would stay overnight in Arnadore at the inn. That way, if they left before dawn, they could get to the orchard at first light rather than late in the morning by riding in from the estate. Gwen was there waiting for them with tools at the ready. Learning their lesson from last autumn, Richen stayed on the ground pruning the shoots sprouting from the roots and base of the trunk while Talon worked the lower branches and Gwen the upper. The area around the trees was mostly clear, but Gwen insisted that they pull any weeds that were beginning to sprout in the moist just-thawed Springtime soil.

By the third tree, the trio was making great progress, and Richen drummed up some conversation. "What's the deal with the slinger and wasting a whole week practicing with it instead of doing your work?" He asked.

"Do you know what a rifle is?" she asked excitedly. Then, not even waiting for a reply, "It's a thing called a firearm, and it works like magic, but there is no magic involved. A dwarf came by with one last Summer and shot a rabbit dead clear across the orchard!" Thorn started to ask a question, but there was no stopping Gwen. "She showed me how it works and said if I could prove my aim next time she stops by, she would let me shoot it. Until then, she gave me this to practice with!" Gwen pulled the mini-slinger out of her pocket.

"So you want one of these firearms?" Talon asked. "What for when you can just shoot a rabbit with a crossbow?"

Gwen shot daggers with her eyes at Talon, "You have no imagination. I could be better than any old wizard with a book, and a crossbow is so ordinary."

"But what if your rifle breaks a string? How do you fix it?" Talon wondered.

"Rifles don't have strings!" Gwen said haughtily.

"Okay, well, what if something else breaks?" Talon retorted.

Gwen, having no answer, got flustered and changed the subject back to pruning the tree, "You aren't doing that right. You need to get the vertical ones *and* the ones that are angled too much."

There was no more talk that day of firearms, but years later, when Talon was a guard and heard that Gwendolyn Milgran had spent a whole harvest's profit on a rifle, he still had the same question.

Present, Year 883 PXF *~ Early Spring*

The sound of the blunderbuss was still echoing in Thorn's ears as he shouted out, "I am looking for Gwen Milgran. Is that you?"

A harsh woman's voice answered back, "What's it to you? What business do you have here?" She then added, "And you just stay right there. That was a warning. I got another one loaded that will take your head off right where you stand."

Thorn took the heavy pack off his back and laid it at his feet. "Well, my business is that I can tell just by the sound of it your blunderbuss muzzle needs reboring, and your powder mix is a bit off." Then, without pause, Thorn continued, "I also see your shed's roof could use some repair, and your trees need a prune and the orchard cleared before first bud."

The woman could not conceal the interest in her voice, "And who are you to know all those things?"

Thorn put a smile in his voice, "I'm a journeyman artificer out of Oldstone looking for work. I have my guild badge if you want to see it." Thorn continued, trying to stay as honest as possible in his story, "I grew up around here, but my family is now scattered to the winds, and over my apprenticeship, I didn't realize just how bad things had gotten in these parts before returning. I used to eat your family's apples when I was younger and remembered your affinity for firearms. So I am looking for a straightforward labor barter. Work for room and board."

The woman exited the farmhouse onto the porch with a rifle in one hand, thankfully not pointed at Thorn. "So what do I call you?"

"You can call me Thorn Berylston."

CHAPTER THIRTY-FIVE

Year 883PXF ~ Early Spring

Gwen took pause at the name Thorn gave, which gave him a moment to take in the woman she had become. The figure who leaned on her gun was sturdy in her build in a way that could make men twice her size cower. She wore a long brushed calfskin skirt paired with an unbleached linen tunic and a turquoise-blue fitted vest fastened with black toggles instead of buttons. She had the confidence of someone who knew their own mental and physical fortitude and openly compared it against those around her—correctly assessing that most she encountered were lacking when measured against her own. Gwen would be just two years younger than Talon, but the last decade of Eleryon's decline had taken an unfair toll. The mousy brown hair of her youth had gone white but for a few locks that had bleached out to light ginger. Thorn was happy to see she still styled it in the braided pigtails of her youth, but Gwen's face had wrinkled beyond its forty-three years, and there was a sorrow about her that she wore like a heavy Winter cloak weighted down with snowmelt.

Curiosity finally loosened Gwen's lips, "That a dwarven name?"

Thorn had hoped that giving Nazge's name would hold off too many questions, as sons who had been sent to apprentice, especially those sent against their will, often denied their birth name, and people considered it rude to ask for it. "My mentor was dragonborn, actually, but the name's roots are dwarven," Thorn answered, hopefully cutting off further questions. However, Thorn could see Gwen's lips purse and thin at the answer, and he wasn't sure if politeness would hold off her desire to know more of who he was, so he offered, "I can show you my journeyman badge with his name on it." Thorn slowly bent down to his pack and began opening a small outside pouch.

Quick as a snake strike, the rifle came up, "Did the Black Court send you?"

Thorn froze with his hands up, "I don't know who or what the Black Court is, but I assure you they did not send me."

Still looking down the barrel of the rifle, she spat out, "Prove it. Tell me something only locals know."

"Lolly Kindervan made the best shepherd pie in town the night before every other Hearth's Rest for people to take home leftovers for the following day." Gwen's gun did not lower with the general knowledge about Lolly. Wracking his brain for something else that would also support his apparent age, he landed on the perfect tidbit, as gossip was always the correct answer. "My mother used to say every time Faldan the weaver's son rolled over in bed, Ella got pregnant."

The rifle returned to Gwen's side with a guffaw and laugh, "Well, that's the damn truth if I ever heard it."

Thorn picked up his pack and stood up, taking a step toward the house.

"Ah ah, nope." Gwen motioned with her rifle toward the large workshed barn with the collapsed roof, "You'll be staying over there and are not invited into my house." Thorn noted the superstition behind those words and pondered why she might include them. "You try to break in. Let me assure you, there are plenty of things that will kill you without me being awake." Gwen then added, "Hope you brought provisions until you actually earn some; otherwise, I hope you don't mind being hungry."

"I have salted meat to share as a good-faith gesture if you would like some." Thorn offered, motioning to his pack.

"Clean meat? Not corrupted?" Gwen eyed Thorn suspiciously.

Thorn tested the waters and gave more information than he intended, "Balanon confirmed it."

"You've been to Arnadore?" Gwen didn't aim the rifle at him, but it came to the ready. "You are more dangerous than you look, then. Thanks for the tip. You can leave a portion of the meat on that bottom porch step. Then, you best prepare your space for the night. I can't vouch that the critters that prowl the darkness won't find you or get in with how things stand over there." Gwen motioned again with the gun to the barn. "We start on the trees tomorrow."

The workshed barn was a long open building with ceilings nearly fifteen feet high. The roof had collapsed over only a third of the structure, and the manner in which it had given away cordoned off the far end of the building, effectively creating a new wall between the intact part of the barn and the area exposed to the elements.

Slipping around the fallen roof section, Thorn found the space behind it spacious, with several areas subdivided by half walls and a loft area built at his chest height that he could use for sleeping off the ground. He did need to seal up some holes around the perimeter of the space, which was easy enough to accomplish with salvaged wood and nails from the roof collapse. Richen's hammer made quick work of the process with its added enchantments. Finally, Thorn made a small hearth from a cobblestone paved area near one wall whose original purpose he could not discern but where he could duct smoke outside relatively easily.

All in all, for a few hours of work, it was an adequate, if not borderline nice, home Thorn had created for as long as he might need it. Later in the evening, it heartened him to catch the smell of roasting meat coming from the main house as he satisfied himself with some road rations by his small fire to keep the chill of the night from his bones before retiring to the loft to sleep.

Thorn was up at first light and just barely beat Gwen to the yard between the house and the barn before she appeared with a pruning blade in one hand, a mug of steaming tea, and a small firearm strapped to her waist.

She nodded to the orchard without saying a word following behind Thorn, obviously not wanting to turn her back on him. Their breath fogged in the cold morning air, and frost crunched underfoot as they walked to the far side of the orchard.

"That one," Gwen gestured at an apple tree at the edge of the neat array of other trees. Thorn obliged and began work as she observed. It might have been thirty years since he last pruned these trees, but the task was still the same. He started at the roots using his sickle to take off sappers and then climbed into the branches to thin out the canopy. Thorn was grateful for Talon's height that, for at least the time being, he still possessed but was just as thankful that he no longer carried the bulk of his former life. There was no way at Talon's size he would have been able to complete the pruning from within the branches as not even the trunk would have supported him. He might wish for the strength of his old life for some jobs that he might encounter in the future during his stay at Milgran's, but it was not the critical factor for this, the most important one.

Gwen gave a grunting snort of approval when she had seen enough of his work to be satisfied, the sound creating a cloud of fog out of her nose, then added, "I will be three trees in that direction," pointing over her shoulder. "You don't get any closer, as I will shoot first. No questions asked." Then, as she walked away, she commanded, "Clear the ground before you move on and pile your trimmings along the main rows."

At first, Thorn bristled a bit at the lack of trust and created in his mind the added insult that she had positioned herself between him and the farmhouse as a further cementing of that fact. But as he worked, he put himself in her position. To have survived this last decade with the orchard mostly intact, and as far as he knew alone for some portion of it, Gwen couldn't afford to trust a stranger. She had known him for less than a day. He would have to earn every drop of trust she might give him, and he could lose all of it instantly. He would be wise to remember that.

The first couple of trees were hard going as he got back into the rhythm of the process, but by the fourth or fifth, he found himself enjoying the work. Seeing the canopy of the trees back in the shape and condition he remembered them from years ago was a comfort to his spirit after the bruises it had taken seeing so much of Eleryon destroyed. There also seemed to be a gratitude from the trees themselves. Whether by some magic or his imagination, he felt his hand guided to where and what the trees wanted and needed pruned. Thorn continued working through the morning with only a brief break for a lunch of jerky and hardtack taken among the branches. With the Springtime sun overhead and a cool breeze lifting his hair, he felt more attached to the world than at any time he could recently recall.

Thorn worked until Gwen came to retrieve him as the sun was just beginning to dip below the far treeline to the west. All in all, he had pruned nine trees, between which he had stacked neat piles of the trimmings and pulled weeds. Gwen walked his work before approaching the tree he was finishing. "Not bad. I got twelve for my part. That means just eight hundred and seventy more to go in the next forty-five days or so to beat the budding. We clear the rows every three days to keep our smoke down from the burn." Then, with a mock genteel gesture, she invited Thorn to lead the way back to the farmhouse and barn.

Thorn had many questions he wanted to ask Gwen regarding the Orchard and her life but felt prying at this juncture could possibly do more harm than good. So they walked in silence back to the yard between the house and the barn, and Gwen, as a dismissal, said only, "Same time tomorrow."

Thorn taking the hint, headed back to his place in the workshed and lit his hearth. As he roasted some of the salted meat he brought with some wild onions he picked while clearing weeds, Thorn heard the telltale sound of a whetstone against a blade from the direction of the house. The cool nighttime air carrying sound further than it should. He pulled his dinner from the fire and wandered out the front of the shed. Gwen's hand went to the rifle by her side as soon as he emerged. Thorn internally mused that Lochlan must have trained her about keeping weapons close. She was sitting on the porch's top step, sharpening the pruning blade she had used that day in the orchard. He raised his hands and didn't get any closer. "I can help with that," he offered.

Insulted, she retorted aggressively, "If you think I can't sharpen my own damn blade..."

Thorn cut her off by raising his fingers and letting them spark with arcane energy, "I mean magically." Then, pointing to himself, "Artificer, remember?"

The pruning blade flew at him almost faster than he could react. Thorn caught it just before it would have plunged into his shoulder. "Look, Thorn whoever-you-really-are, I don't know what your angle is or what kinda trouble you are going to bring on my house, but whatever it is when it comes, I'm gonna shoot you myself." She stood up, gun in hand, and returned inside the house. Thorn could hear Gwen throw the bolts of multiple locks through even the closed door. So, after casting a sharpening spell on the pruning blade, which should now hold its edge for at least a week, he approached the porch, hands raised, and left the blade on the bottom step.

The next day and following week went much the same way, not even a crack forming in Gwen's frosty façade of indifference and hostility toward Thorn. The two pruned another hundred and forty trees between them over that time, and on the seventh day, Thorn awoke to the sound of two rifle shots in the darkness before dawn. He charged out of the workshed, sickle, and hammer at the ready, only to find Gwen standing calmly in the yard. Motioning out to the orchard, she said, "Two suckling hogs out about a hundred fifty yards that way. The big one is yours. Leave the other one by the porch. You can use the butchering rack behind the north side of the shed. Bury or burn the offal so it doesn't attract scavengers. Consider that your board for the first week."

Two nights later, Thorn heard the familiar sound of the whetstone again. He ventured out of the workshed and into the yard to again try and gain a little favor with Gwen. She gave him a piercing look as he took a seat on a small overturned apple crate by the shed's doors. "You're a hard worker. I'll give you that," she stated flatly, then continued accusingly, "why do you give two spits about this orchard? And don't you tell me it's because you like the apples."

Thorn considered concocting a story but then decided the time for lies was long past, so he said the most honest thing he could. "I fell in love under these trees, and now that he's gone, it feels like they are one of the few things I have left."

"Huh," she paused. "A romantic. I wasn't expecting that." There was a wistful scoff to her tone. "Love's something reserved for the young and the bored, two things beyond me in this life." Gwen stood up to leave, but as she seemed in a talking mood, Talon pressed his luck.

"How'd you do it? Keep the orchard from being destroyed, that is?" he asked as genuinely and openly as he could.

"My family never did have time for stupid men and their militias or nobles and their politics, and most knew it." She smiled menacingly, "You drop a few folks at a thousand yards no matter what flag they wave, and the message gets around real fast. Could the Jade Guard have overrun us? Sure, but they had no interest in this land – or any of Eleryon, it seems." Thorn could hear the anger in her voice as she continued, "As for that devil Cour-Vermane, I always knew that bastard was a thief and a liar. He might have put on a show as a guard and hero in the songs, but hells, he even betrayed that traitor Issul in the end." She spat on the ground. "I..." She must have seen Thorn's reaction and pulled her story up short. She seemed to squint at Thorn, searching for something but not finding it. She threw her pruning blade into the wood of the bottom porch step and turned to leave the vibrating steel singing in the twilight gloaming. "That could use another sharpening," she stated and walked inside.

Thorn felt like he had swallowed a boulder the size of Sunhall at Gwen's words. He had hoped to confess to her his true identity and his purpose in Eleryon: to heal the land and eventually face the Vermillion Blade to help rid the region of its corruption. But, while he knew that Talon's name had been soiled after the revolts, he didn't think people would still vilify it. For the next month, Thorn tiptoed his way through his work, keeping his own counsel and not pressing Gwen about details of her life again. Thorn's silence proved to be the trick, and Gwen was a little less frosty each week as they fell into the routine of the work before them. As promised, she provided fresh game each week as board, and Thorn kept her tools enchanted to razor sharpness.

Year 883PXF ~ Spring

They pushed each other hard to make it through all the trees in the orchard, even working over Hearth's Rests without question or complaint. Finally, they finished the last rows just as the trees in them began to bud and Spring's warm rains began. Thorn and Gwen surveyed the orchard in the late afternoon of their last day pruning, both a little amazed at all that they had accomplished. Gwen broke out some sparkling cider for them to share and, never looking at him but instead into the sun's golden light, said, "Why don't you come in for dinner tonight to celebrate?"

Thorn smiled, also looking toward the horizon and the falling sun replied, "I was just going to ask if I could offer you some traditional dragonborn cuisine to do the same."

"Well, how about you cook it up inside then?" she stated in her matter-of-fact way.

"Actually, heat it up. I brought it with me from Oldstone," Thorn admitted.

Now Gwen did look at Thorn, "Yuck, that has got to be months old."

Thorn assured her, "Magically sealed. It should be good as the day Malkidan cooked it. I will warn you, it is spicy, though."

"Ah, I can handle it," Gwen replied confidently. Thorn just nodded and smiled to himself.

Dinner went better than Thorn had hoped. After some well-deserved laughs over Gwen in no way being able to handle Malkidan's spices, Thorn brought up what had been on his mind while cleaning up. "Gwen, there won't be much to do in the orchard other than watch the leaves grow over the Summer, so I want to repair the workshed barn roof next. I am betting the reason you left it still caved in is that you know it is a two-person job. So either someone else walks up to your door without getting shot, or we will have to do it together."

Gwen paused and looked at him piercingly in the eyes. Then, with a slight nod, "Okay," was all she said.

Thorn didn't argue or expound further on the job ahead, just dried off the crockery pot Malkidan had given him, said, "Good night," and headed across the yard to the workshed.

Year 883 PXF *~ Late Summer*

Repairing the workshed and barn proved to be precisely what Thorn and Gwen needed to cement their trust and kinship with one another. Thorn's magic had luckily minimized the need for any new lumber as he could mend much of what had been broken, but no amount of magic could supplement the ingenuity and teamwork it took to raise and install a roof.

Of course, there had been disagreements and arguments, but as often as not, their altercations brought about better solutions to the problems at hand. Conversations remained superficial in nature, neither of them delving too far into the other's past and mainly sticking to the topics of running the orchard or the antics of the small herd of wild goats that had taken up residence under the branches of the apple trees.

It had taken nearly three months, but they had finally completed the last of the work to get the barn and workshed back under one roof again. Sitting on the porch, watching the fireflies out among the apple trees, Gwen stated, "We are going to need people to harvest all these apples."

Thorn, who had inadvertently adopted Gwen's manner of simple statements, replied, "Yes, we are."

"You want to invite people here from Arnadore, like in the old days, don't you?" Gwen said disapprovingly.

"Yes, I do." Thorn said without emotion.

"It is going to draw attention. You saw that rider the other day as well as I did. The Black Court has left us alone because we are staying to ourselves," Gwen chided.

"What if I said let them come? You have never told me anything other than their name. If it's just bandits, you have your guns, and I can defend myself. I don't see what you are so afraid of." Thorn questioned, grasping for understanding.

"They aren't just bandits, and if it were just defending us, I wouldn't be worried. We have to defend all of this." She motioned to the orchard and everything around her. "Can you tell me you can keep every flaming arrow a bandit might shoot out of the house, or the barn, or the trees?" She continued, "And that is not all they will bring at us. Some of them kill the land they walk on. You saw Arnadore. Do you think what plagues the city is just bandits?"

"Well, if we had more people here, they could help protect it," Thorn offered.

"Or they could turn on us, just like before. These are desperate people." Gwen tried to close off the conversation with her tone.

"But..." Gwen cut Thorn off.

"Look, I know who their leader, the Raven Judge, is and we can't beat him. He will come if he senses hope anywhere in Eleryon. He will destroy it just like he did before." To hammer her point home, Gwen paused before her final statement. "The Raven Judge is Talon Cour-Vermane. I know because I saw that damned red glaive of his through my rifle's scope when he cut down my husband."

CHAPTER THIRTY-SIX

Year 883 PXF *~ Late Summer*

Gwen's words struck Thorn speechless. He tried to grasp all the information tied up in her words, but it became a jumble in his head. He was already upset about Gwen's stance on the harvest, but all of this about the Black Court, the Raven Judge being his past self and having the Vermillion Blade was too much to process all at once. Thorn stood up silently and descended the porch steps into the yard. Pouring out his cider that had gone warm, he walked out of the lantern light of the main house and into the orchard.

The night was warm, the fireflies performing their hypnotic dance among the branches laden with tiny apples promising an abundant harvest once autumn arrived. Thorn walked without direction between the rows of apple trees, drawing his hand across their trunks as he passed. So many of them had been restored to vitality by his own hand, and the connection he felt to them was real. He understood Gwen's fear. She had cared for these trees and this land for over thirty years, through times of bounty and hardship. How could he ask her to risk everything she had left in her life, especially when he had an ulterior motive?

Thorn came to the familiar tree in the center of the orchard near the pond; its crown, even after his copious pruning, still stood proud above all the other trees surrounding it. He sat beneath it, back leaning against its wide trunk, and looked up through its branches at the stars and fireflies above him. What was he supposed to do? He had healed the land, at least this small part of it, but now he would have to wager it against the power of the Vermillion Blade and this Raven Judge to save it. Could he ask Gwen to stand with him in this? More importantly, would she if she knew who he truly was? Forearms on knees, Thorn looked out into the rows of trees filling his vision. He tried to summon some ghost or memory of his past to guide him at this moment, but nothing materialized. This was his decision. A choice about the man he was going to be, and while the experiences of the man he was were a part of him, this moment was Thorn's and his alone.

Returning from the orchard, Thorn walked into the farmhouse kitchen, the doors still open wide to catch the cool night air after the heat of the late Summer afternoon. Gwen, with furrowed brow, was leaning against the counter, gazing into the empty water basin, lost in her thoughts. She didn't react to Thorn's entrance, but by the slight tensing of her shoulders, Thorn could tell she knew he was there.

"The Raven Judge is not Talon Cour-Vermane." Thorn paused and took a deep breath, "I know he's not because I am, or more accurately, was." Thorn's voice cut the silence like one of Gwen's gunshots. Gwen's hand found the handle of a carving knife sitting on the counter next to her on a drying towel, and when she raised her eyes, it was not to look at Thorn but to the rifle leaning against the doorjamb behind him. Thorn raised his hands to his sides, careful not to look as though he was going for his sickle whose hilt was perched on his shoulder, as he tried to explain himself, "I have not been plaguing this land for the last decade. I have indeed been in Oldstone. And while Talon..." Thorn paused, unfamiliar with claiming Talon's life but needed to in this moment, "...while I did not follow Duke Issul's command and broke my oath to him, it was because I uncovered my father's plot for the secession and coup. I just discovered it far too late to stop it."

"Get. Out." Gwen spat the words at Thorn through clenched teeth.

Thorn had to continue, "You are right. The red glaive is indeed damned. It is why I look the way I do. I am cursed by it."

Gwen advanced on him with the knife, and he backed away and through the open door. Gwen grabbed the rifle as she followed him outside and aimed it not at his chest but right between the eyes. "I knew you were trouble, but I didn't know your mind was also broken!" she shouted as Thorn stumbled backward down the porch stairs.

"Gwen, listen. Richen and I helped you prune the trees on Hearth's Rest thirty years ago so you wouldn't tell anyone we stole a barrel of apples. You are the person who taught me how to take care of the trees. This is real. Caspharian broke me away from my family's pact with darkness and the Vermillion Blade to let me have a new life as Thorn, but it can't be over until the glaive is contained. They sent me to do that, and I need a place where the land is healed, and here we have done that." Thorn was now pleading.

"I. Don't. Care. And I don't believe in gods anymore," Gwen said dismissively. "I warned you I would shoot you myself when your trouble came to visit, and I don't ever lie." Gwen's eye lowered to the sight of the rifle, and her finger began to tighten on the trigger.

Time seemed to slow as Thorn's sickle fell from its perch on his shoulder, freeing itself in a way it had never done before. Even Gwen's trained eye followed its fall, perhaps worried it was some trick or magic that posed a threat to which she would need to react. As the sickle dropped, it left a trail of tiny blossoms that floated like embers out into the orchard on the warm night air. Then, the sickle hit the ground blade first and slid into it up to the hilt in a way that should not have been possible. The tiny tree planted firmly in the soil, its branches now bare of flowers, began to make a soft humming noise. Thorn, his back to the orchard, only saw Gwen's eyes widen at first. He turned, and spreading across the canopy of the orchard, he saw hundreds and then thousands of blossoms, the color of moonlight, blooming on the trees.

Gwen's rifle lowered to her side, and she began walking toward the miracle happening before her. Thorn, enraptured as well, joined her, walking the rows of the orchard under the moonlight blossoms. Turning around with arms outstretched and looking into the branches, they could see a flower blooming for every one of the tiny apples yet to ripen, the blooms infusing the fruit with their light.

As they ventured deeper into the acres of trees, the hum that had first started at the sickle now seemed to be in front of them. Thorn felt he knew its source and started heading toward the center of the orchard. Beside him, Gwen paused. Thorn had noticed she often bypassed the center tree by happenstance, but now he realized there must be more of a reason behind it. Thorn waited for Gwen to decide whether to come or not and as he waited, what had been the single tone of the humming became a musical note and then a tune.

Gwen raised a shaky hand to her mouth in recognition of the song, and her eyes began to brim with moisture. Even that small act was more tender emotion than Thorn had ever witnessed from her, so he held out his hand and offered to guide her ahead. Gwen's eyes went from his outstretched hand to his face and then up to her trees glowing with ethereal blossoms, and with a slight nod, she grabbed Thorn's hand. When they arrived at the grand tree standing reverently in the center of the orchard bathed in silvery light, a figure made of moonlight and fireflies was waiting there. Thorn's heart leapt, thinking it must be Richen, but as the figure turned to them, he recognized neither the face nor the eyes. Gwen's sharp intake of breath immediately informed Thorn of who it must be. Gwen dropped Thorn's hand and walked the rest of the way alone. The ghost or apparition or memory made manifest smiled as she approached, and Thorn could hear Gwen's wracking sobs as she got closer. Thorn backed away, knowing that this miracle was not for him but for another soul desperately needing healing.

Thorn gave Gwen all the time she needed. He strolled the orchard as the moonlight blossoms faded, the trees slowly drinking in their magic. It was nearly two hours before Gwen caught up to Thorn where he had settled, leaning against one of the trees he had pruned the first day. He looked to her with the unspoken question of if she was okay. Gwen nodded and, with a sniff, added, "He's in a good place." Gwen had pulled the chain she wore around her neck out of her tunic, and Thorn saw the two wedding bands that hung there. She let her hand clutch them to her heart for a moment before tucking them back inside her shirt and attempted to smile at Thorn.

Thorn went to her and embraced her tightly, slowly swaying as Richen and later Rahmed had done for him when he needed comfort. There was one last bout of tears and then a long sigh and sniff. Then, after a pause, she spoke into Thorn's shoulder, "The Raven Judge is coming for you. He can feel where you are."

Thorn immediately replied, "I'll leave now, then. It is too much to risk all this." In Thorn's mind, there was no question about his decision, even if it meant he would be at a disadvantage.

"No, I need you to stay here. I want you to stay." Gwen now looked up into Thorn's eyes. "You are the closest thing I have to family now, and family stands together to protect their home."

The two slowly walked, side by side, back to the farmhouse, the light from the moonlight blossoms no brighter than a fading memory. As they exited the rows of trees, Thorn turned and looked back at the orchard stretching out before him, trying to etch the scene in his mind, just in case. Gwen patted his arm, and Thorn reached down and pulled the sickle from the earth, and as he did so, the sickle opened his senses to the world around him. The orchard shone like a beacon, as did he, as both a call and a challenge that the Vermillion Blade would never leave unanswered. Hooking the sickle under his arm, tree on his shoulder as had become his custom, Thorn looked to Gwen, saying, "I don't know how long we have, but the Raven Judge and the Blade will be here soon. Certainly by nightfall on the morrow."

Thorn turned Gwen toward him, holding both her shoulders and gently looking her in the eye. "The Vermillion Blade can counter any mundane weapon. Your guns alone will be useless. The Raven Judge will know that. One of the reasons I believe he will come so soon is because I suspect through the Vermillion Blade, he also knows I can enchant but a single bullet in that time. So you will have one shot, but listen, I once wielded the Blade, and it will deflect even magical ammunition unless at its weakest." Thorn paused to ensure she heard his next words, "You cannot waste your shot to save me if I fall. The bullet will keep its enchantment even beyond my death, so you must run if I am defeated."

Gwen shook her head, "I won't run. No."

Thorn squeezed her by the shoulders, his thumb digging into her flesh. "*You have to.* If I fall, the Vermillion Blade will gain the power locked inside me and grow even stronger. You will be Eleryon's only hope of stopping the Judge." Thorn's eyes grew wide, "Promise me." When there was no answer, "Promise. Me."

Gwen's eyes closed, and a tear fell across her cheek to the ground. She whispered, "I promise." Thorn pulled her in and hugged her for the second time that evening. The reassuring words he wanted to say got caught in his throat. Thorn didn't want any of the last things he told her to be lies.

Thorn finally broke the embrace and held his hand out to Gwen, his eyes focused on the rifle. She opened the chamber and handed him the single bullet. Wrapping his fingers around the ammunition, he nodded with gratitude and furrowed brow, turning to return to the shed to begin his enchanting. Thorn felt Gwen's eyes on him as he went, then heard the farmhouse door close and its latches being thrown.

Thorn came awake to the sound of a knocking on wood. In the haze between dreaming and awake, he imagined he was in his old rooms at the estate, and it was the Commander knocking on his door for training. He then jumped to alertness, his hand grabbing the sickle by the side of the pallets he slept on in the loft of the orchard's workshed. The smell of coffee filled the workshed. Sunlight was streaming through the cracks in the structure's siding, and Gwen stood across the space he had used as rooms with a steaming mug in her hand. "I thought you might have been up late, and when you didn't appear in the yard earlier, I figured I would let you sleep. It is getting close to noon, though, and I'm not ashamed to admit I am getting jumpy," she said, offering the mug.

Thorn had been up until almost dawn, but the bullet was complete. He sat up and walked to Gwen grabbing the mug, his bare feet carefully padding across the hard-packed earth covered in sawdust from their work on the roof, causing him to step gingerly to get to her. His heart broke a bit as his mind came awake and registered the similarities of his actions to his mornings with Richen a lifetime ago. Gwen must have seen the look on Thorn's face. She gently said, "Memories are the most terrible blessings, aren't they?" Thorn just nodded, his mug no longer smelling of coffee but of spiced tea and sweet cream.

After a gulp from the mug, Thorn went over to a small rune-covered stone tablet and pulled the single bullet from its center. He handed it to Gwen, and she slid it into the chamber, instantly becoming more relieved. Then, he caught her eye and looked at her sternly, "Remember."

She nodded, "I promise."

They didn't know how long they would have to wait or if the Raven Judge would come with the Black Court or alone, so they got into position as soon as they were ready. There was no real need for discussion because there was little choice about where they should be. Gwen went up to the upper floor of the farmhouse to the boarded-up window with her rifle, and Thorn remained on the ground with the orchard at his back.

Thorn thought back over Talon's battles. When Talon had fought devils and raiders and all number of beasts throughout his life, he wore full armor and the Vermillion Blade on his back. If Talon saw Thorn as he prepared to fight the Raven Judge, he would have laughed. A twenty-five-year-old kid wearing a cloth tunic, calfskin leathers, and working boots with a sickle in one hand and a ball-peen hammer in the other. Thorn did get some comfort from the fact that under his tunic was the chainmail gifted him by some different world's Silver Scribe, and his weapon was Caspharian's sickle. But who knew what this Raven Judge might have in addition to the Vermillion Blade, which was dangerous enough alone to make Thorn worry.

Thorn's only other assets were the orchard, which, other than his plan to lure the Judge into it, he didn't know how much more it might help, and a single bullet from Gwen if she got the opportunity. Thorn mentally reminded himself that Gwen would only have a shot if he could get the Raven Judge on the single row of the orchard that lined up with the window she was in. He knew, more likely than not, that shot would never come.

They waited through the afternoon. Sweat dripped off Thorn's brow as the day dragged on, and before his thirst made him delusional, he ran inside to slam down some water and wet his neck. Thorn returned back to his watch as quickly as he could so Gwen could do the same. As the sun dipped below the horizon and the shadows overtook the land, Thorn wondered if he had it wrong. Perhaps the Raven Judge would take time to plan a strategic assault? Perhaps he had greater control over the Vermillion Blade's egocentric will than Talon ever had. Then, as if summoned by the thought, without warning, a shadow near the workshed seemed to coalesce into substance, and a haunted voice called out, "Talon Cour-Vermane, we have come to reclaim what is rightfully ours." The Raven Judge had arrived.

CHAPTER THIRTY-SEVEN

A dark tattered cloak, hanging nearly to the ground, wrapped around the figure that emerged from the shadows; it draped forward over the left shoulder, concealing that arm entirely along with part of the layered black leather breastplate they wore. The armor rippled with spiteful energy seeming to darken the shadows around it, slithering through the night like it was alive. The other arm held the Vermillion Blade in all its crimson malevolence. Its light shone upon the visage of the Raven Judge, but where the face should have been, there was a bleached mask of a distorted raven's skull, empty eyes staring at Thorn.

"You have found him, and what you desire will not be freely given," Thorn bellowed.

Thorn could feel the Raven Judge's eyes surveying him as though seeing him for the first time, "This? *This* is who they warned me about? This is a farce." In response to the dark figure's words, Thorn could almost feel the curse begin to writhe inside him, the eel fighting against the net that captured it. In the fraction of a moment that he recognized the curse stirring, the Raven Judge was upon him. If the sickle hadn't awakened his senses, sending its glowing life force out around him and connecting to every drop of life nearby, it would have been over before it even began.

SCHANGGGG

Thorn's crossed sickle and hammer caught the massive edge of the Vermillion Blade before it could cleave him in two. He used the force of the blow to add momentum to his disengagement as he propelled himself backward out of the shadowy farmyard and toward the added cover and life of trees. The Judge paused for just an instant, but Thorn felt what was happening. He could no longer see them but could feel the Vermillion Blade's web of chains spin their way out of the Raven Judge, beginning their evil work.

"You think your trees will help you? You ridiculous little boy." The Judge's voice echoed out from under the raven mask, then lifting open the cloak with the still concealed left arm, a flood of corpse rats poured forth, scurrying toward Thorn.

Thorn's eyes darted around the hundreds of half-skeletal vermin crashing in his direction. They swarmed at him with their claws and gnashing teeth, clawing over one another to leap to any exposed skin they could find. As their bites tore through his leathers and even his boots, he could feel the poison they carried trying to take hold in his flesh. He slashed through half a dozen or more, retreating backward as he went, then finally had to break and run into the orchard as more and more of the wave of vermin threatened to overrun him.

Thorn didn't know how to deal with the swarm invading the grove, but after hopefully putting enough distance between them, he spun around to make his stand between the trunks of two trees. Instead, what he saw filled him with despair. As the rats flooded into the orchard, a blight spread around them, blackening the trunks. Through his augmented sight, Thorn watched the filaments of life surrounding the trees flicker out at their diseased touch. Beyond them, the Raven Judge slowly advanced, his laughter echoing in the night.

Thorn froze in horror at seeing the trees' life force wither and die, his eyes lifting slightly to the second-floor window where he could see Gwen's face glowing in the moonlight. As the blight reached his feet with the expanding ring of rats behind it, Thorn screamed, "No!" and plunged the sickle into the corrupted earth. A wave of green energy burst from the blade, and as it passed over the rats, they began to spasm and writhe in pain. The first one exploded, revealing an aquamarine bioluminescent mushroom emerging from its corpse, and then two more rats burst open and then even more. Like a chain of fireworks, the rats' undead forms ruptured, creating a ring of sparkling blue, glowing mushrooms in the moonlight. There was no mistaking that they were the same ones that had cleansed the beast he had killed in Arnadore, and as the ring closed, connecting with the first half dozen rats he killed before fleeing, a powerful beam of moonlight descended from the heavens blocking the Raven Judge's path. The Judge's laughter turned to a roar of frustration as he stalked forward. Thorn flashed a smile of relief for small victories as, from across the column of moonlight, he saw that the Raven Judge could not seem to pass through the cleansing ring now healing the trees. Turning, he ran deeper into the rows of the orchard.

Thorn skidded to a stop on the soft earth as he approached the center of the orchard near where the great tree stood. He looked down the row past the fading beam of moonlight and Gwen's perch beyond. *Please wait for the shot, Gwen. He's not nearly done.* Thorn tried to think his plea as loud as he could, hoping she could somehow hear it. Then, catching his breath, Thorn closed his eyes and reached out with the sickle to detect where his foe might be. In his mind, the night ignited with the silver-gold glow of the filaments of life surrounding him, the network of tiny roots and veins covering every surface of the ground, the trees, and even the motes of floating seeds and insects in the air. Thorn reached out through every root, branch, and leaf, searching for even the tiniest movement of earth or air to find the Judge. During his first attack, the Raven Judge had been a black hole in the fabric of life, unmistakable against the backdrop of the sickle's second sight. But try as he might and straining with every fiber of his will,

Thorn could sense nothing of him. Doubt began to creep into Thorn's heart, followed by its companion fear.

"*ABOVE YOU!*" Gwen's scream carried across the field and through the night, saving Thorn as he instinctively dove to one side. The Raven Judge dropped out of the sky like a wyvern diving on its prey, the Vermillion Blade slicing through the sleeve of Thorn's tunic where his chest had just been. The Raven Judge, Vermillion Blade still stuck in the ground having missed its mark, looked back over his shoulder and glared directly at Gwen's position in the window. As he glanced back to Thorn, he sidestepped out of the row lining up with her sightline, recognizing the threat it posed. Disappointed but thankful, Thorn leapt to his feet and looked down at his arm. He saw the enchanted chainmail shining through his tunic. It had protected his flesh, but where the Vermillion Blade had sliced across it, he could see its edge had distorted and bruised the links of the chainmail. While it protected Thorn, he was not invulnerable against the cursed weapon of his family.

The two faced off under the apple trees' low canopy, rotating slowly around each other, trying to gain position, but there was no clearing for a proper duel this deep in the orchard, exactly as Thorn intended. Thorn did not close his eyes but instead split his awareness between what he saw with his eyes and all the information the sickle was giving him through his other senses, the golden roots and veins of life now overlaying his vision. Though he could not see them, he knew the black web of the Vermillion Blade's chains surrounded them. Its chains wrapping around every trunk and limb, the links feeding the Judge every possible attack and defense Thorn might be planning. As the Raven Judge, ever impatient for victory, made the first attack, his cursed glaive clashing with Thorn's sickle and hammer, a battle also waged between the Vermillion Blade's chains of darkness and the sickle's filaments of life.

Through the trees and around their trunks, their weapons clanged against one another, the Vermillion Blade's reach and weight hampered by the tight quarters, while Thorn's lighter, faster weapons excelled. Thorn dove around trunks and swung from familiar limbs as the Raven Judge, even guided by the Vermillion Blade's chains, found his large weapon fouled and confounded by the low canopy. Thorn's sickle against an armed and armored foe who could anticipate every attack was not a weapon of instant death or debilitation but a process of precision strikes slowly opening up access to more vital areas.

As Thorn swung off a tree limb, attempting an acrobatic move worthy of Osman to cut the last strap of one of the Judge's pauldrons, the Raven Judge's tactic changed. Instead of swinging for Thorn, who had prepared his hammer to fend off the strike, the Judge plunged the Vermillion Blade into the apple tree he had just launched from. Thorn landed his strike severing the strap connecting the Judge's left pauldron to his chest piece, but its success was eclipsed into nothingness as Thorn felt and saw the instant death of the apple tree pierced by the cursed edge of the Vermillion Blade. As the tree withered, it left a dark hole in Thorn's vision, and the Raven Judge slipped into that darkness.

Thorn tried to block the Raven Judge's attacks against the orchard, but the power of the thrusts and reach of the Vermillion Blade was unstoppable. Around him, he watched the lifeforce of tree after tree wink out, at least two dozen falling into darkness, their withered brittle branches now crumbling under the weight of the young fruit they carried. Where once life had been abundant, Thorn found himself in a graveyard of death. Withered trunks stood like gravestones around him, and the verdant canopy was gone entirely, its branches now broken and scattered, dead at his feet.

The attack came out of the darkness and death with no warning from the sickle's second sight, now blinded by the decimation around Thorn. The Raven Judge, holding the Vermillion Blade horizontally before him, charged Thorn, pushing him across the desiccated ground, and slammed him into the still-living trunk of the tree at the center of the orchard. The

Raven Judge held Thorn against the tree with the Vermillion Blade's shaft pinning him. He and the Raven Judge were face-to-face, and Thorn could now see beyond the black voids of the raven skull mask and into the eyes of the person beyond. He watched them narrow maliciously and imagined the predatory smile that must be occurring beneath the cowl.

With the Vermillion Blade in such close contact, and the added prodding of the Judge's will, the curse inside Thorn began to thrash into a frenzy. Caspharian's bonds holding it began to fray under the assault. Thorn was in agony, his body trying to both age and regress simultaneously. He couldn't help but let out an anguished scream. With no other option to stop the pain, Thorn's mind grabbed onto the writhing curse and reached through it to the Vermillion Blade. He willed Talon's mark, visualized as the red hot burning curved 'V,' at the blade, trying to brand it again and bring it under his control. Thorn's eyes darted to the cursed weapon where the brand had once been, but nothing marred its smooth surface.

Panicking now, feeling the curse slithering through the gaps in its bonds, Thorn pushed his will with all his might, reinforcing it with his love of Richen and Osman. He pictured Richen in the smithy, shooting smiling glances at him as he worked, and Osman tumbling through the air at the gala in his wondrous outfit. Thorn buttressed his love with the memories of his found family: Nazge's inventiveness and Gwen's resolve and from Talon's life, the guiding hand of Lochlan, the stoic strength of Mikal, and the homespun graciousness of Lolly and Ms. Haddington. Finally, he strangled the curse's slithering form with the resolve of knowing himself. His identity. His truth.

The curse's thrashing lessened, but, gaze locked on the Vermillion Blade, there still was no brand appearing. Desperate, Thorn dared to look to the Judge's eyes and saw them widen with anger and pain. That is when Thorn smelled the burning flesh. The Judge pushed away from Thorn with a scream ripping open the left side of his breastplate where Thorn had cut the last strap, exposing the bare skin beneath, and there, growing red with heat like it had just been pulled from a forge, was the scar of the mark Talon had placed during the duel so many years earlier.

"Rabien!" Thorn exclaimed.

The Raven Judge ripped off the mask as Rabien screamed, "YOU NAMELESS BASTARD!" Rabien swung the Vermillion Blade with the fury of a rabid bear. Thorn barely dove out of the way as his blow struck and nearly cleaved the tree at the center of the orchard in two. Whatever power had imbued the blade to kill the trees before was missing in this strike as the great tree did not immediately wither, but the wound it sustained was surely mortal. Thorn tried to roll towards the still-living portions of the orchard, but the Vermillion Blade slammed into the ground blocking his escape. Thorn scrambled to his feet, and Rabien drove him back into the dead clearing.

Rabien's assault was relentless, fueled by decades of hate and envy. Thorn could do nothing but dodge and parry as Rabien circled and herded him further and further into the center of the blight. No matter what he tried, whether his own tactics from training in Oldstone or strategies Talon had learned from fighting Osman, Thorn could not turn Rabien's offensive. The Vermillion Blade steered Rabien's seething rage expertly. Not only with its knowledge gathered through the centuries of how to counter any weapon, but its chains were also now guiding Rabien's every move with skills learned from Talon himself. Blinded from the sickle's expanded senses, Thorn's speed was the only thing keeping him alive. It was inevitable: too much debris from the destruction of the trees littered the ground, and Rabien's onslaught was too relentless. Thorn finally lost his footing and fell to the ground.

CLANG!

Thorn used the sickle to deflect the Vermillion Blade first to one side, his armor catching the blow, but the mail unraveled from the dark energy now dripping from the cursed edge of the blade. Rabien used the deflection to spin the blade of the cursed glaive back around over his head and down at Thorn.

CLANG!

Thorn swung his hammer backhand across his body to impact with the steel of the Vermillion Blade, driving it from his chest and into the armor on his other arm. While the strikes hadn't penetrated Thorn's blessed armor, the impact of Rabien's cursed weapon had numbed his arms, and neither the sickle nor the hammer was in a position to block as the edge of the Vermillion Blade came around again, descending toward Thorn's head.

BOOM! – TING!

NOOOO! Thorn screamed in his head as he heard Gwen's rifle fire. Time slowed as he saw the bullet ricochet off the cursed steel of the Vermillion Blade and head back along its trajectory. The next sound Thorn heard was the splintering of wood, as he knew precisely from Talon's experience where the bullet had returned to. The unexpected attack gave Thorn time to roll away from Rabien and gain his feet again, but to what end? The Vermillion Blade knew how to counter any weapon, the sickle was blinded, and now there was no second chance.

Thorn scrambled around Rabien to hopefully retreat out of the clearing and back into the trees where the sickle's sight glowed in the distance. As Rabien turned around dramatically, his face was positively feral with delight. "One bullet," was all he said, licking a mixture of spittle and blood off his upper lip.

Thorn looked down at his hammer and sickle and back to Rabien holding the cursed blade of the Cour-Vermane bloodline. How could these tools, no matter their blessings or enchantments, defeat a weapon such as the Vermillion Blade? That is when it hit him; what he wielded weren't weapons but the tools of field and forge—the symbols of Caspharian's domains. Thorn had to stop playing into the Vermillion Blade's strength. He had to trust the tools his love and his deity had placed in his hands.

Thorn didn't need the sickle's sight to know what surrounded him in this dead place created by the weapon he once wielded. A sickle is meant to reap, and it was black chains that Thorn intended to harvest. Circling Rabien at a distance, Thorn visualized the webwork array of dark links that Talon had used and augmented his skills with for decades and swung the sickle in the same sweeping motion he had used to clear the ground of this once fertile land. Caspharian's sickle blazed with its green-gold energy as it swept through the seemingly empty air.

SHATTER! TINK. TINK. TINK. TINK.

Broken iron links forged out of crimson darkness materialized in the sickle's wake, falling to the ground. Around the now corporeal corrupted steel, the young apples touched by the moonlight blossoms the night before littered the clearing. They instantly sprouted and entangled the broken links dragging them down into the earth. Thorn spun and swept the sickle across the darkness again, and more dark links shattered and fell out of the air to be devoured by the soil. Rabien charged across the clearing holding the Vermillion Blade like a lance.

Thorn swept the sickle again, hoping his next gambit would not be his demise. Instead of deflecting Rabien's attack, he let the armor covering his chest take the blow while he let his hammer do its work. Activating the enchantment he had laid into it himself as an act of remembrance of his love for Richen, he swung and struck Rabien's elbow with the ball-peen hammer. With a crack of thunder, the light hammer hit with the force of a twenty-pound sledge wielded by the strongest of smiths. Rabien's elbow exploded in a shower of tendon, ligament, and bone as Thorn was simultaneously thrown backward by the impact of Rabien's charge and clean hit. As he arced through the air, Thorn looked down to see if the

Vermillion Blade had plunged through the blessed chainmail shirt and into his chest. It had not, but the chainmail had dissolved not only over his chest but in a line down to the hem, becoming now more of a vest than a shirt., The flesh of his whole torso was now exposed, including the scar Lochlan had placed over his heart.

Thorn landed on his backside, did a backward roll, and leaped to his feet. Across the dead clearing, Rabien was looking down at his right forearm, which was still attached to him but only by thin ropes of skin and sinew. Thorn saw his hand was still gripping the Vermillion Blade but knew from Balanon's training it should be impossible for anyone to still grasp a weapon after the damage he had caused. It was then that he saw the words glowing on the cursed weapon's shaft.

To break oath is to be doomed even beyond death to walk this land as a blight upon it.

Thorn realized that Rabien's hands weren't gripping the glaive, they were welded there. The original curse meant for Thorn now was enslaving Rabien. Thorn watched in horror as the destroyed elbow knitted itself back together under the malicious light of the glowing words of the curse. Rabien looked up at Thorn once his forearm had fully reattached itself with an evil smile. Thorn's eyes, however, saw what Rabien could not, his face was gaunt like it had aged ten years. The repair of his arm had come with a cost.

It was then that Rabien must have seen Thorn's exposed chest and the scar there. Thorn could see the rage rise in him again. "I. AM. NOT. YOUR. TWIN!" He screeched out of cracking desiccated lips. Swinging the Vermillion Blade wildly, Rabien leaped toward Thorn, his black cloak spreading like his alter ego's namesake's wings blotting out the moon above. Thorn rolled away and swung his sickle to shatter more links of the Vermillion Blade's web. Rabien's raging swings and attacks were now reckless and unguided by the strategies of the Vermillion Blade. Wanting to feed Rabien's rage, Thorn laughed and mockingly shouted, "Who's the farce now? Didn't they tell you? You're not my twin - the Vermillion Blade is! You're just the flesh sack with legs that is going to deliver it to me! *Again!*"

"ARRRRRGHHHHH!" Rabien's mind seemed truly broken as a frenzy overtook him.

Thorn could dive under and around the continuous flurry of his attacks, getting inside Rabien's guard to strike him with his hammer, which now glowed red hot with the power of the other enchantment Thorn had placed upon it. But, Rabien's wounds continued to stitch themselves back together, the toll beginning to show both on him and the dimming curse of the Vermillion Blade. They battled on and on, Rabien's rage and endurance never diminishing and Thorn still breaking the seemingly endless supply of the Vermillion Blade's chains and his hammer unable to overwhelm Rabien's regeneration.

Thorn's muscles were aching, and he knew he soon had to end this, but how? Thorn had one last idea now that Rabien seemed more undead than alive. Instead of using the sickle to break more chains, he dove toward Rabien's left leg with the intent of striking it with both weapons simultaneously to completely separate it and perhaps seed the sickle's mushrooms in the wound. His fatal error was his assumption that Rabien's hands were still welded to the shaft of the Vermillion Blade. Rabien's now mostly skeletal left hand, bones sharpened by the foul curse of the glaive, was there to meet Thorn's forward shoulder roll and plunged deeply into his abdomen.

Thorn hooked his sickle behind Rabien's knee as his undead cousin yanked Thorn upward, skeletal fingers inside his ribcage and lifting him by the sternum. Thorn felt Caspharian's sickle slice clean through Rabien's leg as he was lifted to his feet and then raised toward the sky. From the corner of his eye, Thorn thought he saw an aquamarine glow begin to form below him. He did not know if it would be enough, but at this point, he could only hope the gods chose it to be so. Thorn watched as the remains of life drained from Rabien's undead face as the Vermillion Blade worked to keep Rabien's leg attached and fight the mushrooms now infecting his decaying form. Thorn pressed the glowing red-hot head of his hammer into the scar of Talon's mark on Rabien's chest, trying to perhaps ignite some magic that lay within.

Now he just hoped to overwhelm the Vermillion Blade with damage to his cousin before he died, and Rabien could consume parts of him to bolster himself in this new incarnation, as Talon had seen himself do in the Blade's cursed vision of his future. Thorn was losing consciousness fast as Rabien's left hand dug deeper under his rib cage and his feet dangled above the ground. He lifted his eyes to the sky, trying to conjure Richen's face into existence so it would be the last thing he saw, not the horror of his family's legacy.

BOOM!

Time became liquid glass. Thorn saw the Vermillion Blade reflexively drop into position behind Rabien's head to deflect the incoming shot. Bewildered, Thorn watched as his enchanted bullet burrowed through the cursed steel of the blade, burning a hole clean through it before exploding into and through Rabien's skull. Thorn dropped to the ground, Rabien's undead headless form crumpling beside him, Vermillion Blade still clutched in his right hand.

Thorn could hardly move. Blood and part of his entrails bulged out of the wound in his abdomen. Then, in a determination driven by the knowledge of these being his last moments, he agonizingly lifted his prone form onto his elbows and looked to see if Rabien was somehow being stitched back together by the curse and, if so, for a way he could stop it. Thorn saw no evidence of the flesh clawing its way back together, so he peered at the

Vermillion Blade clutched in Rabien's skeletal right hand. The words of the curse etched on the shaft still glowed but had dimmed to embers. Thorn, unwilling to leave his family's evil legacy free in this world, clenched his teeth and threw his will at the Vermillion Blade to try to bind its power again and place a brand upon it. Tears poured down Thorn's face as a faint smile formed through teeth, nearly cracking under strain as the brand appeared on the neck of the Vermillion Blade.

Thorn collapsed, his last breath escaping his lips as his back hit the ground. Eyes pointed to the sky again; he saw there among the stars a pair of stormcloud eyes looking down on him. Thorn's heart was full of light as darkness overcame him, and he went to meet his Richen again or wait for his love to join him.

CHAPTER THIRTY-EIGHT

After she took the shot, Gwen jumped up from her perch and ran out of the upstairs room. She scrambled down the stairs in whatever way her half-numb legs would navigate them and burst out the farmhouse door, sprinting into the orchard. Lungs pumping like bellows and heartbeats in her ears sounding as loud as one of her gunshots, she charged through the darkness under the still-living trees toward the dead clearing.

She had seen everything through her scope. After the Raven Judge's arrival and his conjuring of the rats and then taking to the sky, she was horrified at what they faced. She knew that she would give away her position by warning Thorn of the Judge's descent from above, but she couldn't not call out. And when the dead eyes of the raven mask looked up at her, she knew she would have to do something more than what she had promised Thorn. That is when Thorn's words came to her: *he knows I can enchant only one bullet.* She unloaded the bullet he had given her and replaced it with a mundane one.

Her feet pounded forward out of the rich soil of the still-living part of the orchard and into the dust of the desiccated clearing. On the side of the dead zone closest to the center of the orchard was the fallen body of Thorn and the crumpled undead corpse of Rabien. She ran to Thorn, who she saw wasn't breathing, the grievous wound in his torso slick with blood and exposed viscera.

"No, no, no, no, no…" She pleaded through sobs as she skidded to her knees and cradled his head. She looked for his sickle that she had seen perform a miracle the night before and found it lying in his open hand, the tiny tree that was its hilt looking sickly and with only a few remaining leaves. She picked up the sickle and laid it on his chest along with the hammer from his other lifeless hand. "Not here. You don't leave me from this dead place. Not while I am with you, you don't," she vowed. Gwen put her hands under Thorn's armpits and dragged him toward the now split largest tree at the center of the orchard that had meant so much to both of them.

Gwen propped Thorn's body against a side of the trunk which was still undamaged and took his hand in both of hers. "Please," was all she said. She didn't know if she was talking to the ghost of her husband, the gods, or even the trees of the orchard. She didn't even know if she had the right to ask, but she still did and, lowering her head, repeated quietly, "Please."

A soft breeze rustled the leaves of the great tree above her, and a weak, gentle hum began beside her from the tiny tree of the sickle as it struggled for life.

Thorn stood at the threshold of a beautiful valley. Towering granite cliffs and monumental rock faces stood sentinel to either side, with shimmering waterfalls cascading off their dizzying heights. He saw a river wound lazily across the valley floor, gurgling across polished stones and gently tumbling around fallen boulders in its path. In the distance, a forest glade stood ahead of him, promising shade and verdant serenity as pink wildflowers carpeted the way toward it.

His consciousness seemed to rush toward the glade as he saw a familiar figure emerge from the welcoming green shadows, and then another, and sadly a final one. Ms. Haddington, Mikal, and Lochlan stood waiting to greet him. Ms. Haddington opened her arms, awaiting a long-missed embrace. With relief for the person he did not see and regret that they had never met again in life, Thorn took a step forward into the valley.

Gwen's eyes looked to the soft musical note coming from beside her. It was the first note of her and her husband's marriage song. Tears coming unbidden to her eyes, she added her voice to the melody. The little tree sang back to her as its tiny form lifted off the blade of the sickle and began to float above Thorn's chest, its remaining leaves glowing with silvery gold light. As the miniature tree slowly rotated, its last leaves detached, evaporating into sparkling motes of light. The rustling in the great tree above her became like a tempest and spread to the orchard around her. The canopies of the trees pulsed with stored moonlight sweeping across the whole orchard towards her. Radiance flowed like a wave over the boughs of the trees and across the dead clearing. It coalesced above her, filtering through the branches of the great tree, its dappled light flashing on Thorn's body with the brilliance of a lightning strike.

From the split in the tree behind her, an ethereal vine reached out and twined its way across the barren clearing. As it grew, it arched over the Raven Judge's corpse and wrapped around the Vermillion Blade, wresting it from the Judge's grasp. The vine picked up the cursed blade and drew it closer, bringing it towards Thorn. Gwen moved to block its path, having seen all the evil that glaive had wrought. This was no salvation. Even if it were the intent of the gods, she would not allow it.

As Thorn lifted his foot to step into the Valley, ready to be at rest and with those who had already arrived, the ground ripped open before him. He stood alone on a stone precipice as the valley, and those waiting for him, began to retreat from his sight. Thorn was not going to lose this family, not now. He leaped across the widening gulf, barely grabbing the edge of the retreating sanctuary, his body hanging over a gray nothingness below him. Thorn scrambled up over the edge and onto stable ground. Lochlan was there before him, waiting with the others behind him.

Ms. Haddington and Mikal began to step around Lochlan, but the Commander blocked them with outstretched arms. "Thorn, you cannot cross to this place unescorted, and you are beyond the Last Friend's reach to guide you. You shouldn't have even made it this far." His voice carried the same force as when training him back in the estate's courtyard.

Thorn, confused and hurt, responded with the words in his heart, "I don't know why I made it this far, but I'm not losing all of you. I am *not* going to be alone. I may not have the Last Friend, but finally, for once in my life, I am *my own friend.*" It was not a plea but an epiphany.

Lochlan's mouth made a slight upward curve of approval. He placed his hand on the chest of the man he thought of as his son and stated, "And that is why you cannot enter." And pushed Thorn over the edge out of the valley and into the void.

Gwen shuffled on her knees into the path of the vine carrying the Vermillion Blade closer toward Thorn. She didn't know what she would do to stop this. She even looked over her shoulder, hoping the tiny tree would help, but it had fallen lifeless onto Thorn's chest, laying on the open wound gaping there. "Stop! No! This can't be what he wanted." She shouted at the oncoming weapon and the vine carrying it.

As it advanced, now at Thorn's feet, she saw the mark branded into the cursed glaive that she knew hadn't been there before. She sat back on her heels, and her arms fell to her sides. Closing her eyes, she let the blade continue on its course. The ethereal vine, still carrying the Vermillion Blade, drifted past Gwen and Thorn, retreating back into the tree from which it had sprouted, taking the glaive with it. It seated the Vermillion Blade deep within the split the weapon had created in the great tree. The mark Thorn had placed upon it glowed brightly: a five-petaled apple blossom, looking like it was painted in full color instead of the black char of a brand.

As the glaive locked into place, crimson-gold light erupted from the great tree. Gwen now witnessed the filaments of life as Thorn did with the sickle, covering and interconnecting everything in its vast webwork. The orchard and all around her was encompassed by the display of the intersection of life's possibility. It pulsed with energy that flowed into the great tree, and she watched the split in its trunk begin to close, encasing the Vermillion Blade within. Then, looking to Thorn's body, she saw that as the wound in the tree healed, so did Thorn.

There was no darkness nor light in the place where he was left. He was adrift in a gray abyss of nothingness. How long Thorn floated there, he did not know, but suddenly he began to fall, and with an impact that vibrated deep in his bones and knocked the breath out of him, he coughed and opened his eyes. His chest hurt like hell. Above him were the branches of an apple tree glowing like brass just pulled from a forge. Ringing in his ears was a fading musical note, and then Gwen was there, her concerned face looking down at him streaked with tears. "THORN? Thorn? Are you there? Are you okay?" She pleaded.

"Yes, I think." He coughed out the words. "What happened? Is Rabien still dead? Where is the Vermillion Blade?" Thorn pushed himself to a sitting position and got to his feet with Gwen's help. He gathered his bearings. The whole orchard looked like it was bathed in sunlight, but the largest tree here at its center glowed the brightest.

"Look," Gwen said as she turned him toward the split in the tree as it closed around the Vermillion Blade. The top of the shaft and all of the steel blade, including the hole made by Gwen's shot, was still visible but wouldn't be for long, and there on the neck, where metal met wood, was the apple blossom seal Thorn had willed upon it.

"It worked," Thorn stated, relieved. "The life of this whole orchard and all connected to it will bind it here." Thorn looked down at his own chest and saw the discoloration and dark scar where his wound had been. It was in the exact shape of the tree that had once been the hilt of his sickle. "Oh no," he whispered as his hand came up to the scar, and he frantically looked around for Caspharian's weapon. The blade portion was on the ground next to where he lay with his hammer beside it, but the tiny tree was nowhere to be found.

Gwen squeezed Thorn's hand, "It's gone. It fulfilled your last wish and used its last bit of life to join the glaive with the tree." Thorn picked up the remainder of the sickle along with his hammer and held them close to his heart.

Thorn and Gwen watched the wound in the tree close until its wood and bark enveloped every inch of the Vermillion Blade, both waiting until the end to ensure it was completely contained. Thorn then looked into the still-dead clearing where Rabien's body had fallen. All that remained was his black cloak, crumbling bones, and a patch of glowing blue mushrooms cleansing the corruption of his remaining flesh. It heartened Thorn to see the mushrooms were beginning to spread beyond Rabien and had started cleansing the desiccated clearing as well. As he scanned the ground, Thorn spotted a tiny apple tree sapling that had already sprouted. With a smile, he carefully scooped it up in his hands, and side by side with Gwen, they walked through the orchard in the moonlight back to the farmhouse.

THE END

EPILOGUE

Six years later - Year 889 PXF *~ Late Autumn*

Osman stepped into the cidery of the bustling Milgran's Orchard. He had been surprised that this orchard and the surrounding farms had recovered so successfully. So much of Eleryon, and especially Arnadore, still struggled to return to prosperity even fifteen years after the rebellion. Osman had little information as distrust of outsiders was still very prevalent; in addition, he was being careful, as while few might remember, he was in breach of his exile by walking these lands. With no truly functional inns or taverns in the region, this cidery might be his only chance to buy some rumors and information.

The cidery was newly built, an additional stand-alone building to the obviously older farmhouse and structures used in the running of the orchard. One of the dozens of workers still harvesting apples from the trees had pointed him to the entrance, and he cautiously stepped inside, not knowing what to expect. He found the cidery well constructed with care and craftsmanship. It gladdened Osman to see it and the hope it meant for the future of the lands around his once home. Half a dozen currently unoccupied small tables filled one side of the room, and a long bar dominated the other, along with stacks of cider barrels behind it.

An older human woman nearing or slightly beyond her mid-fifties was working behind the counter, and another human with wild cascading hair tied up in a loose tangle on his head, perhaps her son of no more than nineteen years, with back to the main room, assisted her. Osman strode to the bar and laid down a golden Uldani coin, "I'll take your best cider," he confidently requested, sliding what must be far more than the payment across to the older barwoman in full offering.

She eyed Osman and the coin and nodded to her assistant to draw the cider into a tankard. "What is it you want, friend? You are a long way from the Isles."

"I am looking for someone. An old rumor came to my homeland regarding the last Knight Captain of Arnadore." Osman said the last part cautiously, judging the barwoman's reaction. When she gave none, he continued, "He would be near your age now, and I have need to find him."

Sliding the tankard across to Osman, the woman wearing the unreadable mask of bartenders and good folk who work the land in all regions replied, "All the traitor Duke's guards either died in the revolt or were executed with him." Osman picked up his tankard to drink, and she wiped the bar clean where it had sat. Then, pocketing the coin, she continued, "I appreciate your business, but you best be moving along, it will be dark soon, and there are no open beds for you here this night."

Osman got the message and drank down the cider in one gulp. He placed the tankard back on the bar and backed away, hands splayed to show he had no ill intention. As he opened the door, feeling there might be more this woman wasn't saying, he looked over his shoulder and said, "Well, if he is alive and you see him, tell him his little brother is looking for him and that he found Richen."

To be continued in

Book II of the A Time of Falcons and Roses Series:

Promise of the Betrayer's Dagger

Thank You, Mom